"Hello," Michael said.

The figure was female in a bizarre sort of way. Her arms hung almost to her knees. Her legs, clothed in ragged pants, were very long in comparison with her torso. She lifted one hand and wriggled spider-leg fingers in front of her flat chest. Another woman with similar features leaned from one window of the hut. Behind Michael a third woman stood on one spindly leg with the other tucked close to her chest.

"Are you Nare, Spart, and . . . Coom?" Michael asked.

"I am Nare," said the Crane woman standing on one leg.

"Spart," said the one at the window, and

"Coom," said the downy-haired figure who had first addressed him. "Want us teach?"

"I don't know what I want," Michael said, "except to get out of here."

The Crane women chuckled, a sound like leaves skittering over rock.

"We don't mind man-childs," said Nare at his side, circling.

"We won't hurt you," Coom said. *"Much."*

THE INFINITY CONCERTO

GREG BEAR

BERKLEY BOOKS, NEW YORK

THE INFINITY CONCERTO

A Berkley Book/published by arrangement with
the author

PRINTING HISTORY
Berkley edition/October 1984

ISBN: 0-425-07308-4

To Betty Chater:
dear friend, teacher, colleague

If a man could pass through Paradise in a dream, and have a flower presented to him as a pledge that his soul had really been there, and if he found that flower in his hand when he awoke—Ay!—and what then?

—Samuel Taylor Coleridge

What song did the sirens sing?

—Ancient Riddle

Chapter One

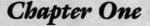

Are you ready?

"Huh?" Michael Perrin twitched in his sleep. An uncertain number of tall white forms stood around his bed, merging with the walls, the dresser, the bookcases and easels.

He's not very impressive.

Michael rolled over and rubbed his nose. His short sandy hair tousled up against his pillow. His thick feathery red eyebrows pulled together as if in minor irritation, but his eyes stayed shut.

Look deeper. Several of the forms bent over him.

He's only a man-child.

Yet he has the hallmark.

What's that? Wasting his talents in all directions instead of concentrating? Never quite able to make up his mind what he is going to be? A ghostly arm waved at the easels and bookcases, at the desk swamped with ragged-edged notebooks, chewed pencils and scraps of paper.

Indeed. That is the hallmark, or one of—

Michael's alarm clock went off with a hideous buzz. He jerked upright in bed and slapped his hand over the cut-off switch, hoping his parents hadn't heard. He sleepily regarded the glowing green numbers; twelve thirty in the morning. He picked up his watch to check. "Damn." The clock was eight minutes late. He only had twenty-two minutes.

He rolled out of bed, kicking a book of Yeats' poems across the floor with one bare foot. He swore under his breath and felt for his pants. The only light he dared use was the Tensor

1

lamp on his desk. He pushed aside the portable typewriter to let the concentrated glow spread farther and spilled a stack of paperbacks on the floor. Bending over to pick them up, he smacked his head on the edge of the desk.

Teeth clenched, Michael grabbed his pants from the back of the chair and slipped them on. One leg on and the other stuck halfway, he lost balance and steadied himself by pushing against the wall.

His fingers brushed a framed print hung slightly off balance against the lines and flowers of the wallpaper. He squinted at the print—a Bonestell rendition of Saturn seen from one of its closer moons. His head throbbed.

A tall, slender figure was walking across the print's cratered moonscape. He blinked. The figure turned and regarded him as if from a considerable distance, then motioned for him to follow. He scrunched his eyes shut, and when he opened them again, the figure had vanished. "Christ," he said softly. "I'm not even awake yet."

He buckled his belt and donned his favorite shirt, a short-sleeved brown pull-over with a V-neck. Socks, gray hush-puppies and tan nylon windbreaker completed the ensemble. But he was forgetting something.

He stood in the middle of the room, trying to remember, when his eyes lit on a small book bound in glossy black leather. He picked it up and stuffed it in his jacket pocket, zipping the pocket shut. He dug in his pants pocket for the note, found it folded neatly next to the key-holder and glanced at his watch again. Twelve forty-five.

He had fifteen minutes.

He trod softly down the wall-edge of the stairs, avoiding most of the squeaks, and half-ran to the front door. The living room was black except for the digital display on the video recorder. Twelve forty-seven, it said.

He opened and closed the door swiftly and ran across the lawn. The neighborhood streetlights had been converted to sodium-vapor bulbs that cast a sour orange glow over the grass and sidewalk. Michael's shadow marched ahead, growing huge before it vanished in the glare of the next light. The orange emphasized the midnight-blue of the sky, dulling the stars.

Four blocks south, the orange lights ended and traditional streetlamps on concrete posts took over. His father said those lights went back to the 1920's and were priceless. They had been installed when the neighborhood houses had first been built; back then, they had stood on a fancy country road, where movie stars and railroad magnates had come to get away from it all.

The houses were imposing at night. Spanish-style white plaster and stucco dominated; some, two stories tall with enclosures over the side driveways. Others were woodsy, shake shingles on walls and roofs and narrow frame windows staring darkly out of dormiers.

All the houses were dark. It was easy to imagine the street was a movie set, with nothing behind the walls but hollowness and crickets.

Twelve fifty-eight. He crossed the last intersection and turned to face his destination. Four houses down and on the opposite side of the street was the white plaster, single-story home of David Clarkham. It had been deserted for over forty years, yet its lawns were immaculately groomed and its hedges trimmed, walls spotless and Spanish wood beams unfaded. Drawn curtains in the tall arched windows hid only emptiness—or so it was realistic to assume. Being realistic hadn't brought him here, however.

For all he knew, the house could be crammed with all manner of things . . . incredible, unpleasant things.

He stood beneath the moon-colored streetlight, half in the shadow of a tall, brown-leafed maple, folding and unfolding the paper in his pants pocket with one sweaty hand.

One o'clock in the morning. He wasn't dressed for adventure. He had the instructions, the book and the leather key-holder with its one old brass key; what he didn't have was conviction.

It was a silly decision. The world was sane; such opportunities didn't present themselves. He withdrew the paper and read it for the hundredth time:

"Use the key to enter the front door. Do not linger. Pass through the house, through the back door and through the side gate to the front door of the neighboring house on the left, as you face the houses. The door to that house will be open. Enter. *Do not stop to look at anything.* Surely, quickly, make your way to the back of the house, through the back door again, and across the rear yard to the wrought-iron gate. Go through the gate and turn to your left. The alley behind the house will take you past many gates on both sides. Enter the sixth gate on your left."

He folded the note and replaced it. What would his parents think, seeing him here, contemplating breaking and entering—or at the very least, entering without breaking?

"There comes a time," Arno Waltiri had said, "when one must disregard the thoughts of one's parents, or the warnings of old men; when caution must be put temporarily aside and instincts followed. In short, when one must rely on one's own judgment. . . ."

Michael's parents gave parties renowned throughout the city. Michael had met the elderly composer Waltiri and his wife, Golda, at one such party in June. The party celebrated the Equinox ("Late," his mother explained, "because nothing we do is prompt"). Michael's father was a carpenter with a reputation for making fine furniture; he had a wide clientele among the rich and glamorous folk of Los Angeles, and Waltiri had commissioned him to make a new bench for his fifty-year-old piano.

Michael had stayed downstairs for the first hour of the party, wandering through the crowd and sipping a bottle of beer. He listened in while the heavily bearded, gray-haired captain of an ocean liner told a young stage actress of his perilous adventures during World War II, "on convoy in the Western Ocean." Michael's attention was evenly divided between them; his breath seemed to shorten, the woman was so beautiful, and he'd always been interested in ships and the sea. When the captain put an arm around the actress and stopped talking of things nautical, Michael moved on. He sat in a folding chair near a noisy group of newspaper people.

Journalists irritated Michael. They came in large numbers to his parents' parties. They were brash and drank a lot and postured and talked more about politics than writing. When their conversation turned to literature (which was seldom), it seemed all they had ever read was Raymond Chandler or Ernest Hemingway or F. Scott Fitzgerald. Michael tried to interject a few words about poetry, but the conversation stopped dead and he moved on again.

The rest of the party was taken up by a councilman and his entourage, a few businessmen and the neighbors, so Michael selected a reserve supply of hors d'ouevres and carried the plate upstairs to his room.

He closed the door and switched on the TV, then sat at his small desk—which he was rapidly outgrowing—and pulled a sheaf of poems from the upper drawer.

Music pounded faintly through the floor. They were dancing.

He found the poem he had written that morning and read it over, frowning. It was yet another in a long line of bad Yeats imitations. He was trying to compress the experiences of a senior in high school into romantic verse, and it wasn't working.

Disgusted, he returned the poems to the drawer and switched the TV channels until he found an old Humphrey Bogart movie. He'd seen it before; Bogart was having woman trouble with Barbara Stanwyck.

Michael's troubles with women had been limited to stuffing love poems into a girl's locker. She had caught him doing it and laughed at him.

There was a soft tap on his door. "Michael?" It was his father.

"Yeah?"

"You receiving visitors?"

"Sure." He opened the door. His father came in first, slightly drunk, and motioned for an old, white-haired man to follow.

"Mike, this is Arno Waltiri, composer. Arno, my son, the poet."

Waltiri shook Michael's hand solemnly. His nose was straight and thin and his lips were full and young-looking. His grip was strong but not painful. "We are not intruding, I hope?" His accent was indefinite middle-European, faded from years in California.

"Not at all," Michael said. He felt a little awkward; his grandparents had died before he was born, and he wasn't used to old people.

Waltiri examined the prints and posters arranged on the walls. He paused before the print of Saturn, glanced at Michael, and nodded. He turned to a framed magazine cover showing insect-like creatures dancing near wave-washed beach rocks and smiled. "Max Ernst," he said. His voice was a soft rumble. "You obviously like to visit strange places."

Michael muttered something about never having actually been to anyplace strange.

"He wants to be a poet," his father said, pointing to the bookcases lining the walls. "A packrat. Keeps everything he's read."

Waltiri regarded the television with a critical eye. Bogart was painstakingly explaining a delicate matter to Stanwyck. "I wrote the score for that one," he said.

Michael brightened immediately. He didn't have much money for records—he spent most of his allowance and summer earnings on books—but the five records he did have consisted of a Bee Gees album, a Ricky Lee Jones concert double, and the soundtrack albums for the original *King Kong, Star Wars* and *Citizen Kane*. "You did? When was that?"

"1940," Waltiri said. "So long ago, now, but seems much closer. I scored over two hundred films before I retired." Waltiri sighed and turned to Michael's father. "Your son is very diverse in his interests."

Waltiri's hands were strong and broad-fingered, Michael noticed, and his clothing was well-tailored and simple. His slate-gray eyes seemed very young. Perhaps the most unusual thing about him were his teeth, which were like gray ivory.

"Ruth would like for him to study law," his father said, grinning. "I hear poets don't make much of a living. Still, it beats wanting to be a rock star."

Waltiri shrugged. "Rock star isn't so bad." He put a hand on Michael's shoulder. Usually Michael resented such familiarities, but not this time. "I like impractical people, people who are willing to rely only on themselves. It was very impractical for me to want to become a composer." He sat on Michael's desk chair, hands on his knees, elbows pointed out, staring at the TV. "So very difficult to get anything performed at all, not to mention by a good orchestra. So I followed my friend Steiner to California—"

"You knew Max Steiner?"

"Indeed. Sometime you must come over to our house, visit Golda and me, perhaps listen to the old scores." At that moment, Waltiri's wife entered the room, a slender, golden-haired woman a few years younger than he. She bore a distinct resemblance to Gloria Swanson, Michael thought, but without the wild look Swanson had had in *Sunset Boulevard*. He liked Golda immediately.

So it had all begun with music. When his father delivered the piano bench, Michael tagged along. Golda met them at the door, and ten minutes later Arno was guiding them around the ground floor of the two-story bungalow. "Arno loves to talk," Golda told Michael as they approached the music room at the rear of the house. "If you love to listen, you'll get along just fine."

Waltiri opened the door with a key and let them enter first.

"I don't go in here very often now," he said. "Golda keeps it dusted. I read nowadays, play the piano in the front room now and then, but I don't need to listen." He tapped his head. "It's all up here, every note."

The walls on three sides were covered with shelves of records. Waltiri pulled down big lacquered masters from a few of his early films, then pointed out the progression to smaller disks, scores released by record companies on seventy-eights, and finally the long-play format Michael was familiar with. For scores composed in the 1950's and 60's, he had tapes neatly labeled and shelved in black and white and plaid boxes. "This was my last score," he said, pulling down a bigger tape box. "Half-inch stereo eight-track master. For William Wyler, you know. In 1963 he asked me to score *Call It Sleep*. Not my finest score, but certainly my favorite film."

Michael ran his finger along the tape box labels. "Look! Mr. Waltiri—"

"Arno, please. Only producers call me Mr. Waltiri."

"You did the music for Bogart in *The Man Who Would Be King*!"

"Certainly. For John Huston, actually. Good score, that one."

"That's my favorite movie," Michael said, awed.

Waltiri's eyes sparkled. For the next two months, Michael spent most of his free time in the Waltiri house, listening to him recite selections on the piano or carefully play the fragile masters of the scores. It had been a wonderful two months, almost a justification for being bookish, something of a loner, buried in his mind instead of hanging out with friends....

Now Michael stood on the porch of Clarkham's house. He tried the handle on the heavy wooden door; locked, as expected. He removed the key from his pants pocket. It was late for the old neighborhood. There was no street traffic, not even the sound of distant airplanes. Everything seemed to have been muffled in a blanket.

Two months before, on a hot, airless August day, Waltiri had taken Michael up to the attic to look through papers and memorabilia. Michael had exulted over letters from Clark Gable, correspondence with Max Steiner and Erich Wolfgang Korngold, a manuscript copy of a Stravinsky oratorio.

"Up here, it feels like it's the forties again," Michael said. Waltiri stared down at lines of light thrown by a wall vent across a stack of boxes and said, "Perhaps it is." He looked

up at Michael. "Let's go downstairs and get some iced tea.
And on the way—instead of my talking about myself—on the
way, I would like you to tell me why you want to be a poet."

That was difficult. Sitting on the porch, Michael sipped
from his glass and shook his head. "I don't know. Mom says
it's because I want to be difficult. She laughs, but I think she
means it." He made a wry face. "As if my folks should worry
about *me* being different. They're not your normal middle-class
couple, either. She might be right. But it's something else,
too. When I write poetry, I'm more in touch with being alive.
I like living here. I have some friends. But...it seems so
limited. I try hard to find the flavor, the richness, but I can't.
There has to be something more." He rubbed his cheek and
looked at the fallen magnolia blossoms on the lawn. "Some of
my friends just go to the movies. That's their idea of magic,
of getting away. I like movies, but I can't live in them."

The composer nodded, his slate-gray eyes focused on the
distance above the hedges bordering the yard. "You think there's
something higher than what we see—or lower—and you want
to find it."

"That's it." Michael nodded.

"Are you a good poet?"

"Not very," Michael said automatically.

"No false modesty now." Waltiri wiped condensation from
his glass on the knee of his pants.

Michael thought for a moment. "I'm going to be."

"Going to be what?"

"I'm going to be a good poet."

"That's a fine thing to say. Now that you've said it, you
know I'll be watching you. You must become a good poet."

Michael shook his head ruefully. "Thanks a lot!"

"Think nothing of it. We all need someone to watch over
us. For me, it was Gustav Mahler. I met him when I was eleven
years old, and he asked me much the same thing. I was a young
piano player—how do they say—a prodigy. 'How good will
you be?' he asked after he heard me perform. I tried to dodge
the question by acting like a young boy, but he turned his very
intense dark eyes on me and said again, 'How *good?*' Because
I was cornered, I puffed up and said, 'I'll be *very* good.' And
he smiled at me! What a benediction that was. Ah, what a
moment! Do you know Mahler?"

He meant Mahler's music, and Michael didn't.

"He was my god. The sad German. I worshiped him. He died a few months after we met, but somehow I felt he still watched me, he would still be disappointed if I didn't make something of myself."

By early September, Waltiri had taken Michael even further into his confidence. "When I began to write music for movies, I was a little ashamed," he said one evening when Michael came over for dinner. "Even though my first score was for a good movie, Trevor Howard in *Ashenden*. Now I have no regrets, but I thought then, what would my heroes say about writing for silly films? Still, it was next to impossible to work otherwise. I had married Golda in 1930, and we had to live. Times were hard then.

"But always before me was the shining splendor of perhaps doing serious music, concert hall material. I wrote some on the side—piano pieces, cantatas, exactly the opposite of the big orchestral scores for the studios. A little has even been recorded recently, because I am so well-known as a film composer. I wanted to do an opera—how I loved the libretti of Hofmannsthal, and how I envied Richard Strauss that he lived in a time when such things were easier! 'Dream and reality are one, together, you and I alone, always together ... to all eternity. ...' *'Geht all's sonst wie ein Traum dahin vor meinem Sinn. ...'"* He laughed and shook his head. "But I am wandering.

"I had one last fling with serious music. And ..." Waltiri paused in the dim, candlelit dining room, his eyes again focused on the distance, this time piercing a framed landscape over the china cupboard. "A very serious fling it was. A man my own age then, perhaps a little older, by the name of David Clarkham approached me at Warner Brothers one day. I remember it was raining, but he didn't wear a raincoat ... just a gray wool suit, without any drips on it. Not wet, you understand?"

Michael nodded.

"We had some mutual acquaintances. At first, I thought maybe he was just another studio vulture. You know the kind, maybe. They hang around, bask in other peoples' fame and fortune, live off parties. 'Lounge lizards,' somebody called them. But it turned out he was knowledgeable about music. A charming fellow. We got along well ... for a time.

"He had some theories about music that were highly unusual, to say the least." Waltiri went to a glassed-in bookcase, lifted a door, and withdrew a small thick volume in a worn wrapper. He held it out for Michael's inspection. The title was *Devil's Music* and the author was Charles Fort.

"We worked together, Clarkham and I. He suggested orchestrations and arrangements; I composed." Waltiri's expression became grim. His next words were clipped and ironic. "'Arno,' he tells me—we are good friends by this time— 'Arno, there shall be no other music like this. Not for millions of years have such sounds been heard on Earth.' I kidded him about dinosaurs breaking wind. He looked at me very seriously and said, 'Someday you will understand what I mean.' I accepted he was a little eccentric, but also brilliant. He appealed directly to my wish to be another Stravinsky. So . . . I was a sucker. I applied his theories to our composition, using what he called 'psychotropic tone structure.'

"'This,' he tells me, 'will do exactly what Scriabin tried to do, and failed.'" Michael didn't know who Scriabin was, but Waltiri continued as if with a long-rehearsed speech.

"The piece we wrote, it was my forty-fifth opus, a concerto for piano and orchestra called 'Infinity.'" He took the book from Michael's hand and opened it to a marked passage, then handed it back. "So we get infamous. Read, please."

Michael read.

"Or of strange things musical.

"A song of enchantment.

"Judge as you will, here is the data:

"That on November 23rd, 1939, a musician created a work of undeniable genius, a work which changed the lives of famous men, fellow musicians. This man was Arno Waltiri, and with his new concerto, Opus 45, he created a suitable atmosphere for musical catastrophe.

"Picture it: a cold night, Los Angeles, the Pandall Theater on Sunset Boulevard. Crowds in black silk hats, white tie and tails, long sheer gowns, pouring in to hear a premier performance. Listen to it: the orchestra tuning, cacophonic. Then Waltiri raising his baton, bringing it down. . . .

"We are told the music was strange, as no music heard before. Sounds grew in that auditorium like apparitions. We are told that a famous composer walked out in disgust. And then, a week later, filed suit against Waltiri! 'I am unable to hear or compose music in a sensible fashion!' he said in the court deposition. And what did he blame? Waltiri's music!

"Consider it.

"What would prompt a well-known and respected composer to sue a fellow composer for an impossible—so doctors tell us—injury? The case was dropped before it ever reached court. But . . . what did that concerto sound like?

"I submit to you, perhaps Waltiri knew the answer to an age-old question, namely, 'What song did the sirens sing?'"

Michael closed the book. "It's not all nonsense," Waltiri said, returning it to the shelf. "That is roughly what happened. And then, months later, twenty people disappear. The only thing they have in common is, they were in the audience for our music." He looked at Michael and lifted his eyebrows. "Most of us live in the real world, my young friend . . . but David Clarkham . . . I am not so sure. The first time I saw him, coming out of the wet with his suit so dry, I thought to myself— 'The man must walk between raindrops.' The last time I saw him it was also raining, in July of 1944. Two years before, he had bought a house a few blocks from here. We didn't see each other often. But this wet summer day he comes to stand on our porch and gives me a key. 'I'm going on a trip,' he says. 'You should have this, in case you ever wish to follow me. The house will be taken care of.' Very mysterious. With the key there is a piece of paper."

Waltiri took a small teak box from the top of the bookshelf and held it before Michael, pulling up the lid. Inside was a yellowed, folded paper, and wrapped partly within, a tarnished brass house key. "I never followed him. I was curious, but I never had the courage. And besides, there was Golda. How could I leave her? But you . . . you are a young man."

"Where did Clarkham go?" Michael asked.

"I don't know. The last words he said to me, he says, 'Arno, should you ever wish to come after me, do everything on the paper. Go to my house between midnight and two in the morning. I will meet you." He removed the note and key from the box and gave them to Michael. "I won't live forever. I will never follow. Perhaps you."

Michael grinned. "It all sounds pretty weird to me."

"It is *very* weird, and silly. That house—he told me he did a great deal of musical experimentation there. I heard very little of it. As I said, we weren't close after the premiere of the concerto. But once he told me, 'The music gets into the walls in time, you know. It haunts the place'

"He was a brilliant man, Michael, but he—how do you say it?—he 'screwed me over.' I took the blame for the concerto. He left for two years. I settled the law suits. Nothing was ever decided in court. I was nearly broke.

"He had made me write music that affects the way a person thinks, as drugs affect the brain. I have written nothing like it since."

"What will happen if I go?"

"I don't know," Waltiri said, staring at him intently. "Perhaps you will find what lives above or below the things we know."

"I mean, if something happened to me, what would my parents think?"

"There comes a time when one must disregard the thoughts of one's parents, or the warnings of old men, when caution must be temporarily put aside and instincts followed. In short, when one must rely on one's own judgment." He opened another door in the bookcase. "Now, my young friend, before we become sententious, I've been thinking there is one other thing I'd like to give to you. A book. One of my favorites." He pulled out a pocket-sized book bound in plain, shiny black leather and held it out for Michael.

"It's very pretty," Michael said. "It looks old."

"Not so very old," Waltiri said. "My father bought it for me when I left for California. It's the finest poetry, in English, all my favorites. A poet should have it. There is a large selection of Coleridge. You've read him, I'm sure."

Michael nodded.

"Then, for me, read him again."

Two weeks later, Michael was swimming in the backyard pool when his mother came out on the patio with a peculiar expression. She brushed back a strand of her red hair nervously and shielded her eyes against the sun. Michael stared at her from poolside, his arm flesh goose-bumping. He almost knew.

"That was Golda on the phone," she said. "Arno's dead."

There was no funeral. Waltiri's ashes were placed in a columbarium at Forest Lawn. There were features on his death in the newspaper and on television.

That had been six weeks before. Michael had last spoken with Golda two days ago. She had sat on the piano bench in her front room, straight-backed and dignified, wearing a cream-colored suit, her golden hair immaculately coifed. Her accent was more pronounced than her husband's.

"He was sitting right here, at the piano," she said, "and he looked at me and said, 'Golda, what have I done, I've given that boy Clarkham's key. Call his parents now.' And his arm stiffened. . . . He said he was in great pain. Then he was on the floor." She looked at Michael earnestly. "But I did not tell your parents. He trusted you. You will make the right decision."

She sat quietly for a time, then continued. "Two days later, a tiny brown sparrow flew into Arno's study, where the library is now. It sat on the piano and plucked at pieces of sheet music. Arno had once made a joke about a bird being a spirit inside an animal body. I tried to shoo it out the window, but it wouldn't go. It perched on the music stand and stayed there for an hour, twisting its head to stare at me. Then it flew away." She began to cry. "I would dearly love for Arno to visit me now and then, even as a sparrow. He is such a fine man." She wiped her eyes and hugged Michael tightly, then let him go and straightened his jacket.

"He trusted you," she had repeated, tugging gently at his lapel. "You will know what is best."

Now he stood on the porch of Clarkham's house, feeling resigned if not calm. Night birds sang in the trees lining the street, a sound that had always intrigued him for the way it carried a bit of daylight into the still darkness.

He couldn't say precisely why he was there. Perhaps it was a tribute to a friend he had known for so short a time. Had Waltiri actually wanted him to follow the instructions? It was all so ambiguous.

He inserted the key in the lock.

To discover what is above or below.

He turned the key.

Music haunts the place now.

The door opened quietly.

Michael entered and shut the door tight behind him. The brass workings clicked.

Walking straight in the darkness was difficult. He brushed against a wall with his shoulder. The touch set off an unexpected *bong,* as if he were inside a giant bell. He didn't know if he had crossed a room or made his way down a hall, but he bumped against another door, fumbled for the knob, and found it. The door opened easily and silently. To Michael's left in the room beyond was another doorway leading into a smaller room. Moonlight spilled through French doors like milk on the bare wood floor. All the rooms were empty of furniture.

The French doors opened onto a bare brick patio and a desolate yard, with a brick wall beyond. The door handles felt like ice in his hands.

He left Clarkham's house. A flagstone path curved around the outside to the side gate. When he had gone through the front door there had been no moon, but now a sullen green orb rose over the silhouettes of the houses on the opposite side of the street. It didn't cast much light. (And yet, the moonlight through the French doors had been bright. . . .) The streetlights were also strangely dim, and yellowish-green in color.

There were fewer trees than he remembered, and those were leafless and skeletal. The air smelled antiseptic, electric and somehow mildewy all at once, as if it had been preserved and then had spoiled for lack of use. The sky was pitch black and starless. Through the windows of the houses across the street came fitful brown glimmers, not at all like electric lights or television—more like reflections off dried blood.

He went to the front door of the house on the left. As predicted in the instructions, the door was open a crack. Warm, welcoming light poured in a narrow shaft from within. Entering, Michael saw a small table sitting on delicately curved and worked legs on the polished wood floor of the hallway. A brass bowl on the table held fruit: oranges, apples, something blue and shiny. Down the hall about eight feet and to the left was the rounded archway leading to the living room. He closed the front door.

The air in the house was stuffy. A faint mildewy smell issued from the walls and floor and hung in transparent wisps through the hall. Michael approached the archway, nose wrinkled. The house was lighted as if somebody lived there, but the only sound he heard was that of his own footsteps.

The living room's only furniture was a chair on a large circular throw rug before the dark fireplace. The throw rug was made of concentric circles of tan and black, resembling a target. The chair had its rear to him and rocked slowly back and forth. He couldn't see who was sitting in it. He had just realized he was not following the instructions when the chair stopped rocking and began to swivel.

Suddenly, Michael didn't want to see or be seen. He ran down the hall, around a short bend and into another empty room. "Do not stop to look at anything," the note had said. He had hesitated, he told himself, not stopped; still, he felt the need to be more cautious. He made sure no one was following him, then exited through the rear door of the house onto yet another brick patio. To his left was a trellis roof overgrown with wisteria. Fireflies danced in oleander bushes to each side. Beyond the patio, glowing paper lanterns hung from strings over a stretch of flower beds.

He was startled to see someone sitting behind a glass-topped wrought-iron table under the wisteria trellis. Except for the wan flicker of the paper lanterns, there was little illumination, but he could make out that the person at the table wore a long dress, pale and flounced, and a broad hat half-obscured by inky shadow.

Michael stared hard at the seated figure, fascinated. Was someone supposed to meet him, take him farther? The note had said nothing about a woman waiting. He tried to discern the face beneath the hat.

The figure rose slowly from the chair. There was a quality to its movement, a loose awkwardness, that made his flesh crawl. He backed up, stumbled down the porch steps into the garden and twisted around to fall on his face. For a second or two he was stunned and breathless. Then he looked over his shoulder.

The figure had left the table and stood at the top of the steps. Even hidden by the dress, every limb was obviously bending in the wrong place. He still couldn't make out the face beneath the hat.

It took the first step down from the patio, and he jumped to his feet. The second, and he ran across the garden to the black wrought-iron gate at the rear. The latch opened easily and he stopped in the alley to get his bearings. "To the left," he said, his breath ragged. He heard footsteps behind, the sound of the latch. Was it the fifth or sixth gate to the left? The alley was too dark to allow him to re-read the note, but he could make out gates—on both sides. Trees loomed thick and black over the opposite wall, absolutely still.

He counted the gates as he ran . . . two, three, four, five. He stopped again, then passed to the sixth.

A lock blocked the iron latch. He knew instinctively he couldn't just climb over—if he did, he would find nothing but darkness on the other side. He fumbled frantically for the key in his pocket, the only key he had been given.

The figure in the flounced dress was six or seven yards behind, lurching slowly and deliberately toward him, as if it had all the time in the world.

The key fit the lock, but just barely. He had to jerk it several times. There was a sigh behind him, long and dry, and he felt a cold pressure on his shoulder, the rasp of something light and hard brushing his jacket sleeve—

Michael pushed the gate open and fell through, crawling and stumbling across broken dirt and withered stubble. The gate shut with a clang and the snick of the latch falling into place again. He closed his eyes and clutched the crumbling clods and twigs, waiting.

Several seconds passed before he even allowed himself to think he hadn't been followed. The quality of the air had changed. He rolled over and looked at the stone wall. The figure should have been visible above the wall, or through the openwork of the gate, but it wasn't.

He let his breath out all at once. He felt safe now—safe for the moment at least. "It worked," he said, standing and brushing off his clothes. "It really worked!" Somehow, he wasn't all that elated. A strange thing had just happened, and he had been badly frightened.

It couldn't have taken Michael more than fifteen minutes to do everything in the instructions, yet dawn was a hazy orange in the east.

He had crossed over. But to where?

Chapter Two

His next thought was how to get back home. He walked cautiously to the gate and peered over. There was no alley, only a broad bank leading down to a gray slow-moving river about a hundred yards from shore to shore. The river flowed hazy in the early dawn light through a hilly landscape devoid of trees, the banks lined with scrubby weeds.

He turned around and surveyed the field before him. It had once been a vineyard but was now overgrown with weeds. The weeds themselves weren't faring too well. The vines had died, leaving thick gray stumps tethered to tilted stakes, surrounded by dead dry leaves and dirt.

As the smoky dawn brightened, he saw that the garden was in the rear of a blocky rectangular mansion. He walked through the dead vineyard, squinting to make out details within the mansion's dark outline. The sun was rising behind the mansion; he couldn't see it clearly until he was about a hundred yards away.

It wasn't in very good repair. One whole wing had been ravaged by fire, leaving only masonry and charred timbers. Michael was no expert on architecture, but the design seemed European, like a chateau in France. It could have been anywhere from a century to three centuries old, even older. There was no sign of life.

He felt he was intruding. He was cold, he hadn't the slightest idea where he was, and now he was getting hungry. For the time being, his only option was to go to the house, see if anyone lived there and try to get his questions answered.

He found a narrow path through the weeds and dead vines.

The house was even larger than he had thought; it was three stories tall. The bottom story was inset five or six feet. Five broad corbeled stone arches supported the overhang; as he approached, he saw that a yard-wide chunk had fallen from the middle arch.

The air of desertion and decay didn't encourage him. The path led up to the central arch, where Michael stopped. A dark oak door was set into the wall beneath, two mirror-image whorls occupying the top and bottom frames, surrounded by intertwining serpents. Two bronze lanterns jutted from the stone beside the door, their glasswork broken and jagged.

Michael made a fist and knocked on the rough, cracked wood. Even after several episodes of heavy pounding, there was no answer. He backed away a step. To each side of the door were bricked-up windows, and beyond them more alcoves in the stone wall. He moved to the next on his right and found another door, again without an exterior handle. He tried prying it open with his fingers but it wouldn't budge. The last door on the right had been plastered over. He returned to the second door and tentatively pushed at it with one hand, feeling the smooth rolls of the serpents beneath his fingers. It swung inward with a whining creak.

He looked behind him anxiously. He was still alone, unobserved, though he couldn't quite help wondering what might be hiding in the ruined vineyard.

With a stronger shove, the door swung all the way open, rebounding with a hollow thud from the wall. He stared into a dark hallway. Back-scattered morning light allowed him to see a couple of yards into the gloom. The walls were simple brickwork, without ornament or furniture. He advanced slowly. About fifteen feet in, the hall turned a corner, and a bar light slanted across the floor from that direction.

Michael peered around the corner. Beyond lay a large and exceedingly abandoned kitchen. He stepped forward gingerly, his feet displacing great wafts of felt-like dust. Yard-wide iron pots and brick-based stoves and ovens filled a chamber at least seventy feet long and sixty wide. Light shafted down through a long, narrow horizontal window about twelve feet above the floor on the opposite wall. Apparently the kitchen was in a kind of basement; from the front it lay below ground level.

The hall through which he had entered flanked a brick enclosure which might have been a storage locker or refrigerator.

A white-enameled metal door hung ajar on corroded hinges, revealing only darkness within.

On the south side of the kitchen a stairwell rose into more shadow. He crossed the cluttered floor between the iron-grilled stove and the enclosure, feet striking mounds of broken crockery and heavy, smaller pots beneath the smooth rivers of dust. He climbed the stair.

Swinging doors waited at the top, one knocked from its hinges and propped against the wall, the other kicked and splintered askew. He pushed the leaning door aside and stepped into a dining hall.

Three long dark wood tables filled about half the space, chairs upended neatly on the table edges. Beyond the tables, the carpet gave way to wooden parquet flooring. The room could have held a respectable-size ball, and stretched to the front of the house, where tall arched windows afforded a view of the rising sun. Morning light smeared silvery-gray across the table tops.

The room smelled of dust and a rather bitter tang of flowers. He looked to both sides and decided to try the broad door on the right.

That took him into an equally decrepit and impressive foyer, with modern-looking overstuffed couches spaced along the walls beneath more tall arched windows. A demolished grand piano cluttered a small stage like a crushed beetle. At the opposite end of the foyer was an immense staircase, transplanted from a castle or luxury liner, with gold banisters mounted on turned pillars of black wood. He looked up. A balustrade ran from the staircase across the length of an upper landing.

"*Ne there! Hoy ac!*"

The largest woman he had ever seen leaned over the stone and metal railing of the balustrade, directly above him. She pulled back. The creak of the floor allowed him to trace her footsteps as she approached the stairs. Through the rails her shapeless body appeared to bulk in at least five hundred pounds; she stood six and a half feet tall, and her arms were thick as hams and like in shape, covered by the long sleeves of a black caftan. Her face was little more than eyes and mouth poked into white dough, topped with well-kept long black hair.

"Hello," he said, his voice cracking.

She paused at the top of the staircase and thumped her palm on the railing. "Hel-lo," she repeated, her tiny eyes growing almost imperceptibly larger. He couldn't decide whether to stay or run. *"Antros.* You're human. Where in hell did you come from?"

He pointed to the rear of the house. "Outside. The vineyard gate."

"You couldn't have come that way," the woman said, her voice deepening. "It's locked."

He took the key-holder from his pants pocket and held it up. "I used this."

"A key!" She made her way down the stairs slowly, taking each step with great care, as well she should have. If she fell, she was heavy enough to kill herself and bring the staircase down with her. "Who gave that to you?"

Michael didn't answer.

"Who gave that to you?"

"Mr. Waltiri," he said in a small voice.

"Waltiri, Waltiri." She reached the bottom and waddled slowly toward him, her arms describing archs with each step to avoid the span of her hips. "Nobody comes here," she said, vibrating to a slow stop a few feet from Michael. "You speak Cascar or Nerb?"

He shook his head, not understanding.

"Only English?"

"I speak a little French," he said. "Took two years in high school. And some Spanish."

She tittered, then abruptly broke into a loud, high, sad cackle. "French, Spanish. You're new. Definitely new."

He couldn't argue with that. "Where am I?"

"When did you get here?" she countered.

"About half an hour ago, I think."

"What time was it when you left?"

"Left where?"

"Your home, boy," she said, some of the gravel tone returning.

"About one in the morning."

"You don't know where you are, or who I am?"

He shook his head. A slow anger grew alongside his fear.

"My name," the huge, corpulent woman said, "is Lamia. Yours?" She lifted one arm and pointed a surprisingly delicate finger at him.

"Michael," he said.

"What did you bring with you?"

He held out his arms. "My clothes, I guess. The key."

"What's that in your coat pocket?"

"A book."

She nodded as best she could; her head was almost immobile on the column of her neck. The effort buried her chin in flesh. "Mr. Waltiri sent you. Where is he?"

"He's dead."

She cackled again, as if that was something ridiculous. "And so am I. Dead as this house, dead as a million dreams!" Her laughter scattered off the walls and ceilings like a flight of desperate birds. "Can you go back?"

"I don't know," he said. "I want to."

"You want to. You come here, and you want to go back. Don't you know *how?*"

He shook his head.

"Then you're dead, too. You're stuck here. Well, at least you have company. But you must leave this house. Nobody stays here come night."

By this time he was trembling, and angry at himself for being afraid. It was all made worse by the way the woman stared at him, saying nothing. "Well," she said finally. "You'll learn soon enough. You'll return to this house tomorrow morning."

"It's only morning now," Michael said.

"And you'll need the rest of the day to straighten out your situation. Come with me."

She walked around the staircase and opened a large door at the front of the house. He followed her shimmying form down a long flight of stone steps to a rocky field, then across a narrow path to a dirt road which wound its way through more low, treeless hills.

"There's a town—a human town—about three miles up this road, beyond the field and over a bridge. Go there quickly. Don't loiter. There are those who have no great love for humans. There's a very ramshackle hotel in town, bed and board; you'll have to work for your keep. They stick together in the town. They have to. Go there, tell them Lamia wants you put up. Tell them you'll work." She stared at the book bulging his jacket pocket. "Are you a student?" she asked.

"I guess so," he said.

"Hide the book. Full morning tomorrow, come back and we'll talk."

She turned without waiting for any reaction and labored up the steps to the door, shutting it behind her. Michael looked this way and that, trying to squeeze meaning out of the barren hills, ruined old house and rocky front yard.

It was all quite real. He wasn't dreaming.

Chapter Three

Michael had not reckoned with feeling scared, being hungry, or facing the acid realization that he had no idea what to do. He had nothing to fall back on, no reasonable guide; he had only Lamia's words. Lamia herself, whatever she had to say, was hardly reassuring. Her brusqueness and her almost certain insanity made Michael all the more desperate to find a way home. He decided to try the gate again, to climb over it if need be; perhaps the river and the countryside beyond the gate were illusory. Perhaps he could just jump and find himself back in the alley. . . .

Back with the figure in the flounced dress and broad hat.

That thought stopped him halfway across the field, behind the ruined mansion. Fists clenched, he turned and trudged back between the dead vines and over the rocks and clods. He was on the dirt road again, following Lamia's directions, when he heard hooves pounding. A group of five horses and riders galloped along about half a mile behind him, raising a small plume of dust. He hid behind a boulder and watched.

The riders approached the narrow path leading to the house and slowed to confer with each other. Michael had never seen horses or men like them. The horses were large and lean, so tightly muscled they looked as if they had been flayed. They were a uniform mottled gray, all but one, a dazzling golden palomino.

The men were tall and thin, with a spectral quality most strikingly evident in their faces. All of them had reddish blond hair, long narrow jaws without beards and square large eyes beneath formidable brows. Their clothing was pearly gray, differing from the horses' coloration only in the way it diffracted the early morning sunlight.

Done conferring, they took the path to the house and dismounted near the steps. The horses kicked at clods of dirt as their masters entered the house without knocking.

Michael squinted from his awkward advantage. He decided it would be best for him to leave the area and get to the village as quickly as possible.

The walk took about forty-five minutes. All the way, he kept glancing over his shoulder to make sure the riders weren't coming up behind him.

His wristwatch wasn't working, he noticed; the sweep-second hand was motionless. The dial read one-sixteen. But he could judge time by his growing hunger.

The village first appeared as an irregular line of brown blocks set against the horizon. The closer he approached, the less impressed he was. The outskirts consisted of small mud-brick houses with thick thatched-straw roofs rising to conical peaks. Tiny columns of smoke crept up from most of the houses. In the still air, the smoke gradually settled into a thin, ground-hugging haze. Beyond the mud-brick houses, larger two-story buildings connected by stone walls presented a unified dreary green-brown exterior.

A low unguarded gate led through the walls into the village proper. He walked between the gateposts, kicking up wisps of moist smoke and ground fog. A sign neatly painted on the gate arch, facing toward the village rather than out, proclaimed:

EUTERPE

Glorious Capital of the Pact Lands

A few people were about in the mid-morning, women carrying baskets and men standing and talking. They all stared at Michael as he passed. He stuck his hands firmly into his pants pockets and returned their stares with furtive glances. The women wore pants or brown, sack-like dresses. The men were dressed in dust-colored pants and dirty tan shirts. Some walked from house to house carrying bundles of dried reeds.

To Michael's discomfort, he was attracting a lot of attention, though nobody advanced to speak to him. The place had a prison's atmosphere, quiet and too orderly, with an undercurrent of tension.

He looked for a sign to show him where the hotel was. There were no signs. Finally he gathered up courage and approached a pale round-faced man with thinning black hair, who stood by a wicker crate to one side of the narrow stone-paved street.

"Excuse me," Michael said. The man regarded him with listless curiosity. "Can you tell me where the hotel is?"

The man smiled and nodded, then began speaking swiftly in a language Michael couldn't understand. Michael shook his head and the man made a few motions in the proper direction, lifting his eyebrows.

"Thanks," Michael said. Luckily, the hotel was nearby and rather obvious; it was the only place that smelled good. There was no sign in front, but the building was slightly more elegant than its neighbors, with a pretense of mud bas-relief ornament over the door and windows. The odor of baking bread poured from the first floor windows in billows. Michael paused, salivating, then walked up the front steps and entered the small lobby.

A short, bulky man wearing a gray kepi and coveralls sat behind the counter. All the furniture was made of woven wicker or—like the counter—of small close-fitting bricks. The carpets in the lobby and hall were thin and worn, and the coarse cloth upholstery on a wicker couch placed near the door was tattered, barbed with feathers and fibers.

"Lamia told me to come here," Michael said.

"Did she now?" the man asked, his gaze fixed on Michael's chest. He seemed unwilling to admit anyone was taller than he.

"You speak English," Michael said. The man agreed with a curt nod. "She said I should work for some food and be put up this evening. I should return to see her tomorrow."

"Did she now?" he repeated.

"She wants me to work."

"Ah." The man turned to look at the rack of keys mounted behind the counter—baked clay keys, bulky and silly-looking. "Lamia." He didn't sound pleased. He wrapped his fingers around a key but didn't remove it from the hook. He stared again at Michael's chest. Michael leaned over until the man could look into his face, and the man beamed a broad smile. "What kind of work?"

"I . . . anything, I guess."

"Lamia." He removed the key and looked at it longingly.

"She never sent anyone here before. You a friend?"

"I don't know," Michael said.

"Then why's she looking after you?" the man went on, as if Michael had answered in the negative.

"I don't know much of anything," Michael said.

"Then you're new." He stated it nonchalantly, then frowned and peered at Michael's face more closely. "By God, you're new! How'd you meet Lamia if you're new? But—" He lifted his hand and shook his head. "No questions. You *are* under her charge, or you wouldn't say so, believe me. Let it stand at that. Since you're new, you'll go in with the teacher." He came around the counter. "Double up. It's a small room and my wife'll work the skin off your fingers and the kink out of your arms. You'll eat plain like the rest of us." He chuckled. "There isn't anything fancy, believe me. This place is quiet at night, you'll sleep on cotton-grass, and when the alarm rings—"

At that instant, a bell clanged loudly. The sound seemed to issue from all directions. "My name," the stout man said, "is Brecker, and we'll be going downstairs now. That's the alarm. Risky!"

Michael thought he was assessing the situation, but he called out, "Risky!" again and a thin worried-looking woman about the same age as Brecker leaped down the stairs, her bandy legs taking them three at a time.

"I heard," she said. Michael looked through the lobby's smoky windows and saw people hurrying about in the streets. "It's Wickmaster Alyons and his coursers again. They must have been at the Isomage's house, and now they're here." Michael followed them down stone steps into a dirt-walled cellar. They squatted by the wall closest to the steps, among large bottles of brown liquid and straw baskets filled with potatoes. Brecker patted the floor beside him and Michael sat.

"Why the alarm?" Michael asked.

Risky tossed her lank hair and spat into a corner. "The riding of the noble Sidhe against the race of man," she said, her voice thick with sarcasm. She appraised Michael with a cool eye. "You're new," she said. "Where's Savarin?"

"Probably watching them from upstairs," Brecker said. "As usual."

Even with the cellar door shut, Michael heard the sharp clatter of hooves. There was a high-pitched keening, and then a voice resonant and hypnotic.

"*Hoy ac!* Meat-eaters, followers of the Serpent! Praise

Adonna, or we unleash your babes and return the Pact Lands to dust and desert!"

Brecker shuddered and Risky's lips became thin and white. The hooves clattered off, and moments later bells rang again throughout the town.

"Welcome to Euterpe," Risky said to Michael as she threw open the cellar door and scrambled up the steps. Brecker followed, motioning for Michael to return with them to the first floor.

"Tomorrow," Brecker told Risky, "our new lodger goes back to the Isomage's house, to Lamia. He's new, you know."

"He's much too young to be anything else," Risky said. "And he's not like the rest of us. Not if *she* wants him." That said, she seemed to make an effort to put everything from her mind. "Show him the double."

"My thought, too. With Savarin."

"Might as well. There's a lot for him to learn."

The double on the second floor was at the end of an ill-lit corridor. The room was small, paneled in thin strips of gray pasteboard. The floor was tiled with mica and flaked under his shoes. There were two beds in the narrow space, stacked bunk-style, and a washbasin on a flimsy stand made of sticks and wicker. At least there were no insects he could see.

As he stood in the doorway, wondering who Savarin was, Risky came up behind him and argued with Brecker over what work he was to do. Brecker gave Michael a nervous glance and took Risky down the corridor, where they whispered.

Michael caught most of the conversation despite their precautions.

"If he's under Lamia's protection, should we work him at all?" Brecker asked.

"Did she forbid it? I say, work him. We can always use hands."

"Yes, but he's different from the rest of us—"

"Only because he came from the Isomage's house."

"And shouldn't that mean something?"

"Lamia doesn't scare me," Risky said. "Now, if Alyons brought him in under his arm and said, 'Show him a good time,' maybe then we'd spare him some labor."

That seemed to settle it. Risky showed him the washroom— "Modern, one upstairs and one down," she said, but no running water and no plumbing—and took him upstairs. He began by wringing fresh-washed linens through stone manglers in a laundry room behind the kitchen. As he turned the handle and fed in sheets and pillow casings, he munched on a piece of bread.

"No crumbs on the sheets," Risky told him, handing him a glass of thin milk. "You look hungry."

"Starved," Michael said.

"Well, don't eat too much. We'll just take it out in more work."

Carrying dried sheets upstairs, Michael noticed that only two rooms were occupied out of the twelve in the building; the double he shared with the unknown Savarin, and the largest, a suite. "We don't go in the suite but once a week," Risky explained.

"Who's in it?"

"Hungry and curious. Hungry and curious. Takes new ones a while to learn how the land lies, doesn't it?" She shook her head. "You'll meet him this evening. Brecker's already planning a gathering."

In the hotel's service court, he was put to chopping sticks— or rather making the attempt. He raised blisters quickly on both hands and felt miserable. He had never enjoyed hard physical labor. As he swung and missed, swung and missed, swung and splintered, swung and finally split a bundle of sticks cleanly, he wanted more than anything to be home again, in bed with a book on his lap and a ginger ale on his nightstand.

By dusk—which came somewhat early, he thought—he had cut thirteen bundles of sticks into sizes that would fit in the hotel stove. Brecker inspected the small pile and shook his head. He stared at Michael's chest as he said, "No doubt you'll do better later. If you get to stay here. But never mind. There's the meeting tonight." His face took on a contented expression and he winked. "Word gets around. You're good for the business, tonight at least."

They allowed Michael a half-hour to clean up for dinner. Having eaten only the bread and drunk two glasses of the translucent bluish milk, he was ravenous again. He went to his assigned room and lay on the lower of the two bunks for a moment, eyes closed, too tired to really want to eat and too hungry to nap. He washed his blistered hands in the basin of water and picked at a splinter beneath his fingernail. A pungent herbal smell came from the basin. Michael sniffed the soap— a fatty, grainy bar with no odor at all—and wiped his hands on a rag. The odor departed rapidly.

He removed his shirt and wiped himself from the waist up

with a damp cloth, then used the primative facilities in the lavatory at the end of the hall. He suspected he would carry the slops bucket downstairs the next day, unless. . . .

What? Unless his talk with Lamia went well? What would she do besides talk to him, and what was her connection with the riders, the Shee as Risky called them?

He was too exhausted to really be curious. He descended the stairs to dinner with drooping eyelids and sat at the smooth-worn stone-top table next to Brecker.

Night had fallen and the table was lit by dozens of tallow candles stuck in holders before each seat. There were twelve seats, each filled, and their occupants—men and women alike—regarded Michael with intense interest whenever his head was turned.

Michael sat as straight as he could, trying to be dignified and not fall asleep. As a bowl of vegetable soup was carried out by Risky, Brecker stood and raised a cup of watered brown ale. "Patrons and matrons," he began. "We have among us this evening a newcomer. His name is Michael, and he's young, as you see; the youngest I've ever met in the Realm. Let us welcome him."

Men and women raised their cups and shouted in a bewildering array of tongues, "Cheers!" "Skaal!" "Slainte!" "Zum Wohl!" "Here's to Michael!" and so on, more than he could separate out. He lifted his cup to them. "Thank you," he murmured.

"Now eat," Risky said. When the soup was consumed, she removed the bowl to the kitchen and brought in the next from the stove. This was a pot filled with cabbage and carrots and large brown beans, as well as a vegetable Michael had never seen before—something resembling a brown-skinned cucumber with a triangular cross-section. There was no meat.

His eyelids drooped and he caught himself just in time to hear, ". . . so you see, lad, we're not in the best situation here." This from the tall, strong-looking fellow with the full salt-and-pepper beard sitting across and one chair left of him.

"Huh? I mean, sorry?" Michael said blinking.

"I say, the town is not in the best of circumstances. Ever since the Isomage lost his war, we've been confined to the Pact Lands in the middle of the Blasted Plain. No children, of course—"

The plump auburn-haired woman next to him shushed him and rolled her eyes. "Except," he continued, giving her a harsh look, "And you'll pardon the indiscretion, but the lad must know his circumstances—"

At this several people called out, "And where's Savarin?"

"He should be the one tutoring the lad," the auburn-haired woman said.

"The lad," the man pushed on, *"must* know that there are children of a sort, to remind us of our peril. They reside in the Yard at the center of Euterpe." The auburn-haired woman crossed herself and bowed her head, moving her lips. "And there's not an instrument in the entire land to play."

"Play?" Michael asked. The group looked at each other around the table.

"Music, you know," Brecker said.

"Music," Michael repeated, still puzzled.

"Lad," the strong fellow said, standing, "you mean to say you don't play an instrument?"

"I don't."

"You don't know music?"

"I like to listen," Michael said, feeling fresh alarm at their amazement. More glances were exchanged around the table. Brecker looked uncomfortable.

"Boy, are you telling us it wasn't music brought you here?"

"I don't think it was," Michael said.

The auburn-haired woman gave a shuddering moan and backed her chair away from the table. Several others did the same. "Then how did you come here?" she asked, no longer looking at him directly.

"He's not a *child*, is he?" a stout woman at the end of the table wailed. Her male companion took hold of her arm and urged her back into the seat. "Obviously not," he said. "We know the children. His face is good."

"How did you get here, then?"

Michael haltingly gave an account of Waltiri, the note, Clarkham's house and the crossing over. For some reason— perhaps his weariness—he didn't mention the figure in the flounced dress. The gathering nodded in unison when he was done.

"That," said the strong man, "is a most unusual path. I've never heard of it."

"No doubt Lamia could tell us more," someone said, Michael couldn't see whom.

"I know," said a deep, gruff voice. The crowd fell silent. Brecker nudged Michael and pointed out a man seated across from them and to the right. "The occupant of the suite," he said.

The man was older than the others, none of whom seemed more than forty or forty-five. His hair was a thin white cap on his head and his almost white face carried an expression of bitter indifference. His pale blue eyes searched from face to astonished face. "He never says *anything*," Brecker said in a whisper.

"Boy," the man said, standing, "my name is Frederick Wolfer. Do you know of me?"

Michael shook his head. The man wore a worn formal black suit. The tuxedo was yellowed and torn and the elbows of the jacket had been patched over with ill-matched gray cloth. "Did Arno Waltiri mention me?"

"No," Michael said.

"He sent me here," Wolfer said, his jaw working. He raised an unsteady hand. "He sent a man already old into a land that doesn't tolerate the old. Fortunately, I have fallen in with good people." A murmur went around the table. "Fortunately, I have withstood the rigors of war, of Clarkham's attempt to build an empire, and the internment of all of us here in the Pact Lands. All of that..." He paused and looked around the ceiling, as if he might find the proper words floating up there. "Because on a summer night, who knows how many decades ago, I went to a concert and listened to a piece of music, music written by Arno Waltiri. I know the name, yes indeed. I am the only one left alive of those who were transported by his music. The only one. Boy, you must understand our circumstances. All of us here, with the exception of you, all the humans in the Realm, or Sidhedark, or Faerie Shadow, or whatever you wish to call this accursed place—we are here because music transported us."

"Enchanted," said the auburn-haired woman.

"Crossed us over," said a plump, black-haired man.

"Me, when I played trumpet," said the strong fellow.

"And I, piano," said another.

Wolfer held up his hand to stop the voices. "I was not a musician. I was a critic of music. I have always believed that Waltiri took his vengeance on me...by setting me among musicians, forever and ever."

"We loved music," Brecker said. "We added something to human music which it does not ordinarily have—"

"Except for Waltiri's concerto," Wolfer interjected.

"We took from ourselves, and made it as the Sidhe have played it for thousands of years, made it whole. And crossed over. All of us love music."

"And here," Risky said, "there is none."

"The Sidhe say their Realm *is* music," the strong man said, "but not for us."

"Ask Lamia why you're here," Risky suggested.

"And be careful of that woman, boy," Wolfer said, seating himself with painful slowness. "Be very careful indeed."

Chapter Four

Michael barely remembered stumbling up to the room after dinner, and he had no memory at all of falling asleep. But he awoke at an unknown hour, in complete darkness, to hear the room door open, footsteps and the clump of something heavy being put down on the mica flooring.

My roommate, he thought. Savarin. He dozed off again with a vague wonder as to what sort of Queequeg the Realm could conjure.

At dawn, his eyes flew open and he stared up at the bulges between the slats on the bunk above. He rolled over beneath the scratchy covers and stared at a trunk over against one wall, beside the washstand. The trunk was made of the ubiquitous wicker, equipped with heavy cloth straps.

He hadn't dreamed at all during the night. Sleep had excavated a pit in his life, a time when he might as well have been dead. Nevertheless, he felt rested. He was contemplating getting out of bed when someone knocked on the door. Simultaneously, a bushy-haired head peered over the edge of the top bunk.

"Lights up," Risky said behind the door. He heard her go down the hall.

"Good morning," said Michael's roommate. He was about forty, with graying brown hair and large bright eyes. His nose was pronounced and his chin withdrawn, set on a thin neck with almost no Adam's apple.

"Good morning," Michael said.

"Ah, American?" the man asked. Michael nodded. "My name is Henrik Savarin. You're in my bunk."

"Michael Perrin. I'm sorry."

"From?"

"Los Angeles."

Savarin nimbly stepped down the bunk ladder and landed on the floor with a plop. He had slept in his brown pants and loose fitting shirt, and had wrapped his feet in felt tied with lengths of rope.

"Short blanket on top," he explained. He untied the knots in the ropes and pulled off the felt, then slipped his feet into canvas shoes without socks. "Musician?"

Michael shook his head. "Student, I suppose."

"A scholar!" Savarin grinned and slid his palms down his pants legs in an effort to remove wrinkles. "In a land full of those crazy about music, a scholar like myself." He held out his hand. "Pleased to acquaint with you."

Michael shook Savarin's hand. "I'm not really a scholar," he said.

"They pry, you know," Savarin said, nodding at the closed door. "Myself, I regard it as most impolite to pry. So no questions for now. But..." He raised his hand and smiled again. "I'll tell you. I study the people here, I study the Sidhe and their languages, and I sometimes teach the new ones. In my day I taught music, but only played a piano poorly. Still, music caught me. I crossed, as they say."

Michael dressed quickly and followed Savarin downstairs into the dining room. The morning sun revealed that the brick walls were covered with faded hand-painted flowers, arranged in decorative rows in imitation of wallpaper. The dinner of the night before had been cleared without a trace. Only Savarin, Michael and the old man Wolfer were in the dining room. Wolfer ignored them. He sat at his own small table near a window and ate his porridge a spoonful every thirty seconds or so, contemplating the indirect morning light with raised eyebrows.

Savarin held his spoon on the table upright in one fist as Risky dropped a starchy sphere of porridge into his bowl, then poured thin milk over it from a clay pitcher. She did the same for Michael. The porridge smelled faintly of horse corral, but it didn't taste bad.

"Lamia wants you this morning," she reminded Michael before returning to the kitchen. Her tone was aloof, as if he were no longer a curiosity or an asset to the inn, and therefore no longer counted for much.

Savarin grinned at Michael and cocked his head to one side. "You have an acquaintance with the large woman at the Isomage's house?"

"That's the way I came here," he said. Savarin stopped eating.

"I'd heard the rumor," he said, frowning. "Most unusual. From the house, you mean?"

"From the gate in the back."

"Most unusual indeed." Savarin said nothing more until Risky came to take the empty bowls. She removed the half-full bowl from under Wolfer's spoon and carried it away, whistling tunelessly.

"Did you know," Savarin said, his voice loud for Risky's benefit, "that the Sidhe feel little affection for humans, one of their many reasons, because we often whistle, as our hostess does this moment?"

Michael shook his head. "Who are the Shee?"

"Alyons and his coursers, among many others. The masters of the Realm. Whistling irritates them greatly. Any human music. Very sensitive. I believe if you had whistled your way across a Faerie path when they lived on Earth, they would just as soon have flattened you with barrow stones as said good night. Angry about spoliation of their art, you see."

Michael nodded. "Who is Lamia?"

Savarin shrugged. "You know more perhaps than I. A large woman who lives in the Isomage's house."

"Who is the Isomage?"

"A sorcerer. He angered the Sidhe far more than someone who simply whistles." Savarin smiled. Risky returned with a pitcher of water, which she poured into clay mugs, setting one before Wolfer, one before Savarin, and one before Michael. Savarin tsked her and shook a finger. "The tune," he said. "Bad luck."

Risky agreed with a nod. "Bad habit," she said.

"The Shee sound like they—" Michael began, but Savarin interrupted.

"Pronounce it correctly. It's spelled S-I-D-H-E, from the ancient Gaelic—or rather, the ancients Gaels heard them calling themselves by that name. They pronounce it as a cross between 'Shee' and 'Sthee.'"

"Yes," Michael said.

"Try it."

He tried it. "The Shthee—"

"Close. Try again."

"The Sidhe——"

"That's it."

"——sound like they're pretty cruel."

"And difficult. But we do, after all, intrude, and I've been told they came to the Realm to escape humanity. There's been enmity between us for a long time."

"But it doesn't seem to me that anyone in Euterpe wanted to come here."

"All the worse, no? Do you speak German?"

"No."

Savarin smiled valiantly, but it was obvious he was disappointed. "So odd," he said. "Only one or two German-speakers in the Realm, and yet Germany was so advanced, musically." He leaned across the table. "So you don't know much about Lamia?"

Michael shook his head.

"Learn as much as you can. Carefully. I hear she has a temper. And when——if——you come back, tell me."

"If?"

Savarin waved the word away. "You'll return. I have a feeling about you . . . you're most unusual."

Michael left the hotel a few minutes later. Brecker followed him into the street and handed him a frayed cloth bag with a piece of bread in it. "I hear Lamia's larder is empty . . . usually," he said. "Good luck."

Michael went back down the road he had taken the day before, his heart pounding and his hands cold. A small crowd gathered at the village outskirts to watch him leave.

He neither saw nor met any Sidhe riders. He saw nothing moving, in fact; neither animals on the ground nor birds in the air. The sky was a pale enameled blue above, and on the horizon greenish-brown mixed with patches of orange, similar to a layer of smog. The sun was warm but not very hot, not very bright in fact——he could look at it almost indefinitely without hurting his eyes.

Yard by yard he returned to the house, feeling as though he were enclosed in a transparent bowl that prevented the Realm from reaching in and making itself real to him, and likewise prevented his thoughts from reaching out to encompass what he saw.

Near the path leading to the house, his vision narrowed. He focused on the front door, which was half-open as if he were expected. He walked down the path.

Pausing on the porch, he took a deep breath. The bowl seemed to keep even the air from his lungs. He breathed again, with little better result.

His room. His books. Saturday afternoon movies on TV. Mother and Father. Golda Waltiri with a tear running down her cheek and more swelling up in her eyes. Michael felt hollow, full of echoes.

He heard horses coming. The door opened and a thick arm reached out to grab him, pulling him inside before he could react. Lamia's grip was painfully strong. She let him go, then took hold of his coat collar and lifted him to her head level, looking at him intensely through her tiny eyes. "Into the closet!" she whispered harshly. She half-dragged, half-pulled him across the floor and opened a narrow closet door behind the grand staircase, thrusting him inside. He fell back against soft dusty things and tried to hold back tears, shaking so hard his teeth chattered.

Through the closet door, he heard footsteps. The front door shut with a click, as if just enough energy had been expended to bring it completely closed, and no more.

He heard Sidhe voices again, commanding and melodic, speaking in a completely unfamiliar language. Lamia, her tone softened, subservient, replied in English. "I've felt nothing." Another voice continued at some length, fluid and high-pitched but distinctively masculine.

"No one's been here, no one's passed through," Lamia said. "I tell you, I felt nothing. I don't care what's happening in town. They're all fools, you know that better than I."

Michael reached out in the darkness to get leverage to stand. His hand touched rough fabric, then something soft and smooth which he couldn't identify, like leather but thinner and supple as silk.

The Sidhe voices took on a snake-like threatening tone.

"I remain at my station, I watch," Lamia said. "You force me to stay here, you keep my sister at the gates; we are your slaves. How can we defy you?"

Michael picked out one word in a rider's response: Clarkham.

"He has not come here," Lamia said. That ended the conversation. The front door swung open and a sound resembling wind announced the rider's exit. Michael felt for a doorknob. There was none.

Lamia opened the closet. "Come out," she said. He blinked and took a step forward, tripping over something soft and tough. Before he could look back in the closet and see what it contained, she whirled him around and slammed the door shut. "They'll raid the town tonight, looking for somebody. They won't raid Halftown; they never do. So I'm sending you there. First, though, listen to me and answer some questions."

Michael shrugged out from under her hand and backed away. "I have questions, too," he said.

"By what right? You've come here, you should know as much as there is to know."

"But *I don't!*" His voice ended in a high wail of frustration. The tears came freely now. "I don't know anything, not even where I am!"

"In Sidhedark," Lamia said, turning from him. "Come with me," she continued, more gently. "In the Faerie Shadow. The Realm. You are no longer on Earth."

"I've been told that. But where is this place?"

"Not on Earth," Lamia repeated. She walked ahead, her bulk rippling.

"Can I go back?" he shouted after her.

"Not this way. Perhaps not at all."

Suddenly deflated, Michael followed her down a broad hallway, into the burnt-out wing of the house.

Chapter Five

"Years ago, there was a war here," Lamia said. "The entire plain was scourged. The river turned to steam, the trees became serpents and crawled away, the land cracked like open wounds, revealing all of Adonna's past indiscretions, its abortions. And in the middle of it . . ." She paused, swinging her thick arms to take in the ruined wing. "In the middle of it, this house stood alone. The Isomage lost everything, almost. But he escaped, and he still had enough power to threaten them with great harm if they didn't make a pact with him. For their part, the Sidhe were to create a liveable territory within the Blasted Plain, and gather all humans here, all those who had crossed over and were being persecuted. The Sidhe were not to harm them, but would tend them. For his part, the Isomage would go far away and work no more magic in this part of the Realm." She turned her tiny eyes on him and Michael saw a gleam of defiance and strength that seemed out of place in the massive doughy face. She closed her eyes and hardly seemed human. "I was young then." She took a deep, quivering breath and let it out through her small, narrow nose with a low whistle.

They stopped by a long charred table with fragments of chairs scattered around it. In the rubble which covered the table, Michael could see glints of tarnished silver plates, bent and melted forks and knives, slumped metal cups and shattered glassware, all dusted with fine gray powder and chunks of wood and plaster. The smell of smoke was still thick in the air.

"Years ago. Ages," Lamia said. Moving one columnar leg at a time, slow and ponderous as an elephant, she swung around to face him and pointed with her quivering left hand in his general vicinity. "You crossed over with something powerful on your person. I know you did. Are you aware of it?"

Michael shook his head.

"You'll know what it is, soon. This is a strange place; take nothing for granted. And above all, *obey*." She growled the last word and advanced on him, stopping a yard away when he began to back up. "You still have a book. I told you to hide it. The Sidhe don't like human words, any more than they like human song. Why didn't you obey me?"

"I don't have anyplace safe to hide it."

"You doubt whether I should be obeyed?" Her voice was not any more menacing than usual, but he felt a tremor up his back nonetheless. He said nothing.

"I am the second guardian. Did you meet the first?"

"I don't know."

"You would know, my boy. Believe me, you would know."

He thought of the figure in the flounced dress. "I think so."

"Were you afraid of her?"

He nodded.

"You're less afraid of me, that's obvious. And yet..." She smiled, the curve of her mouth barely shifting the great flaps of her cheeks and jowls. "I am the one who controls the other. Is that clear?"

"If nobody ever comes this way, why are you here?" Michael asked. Lamia tittered, holding one hand over her mouth and pretending coyness in a way that made his stomach uneasy.

"Now," she said. "There are a number of things you must do. You're new, you can't know half what it takes to simply stay alive. And believe me, you don't want to *die* here. To keep alive, you'll have to be trained."

"I don't want to stay. I want to go back." He clenched his hands. He still couldn't believe the situation was irreversible.

"To go back, you must move ahead," Lamia said. "There's only one person with the power to send you back. He's a great distance from here, and to reach him you'll make an arduous journey. That's why you must be trained. Do you understand me now?" She leaned over and peered at him. "Or are you stupid as well as young?"

"I'm not stupid," Michael said.

"Parts of the Realm are quite beautiful, though few humans cross the Blasted Plain to see them. The Sidhe appreciate beauty. They leave the ruins for humans."

"Are you human?" Michael asked.

Lamia's white skin purpled slightly. "Not now."

"Are you a Sidhe?"

"No." Her laugh was a deep grumble in her massive torso. "Now you have had your questions. Any more and—"

"If I don't ask questions, how will I learn?"

Before he could flinch, her arm struck out like a scorpion's tail and her hand slammed against the side of his face. He spun across the charred floor and fell into a mound of ashes, raising a cloud. She pushed through the cloud and grabbed him with both hands by the shoulders, lifting him clear and dangling him over the floor. Gentle, almost sweet, her voice reached him through the haze as if she were miles away.

"You'll go to Halftown. You'll take instruction from the Crane Women. Got that?"

"The hotel—"

She shook him once, making his bones pop. "You don't deserve the luxury. The Crane Women are called Nare, Spart and Coom. Tell me their names."

He couldn't remember.

"Again, then. Nare, Spart, and Coom."

"Nare, Spart . . ."

"Coom."

"Coom."

"They're expecting you. They'll teach you how to survive. Maybe they'll teach you how to see and hear and remember, how to judge situations better. Think that's possible?" She held him with one hand and brushed him down with the other. Her touch was feverishly warm. She set him down near the table and looked up longingly at the burnt-out rafters.

"It was the middle of a banquet," she said. "They took us by surprise. We used to have parties here often. It was beautiful."

Michael tried to control his trembling but couldn't. He was terrified and furious. He wanted to kill her.

"Go," she said. "Tell the innkeeper and his wife that Lamia no longer needs their services. Take yourself over to Halftown. The Crane Women. What are their names?"

"Nare, Spart and Coom."

She grunted. "Go, before the Sidhe return."

He fled from the ruined wing, through the hall and across the entry to the front door. Book bouncing against his hip, he ran down the road to Euterpe until his lungs were about to burst. His face was streaked with tears of rage. He stopped by a cracked, glazed boulder and pounded on it until his hand bled. "God damn you, God damn you!"

"Better be quiet," the wind whispered. He jumped and whirled around. Nobody.

"Remember where you are."

He screamed. Something luffed his hair and he looked up. There, translucent as a spider's web, was a narrow and colorless face. It rotated and vanished.

Cupping his hands over his mouth, smearing blood on his chin, he stumbled and ran the rest of the way to Euterpe with little concern for his lungs or his legs.

Risky accepted his explanation with seeming indifference. Brecker nodded and accompanied him upstairs to the room. "You didn't come here with anything, so there's no luggage for you to pick up," he said. "But you can help me clean it." They swept the floor in silence. Michael was confused by the token labor.

"It's not my dirt," he said. "I've only been here one night."

"We all do our bit," Brecker said. "It's what keeps us going."

"Even when there's nothing to do?"

Brecker leaned on his straw broom. "Where'd you get that bruise?"

"Lamia hit me."

"Why?"

"I don't know why," Michael lied.

"For asking dumb questions, likely." Brecker resumed his sweeping. "It's a hard land, boy. Wherever you came from, it seems you led an easy life among reasonable people. Not here. Mistakes cost." He held a pan down for Michael to sweep dust and mica flakes into. "Mistakes cost dear."

Savarin was climbing the stairs as they descended. Michael passed him with a shrug. "Moving already?" Savarin asked, peering after them.

"To Halftown," Michael said.

"Might I accompany you?" Savarin asked. Michael shrugged again. "This could be most useful."

The road to Halftown stretched to the east of Euterpe for two miles.

"We call it east, anyway," Savarin explained, walking beside Michael. Michael kept his hands in his coat pockets, one wrapped around the book of poems. "Where the sun rises, you know."

Michael said nothing, staring at the ground as they walked. "Where did you get the bruise?"

"Lamia hit me for asking questions."

Savarin pursed his lips. "Tough customer, Lamia, I hear. Never met her myself. What sort of questions?"

Michael looked suspiciously at Savarin. "What do you know?"

"You might have gathered by now that when new people show up, I am their tutor. I know as much as any human here, I suspect—with the exception of the Isomage, but he's been gone for decades now."

"Where the hell is this place?"

"Some people claim this place *is* hell, but it is not. I would venture a guess that it is the legendary land of Faerie, which some consider the place of the dead; but none of us trapped here died on Earth, so your guess is probably as good as mine. Ask Adonna. Adonna made it."

"Who's Adonna?"

"The *genius loci*, the god of the Realm. Most of the Sidhe pay obeisance to it. From what I gather, it's not in the same league as whatever made our universe. Much cruder." Savarin winked. "But be careful to whom you speak when you make such critiques."

"So we're in a different dimension?"

Savarin held up his hands and shook his head. "Not to be quoted. Scholar that I am, and as hard as I've researched, I'm still remarkably ignorant. Facts are hard to obtain. Frankly, I was hoping you could provide a few."

"Who are the Sidhe?"

"The mortal enemies of humankind," Savarin said, his face suddenly grim. "There are all kinds of Sidhe, not just the ones who bear a passing resemblance to us. There are the Sidhe of the Air, called Meteorals by some—"

"What do they look like?"

"Translucent, drifting creatures, resembling spirits. There are the Sidhe of the forests, called Arborals; they are green as grass. Umbrals will always be found in shadow, and at night can be very powerful. Pelagals are reputed to be ocean-going, but we only have rumors of a distant ocean here. Riverines live in streams and rivers. Amorphals can be a different shape each time you see them. Most of the Sidhe, however, belong to the kind called Faer—like Alyons and his coursers. The Faer resemble you and me and we can even interbreed, but they're a very different race, ages older than the current stock of humanity."

"And what is Halftown?"

"Where the Breeds live. Born of female Sidhe, sired by human males, most often."

"They won't live with humans?"

"They're a sad lot," Savarin said. "They're reputed to live forever, like the Sidhe, and like the Sidhe they have no souls. But like humans, they change—their peculiar way of aging. Humans don't accept them. Sidhe isolate them, but find them useful now and then. Many know Sidhe magic." They walked on in silence for a few minutes. "Who's to watch over you in Halftown?"

"The Crane Women," Michael said.

Savarin was impressed. "Very powerful. Ugly as sin, and they wouldn't mind my saying so. They're the oldest Breeds I've heard of. Was it Lamia who sent you to them?"

Michael nodded. "I don't go anywhere on my own. I mean, I don't have any choice."

"Maybe that's something to be thankful for. Less mistakes made that way."

"Is Lamia a Breed?"

"I don't think so. There are many stories about her, but nobody really knows what she is. I suspect she was human once, but did something the Sidhe didn't like. She was at the Isomage's house when I came here."

Beyond a rise, the road bisected the Breed settlement, which was laid out in an irregular circle. Halftown covered about ten acres, brown and dun and weathered gray buildings arranged along concentric half-circle streets, the ends of each street letting out on the main road. The land around Halftown was hummocky, as if ploughed by a giant and careless farmer, and the ground was poorly drained. Standing pools and puddles lay in the hollows and the air had a marshy green smell. A branch of the river flowed past the other side of the village, little more than a creek.

"Observe the structures," Savarin said, stopping to tie a string on his cloth shoes. "What would you say of them?"

Michael examined the buildings and then, to make sure he had missed nothing, examined them again. "They're shacks," he said. "They look like the houses in Euterpe."

Savarin straightened. "You're still not observing. See with what you already know." He pointed to the barren landscape: grassy shrub, hammocks and puddles, low bushes and scattered boulders.

"Jesus," Michael said under his breath. "They're shacks. Made of wood."

"Wood," Savarin emphasized. "See any trees?"

"No."

"That's how you tell Halftown from Euterpe. Breeds have Sidhe relatives, and that means connections with Arborals. Arborals control all the wood in the Realm. Humans are only allowed sticks and wicker and grass."

Michael felt dizzy. He still hadn't accepted that the Realm was real—yet every moment it became more and more complex.

"There aren't any trees here at all?"

"Away from the Blasted Plain, there are forests everywhere, but no wood for you and me. Very few humans leave the Pact Lands. Sidhe traders bring in goods every fortnight, in accord with the Isomage's pact, but even they face danger on the Blasted Plain."

Michael saw his first Breed as they came within a hundred feet of the outer circle of huts. The Breed was a male, slightly taller than Michael, with long, lank red-brown hair and a powerful build. He stood in the middle of the road, a staff in one hand and a bored expression on his face. He held out his staff to stop them.

"I recognize you, Teacher. I know this young fellow, too. Lamia sends word about him—but not about you."

"I come here often," Savarin said defensively.

"The coursers came last night," the Breed said. "No more humans allowed in Halftown. Except, of course . . ." He pointed his finger at Michael.

"I think you'd better go," Michael told Savarin. "Thanks for helping me."

Savarin frowned at the breed. "Yes. I'm sure discretion is best. But I've never been barred from Halftown. I hope it's not permanent. This is where I get most of my information." He sighed, cast a sunny smile on Michael and turned around. "Learn quickly, friend. And come tell me what you've learned, if you can."

Michael accepted his outstretched hand. Savarin returned the way they had come, leaving him alone with the Breed guard.

A cool breeze rippled their hair and clothes. "So where am I supposed to go?"

"To the Crane Women. Come."

Michael followed him down the road. Through Halftown, the thoroughfare was paved with brown brick and cobbles. The huts seemed cleaner though flimsier than the huts in Euterpe. Small plots around each house were filled with rows of healthy green plants; he couldn't see any flowers.

Other Breeds stared at him through windows and open doors. The men were almost as tall as the Sidhe Michael had glimpsed at the Isomage's house. The women were slender, noble-looking, though few were what Michael would have called pretty. Their faces were hard and sculptured, too much like the men's.

His escort led him out the other side of the village and away from the road, toward the creek. Across the water, perched atop a broad low mound, was a larger hut shaped like a half-deflated soccer ball, covered with sticks, dirt and thatch. Except for two round glass-paned windows and a stone chimney poking through the top, it could have been a yurt—one of the portable dwellings used by central Asian nomads. The yard around the hut was strewn with small boulders and piles of debris, sorted and categorized—a pile of pebbles here, sticks to one side, bones and animal skulls there, other mounds he couldn't identify. The smell was of ancient garbage, richer and more suggestive than dust, but not overtly offensive. Stakes marked the perimeter of the mound and scraps of fabric fluttered from them like sad decrepit banners.

"How do I get across?" Michael asked as they stopped at the water's edge. The Breed pointed out flat stones just beneath the slow-moving surface.

"They await you," he said, and began his walk back to Halftown. Michael swallowed the tightness in his throat and stepped out onto the first stone. The water swirled around his shoes. He thought about falling into the water to force himself to wake up, stop dreaming, but if he hadn't been shocked out of sleep by the things that had already happened, the murky creek was unlikely to do the trick. Besides, he had no idea what lurked in the depths. He was sick of being afraid. He clutched his book tightly and stepped onto the second stone. He concentrated so hard on not falling that he failed to notice a figure standing on the opposite bank until he had crossed. He looked up with a start.

"Hello," he said quickly.

The figure was female in a bizarre sort of way. She still possessed a roundness in her elongated, leather-skinned limbs which demonstrated femininity, but her arms hung almost to her knees. Her face was oblate, wider than tall, with narrow long eyes beneath thin flat brows. She stood an inch or two shorter than Michael, slightly stooped. Her legs, clothed in ragged pants, were very long in comparison with her torso. She lifted one hand and wriggled spider-like fingers in front of her flat chest. The fingers were long and dark and tapered to thin black nails.

"Hello," he repeated. She looked him over slowly, nodding with a steady rhythm as if she were feeble. Her short-cut hair had the color and texture of goose down.

"Jan Antros," she said. "Just man-child." Her voice was a gnarly squeak with undertones of heavy wind.

Michael shook his wet feet and reached with one hand to empty his left shoe, then his right. He never took his eyes off her. The shoes squelched when he put them on again. "I'm Michael," he said, trying to be agreeable.

"You're a delicate, incredibly fragile, very frail indeed piece of tissue," came a melodious voice from the hut. Another woman with similar features leaned from one window. Her face was a puzzle of wrinkles and red and purple tattoos. "You don't look important."

Behind Michael, where she couldn't possibly have snuck up on him, a third woman stood on one spindly leg with the other tucked close to her chest. She had long dusty-red hair tied in a single braid which reached to her knees. "The Flesh Egg sends us a weak man-child. She expects us to process, train?"

"Are you Nare, Spart and . . . Coom?" Michael asked, trying to keep his teeth from chattering.

"I'm Nare," said the Crane woman standing on one leg.

"Spart," said the one at the window, and

"Coom," said the downy-haired figure who had first addressed him. "Want us teach?"

"I don't know what I want," Michael said, "except to get out of here."

The Crane women chuckled, a sound like leaves skittering over rock.

"Won't hurt you," Coom said, backing off a foot. "Much." Her hair seemed alive in the breeze.

"We don't mind man-childs," said Nare at his side, circling.

"But there's one thing you must want," said Spart in her beautiful voice from the window. She spat into a nearby pile of debris.

"To survive," Nare said.

"Live in Sidhedark."

"Fight to live."

"Fight to be human."

"Understood?"

He could do nothing but nod. In the moment he turned away from the hut, Spart left the window and stood between Nare and Coom. She was the tallest of the three and had the longest, most Sidhe-like face. Tattoos formed an intricate tangle of leaves and branches and whorls wherever her skin was bare.

"You'll build a house on this mound, away from ours thirty paces," she said. "Wood will be brought to you this evening. Until you've built your own house, you don't exist."

"What'll I do now?" he asked. He had focused on Spart; he suddenly realized the other two were gone.

"Be patient." Spart's voice had much of the hypnotic quality he'd experienced while listening to Alyons and the coursers. "You can do that, can't you?"

"Yes."

"Go and sit where you want your house. Wood will come."

The Crane Woman returned to their hut, leaving him on the stretch of hard-packed dirt by the creek bank. He shifted from one foot to the other, then looked over the water to Halftown. He shaded his eyes and stared at the sky.

Not a cloud was visible. Enameled sparkling blueness stretched overhead, blending into the orange and green along the horizon. About thirty yards away from the hut, and an equal distance from the creek bank, two boulders nestled against each other, forming a natural seat about a yard wide and two and a half feet tall. Michael crossed to the boulders and sat on them, looking at the sky again. Sometimes it seemed to be made of cross-thatches of colors, hundreds of colors all adding up to blue. Yet it wasn't like a painting. It was very alive, disturbing in the way it seemed to shift, to bulge *down* and retreat *up*.

He felt drugged. Until now, alone, with no instruction but to wait, it was as if he had not seen anything clearly. Now the clarity flooded down on him from the sky. The sky, by its very unreality, seemed to show how real everything was.

But this reality wasn't the same brand he had experienced on Earth. This was more vivid, more apparent and simpler.

He knelt beside the boulders and plucked a blade of grass, peeling it along its fibers, rubbing the ragged edges, smearing the beads of juice. He felt a tickle on his arm and saw a tiny ant crawling among the light, silky hairs. The ant was translucent, rainbow-hued like an opal. Until now, he hadn't thought to wonder if there were insects in Sidhedark. Not many, apparently.

What about birds, cats, dogs, cows? He'd seen horses, but... where did the milk come from?

He was tired. He leaned back on the rocks and closed his eyes. The darkness behind his lids was still and restful. Wind sighed over him.

He had slept. He sat up and rubbed elbows stiff from pressing against the rock. The sun was setting. There were no clouds yet, but unmoving bands of color hung above the horizon, pale pinks and greens at the highest and just above the sun's limb a particularly vivid stripe of orange. Michael had never seen a sunset like it.

He looked to the east. The sky there was an electric blue-gray. Stars were already appearing in the east, as sharp and bright as white-hot needle points. Instead of twinkling, they made little circling motions, as if they were distant tethered fireflies. Michael had sometimes used Whitney's Star Finder on summer nights to pick out the few constellations visible through Los Angeles' thick air. He couldn't recognize any now.

The air had cooled considerably. Orange light flickered in the windows of the Crane Women's hut. He had a notion to peer in and see what they were up to, but he rubbed the bruise on his cheek and thought better of it.

Only then did he notice that his wristwatch was gone. He grabbed for the key in his pants pocket, but it was missing as well. He still had the book.

He felt almost naked without the key. He resented the thievery; he resented everything about the way he was being treated, but there wasn't a thing he could do.

The last of the sun slipped behind distant hills, burning muddy orange through the smoky haze which he surmised lay over the Blasted Plain, beyond the boundary of the Pact Lands. Where the sun had been, a sharply defined ribbon of darkness ascended from the horizon and blended with the zenith; and then another to one side, and yet another on the opposite side, resembling the shadows of cloth streamers in a celestial wind.

Michael listened. The land all around was silent, but from

the sky came a low humming, like wind stroking telephone wires. When the darkness was complete, the humming went away.

Then, starting in the east and progressing westward across the sky, the stars steadied, as if precipitating out of solution and pasting themselves against the bowl of the heavens.

There were stars in the dirt, as well. He pulled his feet up on the boulders and looked down. Things sparkled and glinted between the few blades of grass. Soon these glows faded and the land settled into night with a breezy sigh, as if all the Realm were a woman lying back on a pillow.

No, indeed, Michael thought; this is not Earth, whatever its outward resemblance.

He sat on the rocks for some time before he heard the voices. They came from the creek, but he couldn't see who was speaking; there was no light but the stars and the now-faint glow from the hut's windows. Concentrating on the source, forcing his pupils to their maximum dilation, he discerned a low-slung boat-shadow gliding down the creek, as well as a few figures standing on the prow. The boat nudged the bank and he heard footsteps coming toward him.

He stood up on the rocks. "Who's that?" he called out.

The hut door swung open. Spart stood silhouetted against the swirling, furnace-orange light. The approaching shadows passed through the shaft of light from the door and were outlined briefly. There were four, brownish-green in color—or perhaps solid green—and they were naked. Three were male, one female. They were obviously Sidhe, with the same elongated features and spectral grace, and each carried a broad, stubby log.

They surrounded Michael and at a signal, simultaneously dropped the logs from their shoulders into the dirt.

"*Dura*," said the female. The beauty of her voice made Michael shudder.

"Your wood, boy," the Crane Woman said from the hut door.

He turned and cried out. "What do I do with it?"

But the hut door closed and the naked Sidhe walked away. The female glanced back at him with some sympathy, he thought, but she said nothing more. They were absorbed in the blackness.

He remained standing on the boulder awhile, then sat. The four logs rested on their ends, each about a foot and a half wide and a yard tall. He was no carpenter like his father; he couldn't calculate how many board-feet there were in the logs, or how much of a house he could build with them.

Not a very large one.

He leaned back and closed his eyes again.

"Whose boy are you?"

He thought he was dreaming. He wiped his nose reflexively.

"Hoy ac! Whose house?"

Michael spun around on the boulders and looked in the voice's direction. There was only a log.

"Rup antros, jan wiros," said the voice, like that of the Sidhe woman but with a fuzzy quality. *"Quos maza."*

"Where are you?" Michael asked softly. The night air was quite chilly now.

"All around, antros. It's true. Your words are Anglo-Saxon and Norman and mixes from the misty north and the warm south. Ah, I knew those tongues once, at their very roots . . . affrighted many a Goth and Frank and Jute . . ."

"Who are you? Who?"

There was silence for a moment, then the voice, much weaker, said, *"Maza sed more kay rup antros. It's strange to be broken for a human's house. Why so privileged? Still, all wood is passing; the imprint, must fade . . ."*

The voice did indeed fade. Though it was still and quiet thereafter, Michael got no sleep that night.

Chapter Six

He was almost as cold as the rocks he sat on when the dew settled around him in the early dawn. The sky turned from black to gray and mist slid over the mound and creek in glutinous layers. Narrow vapor trails four or five feet in length shot through the mist with quiet hissing noises. Michael was too chilled to care.

He twisted his stiff neck around and noticed the logs were no longer standing around the boulders. Sometime during the night, they had fallen into jumbles of neatly cut beams and boards. The bark of each log lay folded next to its partitioned innards.

Michael wasn't encouraged. Like a lizard, he waited for the sun to come up and warm his blood. He hadn't resolved anything during the night—the hours had been spent in a cold stupor—but the conviction of his inadequacy had solidified.

The sun appeared in the east, a distant red curve topping a hill beyond the main branch of the river. Without thinking, Michael uncurled his arms and legs and stood on the rock to catch the first rays of warmth. His bones cracked and his legs almost collapsed under him, but he staggered and kept his balance. His clothes were soaked with dew.

The hut was quiet and dark, likewise the village. In a few minutes, however, just when he thought he might be catching some warmth from the new day, he heard activity from the Halftown houses. Curls of smoke began to rise from their stone and mud-brick chimneys.

He heard a woman singing. At first, he was too intent on just getting warm to pay much attention, but as the voice grew near, he angled his head and saw a young Breed female fording the stream on the flat rocks, barefoot. She wore cloth pants ending at the knees and a vest laced together with string. Her hair was raven black—uncharacteristic, he thought—but her face bore the unmistakable mark of the Sidhe, long with prominent cheeks and a narrow, straight nose. She carried four buckets covered with cloth caps, two in each hand. She glanced at Michael on her way to the Crane Women's hut.

"*Hoy,*" she greeted.

"Hello," Michael returned. She stopped before the door, which opened a crack. A long-fingered hand stretched out and took two buckets, withdrew, then emerged to take two more. The door closed and the woman reversed her course. She paused, cocked her head at Michael, then started toward him.

"Oh, God," he said under his breath. He was just warm enough to shiver and he badly needed to piss. He didn't want to talk to anyone, much less a Breed woman.

"You're human," she said, stopping about six paces from the boulders. "Yet they gave you wood."

He nodded, arms still unfolded to catch the warmth.

"You're an English speaker," she continued. "And you come from the Isomage's house. That's all they say about you in Halftown."

He nodded again. Beneath all the cold and misery was a steady current of shyness. Her voice was disarmingly beautiful. He would have to get used to Sidhe and Breed voices.

"It will be warm soon," she said, walking toward the stream. "If you have time today, come to the village and I'll give you a card for milk and cheese. Everybody needs to eat. Just ask for Eleuth."

"I will," he said, his voice cracking. When she had crossed the creek, he clambered down from the rock, walked some distance away, and knelt down to hide himself while he urinated. He felt like some animal, barely domesticated. A pet of the Breeds.

The door to the Crane Women's hut opened and Spart emerged carrying a roll of cloth. She stared at him balefully, unfurled the cloth and flapped it. An exaltation of tiny birds flew from its folds and circled the house, then headed north. Without explanation, Spart returned to the house and closed the door behind.

Massaging blood back into his legs, Michael looked doubtfully at the piles of lumber. He picked up the sheets of bark and discovered that they could be peeled into light, strong strips with a ropy toughness. He thought about how to put a hut together and shook his head. He'd need tools—nails, certainly, and a knife and saw.

Even as he speculated half-heartedly, he asked himself what the hell good it was, building a house where he didn't belong.

"You have a long way to go."

Nare stood behind him. Her eyes were large, like an owl's but mobile. Her long red-gray hair was an unbraided radiance, spreading to its widest point behind her knees. "Now that you have the grace of wood, what are you going to do with it?"

"I need tools."

"I don't think so. Are you aware what the grace of wood means?"

He thought for a moment. "Humans don't get much."

"Humans get scrap. Not even Breeds can get wood all the time. The finest wood is reserved for the Sidhe. Like as not they have ancestors in it."

"I don't understand," Michael said.

"The Sidhe are immortal, but if they die in battle or through some other faulting, the Arborals press them into tree. They dwell there awhile, then request oblivion. Arborals do their work, and we have wood."

"I heard a voice last night."

Nare nodded. Bending over, she picked up a plank and held it out to Michael. One long forefinger pressed against the edge and a notch fell out. "Feel and press. Riddle how it all goes together. Wood was shaped into a house by the Sidhe that dwelled within. Just puzzle it. *Maza.*"

"Today?" Michael asked.

"Today is all the time you have." Nare headed for the creek and dove in like an otter. He didn't see her come up.

For the next few hours, trying to ignore his hunger, Michael took each board and beam and pressed, poked and rubbed the surfaces until he found the removable pieces. At first he took the small pieces and tossed them aside, but thought better of it and gathered them into a small pile.

It became obvious that he could fit some of the pieces into holes in the planks, and use them to slide into notches in the beams. It reminded him of a wooden puzzle he had at home, only much more complex. When the sun was high, he had managed to assemble two planks and one beam, with no idea where to go from there. He didn't even know what shape the house would be.

Spart, the Crane Woman with tattoos all over and the melodious voice, came to him from the hut and offered a wooden bowl. Inside was cold gruel, a piece of fruit and a puddle of thin milk. He ate it without complaint. She watched, one long arm twitching now and then, and removed the bowl from his hands when he was done.

"When you have finished the house, you will go into the village and announce yourself at the market. They will allow for your food. Also, while you're here, you can carry messages for us, and otherwise make yourself useful." She glanced at the pile of wood. "If you haven't puzzled it by dawn tomorrow, it's not your wood any more."

He stared at her tattoos. She didn't seem to mind, but she bent down and tapped the wood meaningfully. He set to work again and she walked back toward the house.

"Is it safe to drink the water?" he called after her.

"I wouldn't know," she said.

By evening, with all his ingenuity he had succeeded in figuring out that the house would be square, about two yards on each side, without a roof or floor. He would apparently have to gather grass or something for the roof, and that discouraged him. He was ravenous, but no more food was brought out.

"Maybe they'll feed me when I'm done," he thought. "If."

He discovered the bark could be used for lashings. As the sun and sky went through the same twilight phenomena of the day before, Michael kicked a beam with one foot and held his hand out in front of him. "It's impossible."

But...

He knelt and picked out a square, thick beam whose use he hadn't discovered. He pressed along the grain and it fell apart in neat, almost paper-thin shingles. Then the plan seemed to come together in his mind. He assembled planks and beams, slipped tenon into mortise, lashed the wood together, and took five long, thin curved pieces to make the framework of the roof. When darkness was complete, he had almost finished putting on the shingles. He had one string of bark and two pieces of pressed-out wood left, yet the house seemed complete.

Spart stood outside when he emerged through the low door. She looked at the string in his hand and shook her head. *"Fera*

antros," she said. "If you had built it right, you wouldn't have
any pieces left over."

For a moment, he was afraid she might have him dismantle
the hut and start all over again, but she pulled a bowl from
behind her back and handed it to him. His meal this time was
vegetable paste and a thick, doughy slice of dark bread. She
squatted down next to him as he ate.

"There are many languages among the Sidhe," Spart said.
"Some are very ancient, some more recent. Nearly all the Sidhe
speak Cascar. It would be an advantage to learn as much Cascar
as you can—and you need all the advantages you can get."

"Some speak English," Michael said.

"Most speak it because it is in your mind. In-speaking. And
English was spoken in the last lands many of us inhabited on
Earth, English and other tongues—Irish, Welsh, French, Ger-
man. We also speak Earth languages you wouldn't be familiar
with, all old, most dead. Languages come easy to the Sidhe.
But no human tongue can replace Cascar."

Not being hungry made Michael bolder. "How old are you?"

"There are no years here," Spart said. "Seasons come and
go at the whim of Adonna. How old are you?"

"Sixteen," Michael said.

She stood and took his empty bowl. "Tonight, in the dark,
one of us will test you. You will not be able to fend us off,
but how you react will shape the way we teach you. Sleep or
not, as you will."

Chapter Seven

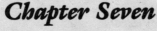

Inside, the house was drafty and small and the floor was no comfort, but it was better than nothing. He sat in a corner, trying not to sleep, awaiting the promised test.

There wasn't much he could do to prepare. He wondered if they would hurt him. He had never been much of a fighter; it had always taken him too long to get angry. Consequently, he had little experience with his fists.

Not having slept the night before, he couldn't keep his eyes from closing. He groaned as he realized he was falling asleep. His head fell against his knees—

And jerked up at the sound of hooves. It was still dark. Something splashed in the river. He heard a horse nicker and sneeze.

He was so tired. Being tired and alert at once gave the experience a surreal edge, as if things weren't bizarre enough already. He had to decide whether to stay in the house—and perhaps have it knocked down around his ears—or go outside.

He stood. The roof was a bare half-inch above the top of his head. All his life he had been slow to act, thoughtful, predictable. Perhaps being unpredictable would give him an advantage. . . .

Hunkering down, he bunched his leg muscles to spring through the doorway. If he could run fast enough, perhaps he could get away.

He leaped through the door, keeping his head down, and ran headlong into someone tall and solid. He rebounded and fell back, clasping his hands to his head. A Sidhe stood over him, wearing bright silver chain mail and sporting a long,

wickedly pointed pike. Michael's vision swam; he barely saw
the Sidhe lower the pike and prod his sternum.

"*Vera ais, sepha jan antros pek,*" said the Sidhe in a low
voice. Michael regained his breath and looked around frantically. A few yards away, a Sidhe horse stood relaxed, pale
gray blankets wrapped around its neck and withers, with a
silvery saddle and no stirrups or reins. "*Vas lenga spu?*" The
pike pressed harder, drawing blood. Michael squirmed and
cried out. "*Vas lenga?*"

"Let me alone!" he shouted. He grabbed the pike but it
seemed to have sharp edges all around and cut his fingers.

"You don't belong here," the Sidhe growled. "Do you know
who I am?"

"No!"

"I am Alyons, Wickmaster of the Blasted Plain and Pact
Lands. Some call me *Scarbita Antros*—Scourge of Men. How
did you get here? Why are you living in a house of wood?"

"I was sent here," Michael said. His fear melted any anger
he felt, but seemed to heighten his perceptions. Even in the
dark he could see Alyons in detail: a spectral face and long,
blood-red hair; huge eyes with reverse epicanthic folds; long-
fingered hands gripping his pike, their nails trimmed to metallic
points; boots made from the same silvery-gray material as the
saddle; pearl-gray cape hanging loose around his shoulders to
his calves. "*Quos fera antros, to suma antros.*"

"The boy is in our charge."

Michael recognized Nare's acid voice. She stood to one
side, between them and the Crane Women's hut, and Spart
stood on the other side. Michael couldn't see Coom. Alyons
made no move, but his hands applied an ounce more pressure
to the pike. Michael felt it scraping bone and tried not to squirm
again. "What is he doing here?" Alyons asked, eyes still on
Michael, like a hunter unwilling to release his prey.

"I have told you," Nare repeated. "He is in our charge."

"He's human. You don't train humans."

There was a rapid exchange in Sidhe between Spart and the
Wickmaster. Alyons' face filled with deep-set lines of hate,
turning his smooth chiseled features into a mummy mask. He
lifted the pike a hair's breadth. "If I kill the boy, I remove a
burden, no?"

"Probably," Spart said. "But what would we do to you, in
turn?"

"You're *t'al antros,*" Alyons said contemptuously. Coom

stepped from the shadows behind him.

"We are very, very old," Spart said, "and the Sidhe of the Irall come to us to ask questions. Would you like your name mentioned when we respond—*horsethief?*"

The lines of Alyons' face deepened, if that were possible. "It wouldn't upset me," he said. He lifted the pike a hair.

"And when Adonna's priest comes for *temelos?*" Spart asked.

Coom cropped a hand on Alyons' shoulder and pulled him roughly away, dragging his face down to her level. "Ours!"

"Then take him," Alyons said with great calmness. He shrugged her off and walked to his horse, seeming to glide on rather than jump. "But I will go to the Arborals and question the grace of wood."

"They brought it," Nare said.

"You are a crude and foolish *fricht,*" Spart said.

"Ours," Coom repeated.

Alyons leaned forward and the horse seemed to turn to smoke, every curve blurring and smoothing. Then, in silence, they were gone. Michael lay on the dirt, his chest bleeding sluggishly, his hands bloody from contact with the pike. The Crane Women were gone, as well.

He got to his feet and made for the shelter of the house. Inside, he tried to keep his lungs from heaving and held his mouth with his bloody hands to stifle sobs. He wasn't sure what had just happened—whether the Crane Women had tested him, or he had actually been visited by Alyons. The Sidhe's voice still haunted his ears, rich and deadly as venom.

Even now, Michael could hardly keep awake. There was a vibrant chirping nearby, repeated several times—birds?—and that was the last thing he remembered until his arm was grabbed.

"Get out of my house," he said groggily.

"*Jan antros.*" Coom leaned over him, the light of dawn through the door outlining the side of her head. "Not eyes-full! We promise test . . ."

He didn't think he was dreaming—dreams seemed to have no place in the Realm—but he wanted to believe he was. "Go away," he said, "please." And he was alone in the hut.

Morning came and went, and the day, and it was near evening again when he awoke, stiff and still exhausted. He felt his chest. The blood had clotted and the wound had been smeared with white paste. It was tender but didn't ache. The cuts on his hands had scabbed over.

There was a bowl of mush and fruit by the door. He ate

slowly with his fingers, his head full of fog. He was past all thought. The temptation to throw it in was strong, congruent with the pain in his body and the tiredness clamped to every muscle.

When he finished eating, he rolled over and looked at the dirt floor. Idly, he drew a line in the dirt with his finger, then wrote a line of words, and another, half-purposefully, until he had scrawled a poem.

> The scraping on the roof at night—
> Chitin or nail or stiff, hot hair—
> In dark of August, summer's heat
> Constructs a limb of dust and air.
>
> If you step out to watch the clouds,
> Silent lightning will prance and grin.
> While on the roof the summer waits
> And if you try to go back in . . .
>
> Why, Hello! The season is a spider.

Half the time, when he wrote a poem, he had no idea what it meant. The back of his head seemed disconnected from all present circumstance, as though facts and images seeped in slowly and were jumbled along the way.

But the menace was obvious. He was scared clear through, and he had no way to fight his fear. Not yet, perhaps not ever.

He stood by the door of his house and watched the sun go down, hands in his pants pocket. Nare came out of the hut and strode toward him. When they were face to face, she took his hands in hers and peered at the palms, then pulled apart his blood-stained shirt and examined his chest.

"How did I do?" Michael asked with an edge of bitterness.

"You are no good to us asleep. You were to go to the market today, get yourself a card."

"I mean, how did I do last night?"

"Terribly," she said. "He would have killed you. And later . . . you are a terrible warrior."

"I never wanted to be a warrior," he said incredulously.

She held out her twiggish fingers and shrugged elegantly. "The choice is to be one, or die," she said. "Your choice."

Coom and Spart crossed the stream and entered the hut.

As Nare stood motionless beside him and Michael waited nervously, the stars twirled into view. Coom and Spart emerged with eight long torches and began staking them in a circle between the house and the stream. They lighted the torches by cupping their hands behind the wick and blowing on them. Sparks and flame shot up into the night and an orange circle of light shimmered within the perimeter.

"Time is difficult to measure in the Realm," Spart said, approaching Michael and taking him by the hand. The sensation of her long, strong fingers around his own quelled any protest. She led him into the circle and motioned for Coom to join them. "You will learn our functions now," Spart said. "Coom is an expert in what the Sidhe call *isray*, physical combat. Nare is versed in *stray*, preparation of the mind. And I will teach *vickay*, the avoidance of battle as a means to victory. Tonight, since it is the simplest and easiest of the three, you will learn from Coom the beginnings of how to survive a fight with human or Sidhe."

Coom walked around Michael slowly, with high, almost prancing steps. Nare and Spart watched from outside the circle of torches. Michael regarded Coom warily, hands at his sides, head inclined slightly. He jumped as she reached down and grabbed a leg to reposition it. "Don't fall over," she said. "Like stool. One leg to be like two." She continued her circling. "Morning, you run to Halftown, run back. Tonight, you just stand up." She shot out one arm and pushed him. He promptly fell on his butt and scrambled to his feet again. She reached out and shoved once more. He stumbled but stayed upright. She circled and shoved from another angle. He toppled forward on his face. "Like stool," she repeated. She shoved again, and again, but he remained standing.

His face was flushed and his jaw hurt from clenching his teeth, but he was surprised at how calm he felt. The methodic circling, shoving, went on for an hour until he kept his balance no matter what angle Coom attacked from.

The torches guttered. "Ears," Coom said. Nare and Spart extinguished the feeble flames. Clouds obscured the stars now; except for the feverish orange glow from the hut windows, there was no illumination. He couldn't see any of the Crane Women. He listened to the sound of their feet moving, trying to guess how many circled him. A hand pushed hard on his back and he went to one knee, then got up quickly.

"Ears," Coom said again. He sensed a footfall nearby and braced himself instinctively in the opposite direction. The blow came, but he kept his balance.

Another hour passed. He was groggy and his legs ached abominably. His shoulders were sore and swollen. For a time he rotated in the darkness, until he realized he couldn't hear their footfalls any more. He was alone. The Crane Women had returned to their hut.

He felt his way to his house and collapsed in a corner. He couldn't sleep. He rubbed his arms and shoulders and contemplated past gym classes, where he had never performed enthusiastically. It wasn't a matter of being weak or gimpy; he could run well enough, and his frame was sound. Michael had just never cared that much, and the gym teachers had seldom inspired confidence in those who didn't profess to be jocks.

Inspiration wasn't the issue here. Whatever he thought, however miserable he was, tomorrow he would run until he dropped—which he was sure he would. No protests, no complaints.

After the incident with Alyons, Michael fully appreciated his position.

Obviously, things could get much worse.

Chapter Eight

"The Sidhe do not use swords," Spart told Michael. They squatted on the ground outside his house, legs crossed, facing each other.

"But Alyons has a pike—"

"That is his wick. He uses it only against humans."

Michael nodded and looked away, resigned to the ambiguities. Spart sighed and leaned toward him.

"You are supposed to wonder what Alyons does with his wick."

"Act wicked?" Michael said, trying for a smile. Spart leaned back and narrowed her eyes to even tighter slits. "Okay," he gave in. "What does he do with it?"

"The wick is his symbol of rank. It confers his power of office, of labor. It signifies that he has the strength to guard the Blasted Plain and the Pact Lands, and to uphold the pact made between Sidhe and the Isomage."

"So why did he stab me with it?"

"He hates humans, like many Sidhe."

"Do you hate humans?"

"T'al antros," she said, tapping her chest with her finger. "I am half-human."

"Why don't Sidhe use swords?"

"They have no need. A Sidhe warrior is frightening enough without. And there is honor involved. Death is final for a Sidhe; there is nothing beyond except being pressed into a tree by the Arborals. That is not even half a life. So it has been established that the Sidhe may combat each other only by means dependent on their own skill and power, by which we mean magic and strength of will."

"I'm going to learn magic?"

Spart shook her head. "No humans ever conquer Sidhe magic. You'll have to learn how to flee, how to be inconspicuous. You cannot hope to best a Sidhe in grand combat. Your only chance is that a Sidhe will consider combat with a human shameful, worth only small effort. Take advantage of that. In the rare instances where you might be called into grand combat—" She slapped her hand against the dirt. "You will simply die. Dying in the Realm is as permanent for humans as death anywhere for a Sidhe. So do not provoke a warrior."

"I don't understand—"

"You will, in time. Now you will go to Halftown, do our errands. After, you will run. There is an order of grains to be delivered here, and you will—"

"I know. Ask for food for myself."

Spart regarded him with infinite patience, blinked slowly and turned away.

Halftown was quiet, matching the somber, overcast morning. Michael tried being cordial to the Breeds, but they returned no greetings; curiosity about him seemed to have lapsed. They were like ghosts intent on some irrevocable task; only a few of the women had any obvious hint of life and joy in them.

Michael followed the curving market street, which branched from the main road near the center of Halftown. The lone market consisted of a house (in Cascar, a *caersidh,* pronounced roughly "ker-shi"), round like most of the others, and a covered courtyard twice the area of the house itself. The courtyard was filled with tables and shelves stacked with provisions—foods in one corner, housewares, liquors (in bottles which looked suspiciously like the ones in Brecker's cellar in Euterpe) in another, and the simple types of clothing in a third. The middle of the courtyard was the counter, and there the market manager held sway.

Spart had said his name was Lirg. He had a daughter, Eleuth, the one who had delivered milk to the Crane Women's hut. Lirg never took cash—the Sidhe abhorred money, which seemed a bit strange to Michael, considering the legends of pots of gold and such—but kept careful track of Halftown's balances. Michael gathered the economy was loosely based on fulfillment of assigned tasks and dispersal of goods according to need.

Not unlike the simpler forms of communism he had learned about in Mr. Wagner's class at school. Allotments of supplies were brought across the Blasted Plain. As Michael skirted the courtyard, three large, big-wheeled wagons, each drawn by two Sidhe horses, lumbered in from the opposite end of the market street.

The wagons were filled with food and supplies. A Sidhe driver sat on the lead wagon, tall and aloof, dressed in iridescent browns, the cut of his clothes not substantially different from that of Alyons, except he wore no armor and carried no wick. The horses were lathered as if they had been driven hard, and a peculiar golden glow lifted from the backs of the wagons like sunlit dust. The glow dissipated, leaving a sweet-bitter scent in the air. Lirg stepped down from his counter and directed the unloading of the supplies. The Sidhe driver took down his tailgates and several passersby pitched in to help. Few words were exchanged. The supplies were either carried into a covered shed in the fourth corner of the courtyard, or placed directly in the market stalls. There was no rush to inspect the goods; they differed not in the slightest from those already available, and assured only continuity, not variety.

Michael watched until the wagons had been unloaded and pulled aside, then entered the courtyard, reluctant to make himself obvious. The driver shut the tailgates and smoothed the wood with his hands, leaving trails of golden glitter on the boards. He then walked around the horses and patted each on the haunch with more precision than affection. Everything he touched was left with a sparkle.

Lirg was back at his counter when Michael approached. The Breed fastened him with a steady gaze, one eye dark and the other half-shut by a scar. Lirg's hair was more brown than red, and his skin tan instead of pale. "Your needs?" he asked, leaning forward on thickly muscled arms.

"I'm here to pick up grain for the Crane Women. And to be put on your list."

"What list?" He examined Michael intensely, then nodded. "The card. I see. Food only...that is all we can spare, even for pets of the Crane Women."

"I'm not a pet," Michael said gritting his teeth. "I'm a student, and I'm doing what they tell me to do." Lirg grinned at that, and Michael blushed.

"I see. Daughter!"

Eleuth emerged from the house with four sacks of grain. She put two of them by Michael's feet and hefted the other two onto her shoulders.

"I can carry them all," Michael said.

"I've told my daughter to help you," Lirg said. That seemed to settle it. Eleuth gave Michael a look suggesting he not argue. Michael picked up his two sacks.

"Am I on your list . . . on the card?"

"You are," Lirg said. He turned to a Breed customer and Michael left the courtyard, Eleuth following a few steps behind.

"What are they teaching you?" Eleuth asked as they approached the creek.

"They're trying to make me stronger," Michael said.

"Why don't you just stay in Euterpe? They have their own allotment. You could do well there."

"That's not the way things worked out," he said. "I suppose I'm being trained so I can go home again. I hope that's the reason, anyway. I have to find the man who can do it."

"A Sidhe magician could send you home," Eleuth said. Her voice was extraordinary; he didn't want to look at her for fear of being unable to look away again. "I think one could, anyway. That's what Lirg says, that the priests of the Irall could send humans home again if they really wanted to. There's something mysterious about that, I can't help thinking. Because, you see, the humans are still here."

Michael considered her words for a moment, then started to cross the stream. "Anyway, I have to learn how to live here."

Eleuth nodded. "If you're new, there's a lot to learn, I guess."

They set the sacks down outside the door of the Crane Women's hut.

"Where's your mother?" Michael asked. Humans didn't live in Halftown; he knew that much.

"I don't know," Eleuth said. Her face was simple and composed. "Most of us have Sidhe mothers, and our fathers are missing—or in Euterpe. We never know who they are. So I suppose I'm unusual, second generation Breed . . . my father a Breed, my mother human."

He knocked on the door and Spart opened it. She peered at Eleuth, Michael and then the sacks and said, "Fine." She closed the door again.

"Does that mean you're free today?"

He shook his head. "I have to run to Euterpe and back."
He walked to his house.

"You built that yourself?" Eleuth asked, following.

"Sort of."

"Like a Sidhe warrior. Must build his own dwelling . . . but
very clever, really, for a human."

Michael glanced at her; Eleuth's expression was still composed and simple. She wasn't ragging him. "Thanks for the
help," he said. He felt very awkward.

She looked around the mound with an expression of awe
mixed with distaste, then smiled at him and said good-by. As
she forded the creek, Michael watched the way her legs moved.
They were long, graceful. His face flushed. She was pretty in
a way; no, not just pretty (perhaps not pretty at all)—but
beautiful. But then, how did he know what passed for beauty
in the Realm?

An attraction to a Breed, he was sure, could be perverse
and would only complicate his life more.

"Man-child!" Nare came toward him, carrying two thick
sticks about seven feet long. "Run to Euterpe. Hold this over
your head going and in front of you returning." She gave him
a stick. He hefted it and groaned inwardly.

"Then what?"

"When you are strong enough, you learn how to use the
stick." With the other stick, she lightly tapped his own just
outside one hand's grip. "Or I break all your fingers. Now go."

Michael began to run. He crossed the stream without slipping and congratulated himself on his newfound coordination.
Leaving wet shoeprints, he took the first hundred yards in
stride, though the stick made his arms ache. Within a half mile
he was still going strong. It was in the third quarter of the first
mile that he was sure the stick would drag him down, and that
once on the ground, he would die.

He tried to remember how to breathe when running: steadily,
without letting his legs pound the air from his lungs.

His mouth was dry and his lungs began to feel as though
they'd been sprayed with acid. His arms were twin upright
pillars of pain, and his knees wobbled; still, he was determined
to keep going. He'd show them he was good for something.
He had had enough humiliation—

His toe caught a rock and he sprawled headlong in the dirt.
The stick bounced end-to-end and rolled ahead of him. He
picked dirt from between his teeth and felt his bruised lips and

nose, trying to control his agonized gulping for air.

A half-hour later, he stood with his hands on his knees before the outskirts of Euterpe, his face beet red and his legs liquid. He dropped the stick on the ground beside him. He wasn't sure he would ever be able to lift it again. "Christ," he said. "I'm nothing but a wimp. He might as well have killed me."

It took him a couple of minutes to become aware of the small crowd standing nearby, just outside one of Euterpe's small pedestrian gates. They watched him curiously, saying nothing at first. He tried to stand upright and winced. The auburn-haired woman he had last seen at the hotel dinner stepped forward. "What are you doing back?" she asked, voice thick with anger. "Breeds not good enough for you?"

He regarded her from under his brows, breath ragged.

"They're getting me in shape," he said. He didn't want anybody to be angry—why should humans be mad at him?

"Why do you need to be in better shape?" a man asked from the back of the group.

"I don't know," Michael said. He picked up the stick, his fingers barely agreeing to close on it, and turned around to start back.

"Michael!"

Savarin came through the gate. Michael leaned on his stick, grateful for a friendly tone and an excuse to rest a bit longer. His chest now felt as if it were filled with water. He coughed and wiped his forehead.

"You're in training?" Savarin asked. Michael nodded and swallowed. "Well, that can't hurt."

"Oh, yeah?"

"They are teaching you . . . how to fight, perhaps, how to fight Sidhe?"

He shook his head. "They're teaching me how to run away from Sidhe."

Savarin scowled. "When can you get back here? There are people I'd like you to meet."

"I don't know. They're going to have me run more errands for them. Maybe later."

"If you can, come to the schoolhouse—it's on the other side of the street from the Yard. In the middle of town. I teach languages, things like that, besides teaching newcomers. Come see me."

Michael agreed and pointed with the stick. "I have to get back now."

"Look at that!" a high-pitched masculine voice shouted from the crowd. "They give the bastard a fortune in wood!"

"Shut up!" Savarin cried, waving his arms and advancing on the crowd. "Go home, shut up, shut up!"

Michael tried to pick up his pace again, what little he had had in the first place. Halfway, the agony began to subside and the run became easier. He had heard of second wind but had never experienced it before. His body seemed to resign itself to the situation and make the best of things.

It was late morning when he came to the creek and crossed it, then clumped to where Spart was standing on the mound. Spart took his stick and called to the other Crane Women with a sharp whistle.

Coom emerged from the hut to inspect him. She palped his legs and arms and shook her head violently, tossing her dust-gray hair. *"Usgal! Nalk,"* she said, pointing to the stream. "You stink."

"That's not fair," he said, frowning resentfully.

"Things won't be fair again until you've bathed," Spart said. "Then follow Coom away from here and you'll keep on working."

"But I'm exhausted."

"You didn't run without stopping," she said. In the hut, Nare cackled and withdrew her face from the window.

Michael dragged his feet to the stream and removed his clothes. He was down to his underpants before any notion of modesty occured to him. He glanced back at Spart, but she was on her haunches plaiting reeds into a mat. She paid him no attention. He kept his underpants on and dipped a foot gingerly into the water.

Of course, it was freezing. He closed his eyes. They would think him an idiot or a coward if he always hesitated. He stepped back and then ran forward, plunging in feet first. The shock was considerable; when he surfaced, he could hardly breath and his teeth chattered like expert telegraphy. Still, it was better to bear the hardship than put up with more ridicule.

As he rubbed the silty, mica-flecked water over his skin, he once again noticed the pungent herbal smell. Apparently that was the nature of water in the Realm. He crawled out of the creek—which was about four feet deep in the middle—

and shook his arms and legs, scattering ribbons of water across the bank. Still damp, he put on his clothes, but held the jacket by its yoke and carried it to where Spart was plaiting her reeds.

She turned her attention away from her work to look him up and down and shook her head pityingly. "Only a fool would dive into water so cold."

Michael nodded without argument. That was their game; he could go along with them. "Thanks," he said.

And so it went for the first five days.

Chapter Nine

The Crane Women ran Michael around the level grasslands, with the stick and without it, sometimes one or two of them pacing him and giving directions. They seemed tireless. When he was near collapse from exertion, they wouldn't even be breathing hard. After a while, Michael suspected Sidhe and Breeds just didn't get tired. He asked about that once, and Nare simply smiled.

He learned the Pact Lands within the vicinity of Euterpe and Halftown quickly. There wasn't all that much to learn—grasslands, the curve of the river, one fork and an oxbow beyond the fork.

He asked about the Blasted Plain, but Spart told him that part of his education would come later. He could see the haze beyond the perimeter of the Pact Lands, and occasionally make out black spires rising through orange-brown clouds, but his radius was never more than six miles from Halftown, and the Pact Lands, he surmised, extended at least ten miles on all sides.

Sometimes, his exercises seemed ridiculous, designed to humiliate him.

"Five times you have missed the mark," Nare said, standing over him. Her shadow bisected four concentric circles drawn in the dirt ten feet from where he squatted. He had been set to tossing pebbles, trying for the central circle. After an hour he had only hit the center three times.

"I've missed more often than that," he said.

"You miss my words, too," Nare said. "You fail to understand anything we've been showing you. Five tests." Michael tried to remember the times he had been tested in any meaningful way. "Not a good sign," she went on. "Don't you see the truth behind the tests? Must we explain in words? Words are so beloved to you!"

"They're clear, at least," Michael said. "What do you want me to know? I've done everything I can to cooperate—"

"Except use your head properly!" Nare grabbed his arm and hauled him to a standing position. "This is not a bullseye. These are not pebbles. You are not training, and this is no series of useless games."

"Funny," Michael said. He regretted saying it immediately; he had vowed that whatever the pressure, he would not behave like a smartass.

"You're a crack-voiced child, and worse, *jan viros*. What have you learned?"

"I think . . . I think you're trying to teach me how to survive by thinking a certain way. But I'm not a magician."

"You are not required to be one. How would we have you think?"

"With confidence."

"Not that alone. What else?"

"I don't know!"

"If we tried to turn you into a magician, we'd be even more doltish than you. You're not special. But Sidhedark is not like Earth. You must learn how the *Realm* is special, how it supports and nurtures us. You cannot be told. Words spoil the knowledge. So we must torment you, boy, to make you see. The Sidhe returned language to humans thousands of years ago, but they never explained how language can destroy. That was deliberate."

"I'm trying to cooperate," Michael said sullenly.

"You cooperate so you can show us you aren't a fool." She smiled, a hideous and revealing expression which didn't reassure him at all, and probably wasn't meant to. Her teeth were cat-sharp and her gums were black as tar.

"In *betlim*, little combat, warriors not kill. Best," Coom said. They circled each other with the sticks held before them in broad-spaced hands. "*Lober*, not hurt. Win. Strategy."

Michael nodded.

"One thing very bad," Coom said. "*Rilu*. Anger. Never let mad control! Mad is poison in *betlim*. In great combat, *rilu* is *mord*. Hear?"

He nodded again. Coom touched his stick with her own. "Disarm you now."

He gripped his stick tighter, but that only made his hands hurt more when, with a whirl and a flourish, she whacked his stick straight up in the air, parallel to the ground. He caught it as it fell, wincing at the pain in his wrists.

"Good," Coom said. "Now you hear why you learn. Hear that stick is wick; you are Sidhe given power of *pais* where you stand. I take wick and take land from you. Stop me— maybe stop me. Hear how I move. Take control of air. Of Realm."

Then she did an amazing thing. She leaped up, braced her feet against nothingness, and sprung at him with her stick. He retreated, but not before receiving another bone-rattling blow. She hung before him a moment and landed on her feet. "Good," she said. "Stronger."

She disarmed him again, this time whacking the stick out of his reach before it came down. He walked over to pick it up and turned to see Coom standing where he had been.

"Gave up ground," she accused, looking disgusted.

"You took away my stick."

"Didn't take away most important weapon." She threw down her stick and backed up a pace. "Come at with *kima*."

He didn't hesitate. She reached around with one spider hand as his stick came down on the spot where she had stood, grabbed hold and slammed it to the ground.

He could feel the bones in his back pop before he let go.

"Little defeats teach potential," Coom said. "Not to waste my time, you will train with this." Spart came from the hut carrying a headless mannikin with bush-branch arms. It held a smaller stick, tied to leafy "hands" with twine. Michael groaned inside, then resigned himself to the indignity.

"Take this off thirty paces and hammer it into the ground. Then fight with it," Spart said.

He did as he was told, clutching the cloth, straw and wood mannikin and using his stick to pound it in like a stake. He assumed a stance before the mannikin, imitating Coom and feeling foolish—

And it promptly swung up its stick and knocked his to the ground. The mannikin vibrated gleefully, twisted on its stake and became limp again.

When the hair on his neck had settled, Michael retrieved his stick and resumed his stance, a little farther back. They sparred for a bit, the mannikin having at least the two disadvantages of being staked to the ground and using a shorter, flimsier stick. Michael wasn't encouraged.

He had no illusions that the fight was fair. He got his lumps.

Chapter Ten

As the pre-dawn light filtered through the plaited reed door cover Spart had given him, Michael scrawled another poem in the dirt floor.

> Night's a friendly sort
> Oh yes likes to throw a
> Fright now and then—when
> The wind hums—but after
> You're dead will gladly
> Share a glass of moon.

Nothing more than exercise, he thought—not worth recording even if he had the means, which he did not—no pencils or writing implements of any sort but the stick, no paper but what was in his black book. And he hardly considered his work worthy of going in the book.

The Crane Women usually arose fifteen minutes before sunrise, which gave him a short time of being alone and at leisure—time more important than sleep. He used the time to read from the book or write in the dirt, or just to savor not having anything in particular to do.

He heard the door to their hut creak open. He took the book, zippered it into his jacket pocket and wrapped it in the folds before hiding it in the rafters overhead.

"Man-child! *Jan wiros!*"

He came out of the house and saw Coom approaching, with Nare two paces behind. They looked like hunters unsure of their prey—and he was their prey. The Crane Women were masters at unnerving him. He could never predict their moods, attitudes. He should have been a nervous wreck, but he found himself adapting.

"More run," Coom said. "To Euterpe and back. With *kima.*"

He grabbed the stick without hesitation and ran. Behind, Nare called out, "This evening is *Kaeli.*" She said it as if some special treat were involved. Michael hefted the stick before him and crossed the creek. He did not see the watery hand which rose up, grasped at his ankle and missed.

He could make it to the town without collapsing now. He took some pride in his improvement. For the first time in his life he felt the exultation of the body in sheer activity, the meshing of breath and legs, the matched, almost pleasant ache in all his muscles.

At first, he stayed away from the outskirts housing, not wanting to bring on another confrontation. But he was curious what Savarin was up to, what the teacher had meant the last time, that there were people he wanted Michael to meet. He decided to enter Euterpe and go to the schoolhouse—and the populace be damned. He had his stick and he felt a little cocky.

He was up to the main gate when he almost bumped into the teacher. They laughed and Michael put down his stick, breathing deeply and wiping sweat from his face with his shirt sleeve.

"I thought I might catch you during your morning constitutional," Savarin said. "And warn you. Best stay out of the town for the next couple of days. Alyons has been harassing us since your arrival. The townspeople are upset. They're liable to strike out at you without being aware of what they're doing."

"I haven't hurt them," Michael said.

"No, but you've brought trouble. Things here are marginal, at best. Alyons threatens to reduce our allotment if anything else happens to upset him."

"Is that why they shouted at me the last time?"

"Yes. I still have people for you to meet, but later. And I also wanted to tell you . . . something's planned for tonight—the Halftown *Kaeli.* Have they invited you?"

"Nare mentioned it before I left. I don't even know what it is."

"It's very important. *Kaeli* is when the Sidhe get together to tell stories, usually about the early times. I'd like you to listen closely and pass on what you hear. I've only heard one—and that from a distance. I was hiding in tall grass. Now, with the Breed guards so tense, I don't dare. Nobody is allowed near Halftown now. . . . That's what makes me think something is afoot."

"What?"

"Best not to ask for trouble yet. But a *grazza,* perhaps. A raid by Riverines and Umbrals. Keep an eye out, and be careful."

"You want me to come back and tell you about the *Kaeli?*"

"Of course," Savarin said, his eyes brightening. "But a couple of days from now, when things are more settled." He looked around nervously. A few faces peered from nearby windows, and two men loitering by the gate cast glances at them. "Until then," the teacher said, gripping Michael's hand and releasing it with a wave as he made for a different gate. Michael picked up the stick, held it over his head, and began the return leg of his run.

His body took over almost immediately and he forgot Savarin, forgot the *Kaeli,* forgot almost everything but the sensation of distance covered.

The Breeds of Halftown marched in double file over the grassland, dressed in dark brown and gray cloaks, conversing casually in Cascar and calling to those farther forward or back in the lines. The air was still and cool; the sun touched distant hills and the ribbons of evening cascaded slowly to the hazy horizon, revealing the stars with their tiny circling motions.

Behind the lines marched the Crane Women. Michael walked abreast of Spart, wearing his jacket. (The book rested in its nook in the tiny house, as secure as he could make it.) He had washed his clothes in the creek earlier, as a concession to formality; they were still slightly damp even after drying near a fire Nare had kindled. Holes revealed his knees and the shoulder of the jacket had separated at the seam.

The Crane Women wore short black coats that emphasized the length of their legs and the shortness of their torsos. They walked with arms folded, jutting elbows making them look more then ever like birds. They seemed to carry more of an ancient reserve with regard to *Kaeli* than the other Breeds, and didn't talk.

Those assigned to choose the site had gone on ahead during the late afternoon. Now a bonfire blazed a few hundred feet down the path, squares of peat and dried brush-wood providing the fuel. Circling the bonfire was a perimeter of poles, each topped by a leafy green branch. When the Breeds had gathered

within the circle, Lirg came forward and paced around the fire.
Michael sat beside the Crane Women, crossing his legs on the
grass stubble and dirt.

Lirg spoke in Cascar for a few minutes. Michael understood
little of what was said; he had difficulty even picking out the
meanings of individual words in the long discourse. There
seemed to be many words in Cascar with the same or subtly
shaded meanings, and the syntax varied as well.

Spart leaned forward from behind him and tapped him on
the shoulder. "You haven't learned the tongue, have you?" she
asked.

"I've only been here a couple of weeks," Michael said
defensively. Nare blew out her breath. The Crane Women
looked at each other, then Spart sidled forward and placed both
her hands around Michael's head.

"Tonight only," she said, "You have a boon. It won't last."
She removed her hands and Michael shook a buzzing out of
his head. When the dizziness passed, he listened to Lirg. The
Breed was still speaking Cascar but the words were limpid;
Michael could understand all of them.

"Tonight," Lirg said, "We invoke the sadness of the time
when we were grand, when the Sidhe marched between the
stars as easily as I circle this fire." He passed around to the
other side, his words piercing the crackle of the flames. "Each
will share the tale, the part of his ancestor, and as conclusion,
I will tell of Queen Elme and her choice."

First to pick up the thread was a tall brown-haired Breed
who announced himself as Manann of the line of Till. As
Manann spoke, Michael was enchanted by the way the language
adapted to poetry—half-singing, half-speaking, until he could
no longer tell the difference.

> The Earth, home to us all, has spun
> A thousand polar dances since
> The war called Westering, won
> First by men, who decreed that none
>
> Of the race called Sidhe should possess
> Souls beyond the border of Death.
> Unwitting, the Mage who made us less,
> Who imposed this inward emptiness,
>
> Gave to the Sidhe life without end.
> And then time came for the wheel to turn

Again. The Sidhe thus damned did send
To defeat the vain and gloating men

Who had in cruel and thoughtless rage
Robbed us of life beyond matter.
The Sidhe bid the responsible Mage
To work their own vengeance and engage

His power to transform men to beasts.
Triumphant Sidhe in sweet passioned
Irony watched mankind decreased.
Yet in the shape of the small, the least

Of claw-foot, scruff-fur animals,
None who had once been men could tell
How to once more open the portals
Of shadowy death; how immortals

Could reclaim the boon of a soul.

Holder of the Wick of Battle,
Ysra Faer of the line of Till
Confined men-beasts and all allies—
Also made beast, and beast-form still—
On Earth, walled-in like cattle.

"How many races were there?" Michael whispered to Spart, uncertain whether he was speaking Cascar or English. She turned her dark eyes on him and answered, "More than four . . . we do not know for sure, now. Much has been forgotten. Many of the animals of Earth were once exalted beings, kin of the Sidhe and humans of old."

Manann sat and another stood, a young woman with beefy arms and a face squatter than usual. "I am Esther of the line of Dravi. I take the challenge of the end-rhymed song, but I *correct* Manann of Till . . ." Laughter rang through the circle. "He forgets my line's honored form, and I follow *that* now."

All tribes, brothers and sisters hand in hand,
In glory Sidhe set out to march the stars.
Through this spacing, histories multiplied
As numberless as the shore's sea-ground sand.
Yet in swifting time, all progress died.

All glorious rise swings back to fall, sure
As the new-born Sidhe on time's cruel road
Came to their doom by chance or anger's blade.
Exaltation turned to slow decay, the pure
And good demeaned, ideals not lived but played.

Lacking worthy goals or adversary,
Star-marcher Faer in easeful ways declined.
None took on the hard discipline of the Sidhe.
Mere sibling strifes trained the warrior wary;
Tribes found bitter freedom in their jealously.

From the line of Dravi, Wickmaster Sum
Foresaw the impending doom; in darkness
Deeper than ever known, against the races
Of the Great Distance he warred, to come
To glory, to draw in battle traces

Of pride and courage lost since war with Man.
The Great Distance breeds minds unlike our own,
With unfamiliar thoughts of foreign
Shape. Of this war called Quandary none can
Recall the tale, only the outcome, when, worn

From victory more costly than defeat,
Destroying what sloth, misrule and ease
Had not already, the wasted Sidhe
Swung Earthward the ravaged Faerie fleet.
Among their dead: Wickmaster Sum, of Dravi.

Having long since beaten humanity,
The last drops from the river of Sidhe
Thought Earth to be their choicest
Harbor, refuge for a well-earned rest.

Esther of the line of Dravi took her seat, and Fared of the
line of Wis continued.

By way of right succession, Krake
Of the line of noble Wis did take
The Wick. As Wickmaster of Sidhe,
Krake brought us home from the endless sea

Of dark-storied, sinister space.
Yet on Earth, no peace, for the race

Of resourceful, unquenchable Man
Had crawled, across an age's span

Up from beast by nature's road
Of Change and Pain, with Death's sharp goad.
While Sidhe declined in sibling strife,
Man struggled back to conscious life.

Though new-born Man was then quite young,
Krake knew on human history hung
The fate of his weary, worn Sidhe,
Too weak for one more victory.

Nizandsa, of Serket's family,
Now extinct, made this plea:
"We must find the one called Mage,
Imprisoned as serpent this long age.

"He has the knowledge to restore our
Souls, whose lack has caused a dour
Decline. Perhaps a trade of liberty
Can return to us the essence of Sidhe!"

But Krake, we are told, did not agree.
"In Man old or new I cannot see
Any answer for our many troubles.
With human help, a problem doubles!

"Power to men, releasing the Mage,
Can only resurrect the rage
Felt in their dread animal fall.
No power to Man! That would end us all."

Nizandsa's faithful lost this debate.
Krake, unhappy still, filled with hate,
Ordered his coursers to halt all
Dissent. In Great Combat, the pall

Of disgrace again gloomed over us.
Nizandsa's murder ended all trust
Between the branches of the Sidhe,
The third curse of a trinity.

Lirg stood now and walked around the fire again. "The new
breed of men," he began, voice low and almost devoid of song,

"had regained their former shape, but not their past glory. They could not keep what had made the men of old the grand enemies of the Sidhe. And the Sidhe, themselves, had long since lost what made them great." He came to the side of the fire where Michael sat between the Crane Women, and looked acrosss the Pact Lands over their heads. "I tell the story now of the family to which we all belong, the line of the mage Tonn's Breath-daughter, Elme.

> Assuming the wick from father Tonn,
> Queen Elme defied the scorners of
> Man, brought Sidhe to new-found
> Harmony, and against the will of
> God-like sire, loved and married—

A distant keening sound carried over the plain, interrupting Lirg and causing the Breeds to stir for the first time in half an hour. Nare, Spart and Coom were on their feet and out of the circle before Michael could blink twice.

Clouds moved quickly across the sky. The keening faded, grew louder, and faded again as if carried on uncertain breezes. From farther away still came the sound of horns unlike any Michael had ever heard; horns that seemed to laugh and cry at once.

As one, the crowd scooped up dirt and put down the bonfire. Michael stood aside, not knowing where he fit in, deciding it was best to keep out of the way.

With the bonfire reduced to embers and smoke, seeing was difficult. A drop of rain struck his forehead, then another. Wind tugged at his jacket—or he thought it was the wind. A green veil of luminosity flashed behind the hills.

"Man-child! This way!" Spart grabbed his arm and pulled him after. *"Kaeli* is over for tonight. Adonna sends its hosts!"

The first burst of rain soaked Michael instantly. He followed the indistinct form of a Crane Woman across the fresh mud and bent, pummeled grass. Puddles were forming everywhere. The wind gusted and pushed him this way and that.

"Where are we going?" Michael asked. The figure didn't answer, but kept running ahead, gesturing. He fell into a hole up to his knees in water, tried to balance and slid up to his thighs. Wiping his eyes, he splashed out of the hole and yelled, "Hey! Wait up!"

The figure paused for him. It gestured again as he clambered after. Running was difficult; the rain was so thick he had to keep his hand before his mouth to keep from breathing water. Still, the figure's pace was relentless.

Sheet-lightning flared again, throwing the landscape into gray brilliance. Michael stopped. He heard something roaring very close—the river, he thought, yet the figure ahead gestured again: Follow. "Where are we?" he cried out. No answer came. He stepped forward tentatively and lost his footing. He yelled in surprise and his mouth instantly filled with rain. Choking, he skidded on scrambling feet and butt down a muddy bank, over an edge and into rain-filled space.

It took him a moment to realize he had passed from rain into flowing water. He kicked and thrashed about, trying to find the shore and grab hold of something, but currents wrapped around his feet and pulled him under. Pressed between thick powerful walls of water, he opened his eyes and felt the darkness of the night pass into blacker insensibility.

His lungs were about to burst when he was propelled from the water like a salmon clawed by a bear. He hit the mud face-down and turned his head just enough to take a breath, inhaling both air and mud tossed up by the weakening rain.

He rubbed his eyes clear. The lightning was continuous, silent and green. In the strobing glare he saw the rushing water a few feet away. Stretching from the water, trying to grasp his legs and retrieve him, were four transparent hands. He jack-knifed his legs and dug his fingers into the mud to pull himself farther up the bank.

One shoulder and an arm struck a cold, solid mass—a boulder, Michael thought. He wrapped his arms around it . . . and the boulder shifted. Looking up, blinking at the remaining drops of rain, he saw a man-shaped piece of night towering over him. Its outline changed and he felt steely, bone-chilling hands lift him from the bank. He tried to scream for help but a hard, cold palm clamped over his mouth, numbing his lips and jamming his tongue against his teeth.

His head was immediately wrapped in a thick cloak.

Then, feeling him roughly through the icy fabric, the shape hesitated. It pulled Michael's head into the open and he stared into a face as black as the bottom of the sea, with two star-like points for eyes. Harsh breath like a freezer's charge of air prickled his nose.

"Antros! Wiros antros!"

With a cry of rage, the frigid shadow flung him aside. He rolled through space, rotating in a world of lightning and darkness, drops of water on his lips and mud in his eyes. The impact seemed to come after the mud, but everything was confused.

Michael lay on his back, certain that every bone in his body was broken. Far away, and growing fainter, the keening wavered with the wind until both were gone, and silence covered the wet, tormented land.

Chapter Eleven

Caught in a beam of sunlight, a drop of water hung from the tip of a blade of grass, more beautiful than any diamond. Round, filled with shimmering life, the drop grew until its freedom was assured. It fell in a quivering sphere and broke over his forehead, cool and gently insistent.

Michael saw a glowing mist, golden above and blue to either side, surrounding the new droplet on the grass blade. He blinked and the mist resolved into sun half-hidden by clouds. Tall green grass rose on all sides. For a moment, he felt no need to do anything but stare. Indeed, it seemed that all his life he had been only a pair of eyes.

But soon he remembered his hands and they twitched. There was some reason he was reluctant to remember his body, and when he moved his legs the reason became clear: pain. His torso, as he lifted his head and looked down on it, was surprisingly clean. Rain had rinsed the mud from his jacket. He tried to sit up, then gritted his teeth and fell back.

Limb by limb, he took inventory until he was sure nothing was broken. Pulling back his jacket and shirt, he found a mass of welts on his side. His arms felt bruised beneath the sleeves, too—especially under his armpits, where he had been hoisted by the shadow. His teeth felt as if they were on fire. He vaguely remembered being slapped from the river, and the hands rising from the water to pull him back . . . the shadow with eyes like stars.

He stood, legs wobbly and vision spinning. The river was down an embankment and about fifty yards away. He must have walked the distance; there was no sign in the unbent grass

that the water had flowed so high as to carry him here. Or—
the shadow had flung him clear.

Had he encountered another kind of Sidhe—an Umbral?

Shading his eyes against the cloudy glare, he looked from
his elevated advantage across the plain. He stood on an island
of grass in the yellow-green sea of mire. For as far as he could
see there was nothing but the storm-soaked plain and the distant
hills. No sign of Euterpe or Halftown; no sign of anyone.

It seemed he was the only living thing besides the grass.
Black curls of flood water still wandered from the low hills to
the river. The river itself had returned to its channel, once more
slow and sluggish.

Michael sat. River-bourne, he must have come from up-
stream, and that was where he would return when he was strong
enough.

His back prickled as if somebody watched. He turned stiffly
to look in the opposite direction. Less than a hundred yards
beyond the grassy knoll, the Pact Lands came to an end. He
had almost been washed onto the Blasted Plain.

The air beyond the border was thick and gray-orange. The
river waters were a muddy gray-blue right up to the demar-
cation, then flowed turgid yellow-green and sickly purple, like
pus from a long-infected wound.

The Blasted Plain itself was an expanse of black, gray and
brown boulders spread across glistening, powdery umber sand.
Through the murky air, he could see tall curling spires of rock
like broken strands of glue left over from a badly managed
patch job. The place was more than the sum of its parts; it was
more living than dead, but nothing alive was visible. It was
malevolent, made of things long buried, hard emotions long
suppressed, mistakes covered over.

Death, despair, foulness and horror.

Michael shuddered and the shudder turned into shivers of
delayed shock. He descended the knoll as quickly as his unstable legs allowed and began his march over the grassland,
upriver to Euterpe and Halftown—or so he hoped—and away
from the desolation of a war he could hardly imagine.

After a few minutes, he began to draw on reserves he had
built up during the past weeks of training. He walked for the
hour or so remaining until dark, then slept fitfully under the
open night sky, and resumed at dawn. He would not die. He
would not starve.

He had survived; and in that simple fact, Michael found a dismaying, pleasurable pride.

Thick swaths of fog shouldered in over the plain, driven before the sun's warmth. Michael followed the sandy river bank, crossed the shallow ox-bow where the river rippled and glittered over rocks and pebbles, and climbed another hill to get his bearings.

The roofs of Halftown were about two miles away. He broke into a run along a trail of hard, clayey sand.

In Halftown, things seemed to be carrying on as usual. There was rain and wind damage to several of the buildings, and Lirg's market courtyard had nearly been flattened, but the Breeds went about their business as if the night before had been commonplace.

The hut of the Crane Women was unscathed. Nare wove reeds into thick sitting mats, squatting between two piles of animal bones, holding a long reed in her teeth and plaiting steadily. Coom was nowhere to be seen. Spart, he discovered, was walking behind him as he approached the mound. Michael grinned at her over his shoulder.

"Worried about me?" he asked. Spart's eyes widened and she bared her black gums.

"It wasn't you they were after, nor any human," she said.

"I got that impression," Michael said. He stopped before his house and lifted one foot to scrape mud from his shoe. "What happened?"

"There was a raid on the Breeds," Spart said. She walked toward the door of the hut with jaw working as if chewing cud. She hardly seemed glad to see him.

"I took care of myself," he said.

"You were very, very lucky." She turned at the doorway. "You escaped Umbrals and Riverines. They're branches of the Sidhe who worship Adonna most fervently. Adonna needs Sidhe blood to do its work, but it cannot touch the pure Sidhe. So it comes for us. We're adequate for its needs, and few care if a Breed is lost. You were lucky, man-child, not skilled."

Michael looked between the two Crane Women, his face reddening. "I survived," he said. "God dammit, I survived! I'm not just some piece of garbage everybody kicks around! I have my rights and I...I—" But he was speechless. Spart shrugged and entered the hut. Nare cocked a glance at him, smiling around the reed in her teeth. She removed the reed and spat into the dirt.

"You survived, boy," she said. "But you did not help anybody else. Three Breeds were taken last night, including Lirg of the line of Wis."

"What will happen to them?"

"Adonna has its uses for them. We said that, boy. You don't listen."

Michael suddenly felt exhausted and discouraged. He had never lived in a place so cruel and unpredictable. The thought of continuing to struggle seemed to pull wool around his brain. He sat before his hut and held his chin in his hands. "What about Eleuth?" he asked a few moments later.

"She was not taken," Nare said. "She is only one-quarter Sidhe. Her uses would be limited."

"Do they always attack on a night of *Kaeli*?"

"Not always. Often enough."

"So why so you still hold them out in the open?"

"We are still of the Sidhe," Nare said. "We must keep the customs, even when it is dangerous."

Michael pondered that for a time, and decided it didn't really make sense. But he didn't want to pursue that line of questioning. "I'm going to run now," he said. Nare didn't react. He wanted to get into Euterpe and talk with Savarin, find out what happened to the humans. At least with Savarin, he could ask questions and not be ridiculed.

He started off at a gentle lope, hoping to ease the exhaustion and funk from his body. As he approached Halftown again, he slowed. Glancing behind to see if he was watched, he took the path leading through the village.

Eleuth swept debris from the courtyard as Michael approached. She glanced at him without slowing her broom.

"I heard," Michael said. "I'm sorry."

"He serves the god now," Eleuth said. Sad, her voice was even more beautiful.

"Are you going to work the market alone?"

"I'll try."

He opened his mouth, but decided he really had nothing to say. He bent down to pick up a piece of timber.

"Put it in the pile," she said, gesturing with the broom end to a neat stack of ruined boards.

"If I can help . . ."

She regarded him with a calm, still expression, though her

cheeks were wet. He had never seen a Sidhe or a Breed cry before. He filed the information away; perhaps it was because she was three-quarters human.

"I mean, anything I can do," he said awkwardly.

She shook her head and continued sweeping. As he turned to walk away, she said, "Michael."

"Yes?"

"I will take my rest later this day. May we visit then? I'll be better."

"Sure. I'll be back by my place at—"

"No. Away from the Crane Women."

That suited him. "I'll meet you here."

Though every muscle ached, it was the sort of pain he felt might be driven away by exercise. Once outside Halftown and on the road, he picked up his jogging pace, slowly increasing speed as ache gave way to exertion.

Twice now his life had been threatened. Such things seemed to be expected in the Realm. The Crane Women, each time, had treated his horrible experiences as just another minor hurdle. Michael couldn't accept that.

He wasn't sure he could trust the Crane Women to help him to his goal; he knew he couldn't trust Lamia. Even the humans had little altruistic interest in his fate; Savarin probably cared for Michael only so long as he gathered information. Only Eleuth accepted him for what he was, and desired his company. He ran even faster.

Whatever else he thought about them, one thing was obvious: the Crane Women were doing him no harm by training him. He felt better, stronger; on Earth, he might have been laid up for a week after nearly drowning and being roughed up.

Euterpe had come through the storm with little damage. Some of the walls were water-stained, and one or two had been shored up after the dissolution of a few bricks, but little more. Obviously, what Nare had said was true: the Umbrals and Riverines sought Breeds, not men.

Michael made his way through the streets, walking quickly to avoid curious onlookers. Even so, he was heckled a few times. He hunched his shoulders and felt the helpless anger build.

He shook his head to clear his thoughts and crossed a narrow, cheerless triangle adjacent to a large, low one-story ochre brick building.

There were no signs announcing the fact, but Michael supposed this was the dreaded Yard. He circled the building, found Savarin's school on the opposite side, a square, low-roofed structure with a clumsy steeple rising over one corner. As he climbed the brick steps, he heard a high-pitched warbling wail from the depths of the Yard and the muffled slam of a heavy door.

Savarin stood near a wicker lectern in the empty single classroom, leafing through a small pile of gray paper. The teacher looked up as Michael entered, his eyes widening at the bruises on his face and the state of the boy's clothing: muddy grass-stained pants, torn shirt and jacket. "You look more like a savage every day," Savarin said. "Was I right about last night—more than a storm?"

"A—what did you call it?—a raid."

Savarin nodded, circling Michael and touching his jacket solicitously. *"Grazza,* similar to the Arabic *grazzu,* you know. My God. I knew Halftown was hit—"

"Right in the middle of *Kaeli,"* Michael said. "They took three Breeds, including the market manager. How often do these raids happen?"

"Often enough to make me suspect Alyons cares little for the Breeds, and that the Pact does not fully apply to them. Yet they follow Sidhe customs—"

"He doesn't give a damn for them," Michael said, surprised by his anger. "I'd like to kill that sonofabitch."

Savarin looked Michael over solemnly for a moment. "I hope your memory of the events was not affected."

"I remember well enough," Michael said. "The Crane Women even let me understand Cascar for a while."

Savarin's face betrayed almost comic envy. "Then tell," he said. "Do tell all."

For an hour and a half, Michael reconstructed the *Kaeli* and the events after. Savarin grabbed his sheaf of gray papers and scribbled notes frantically with a sharp stick of hardened charcoal. "Marvelous," he said several times throughout. "Names I've never heard before, connections made! Marvelous!"

When Michael finished, Savarin said, "I suspect Adonna would have done with us all, Breed and human. But it acts very slowly. A god's time must be different from ours. In its moment of hesitation, we might fit our entire history in the Realm. . . ."

"What happens to the Breeds they took?"

"I've heard the Umbrals and Riverines share them in their temples. Work magic with them. I know little beyond that. Perhaps some are taken to the Irall."

"What's the Irall?"

"Adonna's greatest temple, ruled by the Faer but accessible to all Sidhe. How many did you say were taken?"

"Three."

"Then it might not be an even split. Perhaps the raiders had a tiff of their own, dividing the captives."

Michael didn't like the word, *divide*. It sounded entirely too accurate.

"As for *Kaeli* songs, I've heard some outlines before but never so many details. You help me assemble many separate elements. A shame Lirg didn't have time to tell more about Elme. I suspect some very important history is connected with her." He put his notes on the lectern and sat beside Michael on the classroom's front bench. "Questions are going around town. Why are you here, and why are you with the Crane Women and not your own kind? The townspeople resent you because they fear Alyon's displeasure. Our position is precarious, and you introduce an element of uncertainty."

"Is there anything I can do?" Michael asked.

"Perhaps." Savarin smiled, then frowned as he inspected Michael's bruises. "You should be resting, not up and about."

"I'm fine. Tell me more about the Crane Women." *Come on, teacher*, he thought. *Teach.* "Why are they so old . . . and how old are they?"

"I'm not positive," Savarin said, "but I believe they date back to the time of Queen Elme herself. For all I've heard, they're Elme's daughters, but that hasn't been substantiated, and of course they'll never tell. Sometimes the Sidhe send their priest initiates, or their most promising young warriors, across the Blasted Plain to the Crane Women for training."

"Well, I'm no warrior and certainly no Sidhe. The Crane Women make me feel stupid. If the Sidhe hate humans and Breeds so much, why is Alyons supposed to be protecting us? Does he protect anybody, really?"

"Yes," Savarin said, scratching his nose between two fingers. "Somewhat. Things here would be much worse without him, much as I have a difficult time saying it. But he hates us. He makes sure we stay put, and between whatever protecting he does, he harasses. Makes life miserable."

"He wanted to kill me."

"I'm sure you go against everything he holds dear," Savarin said, chuckling. "You are being treated in a most unusual way—like a Sidhe in many respects."

Michael looked down at the hard-packed dirt floor. "I must have a million questions, and nobody knows the answers, or will tell me if they do."

"If the Crane Women haven't told you by now," Savarin said, "perhaps being ignorant is part of the training." He stood. "Ignorance loves company. I've someone I want you to meet . . . if you're free, that is."

"I'm free," Michael said with a touch too much defiance.

Chapter Twelve

"The last person to arrive in the Realm before you was—is—a young woman." Savarin led Michael down a narrow alley. Their feet squelched in the still-damp mud. "She's been here two years, counting by days—which is more reliable than counting by seasons. I've told her about you, and she wishes to meet you. She is from your country, the United States."

"Where in the United States?"

"New York."

"Savarin, how long have you been here?"

"Perhaps thirty, thirty-five years."

"You don't look old enough," Michael said, astonished.

"Here, we get old to a point, then no older. Our souls are aware there is no place for them to go, and so they take better care of our bodies. Aging stops, even for old Wolfer."

Michael was silent for a moment, letting that sink in. "What's her name?"

"Helena." Savarin turned left and waved for him to follow. At the end of an even narrower, T-shaped alley, a door was set into a mud-brick wall. The T's extensions branched to the right and left, ending in blind walls. Within the doorway a flight of steps led up into shadows. The feeble glow of a candle in a sconce at the top of the stairs lit their way as they climbed.

Savarin straightened Michael's coat collar and tugged his shirt collar out around it, shook his head at the hopeless task of making him presentable, then turned to a fabric-covered wicker door and lightly rapped it with his knuckles.

"Yes? Who is it?"

"I've brought a visitor," Savarin said, winking at Michael.

The door opened with a dry scrape and a young woman, not much older than Michael, stood in the frame. She smiled nervously and glanced at Savarin, smoothed the lower half of her blouse with her hands, and glanced at Michael. She wore a short skirt made of the same dun-colored cloth most of the human and breeds had to make do with. Her blouse, however, was white and cottony, cut short around her shoulders. Her face was broad, with generous black eyes and wide full lips. Her hair was dark brown with hints of red. She was well-formed, slightly plump, but as tall as Michael and able to carry her figure well.

"Helena Davies, this is Michael Perrin." Savarin waved his hand between them.

"Hello," Michael said, offering his hand. Helena took it—her fingers were warm and dry, slightly callused—and stepped back.

"Please come in. Savarin's told me about you."

The apartment was separated into two rooms by a plastered brick wall, the door between hung with curtains made of pieces of hollow twig strung on twine. Two chairs of woven cane stood in opposite corners, covered with tiny gray pillows. In another corner, a washbasin sat on a stand made of sticks, much like the one in the inn room Michael had first shared with Savarin.

"I'm brewing herb tea," Helena said, showing them to the seats. She pulled out a bedroll and went behind the curtain to retrieve a white ceramic pot and three mugs. She set them down on a second wicker stand and pulled the bedroll close to Michael's chair, then sat on it, serving the tea and handing them their mugs. She stood abruptly, her hands going this way and that as she searched for something with her eyes. She said, "Ah!" and walked briskly to a box on the window ledge, from which she withdrew honeycomb wrapped in waxed cloth. "Honey for your tea?"

"Please," Michael said. She broke off a bit of comb and handed it to him. He dropped it into his mug. Realizing his mistake, he started to fish out the melting bits of wax, then gave it up. Helena laughed, but not unkindly, and sat down again.

"I'm so *nervous*," Helena said to Savarin. "Henrik tells me you didn't come here the way the rest of us did."

Michael didn't want to repeat what was becoming, to him, a tiresome story. "How did you get here?" he asked.

"Helena was a budding concerto pianist," Savarin said. She shrugged with false modesty and held her mug to her lips, looking at Michael over the rim.

"Prokofiev," she said.

"Pardon?"

"I was playing Prokofiev. I'd been practicing the Piano Concerto Number Three for a month, preparing for a recital. I was very tired. Up in the morning with Bach, and around all afternoon with Prokofiev."

Michael waited for her to continue. She returned his gaze intently, then laughed and went on. "My hands felt all numb, so I decided to take a walk. The music was in my head. I could feel it. In my body, too, especially my chest and arms." She touched a spot above her right breast. Her breasts swung enticingly free beneath the blouse. "Like I was having a musical heart attack, you know?"

Michael shook his head.

"Perhaps not. Anyway, I was dizzy. I stood at the top of a flight of stairs in my apartment building, and at the bottom was nothing but a pool of mercury—you know, quicksilver— and I stumbled. Put my foot in it. Woke up here." She set her cup down and wiped her lips delicately with a forefinger. "I still don't like stairs, even living on an upper floor."

"That was two years ago?" Michael asked.

"Give or take. Now—how did *you* get here? I mean. Henrik explained, but I'd like to hear it from you."

All of Michael's confidence, built up (he had thought) during the weeks of training, dissolved in her presence. She was fresh, lively, young and completely human. He stumbled over his words, then bore down on memories and produced a passable re-telling of his experiences. When he had finished, Helena looked out the small curtained window, the subdued light from the alley softly dividing her face.

"We really don't understand anything about life, do we?" she said. "I thought this was like purgatory for those who spent too much time with music and too little time in church. At first, I mean. I was that naive."

"Many people feel a religious confusion when they first arrive," Savarin said. "I'm studying it."

"You study *everything*," Helena said, reaching out with a slender hand to touch Savarin's arm. Michael focused on the contact, with a twinge of jealousy. "Isn't he too much?"

"You're from New York?"

"Brooklyn. And you?"

"Los Angeles."

"Oh my *gawd,*" she said, shaking her head. "A crazy Californian. I've never heard of Arno Walt . . . what's his name. Did he ever write serious music?"

"For movies," Michael said.

"Nothing else?"

"Well, the concerto . . ."

"Funny, I've never heard of that, either."

"I think it was suppressed or something. It got him into a lot of trouble."

"Well, music's a big world. And I do suppose composers have a hard time, even harder than pianists. What are you doing now that you're here?"

"I'm training," Michael said before he had a chance to think.

"Training for what?"

"I don't know." He grinned sheepishly. Helena regarded him with apparent shocked surprise.

"You *must* know what you're training for," she said.

"To get my strength up, I suppose."

"You don't look particularly sick to me."

"Weak," he said. "I mean, I just never did much physical exercise."

"A bookworm like Henrik, I suppose," Helena said. "Well, then it's good for you there are so few books here."

"Michael brought one with him."

"Oh, did you? Can I see it?"

"I don't have it with me." He was surprised how touchy the subject was to him; he recalled Lamia's expression when he told her he had a book. "It's just a volume of poetry."

"More's the pity it's not a book of music. I'm terribly out of practice." She held up her hands and spread her fingers, crooking the pinkies slightly. "I'll bet you think musicians are terribly vain," she said, sighing. "Talk too much."

"No, not at all."

"Most of the people here are older than me. Some have been here for a hundred years or more. Isn't that amazing? Yet most don't look any older than Henrik, and those who do, were older when they came here. I think it's all very profound."

"It is," Michael agreed, though he might have chosen a different word. He could hardly keep his eyes off of her. To his embarrassment, he was getting an erection. He held his hands in his lap and tried concentrating on other things—Alyons and his coursers, the Umbral.

"I wonder if we'll ever figure it all out," Helena continued. She seemed aware Michael's shyness—even of his predicament—and appeared to enjoy it. "Will you be staying with the Crane Women for long? I mean, will they let you live in town?"

"I don't know. I don't really know much of anything. I'm so ignorant, but . . ." He wanted to just blurt everything out to her, bury his head in her—He raised his eyes from the blouse. "I have to go," he said. The thought of Alyons had made him presentable again. "They might need me for something. Maybe."

"Oh, I'm sorry," Helena said, standing. He glanced down at her knees, then at her eyes. No doubt about it. She was beautiful. He wondered what Savarin was to her—just a friend? "Can you come back? I'd like to talk some more—remember old times."

"I'll try," Michael said. "When would . . . uh . . . be convenient?"

"I work early mornings doing laundry." She displayed her hands. "Ugly, aren't they?" she said, holding them up before his face again. "No labor-saving devices in the Realm. You can come in the afternoon. I'm usually here otherwise. Do call." She smiled radiantly.

"I have to go," Michael said to Savarin.

"Certainly," Savarin said. He accompanied Michael.

"Good-by, until later," Helena said.

"By," Michael said, waving awkwardly. At the end of the alley, Savarin chuckled.

"She likes you, my boy."

Michael merely nodded.

"And I suppose you won't be seeing me as much, telling me so many interesting things?"

"I'll tell you whatever I learn," Michael said.

"After you tell Helena." Savarin cut off Michael's weak protest with a smile. "No, I well understand. Everybody's priorities are for the immediate. I am cursed, in the meanwhile, with an interest in the long-term."

They parted at the outskirts of Euterpe and Michael returned to Halftown, his thoughts crowded and confused.

Chapter Thirteen

For the first time, life in the Realm had some purpose besides survival and the now-distant goal of returning home. Michael wandered down Halftown's curving market street, thinking of Helena's face, of her lips and the way they moved when she talked to him.

He found the flattened courtyard and picked through the rubble to the front door of Lirg's—now Eleuth's—house. He knocked on the doorframe. There was no answer for a moment, then Eleuth swung the door wide open and stared at him, blinking wide-eyed.

"Hello," she said. Her face seemed older, worn.

"You wanted to talk with me?" Michael asked. He compared Eleuth's strange beauty with Helena's brisk familiarity and felt slightly repelled.

"I need company," Eleuth said. "But if you have something to do..."

"No," Michael said. Queerly, the repulsion was turning itself around now to attraction, but a distanced kind of attraction, something he could handle. Eleuth motioned for him to come in and closed the door softly behind.

The house was decorated very differently from the human dwellings he had seen: solid-looking, clean wooden furniture draped with rugs and fabrics, lamps burning sweet-scented wax in corners away from the windows, a ceramic brick firepit in the center of the house with a chimney poking through the roof. Thick, intricately patterned rugs hung from iron rods between wall and chimney, dividing the interior into four rooms. He sat on a bench and Eleuth sat across from him on the edge of the firepit, which was dark and covered with a brass mesh screen.

"It's not as if Lirg's dead," she said after a few awkward minutes of silence.

"What will they do with him?" Michael asked.

Eleuth lowered her gaze and reached down to adjust a boot. "He will serve Adonna."

"Whatever that means," Michael said.

"It means he will add his magic to the rituals. That will weaken him. Breeds are not like Sidhe full-bloods. Magic tires us. The more human blood we have, the less power to spare."

"And after that?"

"These are cruel thoughts," Eleuth said. "I'll never see him again, either way. He was a good father."

Her words were slow and sweet. The sadder she became, the more he was attracted to her. It took very little effort to sit beside her and reach for her hand. For the first time, he felt he was in control. She looked up at him and there were tears in her eyes. "What is death like on Earth?"

That took Michael aback. Except for Waltiri, he had never experienced the death of a loved one on Earth. Friends, parents, grandparents were all still living, as far as he knew. Death was an intellectual exercise, something to be imagined and not deeply felt. "Final," he said. "Everybody keeps saying humans have souls and Sidhe don't, but I know a lot of humans who would disagree."

"It makes no difference here," Eleuth said. "So I'm told. Young people must rely a lot on what they're told, no?"

Michael lifted his shoulders. "I suppose."

"And what they're told not to do. Breeds are less constrained then Sidhe. We are already among the low. We don't have much farther to fall."

"Humans aren't exactly respected here, either," Michael reminded her.

"But the Sidhe leave them alone. The Umbrals don't come to snatch them away."

"That's because we're useless. We have no magic. Have you done magic?"

Eleuth nodded slowly. "A little. I'm learning, but not quickly."

Michael patted her arm and stood. "I should get back to the Crane Women." He didn't particularly want to, but it was an excuse; he had no idea what more he could do here.

Eleuth stood, eyes still lowered, and reached out to touch the back of his hand with one finger. "When we are alone, we are most vulnerable," she said. She looked up at him. "Both of us need strength."

"I guess that's true," Michael said. There was an awkward moment as he tried to figure out how to say good-by. Finally, he just smiled and sidled out the door. She looked after him, eyes wide as when he had entered. Just before the door closed, he saw her turn away with a slow elegance that sent shivers down his arms.

His confusion multiplied as he crossed the stream and walked across the mound to the huts. Grateful none of the Crane Women were outside, he entered his small dwelling and stood with head brushing the ceiling rafters. His face was marked by lines of reddened sunlight gliding down the opposite wall.

Michael wasn't disturbed that night, except by a distant, deep hum that filled the land for a second or two. When that passed, he lay on the plaited reeds and stared up into darkness. For a dizzying moment, it seemed that it wasn't the world that had changed, but himself; that somehow he had twisted around to present a new face. He didn't feel sixteen years old.

He felt full, expectant . . . waiting.

Chapter Fourteen

Spart roused Michael early the next morning, taking him by the hand and dragging him from his hut, all the while making strange half-humming, half-whistling noises. She seemed to be trying for a tune and not quite finding it, but the closer he listened, the more he realized the sound went beyond tunes. Before he was awake enough to think clearly, she stopped and strutted around him, her critical eye sweeping him from head to foot. "Ready?" she asked, halting before him with hands on hips.

"I suppose I must be," he said.

"We are going on a trip. We will cross the Blasted Plain. You will come with."

"Okay," he said, swallowing. "Breakfast first?"

Coom emerged from the hut and tossed him a gray-green lime the size of an orange. Nare offered a crust of bread from the window. He knew better than to protest; besides, Sidhe food seemed to satisfy more. At least, he was seldom ravenous, and on bulk alone he should have starved by now.

They walked along the banks of the river in the early morning sun, through waist-high reeds and feathery-fronded water plants he couldn't identify. Creepers like green rubber hoses slithered down to the water. Ahead, to the northeast, a patch of intense blue coruscated above the faded orange ribbon which hung over the Blasted Plain.

The Crane Women plunged along ahead and behind him. He remembered some of the landscape from his unexpected journey during the *Kaeli*. After two hours of steady hiking, they reached the grassland that had been most stricken by the storm. The grass was still bent and disheveled. Four hours later, he recognized the mound where he had awoken, with its topknot of greener grass, and he saw the border. But the Crane Women veered northwest, clambering out of the reeds and following a winding trail.

Three hours later, always coming within view of the border only to veer away, Michael was tired enough to halt and utter a weak protest. The Crane Women had been bounding along like children on an outing, acting much younger than they looked (if he could apply any human age at all to them—he wasn't sure he could). "Please!" Michael called out after them. "What are we doing, where are we going?"

Spart waved him along. Michael sighed. He'd given up trying to find motives for what they did. At the very least, the Crane Women were elusive.

And now they eluded him. He had bent down for a second to untangle his foot from a root, and when he looked up, they were gone. Instead, at the top of a low hill about half a mile away, was a horse—a Sidhe horse, its rider nowhere in sight.

Michael searched the hill nervously with his eyes, then walked toward the animal. An unaccompanied Sidhe horse was probably most unusual in the Pact Lands. He had never seen one, at any rate. As he climbed the gentle slope, the horse lifted its head and whinnied. It trained its ears in his direction and turned on pumping legs to face him. Michael stopped; he felt no need to approach any closer. It might be a trap. A Sidhe could be lying on the other side of the hill, waiting for someone just as curious as he.

"Right you are to be cautious," Spart said, a yard behind him. "Do you know what that is? Do they still have them on Earth?"

"Of course," Michael said. "But not exactly . . . it's a horse."

"The Cascar word is *epon*," Spart said, "a word so old it predates the earliest horses. There were other steeds in those times, stronger, even more noble. They did not last the wars. Shall we have a closer look?"

"If you say so."

"Yes," Spart said. "It is part of what you must learn."

The horse pawed at the dirt and bent to nip blades of grass. As they drew closer, it reared up briefly, then cantered straight for Spart. She held out her broad hand and it buried its nose in her palm, closing its eyes and nuzzling.

The horse's coat, up close, was velvety-shiny, the muscles

packed tight beneath. Its legs were long and its head narrow, almost bony. The mane hung low on the neck but was well-kept; the horse had obviously been curried recently.

"Where is it from?" he asked.

"It crossed the Blasted Plain just a short while ago," Spart said. She patted golden dust from its withers. "Its masters await us beyond the borders. It will guide us across, and if we stay close, the *sani* will protect us." She held her palm out to him; there were sparkles in it like flecks of mica. "Would you like to ride?"

Michael shook his head. "I've never ridden a horse."

"You'll have to learn. Should it be now?" She wasn't asking Michael; she was addressing Coom and Nare, who walked casually up the other side of the hill, Nare with a blade of grass between her lips. They nodded noncommitally.

Spart squinted at Michael and shrugged. "His choice," she said. "The horse is borrowed, after all." She walked around the animal, feelings its flanks and withers, caressing its hind-quarters.

Nare chuckled throatily and squatted a few yards away, pulling the grass from her lips and inspecting it. "When you plan to ride a horse," she said, "you walk up to it, look it in the eye, say to it, 'You are my soul, I am your master!' Believe it when you say it. Then . . . you mount."

"Is that all?" Michael asked. Coom laughed, a sound like dragging slate between clenched teeth.

"Yes," Spart said. "But to believe it, you must be able to ride like the Sidhe. No human can ride like the Sidhe. You already have souls. There is little room for a horse."

"I might be able to learn," Michael said defiantly. "Maybe I'll ride just as well."

"Then try." Spart cupped her hands to provide a stirrup. "Left foot up, right foot over."

"No saddle?"

"Unless you're carrying one with you."

He put his left foot in her hands, grabbed hold of the lower neck and swung up and over. For a moment he hung in empty air, and then he landed on his hands and knees, the wind knocked out of him. The horse stood a few paces away, shaking its head and snorting.

"If you can't ride a horse," Nare said, observing him from where she sat, "act like one."

Michael got to his feet. "It's fast," he said.

"Some other time," Spart said. Once again, he felt his worth drop to zero. To regain some of his pride, he approached the horse a second time and patted its flank. It turned its pearly gray head toward him, large silver eyes blinking enigmatically. "Ho," he said. "Or something like that. Are we going to be friends?"

The Sidhe horse flicked its tail at an imaginary fly and lifted one foreleg. "Listen," Michael whispered in its ear, after pulling the head down gently to his level with one hand on its nose. "I'm in bad enough shape without your dragging me any lower. They think I'm a klutz," he nodded at the Crane Women, "and I agree. If you won't be my soul, how about just being my buddy?"

The horse raised its head, butting his hand away, then cocked its ears in his direction and gently bumped its nose into his chest.

"Is it possible you have a way with horses?" Spart asked.

"I wouldn't know; this is the first time."

"Try again," Spart suggested. "If you succeed, maybe you won't have to cross the Blasted Plain on foot." She held her hands out to form a stirrup again. He stepped up and swung over onto the horse's back. The horse wriggled its back muscles and shook its head but stood steady. Michael wrapped his legs tighter and asked, a small quaver in his voice. "Do I ride it now?"

Spart's eyes turned to the west, where a cluster of three Sidhe horsemen moved slowly across the grassland about a mile away.

"Who is that?" Michael asked.

"The Wickmaster," Spart said, blinking slowly and reaching to take the horse by the chin.

"Why is he here?"

"Wants to meet the ones who wait for us," Nare said, standing. "Come. Let's cross now."

The Crane Women walked down the opposite side of the hill. The horse followed, walking under Michael more than being directed by him. He had no idea how to give it directions, and he didn't feel now was the appropriate time to ask. Alyons and two coursers paced their animals about a hundred yards from them, both groups heading toward the edge of the Pact Lands and the smoggy region beyond.

The Crane Women paused at the border. The green grass

stopped along a geometrically perfect line, to be replaced by the glistening black and umber sand of the Blasted Plain. Nare bent to scoop up some of the sand; it trickled between her fingers as lifeless as the dust in a vacuum cleaner bag. She brushed her hand off on her pants, face creased with distaste.

"We'll walk close to you, to the horse," Spart said. Coom inspected the horse's flanks closely.

"Is it the dust that protects us? I mean, the *sani*."

"Part," Coom said. She, too, kept an eye on Alyons and the coursers, who had stopped at the border about sixty yards to the north. Alyons eyed them coldly, caressing his golden horse's shoulder with sure, smooth strokes. Michael wondered why the Wickmaster wasn't acting more boldly.

Nare was the first to cross. The horse followed reluctantly, its flanks rippling. "Forty miles," Spart said, pointing east. "Desolation. Ruin of war. Good training ground. But you should be careful. Adonna buries its mistakes; dig or blast deep enough beneath the ground of the Realm, and you'll find them again."

The tortured spires of once-molten rock rose on all sides, some bending back on themselves to form loops and arches. The ground opened up in cracks and chasms, emitting sulfurous wisps and acrid mists. Scattered over the terrain were pools of churning yellow-orange liquid like pus-filled wounds. Michael's eyes smarted sharply until Spart told him to bend down and administered a dark viscous cream high on each cheek. There was nothing she could do for his sense of smell, however. His nose ran constantly, and whatever dignity he gained by being on horseback was lost in snuffling.

Michael worried that they weren't carrying food and water. If they stayed for any length of time, the oversight would be unfortunate; they would find no sustenance on the Blasted Plain.

The dust billowed thick and irritating around them. Michael took a strip of cloth from Coom and tied it over his nose and mouth; the others did the same.

By dusk, they had made it to a flat pan of rock topped with smaller, sharp-edged boulders. Michael dismounted to help them clear a space about four yards across, lifting and tossing the boulders carefully to avoid cutting his hands. Then Coom took a small wood wand from her pouch and drew a circle in the dirt around the clearing. "Rest here," she said.

"Will that line keep things out?" Michael asked, thinking of pentagrams.

"No," Coom said. She didn't elaborate on its purpose. Twenty yards behind them, Alyons and his coursers halted but did not bother to dismount.

The orange light was oppressive. Michael was anxious to move on and suggested they do so but Nare shook her head firmly. The Crane Women sat within the circle and Michael stood near the center. The horse stood beside him with its head lowered, eyes half-closed. It looked very tired. "Are we resting for the horse's sake?" he said, his voice muffled by the scarf. The Crane Women had also lowered their heads. None of them answered. "I get it," he said. "Something saps the horse's strength when it's here, but it protects us . . ." They neither affirmed nor denied his theory.

A heavy brown cloud moved in over their heads, riding a pseudopod of gray-orange mist. Each liquid particle in the mist was as large as a drop of rain but did not fall. The mist swung around the circle but did not enter.

Alyons and his coursers were outside the periphery of the cloud. They stared intently at the Crane Women and Michael, who fancied he could feel Alyon's hatred even at this distance.

An hour later, Spart and Coom stood up abruptly. Michael shook his head; to his surprise, he had fallen asleep standing up.

He offered the horse to Nare, who mounted without comment. Spart broke the drawn circle with her foot and they continued east. The Sidhe followed not far behind.

Darkness was coming, and the Crane Women hastened to leave the Blasted Plain before nightfall. Michael's feet kept getting stuck in the dust, much worse than sand at a beach; he was soon exhausted and regretted giving up the horse.

With sunset—transformed by the orange haze into a sinister ritual of darkening brown sky and ribbons of ascending tan and ochre—they neared another sharply defined border. What lay beyond wasn't clear; the air thickened at that point, revealing only shadowy presences that could have been tall boulders, or trees.

The horse picked up its pace and they had to run to keep up. Michael did his best, but was the last across the border. For a second, he had a terrifying notion that if the Crane Women left him behind, he might not be able to cross by himself; but there was no noticeable force to prevent him from stepping over.

"Welcome to the Realm, proper," Spart said.

Trees! Huge, spreading leafy canopies rose before them, muting the last of the daylight into green murkiness. The air was clean and sweet. Even the Dust which had accumulated on their skin and clothing sloughed off, leaving them hot and sweaty, but not besmirched.

The horse cantered to a grassy glade to crop an emerald-green dinner. Nare hopped off her mount and sauntered up to a tree, which she patted with her long-fingered hand, grinning broadly. Michael stretched out his arms and inhaled, soaking up the coolness and greenness and peace.

For as far as he could see in the dusk, the trunks of trees rose in well-spaced disorder. Between them were shrubs thick with red and purple berries, tall lilies with white flowers delicately fringed blood-red, patches of blue flowers abutting the glades.

The forest was more than Earth-like; it was surreal, too perfect. After a few minutes, Michael became uneasy again. He looked back to the border, with its abrupt transition to orange haze, to see where Alyons and the coursers were. They were not in sight.

Spart approached him with both hands behind her back. Her grin was more subtle than Nare's. Coom sat on the lowest limb of a tree, watching him like a bird.

Withdrawing her left hand, Spart revealed a flower. It didn't belong to any of the flowering plants he had spotted—it was translucent, as if made from a soft glass. It could have been plastic except for the delicate tracery on its petals. She seemed to be offering it to him, so he reached out to accept. She snatched it back and hid it behind long, fanned fingers.

"What color is it?" she asked.

"Yellow," he said. She pulled away her hand. The flower was bright blue. "Okay, blue, but it looked like—"

"The Realm is not like Earth. On Earth, all things sit on a base of chaos, as here, but the foundations are much finer. The foundations of the Realm are coarse. Everything is much more open to suggestion. On Earth, the chaos is hooked into stability by a law which says you can never win . . . you understand?"

Michael shook his head, no.

Spart held the flower closer. "Earth is a much more accomplished creation. In the Realm, everything is more fluid. Look. What color is the flower?"

"Still blue," he said, but as he said it, he realized the flower had been yellow all along. "I'm . . . I'm sorry. It's yellow."

"Since you cannot win even *betlim*, a small combat," Spart said, "you must be like the flower. Suggest! Take advantage of the fluidity, the seams of the Realm. Magic may be beyond your reach, but not suggestion." She held the yellow flower out to him. This time she let him hold it, but as her fingers released it, Spart herself vanished. Nare and Coom and the horse as well were gone. Michael fumbled the flower and it fell to the long green grass, landing on three dew-flecked stalks.

The flower was pink.

He sat, then lay back on the grass, puzzled over what Spart had just told him. Nearby, the flower wavered on its tripod of grass stalks in a lazy, rich breeze. He smelled the mingled scent of tea roses and jasmine. Night was falling rapidly and the sky above had turned deep blue, with subtle highlights of magenta. The woods were almost black. Wind soughed between the trees, waving the shadow limbs back and forth hypnotically. Michael felt his eyelids closing. . . .

"We have company."

He jerked awake. Nare squatted beside him with another stalk of grass held in her lips. She pointed to a group gathered around a small, bright fire about forty feet away.

"They're Sidhe!" Michael said. But they weren't Alyons and his coursers, who were still not to be seen. Five males with long hair and beards, dressed in gorgeous metallic reds and greens and blues, circled the fire, glancing into the darkness in the direction of Nare and Michael. A sixth appeared, younger than the others; his suit was white with black checks. Whether their clothing was armor or thick garments, Michael couldn't tell, but the portions limned by the fire were dazzling.

He turned his head and saw Coom to one side of the group, conferring with a white-haired, white-faced Sidhe wearing velvety black robes. When the Sidhe moved, Michael saw rich gray patterns in his robes—or rather, suspended just above the fabric, for they seemed to float and changed with every motion.

"Who are they?" Michael asked.

"They are from the Irall," Nare said. "They've chosen an initiate, and they bring him to us for training."

"Why to you?"

"Because we're older than most Sidhe. We know the old ways, the old disciplines." Her expression spoke volumes to Michael: At last, the Crane Women had someone interesting to train, someone worth the bother.

The younger Sidhe detached himself from the fire and walked

to the perimeter of the encampment. He braced against the smooth massive trunk of a tree and let himself slide down on his haunches. He peeled a piece of fruit, seemingly unaware that Nare and Michael were just a few yards away.

"What is he being initiated into?" Michael asked.

"The young one is entering *temelos*, the circuit around priesthood. He is in for some rough times, very rough indeed. The priesthood is not easily arrived at, nor easily kept."

"What's his name?"

"Biridashwa," she said. "We will call him Biri."

Michael looked back toward the border and the brown darkness of the Blasted Plain. He could make out distant red glows like lava fissures creeping up the spires of rock; flitting green balls; and high above the plain, a small lone sphere of lightning, silently flashing.

Then he spotted another fire glowing deep in the woods. Its light was broken by three shapes: Alyons and his coursers.

"What do they want?" Michael asked, gesturing. "They keep following, waiting."

Nare shook her head. "The Wickmaster wishes to speak to the Sidhe of the Irall. He won't get a chance."

"Why?"

Nare smiled a crooked smile like the one she often used to express her opinion of Michael's abilities. "Why do you think Alyons is Wickmaster of the Pact Lands, and not of his own circuit in the Realm proper?"

"I don't know," Michael said. "Why?"

"Too many questions," Nare said, and kept silent for the rest of the night.

Chapter Fifteen

Fog drifted through the trees and over the camps, leaving a glistening layer of drops on the grass, flowers and Michael. He came awake to the sound of heavy bootsteps nearby and rolled onto his back, alarmed. The young Sidhe stood two steps away, white and black against the gray, face pale in the early morning.

"I am requested to see you are awake," Biri said. He looked tense, unhappy. The forefingers and thumbs on both his hands rubbed together.

"I'm awake," Michael said, getting to his knees. He was a little in awe of the young Sidhe. His companions seemed so different from Alyons and his coursers. At that thought, Michael tried to penetrate the fog and see where the Wickmaster was, but there was only bright silver and great tree shadows. He brushed the dew from his face and arms and shivered.

"They haven't taught you *hyloka?*" Biri asked.

Michael shook his head. "Whatever that is."

"I'm told we will train together. Perhaps we can help each other."

"You're going to be a priest."

Biri looked at the ground "My guardians will leave soon. I'll cross the Blasted Plain with you. Where are the *Geen Krona?*"

"What?"

"The Crane Women."

"I don't know. Not far, I'm sure." But he was never sure about the Crane Women.

Three tall figures came out of the mist, approaching the

camp. Michael stood quickly. He immediately recognized Alyons' slender, powerful shape. They passed within five or six paces of Michael and Biri, ignoring them, and stopped just beyond the Sidhe camp. Biri backed up and whispered to Michael. "They followed you here?"

Michael nodded. "Alyons doesn't like me."

The Wickmaster spoke in Cascar with the guardian dressed in black. The coursers stood motionless to one side, in casually defensive poses, while the guardians looked upon them with unconcealed distaste.

"He's asking for a new audience with the *Darud*," Biri said.

"Who's that?"

"The chief of the *Maln*, the Black order. That's Tarax—the one in the black *sepla*. Alyons used to be a member, but he committed some crime. He was punished by being sent to the Pact Lands to oversee humans and breeds."

"What are they saying now?"

Tarax had half-turned from Alyons and approached one of the coursers. A few words were exchanged and the courser backed away, bowing slightly.

"Tarax has told Alyons to be thankful for what he has. I think Tarax berates the courser for some error in ritual before a member of the *Maln*."

Michael watched Tarax closely, fascinated by the movements of the white-haired Sidhe. "Is he older than the others?"

"A human might think so. Age doesn't matter much to the Sidhe, give or take a few thousand years. Especially here."

"Well, is he?" Michael persisted.

"I don't know," Biri said. As if suddenly aware he was speaking to a human, Biri stiffened and took a step away. Alyons bowed to Tarax and turned, gesturing for his Sidhe to follow him away from the camp. His eye caught Michael's and held; Alyons' face showed no expression, but Michael felt a flash of hatred nonetheless.

"He's very angry now," Biri said. "I think the Crane Women have been talking with Tarax. Alyons was hoping for leniency. Tarax told him there is no such thing among the Sidhe."

"Great," Michael said. "Now he'll really get down on us."

"I don't think so," Biri said. "Not so long as I'm here. The Crane Women have an honored status, especially when they train a novice. They are no longer just old Breeds. Alyons doesn't dare displease them."

"And when you're gone?"

Coom descended the trunk of a nearby tree and jumped to the ground with a thump. She brushed bits of bark from her clothing and squinted at Alyons and his coursers as they vanished into the fog. Nare walked up behind Michael and Biri, carrying fruit in a newly-plaited grass mat.

"Breakfast," she said, laying it between them. "Eat well. We cross the border this evening, and it's best to be nourished, but not full, when we do so. This is our last meal today."

"Why this evening?" Michael asked. "Isn't it more dangerous?"

Coom snorted. Nare tossed him a blue fruit similar to the one he had seen in the between-house. He caught the fruit and turned it in his hands. Half of it was furry and soft like a peach, though colored pale sky-blue. The other half was dark blue, apple-hard and shiny. At no point on its surface did it show a stem or other blemish. "Eat," Spart said, standing a few yards away, near a sapling.

At mid-day, the Sidhe brought their horses forward and mounted. Tarax approached Spart and handed her a packet of *sani;* there would be no horse to protect them on the return trip. Instead, they would have to rely on Biri's pure Sidhe magic, undeveloped as it was.

Tarax held his hands out and Biri clasped them. The looks that passed between them was one of long acquaintance, even dedication, but no apparent affection. Tarax broke the clasp first. Before departing, he turned to Michael and surveyed him coldly. "So this is the Flesh Egg's favored, is it?" he said, his voice deep and level. "To be trained with my Biri, by the oldest of the Breeds."

Having delivered these few obvious words, Tarax returned to his group and they mounted. The shadows around the trees seemed to double and shift—and horses and Sidhe were gone.

Biri sighed. "You are the first human he has spoken to in centuries. The last one . . . best not to describe what happened to him."

When the shadows of the trees were long and the sky was changing hue, the Crane Women led Biri and Michael from the forest, moving south to cross the border at another point. Michael paced steadily behind Spart as they traversed a brief, emerald-azure savannah. Beyond the high, moist grassland stood an orderly row of waxy brown rocks, shining in the sunset like polished wood. The highest was about thirty feet, the lowest barely a stepping stone. Where the rocks crossed the border, they became blackened and cracked, tumbled to one side or the other. Nare took the giant slabs one by one, climbing to the highest and jumping from rock to rock, the others following until they stood on the border, which plainly divided one boulder about ten feet tall.

Beyond the border, dust piled up on each side of the rocks. Biri crossed first, staying upright as he slid and ran down an incline of dust. Coom and Nare followed. Spart tapped Michael on the shoulder, urging him ahead. He tried to imitate Biri's grace but ended up sliding down the incline on his butt. They quickly ran ahead to avoid the acrid clouds they had raised.

"Now we move as a group," Spart said. "Close together." Biri brought out the bag of *sani* and sprinkled a little on each of them, muttering something in Cascar as he did so. They walked due west until the dusk settled into darkness, and then halted. Michael looked around at the orange band of fading light on the horizon, at the dust now inky black, at the gluey arches and spires to the north, and shivered.

"Why are we stopping?"

"Because we won't be able to see much longer," Spart said. This time it was Biri who removed a wand from his white-and-black checked coat and drew a circle around them. Where the lines joined, he sprinkled more *sani,* then stepped back.

"Now watch," Spart said as they gathered and sat in the middle of the circle. "See what even a young Sidhe can do in the Realm."

Biri reached out with his long, muscle-knotted arms and touched a spot directly before him with his index finger. The muscles in his face tightened and his lips moved silently. The rock began to glow, and presently the cold was dispelled by a steady pulse of heat. Michael was mesmerized by the glowing spot. "Will I ever be able to do that?" he asked Spart in a whisper.

She shook her head, not in definite denial, but as if the question irritated her. Michael leaned back, frowning. *Well, will I?* he asked himself. He held his hands out to the warmth. He was thirsty—he had swallowed some dust and it tasted like the bitter part of a bad apple—and hungry, but he knew better than to ask about food.

Presently his legs cramped and he unfolded them and lay

back. The others remained sitting, staring at the glow. He
leaned on his elbow, stretching his legs behind Spart. His
eyelids began to droop.

He awoke, his whole body jerking and trembling. His eyes
opened and he became aware that he was standing, the toes of
his shoes on the edge of the circle Biri had drawn. He faced
away from the heat into darkness. Something urged him to
cross over the line, but he couldn't.

In the fixed starglow, Michael made out a purple shape
beyond the circle. Each time he blinked, it changed form and
appeared closer. The battle between the urges to step over the
line and to stay inside the circle jerked him harder now; his
legs and arms twitched like marionette limbs in the hands of
an inept puppeteer.

The purplish shape was close enough now to stand face to
face with him, but it had no face. The shape consisted of smooth
rings of varying sizes stacked atop each other, with several
more rings gliding up and down the thing's exterior. Michael
blinked and the shape became an assemblage of irregular rounded
blobs.

He blinked again, and the shape was his mother, smiling at
him and holding out her arms.

Again, and it was Helena, waving for him to follow her as
she stepped back.

"It's quite obvious, isn't it?" Biri said, standing beside him.
"You haven't met one of these before?"

Michael shook his head. "What is it?"

"An abortion. A creation too inconsistent to match up with
the Realm."

"One of Adonna's mistakes?"

"Gods don't make mistakes," Biri said. "What are you going
to do?"

Michael laughed hysterically. "What should I do?"

"Do you wish to see it as it really is?"

"Should I? I mean no, no."

"I've seen them many times," Biri said. "They are mostly
harmless to a Sidhe, even to capable Breeds. Only humans are
susceptible. It was the power of the Isomage that liberated them
from their deep tombs. The Blasted Plain has much worse to
offer."

"Can it hurt me?"

"It can do worse than kill you. Whenever a human child is
born, one of these is liberated. The child has no reservoir of

waiting souls from which to draw, so its search allows certain patterns within one of these to enter the Pact Lands. The child is branded. The same could happen to you if you slept here and did not have a circle."

"You mean, I'd be possessed?"

"These are not intelligences. They are abortions. You would be more eaten than possessed. Your soul is a rare thing here, heavily armored within your body. What happens to it when they crack that armor is not explainable in your languages."

Michael tried to retreat from the edge of the circle, but couldn't. "I'm stuck."

"It cannot hurt you in here. You can play with it, in a sense; it can no more leave you than you can back away. So you can learn from it."

"I don't want to learn. I want it to go away and leave me alone."

"A Sidhe uses the abortions to prove his interior—"

"I don't care!" Michael shouted. "I'm not a Sidhe! Make it go away."

"I can't," Biri said. "Only you can release it." The novice walked away and squatted near the glowing rock.

"Spart," Michael said, "help me!"

There was no reply, and he couldn't turn his head to see the Crane Women. The shape now resembled Eleuth. She looked very sad, as if she had lost something vital and he was responsible. She looked down. She became a cylindrical something, lines of light crawling up its surface like worms, leaving trails of fire behind.

He tried to find a clue within himself. They wouldn't leave him in this fix (he hoped) if they didn't believe he had some way of getting out of it. He had to think it through. . . .

No, in an emergency, thought would be too slow. What if humans had something to make up for their lack of magic, something instinctive? He searched, waited, but the necessary remedy wouldn't come forth.

The cylinder split like a pared cucumber, revealing an interior compounded of offal and tiny, unidentifiable skeletons. The bones of the skeletons linked and spun, churning the fleshy parts into liquid, which streamed through the lengthening slits and spattered on the dark ground. The segments turned into slithering smooth snakes without discernible head or tail. They rolled into spirals and the spirals lifted to vertical positions, then met at their edges.

They flowed into the shape of Arno Waltiri. He sat upright in a coffin, sallow-fleshed, eyes open but dead and sunken. His mouth fell open abruptly and music came out, sharp and painful. Michael's skin seemed to blister as the music surrounded him. The corpse fell forward, draped over the lower half of the coffin lid, and revealed another body behind it: his own.

"Wait," Michael protested. It was stealing all these images from inside him. If he could stop the flow . . .

"Wait," the ragged Michael in the coffin mimicked, shaking its head from side to side.

"Stop," Michael said. He shut his eyes and concentrated on doors closing, dams cutting off water at their sluice gates, capping toothpaste tubes, corking bottles. He tightened his mind down until his entire brain seemed to contract. *You can't steal anything more. I've put a lock on it. Loose minds must not entwine, must not combine—*

Michael opened his eyes and saw nothing but darkness beyond the circle. He relaxed; he was in control again. He backed away and lay down again by the glowing rock, glancing at Biri, who lay on his back, head turned in Michael's direction.

The Sidhe nodded and closed his eyes.

They spent two days and three nights in the desolation, Spart engaging Michael in endless and repetitive drill with sticks, running him over the sharp boulders until his feet were in agony and his shins and hands were scraped raw. The dust in his wounds stung like acid and left tiny black lines that were slow to fade.

When he wasn't training, Michael watched Nare and Coom preparing Biri. The young Sidhe endured everything stoically and performed his exercises flawlessly. The most spectacular thing he did was to reduce a boulder nine or ten yards across to rubble by running around it and chanting. When the dust had cleared, Biri stood atop the heap, brushing his clothes down. Nare and Coom walked around him, features blank.

Michael knew they were much more pleased with Biri than they were with him, and it was obvious why.

Despite Biri's apparent ease with Michael, he was seldom able to engage the Sidhe in any meaningful conversation beyond amenities and occasional advice, which galled Michael even more than silence.

"Why do you even bother with me?" Michael asked Spart.

"You could train the Sidhe to do whatever you want." Spart agreed and shook her head in despair.

"We do indeed waste our time," she admitted. "It's fortunate we are immortal and can afford to be foolish."

Only on the last night on the Plain did Biri open up a bit, as they were preparing to cross the border into the Pact Lands. "When I am done here, I have a good thought, and a bad," he told Michael.

"What are those?" Michael asked, his tone hardly concealing his resentment. If Biri had not answered, he would not have much cared, but the Sidhe pointed across the Plain and said softly, "It is good to go back to the Sidhe territories, but it is less good to fulfill my purpose there."

"What will you do with the Breeds you've had captured?" Michael blurted. "When you're a priest, I mean."

For the first time, Michael saw Biri become visibly angry. He advanced on Michael and stood over him. "The Faer do not worship Adonna that way," he said, his voice cold and crisp.

"Some of the Sidhe do," Michael said. Spart looked between them curiously, as if anticipating some kind of fight, and perhaps welcoming it.

"Not the Faer," Biri reiterated, backing away. He glanced at Michael from under his brows and went back to his preparations. Michael took a deep breath.

"Hold it in," Spart said, continuing to stare at him curiously. Michael held his breath, inwardly fuming at the indignity. "Not your breath, your mind. Hold it in again."

"I don't understand," Michael said.

"Just now. Biri probed you to see what your intentions were. It was a very young thing for him to do, and he didn't succeed."

"He tried to read my mind?"

Spart shrugged and took Michael's hand. "You are indeed a man-child," she said. No further explanation was offered.

Night had fallen when Nare told them to follow behind her. Michael walked ahead of Spart, who was at the end of the line, and he stumbled less often than he expected. "I'm getting more agile," he said to no one in particular, enjoying this small accomplishment. And he had to try extra hard for the next few minutes to keep from making himself a liar.

Coom carried a stick which she had caused to glow at one end. The dim yellow luminosity was all they had to travel by. Michael didn't ask why they couldn't wait until morning. He felt some trepidation about what they might encounter, with no circle to protect them, but it seemed part of the plan, the test.

They marched down a gully and then followed the long depression. The plain was silent except for the sound of their footsteps. Michael lost himself in the rhythm of putting one foot ahead of the other, keeping up with the circle of light from the glowing stick.

"Ssst," Nare hissed. Michael looked up and followed the direction of the eyes of those ahead. On the edge of the gully, outlined against the stars, was a giant inverted skull, its blunt jaw poking at the sky.

The group stopped and Coom raised the stick higher. The object was at least thirty feet high. As Michael peered closer, he saw it wasn't a skull, but a huge shell. The occupant—or occupants—of the shell rose over the rim of the gully, protruding from the "eyes," long blue-black slug-like things. They joined just beyond the two holes, forming an elongated body which split again near a triplet of heads. The heads were further divided into three stalks, each sporting a mouth like a pair of toothed dinner plates hinged with filamented flesh. The heads and stalks waved above the group, plates opening and closing with faint clacking sounds. Where the skull's nose would have been, an arm with a triangular cross-section slithered, its end covered with tentacles, each tentacle tipped with a blob of flesh that glowed in the dark. The creature or creatures waved this arm as a watchman would his lantern.

Michael stood his ground only because the others did so. His instinct was to either run or have a heart attack. He could hear the breath in his lungs rasping like a file cutting steel. His pumping blood sounded loud enough to shake the rocks loose. Indeed, a few pebbles clattered down into the gully as the thing slithered on, and it turned its heads to peer after them.

There was a look of awe on Biri's face, intensely watchful, fascinated.

The monstrosity either didn't see them or ignored them, passing with cruel slowness. More rocks clattered down, the heads swiveled again, and then it dragged its shell away from the gully with the sound of huge fingernails on acres of sandpaper. Michael shuddered uncontrollably and sat down. Biri looked back at him and made as if to wipe his own brow, a gesture which endeared him to Michael enormously. Spart poked Michael in the ribs to get him moving again.

Only a few minutes later, they crossed over into the grassy prairie of the Pact Lands, not far from the river. The group made it to the mound by early morning, and Michael went to his hut and collapsed.

He was shaking. Not until his body had shivered itself free of every vestige of emotion and tremor of memory did he fall over on his side and sleep.

Outside the hut, Biri stood to face the newly risen sun, holding his small wand high in the air. He then sat on his chosen spot and his head slumped forward. He, too, slept.

Chapter Sixteen

Michael sat up and rubbed his eyes; he had felt, rather than heard, Biri's presence outside his hut. "Yes? What is it?"

"My wood was delivered last night," Biri said. "I've built my quarters."

Michael pushed through the doorway cover. A new hut, little different from his own, sat on the mound about twenty feet away. He was not fully awake and felt awkward in the Sidhe's presence. "Good."

"Before you, I'd never spoken to a human being. I'd never even heard of the Pact Lands until my journey began.".

Michael's bowl of porridge waited to one side of his door. He bent over to pick it up and began scooping it into his mouth with two fingers. "Where are you from? I mean, not that it would do me any good to know. . . . I'm pretty ignorant about everything outside the Pact Lands."

"Shall we trade stories?" Biri asked. "The *Geen Krona* believe if we train together, we should behave honorably, and not dispute. I am very interested in where *you* are from, and how you came here."

Michael agreed, and told Biri about his circuitous route to the Realm. Biri nodded at the key points, and frowned when Michael mentioned the figure in the flounced dress. Michael put aside his empty bowl and said, "Now, you."

"To the north, across savannahs and beyond *Nebchat Len*— that's a lake, almost a sea, very deep—there is a forest called *Konhem*. That's where I was born." He paused, glancing at Michael from the corners of his deep-set eyes. "Do you know much about the Sidhe?"

Michael shook his head. "Not really."

"We are seldom told who our parents are, especially when we've been chosen before birth, sometimes before conception. for the priesthood. By tradition, our fathers are ashamed of showing weakness by loving a female and getting her with child. That is why young Sidhe are so rare." He turned his gaze toward Halftown. "I think there are more Breeds born than Sidhe. At any rate, I've never met another Sidhe younger than myself. And our mothers return to their clan after giving birth, leaving the children to be cared for by the *Ban Sidhe*. They are the *Mafoc Mar*, the Bag Mothers, clanless females who serve the members of the *Maln*, the Black Order." He stopped and sketched a design in the dirt with his wand. When he lifted his wand up, the design rubbed itself out. "Do you understand?"

"I think so," Michael said. "I don't speak Cascar much at all, but I've heard of the *Ban Sidhe*. On Earth, they're supposed to come and claim the dead."

Biri's ears cocked forward slightly, something Michael had never seen a Breed's ears do. "The Clanless Bans not in charge of raising young take Sidhe dead to the Arborals, or to their tombs, whichever is willed."

"Where is this forest, and the savannah? We met in a forest . . ."

"A small forest, just a patch. The savannah—the *Plata*—stretches around and beyond this patch, to *Konhem*, the deepest, darkest forest in the Realm. I lived in *konhem* for a time. Then I was taken into the mountains called *Chebal Malen*, the Black Mountains. I was given up to Tarax . . ."

Biri leaned forward and stared into Michael's eyes. An extraordinary thing happened. Michael's view of the mound and the Crane Women's hut faded and he seemed to stand before the white-haired, black-robed Sidhe, peering up from a low angle. Tarax bent down and took a small, slender hand—his own, or rather Biri's. That faded—Michael could vaguely see the hut again—and was replaced by the vista of an enormous flat-topped mountain with jagged slopes dusted by swirling drifts of snow. Then he stood on a perfectly flat plain, surfaced with cyclopean blocks of stone stretching for miles on all sides, cloud shadows flowing over the stonework. Ribbons of cloud flew straight up from the slopes on the opposite side. "The Stone Field is not on the highest mountain in the *Chebal Malen*, but it is very cold and harsh there. Tarax built a four-room *caersidh* out of stone and I lived there for many seasons while he tutored me. Finally, I was considered worthy and he took me to the *Sklassa*, the fortress of the Black Order. Until now, I have never known anything else." He smiled at Michael. "The trip across the forest and savannah was wonderful. I have never seen so much change."

"What does a priest do?" Michael asked.

Biri drew back and sighed. "That I cannot tell you."

"I mean, do you attend Adonna, take care of sacrifices, that sort of thing? I'm just curious what—"

"I cannot tell!" Biri said, standing swiftly. "I've spoken too freely already. No human must ever know what happens in the Irall." He stalked off to his own hut, leaving Michael to ponder Sidhe moods and Sidhe secrets.

If anything, he thought, it was the Black Order, the *Maln*, that sounded like it should be kept secret. Was training novices the only thing the Black Order did? Even among the Sidhe, Tarax had been impressive—if only for overshadowing and cowing Alyons.

The Crane Women walked up the side of the mound opposite Halftown, pushing their knobby knees with their hands as if going up some long, exhausting grade. They cackled softly among themselves and shook their heads. Nare saw Michael sitting on his boulder and straightened sharply, regarding him with large, piercing eyes.

Their faces are so strange, he thought. *So human, but the way their eyes curve up, the way they blink almost from three-quarters to one side....*

Spart called across the mound, "Boy! You'll come with us today." He sighed, climbed down from the rock, and reached into the hut for his shoes.

They walked several miles away from Halftown, due east. He wondered why Biri wasn't going with them and Coom seemed to hear him think. "Sidhe trains different," she said. "Share some, not today." She cackled softly again and Michael felt his neckhair rise.

"He already knows what you'll need to learn today," Spart said. She walked ahead of the rest, holding out her wand and pointing it here and there at the horizon. Soon a mist began to rise, swooping across the river and enveloping them. Spart rejoined the group, and they squatted to rest—all for Michael's sake, he imagined, since the Crane Women never seemed to tire.

"Do you remember the color of the flower, boy?" Spart asked, shuffling nearer to him and peering intently at his face. She grimaced, wrinkles distorting the snakes and vines tattooed in red and purple across her features.

"I remember it changing," he said.

"What advantage does the Realm give you?" she asked.

"There are ways to change it."

"What is magic, boy?"

"I . . . I don't know. Yet."

"Will you ever know?"

He didn't answer. Coom came closer, her goosedown hair curling in the mist. Nare stood behind him; he could hear her breathing.

"Some think the Crane Women will be here forever, training and teaching," Spart said. "Do you believe that?"

Michael nodded. "I don't see why not."

Spart chuckled in the back of her throat and pushed her wand into the dirt. "Biri is a curious novice. He made you see today. What do you think of the Sidhe now?"

"Strange," Michael said, squinting in a stray shaft of sunlight.

"Will you ever understand Sidhe, or Breeds?"

"Probably not," Michael said.

"Because you're human," Nare offered.

"No, because you're Breeds . . . and he's Sidhe," Michael countered, uncertain what he meant.

"At this stage, your mind is all confusion," Spart said, tying in to his uncertainty. "You don't think clearly. You are slack. You can't feel what we teach. You spirit is like a limp sail on *Nebchat Len*."

"You have sailboats?" Michael asked.

Spart sighed. "You see? Every breeze pushes you this way and that. No listen close. We have less time to teach you now. Other tasks await us." She looked at her companions. "Less time than you think. You must learn quickly. Remember the flower. Remember, the Realm works for you. And *you* . . ." She stood. "You have less time." She pulled a flower from her pouch and dropped it to the ground before him. "What color?"

"Blue," he said. He looked up from the flower. The Crane Women were gone. He turned quickly, trying to catch some glimpse of them in the mist. They had deserted him.

The flower was yellow.

A deep, bass humming ascended and swept over the grass

like the passage of a huge helicopter. The mist swirled and was blown away in translucent spirals. The grass began to fan out and wind scoured at his face.

Michael walked a few steps backward and came up against a square-cut stone marker about as tall as he was. A few yards away, emerging form the mist, was another. Both had been carved with circled swastikas that faced each other over a stretch of fresh-cropped grass.

The more the mist cleared, the more obvious it became that a kind of path was aligned between the markers; not a path traveled by horses, people or even carts, however. The grass had not been trampled—only neatly cut short.

Again came the humming and the sensation of motion overhead. The hair on his arms erected and his whole body tingled.

Something white wavered at the boundary of the mist, a few dozen feet down the path. It detached itself and swept along, a human-like figure from the waist up, a trailing blur from the waist down. As if Michael didn't exist, the figure passed by and vanished in the opposite haze.

The Sidhe of the air, Michael thought—a Meteoral like the one he had seen on the road from Lamia's house. He picked up his stick and scurried to the edge of the path, where he squatted in the taller grass, shivering, trying to be inconspicuous.

Several more flew by, the air swirling in their wake. They weren't immaterial but he could almost see through them. They cast only the vaguest of shadows in the muted sunlight. The tops of their heads floated a good eight feet above the ground, and they seemed in proportion to that height. At first he could not tell whether they had male or female features, but he soon realized they were all female, with slender, hard-edged faces and somber expressions. Soon, a steady stream of Meteorals came down the path, growing more and more distinct as the sun burned away the mist.

At first, none of them paid him any attention. He tried to hide in the deeper grass, however, and stepped on a dry stick. It snapped loudly. He felt his heart convulse around his blood like a closing fist.

The stream of Meteorals scattered in all directions. Michael heard whisperings overhead, then all around, as if they had regrouped and were lowering themselves in a surrounding canopy.

Directly in front of him, the air glimmered and crackled.

His skin tingled painfully as a rush of white filled his view. He caught a glimpse of a hideous, angry long face drawn into a scream, fingers shaped into claws. His cheek stung and he grabbed it with his hand. His fingers came away bloody.

"Sed ac, par na antros sed via?" The voices came from all directions, from a hissing multitude, exhaled like a chill wind.

"You are on a trod," came a softer, no less menacing single voice right next to his ear. He turned slowly to face a Meteoral stooping in the grass. The grass seemed to pass right through her. He could feel her breathing on him, the breath sweet as ether. "You are the human from the house of the Isomage, no?"

Michael nodded. His legs froze and pins and needles traveled up his thighs.

"You should not be here."

"The Crane Women—"

"Have no power over us." The face shimmered and stretched, becoming even more hideous. The eyes were large, the most substantial things in the face, completely white and without pupils. A hand rose to one side of his head and the fingers stretched and clenched. Blood from Michael's cheek dripped onto his jacket.

"They brought me here. Talk to them—"

"We despise Breeds as much as we despise you."

The face vanished. Michael's legs were too numb to support him. He fell back into the grass and cried out through clenched teeth at the pain as the circulation returned to his legs. He looked down at the spots of blood on his shoulder and the front of his jacket, and saw that his clothing had been neatly sliced to ribbons. The leather of his shoes was in shreds, as well.

"Help me," he murmured, crawling away from the trod. He left scraps of cloth behind. "Please help me. God, please take me back...."

A long ribbon of pearly white formed over his head. He looked up, cringing, and saw a chain of meteorals swooping low above him, each face conveying some new expression of curiosity, anger, irritation, even humor. And with each passage, his clothes became more and more ragged. Their trailing arms drifted over him like smoke, silently slashing, flaying.

He closed his eyes and leaned on his arms, lowering himself to the ground. He buried his face in the grass, certain he was going to die. He just didn't want to see it happen. Where were the Crane Women? Had they done all their work, the weeks of training, just to let him be sectioned like bologna in a deli?

He felt a rush of cold air on his naked back. His jacket and shirt had completely fallen away. The first stab of pain hit him, slow, excruciating, as something moved along his back. *No.* He felt a burst of anger. *God damn them all. Why did everyone have to be so cruel, so full of hate? He didn't hate them.*

Suddenly, he seemed to be sitting somewhere else, watching but not seeing in the midst of incredible stillness and calm. He had had the same feeling when poetry flowed from his pencil so fast he couldn't tell where it was coming from.

It was a kind of looseness, in his hands as much as his head. He watched himself stand, sweep at the air with his stick, grimace. He seemed to be grinning back at the Sidhe hovering around him.

The stick was little use. He'd have to take advantage of the chaos. Blue flower, yellow, really pink.

Grass, actually, and air, right here.

He ran, holding the stick before him, knees parting the hip-high grass smoothly. Part of himself had been left behind like a squid's decoy cloud of ink. Not magic, but interesting; the Meteorals didn't seem to notice where he really was.

Naked, he ran through the sunlight and warm gentle breezes, legs pumping on their own, lungs drawing in and growing, heart strong and leonine. He imagined his heart growling, surrounded by a wind-tossed mane. He imagined himself a glass gazelle, a Sidhe horse turning into a quicksilver blur. The grassland fled beneath him, afraid of his feet; he was the center and the Realm passed under, not the other way around.

Meteorals flanked him. He dodged. Blue flower, pink.

Here, he thought in a place below thought, you can reach down and use your mind to accomplish things impossible on Earth. Because Adonna is not a mature god, and the Realm isn't quite polished. Was that what the Crane Women wanted him to learn?

He dodged, leaving shadows. The Meteorals were farther away, swirling around one of the shadows like a snow-devil.

Long after he knew he had escaped, he continued to run. There was no body carrying him, only eyes. He could not feel his muscles, only the stick he held before him. He was the stick, and his body was the comet's tail of its flight.

Michael Perrin fell down and rolled, stuffing grass and dirt into his mouth. The stick bruised his ribs. He came up squatting with legs and arms splayed. His head fell forward and his arms went out from under him.

The whole world was suddenly filled with agony. His body wanted to curl up like ash, his muscles burned so badly. His vision was red and uncertain.

And he was scared again. His heart was a small, tight snake, not a lion. "God," he gasped. "God please."

"Quiet." Spart stood over him, hands on hips, arms elbowed out like bird wings. She bent down and felt his arms and back with a worried frown. He heard Nare and Coom conversing in Cascar to one side.

"You did well," Spart said. "Much too well, actually."

The agony and fear faded. *Is it night?*

No.

Chapter Seventeen

Did they want him dead? Why did they leave him between the markers—to put him out of the way, so they could concentrate on Biri? Or was there something else—a conspiracy, perhaps—of which Michael knew nothing?

When he opened his eyes and stared at the roof of his hut, it all seemed like a dream. In the Realm, however, there was no dreaming . . . perhaps because one cannot dream within a dream. In the mind, anything can happen. Anything can be accomplished, given control of the milieu. Was that what the Crane Women were trying to tell him?

Spart leaned over him and peered into his face, making him jump. He hadn't been aware she was in the hut.

"I was good, huh?"

"Survived again," Spart said laconically. "When you can do what do did at will, you will be acceptable."

"What did I do?"

"Out-seeing. In Cascar, *evisa*. You threw a shadow. Do you remember what it felt like?"

He tried to recall the sensation, like picking out the muscles to make ears wriggle. He had never been able to make his ears wriggle, however, or his nose. On Earth, he had often dreamed of flying. It had been so simple to fly: Just by discovering and flexing a certain muscle in his neck and head, he could lift himself from the ground a yard, two yards, higher with more strain. Upon waking, he could never locate the muscle—nor could he now.

"I'm awake," he said. Spart pulled her hand away from his

chest. "Maybe I'll just do it when I really need to." He sat up on his elbows.

"What if you do not know you need to until it is too late? You are just beginning. Don't get your hopes up."

"What hopes? I haven't had any hope since I came to this place."

"Ah!" Spart pulled her lips back from her black gums and long teeth. "You hope for those *geen*."

"Who?"

He felt weak and fell back. As he twisted his head, he saw Nare on one side of him, Coom on the other. *"Ba* (click) *dan,"* Coom said. "Okay?" Nare bent closer to examine his limbs.

"Other than being a little banged up, I'm fine," Michael said quietly.

"Something," Coom said. "Did something."

"What?"

"Up. Outside."

He stood awkwardly and realized he was naked. Spart pushed him through the doorway and they pulled him forward by his arms until he stood in the middle of the mound. "Do you feel anything?" Spart asked as they circled him. Coom made soft clucking sounds. "Anything odd?"

"No. Nothing. Why?"

"Be certain!" Nare snapped. "Where is it?"

"On one of his limbs, probably," Spart said. "Hiding."

"Daggu," Coom said. It sounded like a curse. He was filthy, stained with grass juice and blood, but he didn't feel badly injured. Still, the way the Crane Women regarded him, with tight narrow expressions, worried him. Coom glanced down at his calf and bent over. She held out her left hand, wriggling her fingers slowly, and suddenly snapped it down to his ankle, plucking something up and holding it at arm's length.

"Do you see it?" Spart asked.

"What?" He tried to make out what Coom was holding but was too nervous to approach close enough.

"In the sun," Nare said. Something about two inches long glinted in Coom's long fingers. He squinted and traced its silhouette. It resembled a slender crab, translucent, almost invisible. In all the dirt and mess, he wouldn't have noticed it at all; he certainly hadn't felt it.

"What is it?" he asked, shivering.

"This night, while you sleep," Nare said, "it would kill you.

It's a gift from the Meteorals. When they give one of these to another Sidhe, the bite produces mystic dreams. Humans can't dream here, so it kills them."

"Jesus," Michael said.

"Remember," Spart said, her eyes fixed on his. "You cannot dream here. There are no dreams."

Coom carried the tiny creature into their hut. "It will entertain us tonight . . . and then, we'll add it to our collection," Spart said.

Biri had watched all this from the door of his hut. The young Sidhe drew his reed curtain closed and Michael stood alone and naked, as hollow as a dead tree.

Inside his hut, stashed in a corner, was a change of clothing. The pants, shirt and cloth shoes resembled what the Crane Women wore but were even more ragged. Still, they were clean. He put them on. The fit was tolerable.

Michael felt the by now very familiar sensation of apprehension and helplessness. He had survived. He had done something strange, something he wasn't sure he would ever be able to repeat; yet in the face of the Realm's mystery, he had not learned much.

What he had learned was that the Crane Women cared little for his safety—or they were crazy enough to put him into situations where he could get killed.

He came out of the hut again to see that the sky was brightening. He had slept all day after his ordeal. After eating the fruit and porridge Nare had left for him, he went to the stream to bathe. He scrubbed off all the dry grass and dirt stains, then poured water over himself. When he had shivered dry, he went to a relatively calm pool and peered at his reflection.

His cheek was swollen and the scratches were pink and puffy, but they didn't seem infected. His forehead was bruised, as were his ribs and feet.

Biri came up to him as he finished dressing. "What do you want?" Michael asked, looking off to one side.

"They played games with you. Not the Crane Women— the Meteorals."

"Everybody plays games with me."

"If they had meant to kill you, you wouldn't have escaped."

"Maybe they did try to kill me, and I'm just better than anybody thinks."

Biri shook his head.

"Dammit, nobody believes I'm worth a crap! Why can't I

just do something right and be recognized for it?"

"Do you know what you did?"

"Yeah. I survived. We've been through all that."

"The Crane Women were—"

"I don't give a damn what they were doing. I'm not wanted around here. Tell them," he nodded at the hut, "tell them I'm going to spend the night with my own people. Not with Breeds." He hesitated. "Not with Sidhe."

"I'll tell them. And after tonight?"

"I'll worry about that later."

"What will Lamia do?" Biri asked.

"What do you know about her, or care? I don't want to be here, that's all."

Biri watched as Michael crossed the river and walked west. He carried his book in one frayed pocket; it slapped against his hip with every step.

In Euterpe, Michael located the alley where Savarin had led him, turned left into it and at the end walked up the flight of steps to Helena's doorway. He knocked on the frame but received no answer. Standing for a moment, convinced his luck wasn't going to improve for some time, he descended the stairs and nearly walked into her.

"Michael! What's happened to you?" She reached up and touched her fingers solicitously to his face.

"I'm leaving the Crane Women," he said. "I want to live in town. I thought you might be able to help me find a place."

"Maybe. Maybe Savarin can help you."

"I thought..." He was too numb to consider finesse. "I thought maybe I could stay here."

"Oh, I don't think so," Helena said, smiling broadly. She patted him on the shoulder. "Come on. Let's find Savarin."

At the hotel, Risky told them the scholar was teaching classes. "Why did you decide to leave?" Helena asked as they walked through the streets.

"Sick of it," he said. "I just want to find some way to go home."

"So do we all," Helena said ruefully. "But most of us have learned to accept that there's no going back."

"Someone could send us back."

"That hasn't happened yet. What did they do to your face?"

"They took me out on a hike and left me on a trod. I was almost killed. That's part of the training."

Helena shook her head sympathetically.

The school was in worse repair than most of the buildings in town. There were no windows in the brick frames and the door hung askew, allowing Savarin's dulcet tones to escape across the clear sunny morning.

They waited for Savarin's lecture—conducted mostly in French—to end. The five townsfolk sitting on the brick pews got up and shuffled out, their expressions resigned. Savarin lifted his arms in greeting. "My flock," he said, pointing to the backs of the departing five. "Enthusiasm incarnate."

"Michael needs a place to stay," Helena said.

"Why? You have your place outside Halftown."

"I don't want to be there," Michael said. "I'm leaving the Crane Women."

Savarin frowned. "That's not good," he said. "I'm afraid there's no place in town for you. You don't have a job, and jobs are important. Outsiders are few and the accommodations are slim even for those living here."

"I'll work at something."

"You don't understand." Savarin sat on the end of a pew and spread his hands. "Lamia ordered you to the Crane Women. The townsfolk are in awe of Lamia, no matter how irreverent they may seem. If you displease her, you have no place here. Go back."

Michael shook his head.

"Savarin is right," Helena said. "I mean, I've only been here for a short time, and I have to accept things as they are. Getting along, doing things the accepted way."

"Can't I share your room? Michael asked, glancing from one to the other. Helena's sympathetic smile was weaker this time.

"You're young," Savarin said. Michael turned away, unable to bear the thought of another lecture.

"Look," he said, "I know I'm young, I'm stupid, I'm clumsy. So what? I need a place to stay. I need some freedom."

Savarin laughed bitterly. "Freedom? Show me a human in the Realm who has any freedom. Why should you be different?"

"I didn't want to come here! Music didn't bring me here."

"No," Savarin said. "You walked here, on your own volition. You knew you were going someplace. You tried harder to get here than we did. So you are a little less free. There's no place for you here in town." He tried to soften his words by adding, "Not that we wouldn't put you up if we could. But things are balanced very delicately now."

"We can't afford to rock the boat," Helena restated.

"I might manage to get you some food," Savarin said.

"Me, too," Helena said. "And maybe some better clothes. Where did you get those?"

Michael didn't answer. He looked at Helena imploringly, and realized his few hopes had been exploded. Without a word, he turned and left the school.

"Michael—"

He ran. Letting the familiar pleasures and pains of exertion fill him, blanking out his worries, he covered most of the distance to Halftown before forcing himself to slow to a walk.

He didn't even know who he was any more. At one time he had been the young, bright son of well-to-do, talented parents, living in a prosperous neighborhood in a famous city, hoping—trying—to be a poet. Now he was ragged, bruised . . . yet stronger and swifter, and he had been forced to do something quite wonderful . . . or die. He didn't know who his friends were. He was angry at Savarin and Helena, but he didn't actually blame them. . . .

The Realm was a tough place to live.

He entered the market courtyard in Halftown. The Breeds paid little attention to him; he was none of their concern. But Eleuth saw him from the workshed, where she was wrapping cloth goods for a customer, and her face lit up with a smile. When she saw his bruises, the smile changed to a look of concern. She finished tying the package and handed it to the tall Breed woman, who glanced at Michael sternly in passing.

"Hello," Michael said.

"They've been testing you again," Eleuth said, perching on a stool in front of him. Standing, she was a couple of inches taller. On the stool, her face was level with his.

"How'd you guess?" He smirked, holding out his tattered sleeves.

"And they won't let you stay in Euterpe."

"Did you see me going there?"

She shook her head. "I'm learning. Very slow, very difficult, but just looking at you I can tell a little of what happened. Why did you leave them?"

"I don't want to die," Michael said. "And I don't think they much care if I do."

"You could be wrong," Eleuth said. "But stay here. I have to work for a while."

"I don't have anyplace else to go," Michael said.

Eleuth smiled. "I mean, stay here with me. You can help. As long as they let you."

Michael watched her return to her customers. Suddenly, a different kind of panic assailed him. What was he going to do, living with a Breed woman under the same roof?

What would she expect him to do?

Chapter Eighteen

"I'm closing now," Eleuth told Michael as dusk settled. "Today seemed shorter than usual, didn't it? Adonna's whim, I suppose."

She showed him how to pick up the baskets of merchandise from the board tables and where to put them in the shed, away from the elements. He helped her draw a tarp over the displays of heavier merchandise. "Nobody steals anything here?"

"Certainly," Eleuth said. "But even Breeds can afford a few safeguards." She didn't explain, simply grinned at him as she closed the gate to the market courtyard. "Now. How long has it been since you ate?"

"About a day and a half," he said. He hadn't noticed, but the reminder awoke his hunger.

"I have some broth cooking, some Faer dishes . . . I hope it will be enough. I mean good enough for you."

The house next to the market square was soon lit with oil lanterns and candles and a fire was kindled in the pit. Eleuth placed bread on the bricks to warm and stirred a pot suspended over a circle of embers. She offered Michael a cup of water from a cloth bag, cooled by evaporation, and asked him to sit on one of the two wooden chairs.

"How old are you?" Michael asked as she finished gathering utensils and set a wicker table for them.

"Oh, that's not a definite thing here," she said.

"Can you guess?"

"Not much older than you, by the looks."

"But I'm sixteen, and you're . . . bigger."

"That's natural for those with Sidhe blood. We grow up very fast."

"Your father was half Sidhe?"

Eleuth nodded. "My mother was human. She died long ago. I don't remember her very well. Now if I were full Sidhe, I'd either remember everything, or nothing. Depending on what I choose."

"I feel so stupid, living in the Realm," Michael said quietly. Eleuth handed him a ceramic bowl filled with vegetable broth. It smelled spicy and was; his tongue was aflame after a few swallows.

"Bread?" she offered. He tried to hide his discomfort by chewing on the durable, brown-crusted bread. "We all learn here, all the time," she continued, sitting across from him. "Isn't that true on Earth? I mean, mortals have finite lives; they must spend all their short years thinking themselves to be very ignorant."

"I guess." A few more swallows and he seemed to get used to the spiciness. The warmth passed up his neck and into his head. His scalp was sweating.

"As for me, I'm not terribly bright, even for a Breed. By Sidhe standards, I'm very slow. My father was a fine parent, but I think I was a disappointment to him."

"He'd rather have had a son?"

"Oh, no!" Eleuth laughed. "Sidhe always prefer daughters. Magic is more powerful in a family with daughters. But in my case, I inherited very little."

"What can you do with magic?" Michael asked "I've seen some things, but . . ." He trailed off.

"We probably shouldn't talk about it," Eleuth said. She took his empty bowl and filled it again. "You're not a Breed. I'm not sure why you're here or why they tolerate you. Do you know?"

Michael shook his head. "I wish I did. I mean, I think I wish I knew. Maybe I don't want to know."

"You must know eventually," Eleuth said. They ate in silence for a while. Then she picked up their empty bowls and stuck them in a pot of sand. She spun the pot on its pedestal and plucked the bowls out, clean.

"You can sleep next to the hearth," she said. She took a rug down from its bar and laid it on the floor, then produced two blankets and a robe. "This was Lirg's," she said, handing the robe to him. "I'll sleep now. In the morning, you can pick out some other clothes. Good night."

He lay on the rug and pulled the blankets over him. Eleuth

put out the fire in the pit and pulled the screen over it, then slipped behind another hanging into her room.

He lay in the ember-lit dark for a few minutes, his mind turbulent but blank. His eyes shut.

Sleep without dreams occupied no time at all. He came awake to the sound of weeping. It was Eleuth. Groggy, uncertain what to do, he sat up on the floor and listened for a minute, chin on his knees. Finally he stood, the old clothes binding him where he had twisted in his sleep. He approached the hanging.

"Eleuth?"

The sobbing became softer. "Eleuth, what's wrong?"

"I'll be quiet," she said, her voice muffled.

"No, what's wrong?"

He pulled aside the hanging and saw her lying on a wooden pallet, blankets pulled up around her neck. Her face was streaked with tears which glinted in the light of the room's single candle.

"I can't remember all the transactions," she said. "No matter how hard I try, I can't keep the accounts in my head."

Michael leaned sleepily against the wall. "Then use paper."

"Oh, no!" Eleuth said, shuddering as she wept. "We do not write anything down. That is . . . wrong. Lirg would be very disappointed in me." She wiped her face with her hands.

"So you're different. Everybody's different."

"I'll be all right," she said. "Go back to sleep now." She lay on her back and stared at the ceiling. He let the hanging slip back.

"Michael?"

He stopped at the edge of his bedclothes. "What?"

"Are you afraid of Breeds? I mean, do you hate us?"

"No," he said. "They're no worse than humans. Better than Sidhe, as near as I can tell."

He heard her bare feet on the floor. She pulled back the hanging and stared out at him. Nothing was said for a time, then she motioned for him to come join her.

"I'm mostly human," she said as she held back the blankets for him. He started to climb in with his clothes still on, but she made a face and pushed him gently back. "Not with those," she said, undoing the strings which belted his pants. "Take off that shirt. You deserve much better."

He felt very strange, excited but sleepy, afraid but calm. She smiled at his underclothes as he untied the fabric and let it hang in front of him. She took his hand and pulled him down beside her, then kissed his forehead.

"You're tired," she said. "Tonight we sleep."

"I don't want to sleep just yet," he said. He put his arms around her, bunching the coarse, pliant fabric of her gown in one fist. He nuzzled her neck and she lifted her chin, closing her eyes. Then he kissed her. She tasted slightly electric, as if he were licking a dime. With one hand he undid the ties on the upper portion of her gown, revealing her breasts. They were dotted with pearly-gray freckles and her sternum rippled in the hollow between. He touched her skin gently with one finger, then rubbed his cheek against her breasts, feeling her warmth. She held his head and squeezed him closer, kissing his hair.

"Sweet," she said. *"Sona, dosa, sona."*

"What do I do now?" he asked, looking up at her, eyes half-closed.

"Sleep, Michael," she crooned, stroking his brow. She nestled down beside him and he felt the bare stretch of her leg against his. He moved instinctively, but she restrained him. "Sleep," she repeated, but he didn't hear her finish the word.

The morning began as a patch of gray light shining on the floor. Michael opened his eyes and looked at the light from where his head lolled over the side of the bed. He rolled on his back and saw Eleuth leaning on her elbow next to him, hair concealing her hand. She smiled and bent to kiss him. "You kept me very warm," she said. She ran her hand down his arm, tickling the hairs.

They made love. It was the most wonderful thing, and the most silly thing. It had nothing of lust in it, only necessity. They lay holding each other and he secretly surveyed her breasts and stomach, and she secretly enjoyed him looking at her.

Eleuth got out of bed, climbing over him with her hand cupped between her legs. She dipped a white cloth in a ceramic jar full of water and cleaned him off, then slipped on her pants and shirt. "No market this day," she said. "But I have a few things to do."

He lay on the cot, half-covered with blankets, watching as the gray light became yellow.

It was one of the most—no, the single most wonderful thing that had happened to him. He was pretty convinced of that. He couldn't remember anything finer, and yet...

It had its drawbacks. In all the time he had spent here, there had always been some hope that it was all a dream, some long-play fantasy. But throughout his few pubescent years, he had never been able to have a fantasy so real or vivid as what had happened this morning.

Ergo, he was not fantasizing. He had more than suspected as much. The drawback was that it was now proven.

And yet . . .

A certain hollowness remained. He was relaxed, as if a knot had been untied between his legs, a knot he had hardly realized was there until now. He had acquitted himself well; Eleuth had enjoyed him, and he sensed the knot flex and tighten as he remembered her enjoyment. His pleasure had been real but unspectacular, sure to get better with practice. Hers had been real and prolonged.

So what about the hollowness? He couldn't put his finger on it. Like everything else in Sidhedark, the accomplishment (and that seemed a truthful but ridiculous word to use) came with a little hard gnurl of unease, of impending disaster.

Michael realized that even if he made it back to Earth, he would still have that gnurl buried inside of him.

Maybe that was part of growing up. Oddly enough, making love didn't make him feel any more adult. It was perhaps the most childish part of being grown-up.

He was dozing when Eleuth entered, carrying three pieces of fruit. She handed him two of them and he smiled at her.

"There's a legend on Earth, saying that if I eat this, I have to stay here forever."

"I wouldn't object," Eleuth said, sitting on the bed beside him. "But you've already eaten fruit here, haven't you?"

He nodded. "Could you teach me to speak Sidhe?"

She shook her head slowly. "It's more difficult than a human language. Lirg tried teaching my mother. Only the Sidhe have a real knack. Sometimes, it's not even a language in your sense."

"But I've been able to make out words."

"Yes. Sometimes we use different words to mean the same things. . . . And when we communicate, we in-speak. You allow me to speak your language. I in-speak . . . look into your mind, and find the words. I wish Lirg were here to explain it to you." Her eyes moistened again and he reached out to touch her shoulder. She lay down beside him. "What will you do today?"

"Go to Savarin, I think," Michael said. "He didn't help me

yesterday, but there are still things I need to know."

"I'll teach you what I know," Eleuth said.

"I'm grateful for that, but he may be able to explain things more clearly. He's a teacher."

"Oh." They ate their fruit. "Can you help me here?"

"Sure," Michael said. "Why don't you tell me what you need done before I go to Euterpe?"

Together they counted rolls of fabric and pots. Eleuth brought out pants and shirts for him to try on, and he found a pair that fit reasonably well. Shoes were more difficult. Sidhe and Breed feet were longer and narrower than human feet. Michael found a pair made out of canvas-like material that didn't actually pinch his toes, and Eleuth watched him with her vague puzzled expression as he stamped about, trying to get them to fit. "They'll never believe it back on Earth," he said. "Faeries wear tennis shoes." Then he laughed at the thought of trying to explain things at home. It was the first time he remembered laughing in the Realm. Eleuth smiled.

She sewed a pocket into his shirt to hold the book and as she cut the thread with her teeth and tied it off, she said, "This afternoon I'm expecting a shipment. Could you be back by then to help?"

"Sure. I thought everything just appeared out of nowhere," he teased. He pointed at the covered racks of merchandise in the storage room.

"Oh, no," Eleuth said, her long face betraying distress. "I'm not nearly that skilled."

He left when the sun was just below zenith and walked the distance to the human town at a leisurely pace. Something had loosened in him; he could observe things without the nervous tightness that had prevailed before. It seemed he now had the time to put everything in perspective.

He also confronted the fact that he would soon have to tell Eleuth he couldn't stay forever, that he didn't love her. He wasn't sure what he felt for her; gratitude, affection.

But there was one image he couldn't erase from his mind: that of the Crane Women—immortal, but because of their human blood, changing with age. How long would it take for Eleuth to change?

A few Breeds—a male and two females, all of that cast of features that indicated they were older than Eleuth, but how how much older he couldn't tell—were directing a horse cart along the road. They passed Michael without acknowledging his presence, holding their long heads high, their dull brown clothes rippling like fur beneath an unwanted touch. He turned to watch the cart, noting the wood-spoke wheels, the well-fitted but unornamented frame, the simplicity of the harness.

At the inn, Brecker greeted him civilly while sweeping out the small lobby and told him Savarin was indeed back in his room. Michael climbed the stairs. Behind the wicker door, he heard Savarin humming to himself. Michael knocked on the wicker. "It's me."

Savarin swung the door wide and smiled at him. "You've forgiven us, I hope?"

"Yeah," Michael said. "I found a place in Halftown."

Savarin invited him in and looked down the hall to see if anyone followed. "We want you to understand, it's not you we're afraid of."

"I know," Michael said. He didn't want to discuss it, but he knew Savarin would air the issue for a while. He sat on the edge of the washstand, lightly so as not to crush it.

"It's just that we have to be careful. We stand between Lamia and the Sidhe, between rules that change from day to day. Have you had any trouble from the Crane Women?"

Michael shook his head. "I haven't seen them. I came here—"

"You still have to be careful. Where are you staying in Halftown?"

"That isn't important," Michael said. "I want you to tell me what you know about Sidhe language. I can't get anywhere if I can't understand what they're saying."

Savarin cocked his head to one side and lifted his eyebrows. "Tall order. You have to be largely Sidhe to pick up on all of the tongues. I'd say the resemblances between Sidhe and human languages are strong, but the syntax and methods of understanding are quite different. For example, the Sidhe use a meta-language . . . a language of contexts. And Cascar is like a hundred languages thrown together. They never run out of words that mean the same thing, or very nearly. I can't speak it well. I can sometimes make myself understood, but . . ."

"I understood it for a time," Michael said. "During the *Kaeli*. One of the Crane Women touched my head, and I understood everything they said."

"And what was that like?"

Michael thought back. "Like listening to music. Each word seemed to be the equivalent of a note. Notes are always the same in music, but place them next to each other and they sound different...or lengthen the notes, shorten them. Use the same word in a different context, and it means something else...sounds different."

"Perhaps you should be educating me," Savarin said.

"But it didn't last. I don't remember anything from that night, except what they said...and even that's fuzzy. They were singing, but not singing. I need to know so—" He stopped himself. "I just need to know."

"Because you still plan on leaving the Realm," Savarin said.

Michael turned his eyes away and pointed his index fingers together.

"I don't recommend that. First of all, Alyons will hunt you. No human can escape his coursers. Second, Lamia will resent even the attempt—and, as I've said before, I wouldn't want to cross her. I don't know what the Crane Women will do."

"I haven't thought much about that," Michael said. "I'm just struggling. I don't want to be anyone's responsibility."

"Just thank the stars you are," Savarin said. "I've known people to come here, Alyons takes them—and we never see them again—despite the Pact! We dare not object. To what end does he take them? Nobody knows. But you! You seem to be protected. He has not taken you...even though he's tried." He put his hand on Michael's knee and stared at him earnestly. "Go back. Keep up the training. It's for a purpose, I'm sure."

"I don't see it that way," Michael said. Savarin shrugged.

"Then we'll discuss Cascar and Nerb. Do you know the difference?"

"No."

Savarin explained that Cascar was a younger, less formal language. He believed it had arisen after the Sidhe returned to Earth, and that it was the proto-language out of which had arisen several of the major human language groups, the most familiar of them, for Savarin, belonging to the Indo-European branch. "Certainly the words sound familiar," he said. "Their word for us—a word which never changes, you notice?—is *antros*. Sometimes they call us males—*wiros,* as in virile, no?—or female, *geen,* and the latter they apply to their females as well—but as a kind, we are always *antros*. A spit-word, so to speak.

"As for Nerb, not many Breeds speak it, and none of the Sidhe I've encountered."

"I haven't heard much about it, if anything. So say something to me in Cascar."

"Pir na? Sed antros lingas ta rup ta pistr."

"What's that mean?"

"'Why? Humans talk as if they have stone tongues.' It's something a Breed once told me. Lingas means both language and speaking and tongue. Context is important, and pitch, as in Chinese. There are other Cascar words for language, meaning eating with the tongue, spitting with the tongue, magic with the tongue. Calling birds with the tongue. All different."

"How do they learn it?"

"They're Sidhe," Savarin said laconically. "It comes naturally to them. Nearly every Sidhe and Breed I've met knows how to speak the human languages I'm familiar with. Do they suck the knowledge out of my mind? I don't know. But they only speak Cascar to us when they don't want us to understand, or when they wish to be belligerent." He paused, looking almost sad. "There's another language I've heard hinted at. I know almost nothing about it but that it exists. One of its many names is Kesh. An unspoken language, used during the star-marches. Not, as you might suspect, a kind of ESP, but something different.

"And to make things even more confusing, I'm tracking down evidence that the Sidhe picked up words from humans—words from tinker's cant, Celtic languages, etc.; picked them up during their last centuries on Earth. There is a section in 'Hudibras' by Samuel Butler—if I can remember..." He screwed up his face in concentration and peered at the ceiling. "'But when he pleased to shew't, his speech/ In loftiness of sound was rich;

> A Babylonish dialect
> Which learned pedants much affect;
> It was a party coloured dress
> Of patch'd and py-ball'd languages;
> 'Twas (Irish) cut on Greek and Latin
> Like fustian heretofore on sattin.
> It had an odd promiscuous tone,
> As if h' had talk'd three parts in one;
> Which made some think, when he did gabble,
> Th' had heard three labourers of Babel;
> Or Cerberus himself pronounce
> A leash of languages at once.'"

"We're like little babies here," Michael said, sighing.

Savarin nodded. "Now perhaps you can tell me why they simply haven't slaughtered us all?"

"Do they hate us that much?"

Savarin's expression brightened "Can you tell me anything about the Council of Eleu? Does that sound familiar?"

Michael couldn't remember hearing anything about it.

"Then listen closely. You're going to be associating with Breed and Sidhe more and more, whatever your personal wishes may be. Just listen for it. 'Council of Eleu.' And if you find out anything, tell me immediately! To answer your question, no, not all of them hate us. And the Council of Eleu has something to do with those who tolerate us."

Something flashed into Michael's head and he struggled to keep it, to clarify it. A group of tall, pale figures talking about him. Something about his room in the house on Earth . . . but it was gone before he could grasp it. "I'll let you know if I hear anything," he said. "How's Helena?"

"Well," Savarin said. "She worries we gave you the wrong impression, that you hate us, hate her."

"I don't hate anybody," Michael said. "I'd like to talk to her some more."

"Certainly. She's working now, I'm sure, but we could walk over later—"

"No. I'll go myself. I have to ask her some things."

"Certainly," Savarin said. His lips normally carried a slight sardonic smile; now the expression took on significance. "I believe there is something you must know, very soon."

"What?"

"Human sex is dangerous here."

"Why?"

"Such things are closely regulated. We do not want children. The Sidhe and Breeds can have young—we cannot."

Michael just looked at him.

"The people who have been here longest, and the Breeds, say it is because there are no seedling souls in the Realm. A human child is born empty. A Sidhe or Breed child is expected to be that way, and already has an internal . . . how would we say . . . compensation. But human children are vessels waiting to be filled. They are filled by creatures from the Blasted Plain—Adonna's own aborted children, some say." He set his lips and waved off any further inquiry. "Talk about it is considered obscene. No more."

"There's just one other thing," Michael said. "I'm a young fellow—everyone keeps saying that—but why do humans put up with all this crap?"

"What else can we do?" Savarin scrutinized him intensely, as if looking for something hidden in his face. Then the perpetual half-smile returned and the scholar leaned back, folding his hands in front of him and cracking his knuckles. "You'll learn soon enough," he said in a low voice. "Why not go and talk with Helena now. She should be done with her work."

Michael didn't expect to be dismissed, but Savarin was obviously thinking about other things. Michael stood and held out his hand. Savarin grasped it and shook it loosely, then fluttered his fingers in the direction of the doorway. "Go on," he said. "And thank you for coming back. We thought we'd lost you when you ran away."

Michael nodded and shut the wicker door behind him. Savarin resumed humming, keeping it low enough so it couldn't be heard more than a few feet outside.

He snapped his fingers while he walked, caught himself, and stuffed his thumb into the fabric tie of his pants. It was early afternoon and the town was slowing down; shops were closing, people were strolling in pairs down the narrow streets, some heading for the ramshackle school, others just walking, talking. Michael saw an oriental man and woman speaking what sounded like Chinese.

His last question—and Savarin's subsequent expression—kept echoing in his mind. Resistance seemed only natural when somebody oppressed you. Michael's father had often talked about his student days at UCLA—talk which had bored Michael slightly, but came back to him now as a model of how Americans, at least, behaved when they thought something was wrong. Michael wondered if the humans in the Realm could organize a protest, maybe set up a blockade. Keep Sidhe out of Euterpe at least . . . passive resistance.

He grinned at how silly it sounded. Alyons would handle a blockade in short order. Some people would probably get killed. Maybe he'd be the first.

He still found it hard to believe that he could die in the Realm. Death had been a difficult enough concept on Earth, but here, with everything topsy-turvy and so many fantastic phenomena, how could anyone actually *die?* So what if it wasn't a dream, he told himself. It wasn't exactly reality either.

His reverie carried him to the steps below Helena's doorway.

He walked up slowly, apprehensive. He rubbed his chin to check the length of peach-fuzz. A few of the real whiskers he had started were getting quite long now; he hadn't thought about them until this moment, but he wished he had a mirror and a pair of scissors to snip them off.

He had a panicky moment just before knocking, when he told himself it would be best just to run away, head out across the—

Helena opened the door.

"Hi," he said, dropping his hand from his chin.

"Hi yourself. I heard you breathing."

"Yeah," Michael said. "I wanted to apologize for running away like that."

"No apology needed," Helena said. She seemed subdued. She opened the door wider and invited him in, then left the door open and blocked it with a brick. "It must be rough on you. Confusing."

"I guess. Anyway, that's no excuse to act like a little kid. To be rude, I mean."

"I'm glad you came back," she said, standing a few feet away. "Would you like to sit?" They sat and Helena bit on a thumbnail, watching him but not really seeing him.

"Is something wrong?" he asked.

She seemed to reach a decision and leaned forward, staring at him earnestly. "Michael, will you swear something for me? Double swear? Because I'm taking a big risk."

"What risk?"

"Will you swear?"

"Swear to what, Helena?"

She stood nervously and paced in front of him, waving her arms as she spoke. "You're a sweet fellow, but you didn't understand what we meant yesterday. You know how strange you are, being taken care of by Breeds and so on."

"I guess," Michael said.

"Don't guess. Do you *know*?"

"It's strange to me, that's for sure."

"Well, it's even stranger for us. Nobody from here—I mean humans—has ever been given that treatment before. So it makes us wonder, are you a double agent or what? A Sidhe who just looks human?"

"I'm not a Sidhe," Michael said, laughing.

"No, I don't think you are. You sweat when you're nervous." She giggled and placed her hand reassuringly on his shoulder, letting the fingers linger, gripping him. "So you have to swear to me, you're not a double agent, you're not a plant or whatever put here to catch us."

"I swear," Michael said.

"Your eyes look so human," Helena said. "Such a nice green color. What's happened to you since yesterday?"

Michael blinked at the change in subject. "I found a place to live in Halftown."

"Oh, where?"

"You wanted me to swear. I did. So what next?"

Helena kneeled down before him. "You know Savarin. He's a scholar. There are other people you haven't met, except one of them came to see you that night they gave the dinner. When you came to town. A short, heavy fellow with black hair."

Michael didn't remember him.

"Well, anyway, he saw you, and thought sometime we'd have to decide whether to contact you."

A bell rang in the town plaza. Michael went to the window to listen.

"So you're contacting me," he said.

Helena stepped up beside him. "That's the warning bell," she said, her voice quavering. "Alyons is here, or some of his riders. So I'll tell you quickly. We found a cache of Sidhe metal. Never mind where. Some people here are keeping it, making it into . . . things. A piano, for one. What I wouldn't give to hear a piano again! But they won't let us play it, of course, until after—" She stopped abruptly, her face paling. Hoofsteps sounded in the narrow alleyway. "Michael!"

"What?"

"Are they after you, or did you bring them here?"

"I'm *not* one of them," Michael said. She grasped his arm. "They're outside!"

Alyons and two of his coursers paced at leisure on horseback toward the door at the end of the alleyway. Alyons glanced up and spotted Michael in the window. Michael pulled back.

"*Antros!* Your presence is requested!"

"They *do* want you," Helena said.

"It looks that way."

"Oh, don't tell them anything. I'm so frightened. Where will they take you?"

"I don't know," Michael said. He stepped out into the hall and looked the opposite way. If he could only get back into that mindset again. . . . He turned to Helena and took her hand clumsily in his, having to grasp it twice before holding it firm. He had a crazy urge to laugh. "A piano, eh?"

"Shh!"

"That's not what I had in mind, but I guess that's pretty subversive."

"Man-child!" Alyons called.

He kissed her hand and felt a flush of pride mix with his fear. A Sidhe appeared in the door at the bottom of the stairs. Michael unceremoniously pushed Helena back into her room and shut the door. He stood at the top of the steps, looking down on the courser with what he hoped passed for imperious disdain. "What do you want?"

The courser began climbing, giving no answer. Michael looked to either side of the Sidhe, wondering if he could play the uncertain flower down the stairs. There was only one way to find out. With all his speed and concentration, he dashed down the steps, trying to send a shadow to one side and swerve himself to the other. The courser grabbed him without hesitation and placed him under one arm as easily as if he carried a trussed pig, then turned and marched out the door, presenting him to the Wickmaster.

They exchanged a few words in Cascar and Michael looked directly at Alyons.

"So you're learning from the Crane Women," the Wickmaster said. "But not too well."

The courser spoke again and they laughed. "Never make a shadow when there are only two ways to send it," Alyons advised. He hefted his wick and motioned for Michael to be tied behind his horse. They skillfully reversed the horses in the narrow alley and left with Michael in tow. He looked over his shoulder and saw Helena at the window, her face pale. His hands were tied by the trailing rope; he could do nothing. For a moment, he had feared the Sidhe would take her, as well.

They pulled him out of town, walking their horses just fast enough to keep him half-running. They joined another group of four, making a total of seven Sidhe, and jerked Michael down the road to the Isomage's mansion.

Chapter Nineteen

The troop led Michael up the path to the Isomage's house, jerking sharply on his rope as he fell back. Alyons dismounted and went inside while the others waited, silent and aloof even from each other.

After some minutes, Alyons emerged and took the end of Michael's rope. He reeled it in until he stood just two feet from Michael, towering over him. "She wants to speak with you, man-child." His expression was stony and his eyes seemed fixed in their sockets as he turned away, pulling Michael by his tied and outstretched hands. Alyons seemed to be in a state of controlled rage, which perversely made Michael more optimistic; if the circumstances weren't to Alyons' liking, perhaps he wasn't in as much trouble as he'd thought.

The interior of the house was as he remembered, only darker and cooler. The sun was now on the horizon. The day had been particularly short.

The staircase led up into brighter light from the narrow windows along the entryway. Lamia stood on the balcony, her tiny, finely molded hands gripping the railing.

"Is he down there?" she asked.

"As you requested," Alyons said, his tone dripping contempt.

"Send him up to me."

The Wickmaster took his time undoing the rope, his long corded fingers cool against Michael's arms. "Go," he said. He gave Michael an unnecessarily hard push and pointed up the stairs. Michael ascended, rubbing his reddened wrists and watching the daylight grow dull in the upper reaches. He didn't fancy staying in the house after dark, but even less did he fancy traveling with the coursers at night, or walking back to the town alone. He met Lamia on the landing.

A change had come over her. He could see it even in the fading light. Her skin was waxen, her face tighter, as if she wore a restraining mask. Around her eyes, scaly patches had started to flake away and her hands were criss-crossed with tiny thin wrinkles like cracks in bread dough. He stopped five paces from her. Lamia made no move toward him, instead regarding him with a wavering gaze. She seemed deadly tired.

"You grieve me, boy," she said softly. "I set you a task and you run from it."

"I don't like being a slave," he said.

"You're . . . no . . . slave." Her voice carried bitter humor. "You're freer than I am, freer than Alyons down there." She gestured with a trembling hand and immediately returned it to the railing to support herself. Michael stared down into the lower floor's gloom. Alyons stood at the foot of the stairs, head bowed, twisting the rope and coiling it in his fingers.

"They keep trying to kill me," Michael said.

"Who, the Crane Women?" Lamia tittered, a dead dry sound of rolling pebbles. She motioned for him to come closer. He hesitated and she made as if to reach out with one hand and strangle him. "Closer!" she growled.

He moved one stride. She edged a few inches along the railing, making it creak beneath her weight. Her arms bounced in slow, oily waves beneath the fabric of her gown. "They are teaching you how to stay alive."

"I can stay alive on my own, in Euterpe with all the others."

"You will not stay in the town. The town is for fools, cowards too afraid to make their own way."

"I'm not too afraid."

"You're too stupid to succeed, then." She lowered her voice and pushed back from the railing, tottering for one awful moment. "You require tempering." Michael retreated two steps in case she fell; he saw her as a poorly balanced sack of venomous fluids, about to topple and burst. But Lamia kept her balance. "Come with me," she said. "We have to talk alone."

She wobbled and thumped through a doorway leading to a second floor hallway. This part of the house seemed in better condition than the ground floor; as far as he could tell in the twilight, the walls were unmarked, and the floor was carpeted, muffling her ponderous steps. She reached out with her left hand and pushed wide a door, motioning for Michael to enter first. He sidled past her and stood in a broad empty room. Lighted candles were placed high on all four walls in sconces at intervals of several feet. The floor was hardwood, brilliantly polished. A second Lamia labored upside down in the depths of the wood as she followed him. She closed the door and leaned against it, breathing heavily.

"Are you sick?" he asked.

She shook her head. Her small eyes, enclosed in scaly flesh, saddened as she looked beyond him at the empty room.

"You have a duty, boy," she said distantly. "Have you learned more about this house, about the Realm?"

"A little," Michael said. "Not nearly enough."

"You know that the Isomage lived here?"

He nodded. "I don't know who he was. . . . Was he David Clarkham?"

"Is, boy. He is." Her lips formed an upward-tilting curve suggesting a smile. To each side, the skin of her cheeks separated in fine cracks. "You know that he wishes to save us?"

Michael shook his head. "Why isn't he here, then?"

"He was driven off by his enemies. I told you. The battle that destroyed this entire plain. They forced all the humans in their control to live here afterward, in desolation and pain. I've never been to the town; I cannot leave this house. But from this house I have a . . . small influence. In my cursed condition, I can help. Do you understand?"

"No." There was pleasant defiance in his ignorance. It warmed him.

She rolled her hips and dragged her legs to the middle of the room. He caught a whiff of her odor, unpleasant and dead sweet, like decaying flowers. "You must not defy the plan," she said. "The Sidhe opposed to us simply wait for their chance to . . ." She shook her head and the skin of her neck crackled.

"Then why do they give you any power at all?" Michael asked.

"They cannot hurt me more than they already have. There is a treaty over this land, over the plain. We suffer our punishment, but if they make any further moves against us, the treaty crumbles . . . and a power buried deep in the land is unleashed against the transgressors. There is a stalemate. To the Sidhe, it seems we are defeated. Perhaps we are . . . and perhaps not. But should humans break the treaty . . ." Her voice trailed off again.

"Why am I so important?"

"Important?" She spat on the floor, then walked to the spot where her spittle beaded on the polished surface and with infinite pains, bent down to wipe it with the hem of her gown. Her skin crackled again as she returned to her upright posture. "You are not crucial. You are simply a messenger. But to help at all, you must survive. You must continue to train with the Crane Women."

"Do I have any choice?"

Lamia turned her back on him. "I have some influence over the Wickmaster; but only some. If you do not return to the Crane Women, he will take charge of you. What he'll do with you, I don't know."

"No choice, then."

She swiveled slowly, in grotesque parody of a pirouette. Michael looked at the far wall and saw a long, horizontal bar mounted beneath the candles—a practice bar for dancers. "May you never know how cruel life is," she said. "Or what can be lost . . . and yet remain alive. Go back to the Crane Women. Resume your training."

Michael stood silent in the candlelight, then turned and left the room. He descended the stairs and stopped before Alyons, who let the rope fall free from one hand.

"Jakap?" the Wickmaster asked. The rope unwound like a struggling snake.

"Lamia orders me to go back to the Crane Women."

"She orders nothing," Alyons said. "I am Wickmaster."

"You can't hurt me," Michael said.

The Sidhe leaned over, bringing his face level with Michael's. "You are right, man-child. I can't hurt you if you do as she wishes. But step out of line, just once . . ."

"Wickmaster!" Lamia stood by the balustrade, limned by the faint glow from the dancing room. "Obey the Pact."

Michael dodged the Sidhe's grasping hand and walked out the door. "I'll ride back," he said, trying to conceal the tremble of anger and fear in his voice.

"On which horse?" Alyons asked, closing the front door with a solid thump. "Where is your horse?"

"Your horse," Michael said.

Behind him, Alyons barked a short laugh. "My horse. Such a beautiful and golden horse, such a temptation, my horse . . . even for humans. Mount then, *Antros*, show us your skill."

Michael touched the golden Sidhe horse delicately, then

mounted as he had been instructed. He wondered idly if it were possible to steal the horse, and decided that would be very unwise. But his feet kicked out of their own volition, gouging the animal in the flanks.

The landscape, locked in long, gray twilight, suddenly blurred around him. The horse's flesh became like flowing steel under the saddle and between his calves, and Michael felt an incredible pulse of power as they streaked along the road. His body seemed to melt and he grasped the horse with his arms and legs in sheer terror, shouting for it to stop. His words were drowned in the wind.

Michael had an impression the coursers were right behind him, but when he tried to turn and look, the landscape made such bizarre gyrations that he closed his eyes.

Suddenly, everything settled. He clung to the back of the horse to keep from sliding off. They stood on the mound, the horse's breathing shallow and steady. It jerked its head and shivered. He slid from the saddle and barely managed to land on his feet.

Alyons' mount rejoined the coursers standing around the Crane Women's hut. The horses' skins gleamed in the furnace glow from the window; the Wickmaster's cape reflected the myriad tiny glimmers in the dirt of the mound as he dismounted from a borrowed animal. The courser without a horse ran gracefully and swiftly over the road and across the creek, stopping at the edge of the mound.

Banners of dark glided up from the horizon, announcing night.

Spart emerged from the hut, glanced at Michael without comment, and turned to Alyons. They spoke in Cascar for several minutes. Michael shivered in the river of cool air flowing from the south. The coursers murmured among themselves.

Nare called to him from the window. He walked unsteadily to the hut. The Crane Woman's luxuriant hair was animated by a current of warm air flowing through the window and caught the inner glow, forming a golden nimbus around her face.

"To Lamia?" she asked. Michael nodded. "Is she different?"

"She's sick, I think. Her skin's all patchy." He was relieved. Apparently he was not going to be chided for running away. "I didn't want to come back," he said, the words tumbling out all at once.

"Of course," she said. She closed the window.

Alyons glided aboard his horse and the coursers moved off

slowly into the dark. For a moment, Michael stood by the hut, then returned to his own shelter. Biri was nowhere to be seen. There was no one to talk to, not even a target for defiance.

He thought of Eleuth and Helena. He hoped Helena wasn't worried—and then hoped she was. He pondered his own neutral feelings. All emotion seemed to have drained out of him.

"Wait and see," he said again and again until sleep overtook him.

That night, before sleep, the darkness behind his eyelids roiled with thoughts of home, the Isomage's mansion, the flaking rims of Lamia's eyes. He awoke before dawn and listened to the humming sky. As the humming faded, he peered out his door to see a pale band of gray on the horizon. Clouds had moved in during the night, and though the air wasn't exceptionally cold, flakes of snow were falling. The flakes melted as soon as they touched the dirt.

Eleuth came from Halftown about an hour later, wrapped in a light shawl and wearing knee-high boots. She carried four buckets of milk, as on the day Michael had first seen her. He stood in front of his hut but she barely looked at him as she walked past. Biri watched both of them from his door. When the buckets had been deposited outside the Crane Women's hut, she began her return trip.

"Eleuth," Michael said. She stopped, still not looking at him. "I couldn't come yesterday."

"So I heard."

"I want to thank you." Those words sounded particularly callous, as if his need to say them belied their meaning.

"Are you all right?" she asked. "I heard Alyons took you from the human town."

"I'm fine. I'll try to see you today."

She finally turned to him and nodded. Biri regarded her with seeming disinterest. To Michael's surprise, a flash of hatred crossed Eleuth's face. She ran across the stream.

Spart stood beside him, holding a cup of milk.

"Where does the milk come from?" he asked, sipping.

"Always questions."

"Always."

"From herds of horses beyond the Blasted Plain. It is brought into Halftown and Euterpe twice each month. It keeps well, and it nourishes." She sighed. "But I remember the fine milk of Earth, rich and full of the taste of the plants cows and goats ate." She smacked her lips and took the empty cup. "You kept the Breed woman company?"

Michael nodded. He wasn't embarrassed; he saw no reason to worry about appearances in front of the Crane Women.

"The Sidhe never eat meat?" Michael asked. The question had waited for weeks. Spart jerked and turned slowly to look at Biri's hut. The door cover was drawn and all was silent within. "No," she said. "Even in-speaking the thought is painful. Never eat flesh. Only humans eat meat. It is the sign of their defeat."

"All Sidhe are vegetarians?"

Spart looked him firmly in the eye. "Always and ever. That is why we have magic and you do not."

"Never?" Michael pursued, sensing something unsaid.

Spart moved away, shaking her head. "The subject is not fit for discussion."

"What do they sacrifice to Adonna?" He thought of Lirg.

Spart turned on him and advanced until her nose was close to his chin. "Always forbidden, on occasion mandatory," she said. "Do you know that law?"

"I don't think so."

Spart glanced at Biri's hut once more, then walked back to her own.

"Can't we even hold a discussion longer than four sentences?" Michael called out after her. "Jesus." Out of habit, he began his warm-up exercises. Tiring soon of that, wondering when his training would continue, he entered his hut and lay on the reed mats, clearing a space to reveal bare dirt. He picked up one of the pieces of wood he hadn't fitted properly into the framework and drew a line in the dust. "I'm a poet," he said to himself, quiet but firm. "I'm not a soldier. I'm not a God damn jock. I'm a poet." He closed his eyes and tried to think of something. Surely he could write about what was happening to him. About Helena, Eleuth. About what Biri had told him.

But it was all a tangle. Their faces came and went, bringing no words with them, not even suggesting. Instead, he began to recall things about Earth. The sadness almost overwhelmed him. His missed his father and mother, the school—he even missed the ridicule and being a dreamy kid in a world of jocks and New Wave robots. He felt like crying. He was being asked—no, forced—to think and behave like an adult, to make life-and-death decisions, to *choose,* and he was not at all sure he was ready to give up childhood.

Michael had always been mature, in the sense of being able to think things out for himself. Given time enough, and equanimity, he could puzzle through most things and reach a conclusion others might regard as advanced for his age. But confronted with love, violence, sex—miscegenation—what could he conclude?

Only that home was better. Safer. How could one ask for more than warmth, food, peace and quiet, a chance to learn and work?

"There's no place like home," he murmured, and snickered. He tapped his heels together. Oz was a National Park compared with Sidhedark. He had never read much fantasy, outside of what he found in poetry, but the Realm was like nothing he had ever heard of. It was something out of a history lesson, not fairy tales—something out of World War II. Internment camps—the Pact Lands. The Blasted Plain, like some bizarre crater from an even more bizarre bomb, filled with mutated monsters. The Crane Women—drill sargeants.

Surely he could write about that.

The stick began to move. He applied it to the dirt and was pleased with the old, familiar feeling of tapping Death's Radio, the source of poetry. In *Orphee*, a film he had first seen at age thirteen, Death had come for the modern beat poet Orpheus in the form of a woman in a large black limousine. The limousine's radio played nothing but provocative nonsense phrases . . . which impressed Orpheus with their purity and poetic essence. Michael sometimes felt he was tuned in to Death's Radio when the poetry came pure and clean.

> Here she comes
> Bottle in hand
> To the mike
> Swaying now
> Gravel voice
> Filmy gown
> She will die
> Her singing
> Will kill her
> We will all
> Listen, her
> Blood and boozy breath
> On our savage ears.

The wood came to a halt and he tapped it on the final period, the tiny hole in the dirt which concluded the poem. He had written a similar poem a year ago, after seeing Ricky Lee Jones in concert. But that poem had been flowery and melancholy-sweet, like bad Wordsworth, and this version was lean, essential—almost too spare for his tastes. No masterpiece, but a tugger. He frowned.

Sometimes he had the impression that he wasn't really the author of a poem, that Death's Radio allocated poems by queue number and not personality. But this was a particularly strong sensation. He hadn't written this poem. Somebody, somewhere, had heard his in-speaking and transformed it for him.

His hand reached out and scrawled *Just ask* beneath the poem. Ask what?

> Gnomisms. Puzzlements.
> Names are but the robes of fools,
> And words the death of thought.
> Your realm lies not in matter's tools
> But in what song has wrought.

He dropped the wood. The letters had gathered all the dirt's sparkles into their tiny valleys and banks. They blazed in the hut's gloom. He hadn't written them; it was more as if he had been conversing with someone.

"Man-child!"

He left the burning words in the dirt and backed away from the bare space. He pulled open the reed door-cover. Spart stood before his hut. "Yes?"

"You will not be trained today," she said.

He stood with the chill draft circulating around him. "So?"

"You are not a prisoner. Just don't attract Lamia's attention again, and don't say you plan to run away. The Wickmaster has enough chores." Her face briefly pruned up into a grin. "When you are not training, you are free to leave the mound. Without our company." She paused and looked around meaningfully. "After all, where will you go? Not far. Not far."

"I could cross the Blasted Plain, like when we went to meet Biri," he said. She laughed.

"I think you are too smart to try that. Not yet."

That was certainly true enough. "What will you do with Biri today?"

Spart shook her head and held her finger to her lips. "Not

for humans to know." She walked off and he dropped the door
cover, then looked back at the words in the dirt, now dark. He
reached out with his foot to erase them, but thought better of
it and pulled the book from its hiding place under the rafters.
It opened in his hands to Keats' long poem, "Lamia," which
he had first read a few years before and forgotten. It didn't
illuminate his situation, nor did it shed much light on Lamia;
it did, however, raise his curiosity as to why she was called
that. No part of her was serpentine.

Except that she was shedding her skin. He closed the book
and put it in his new-sewn pocket. Outside, the mound seemed
deserted. For a second he had a crazy notion to search for the
Crane Women and Biri, observe them secretly—but that was
as unlikely as escaping across the Blasted Plain alone.

He set out for Halftown.

As he approached the market square he heard a commotion.
Three tall Breed males—including the guard who had first met
Savarin and Michael on the outskirts of Halftown—stood at
the gates to the market, glaring at a small crowd gathered
around. The discussion was in Cascar and it sounded heated.

Eleuth stood to one side, head bowed. Michael walked up
to her. "What's going on?"

"The market is no longer mine to manage," she said. She
tried to smile but her lips wouldn't cooperate. "Since Lirg was
taken away, I haven't been running it at all well. So the Breed
Council claims."

Michael looked at the guards and the crowds and felt his
face redden. "What will you do now?"

"They'll assign me a new house and find a new manager.
I'll move."

"Can't you fight it?"

She shook her head as if shocked by the idea. "No! The
council's decisions are final."

"Who's in charge of the council?"

"Haldan. But he takes direction from Alyons, who oversees
everything in the Pact Lands, especially in Halftown."

"Is there anything I can do?"

She touched his cheek appreciatively. "No. I will be assigned another job, one better suited to my abilities."

He felt a surge of guilt as she stroked his cheek.

"I'm learning more rapidly," she said, her voice distant.
"Soon I'll be able to do things a young Sidhe can do."

"Magic, you mean."

"Yes. Michael, we could go away today..." The look of misery in her face, the desperation, was more than he could stand. "To the river. It looks like it will be warmer... perhaps we could swim."

Michael grimaced and shook his head. "I'm not sure I'll ever swim again."

"Oh, the Riverines are seldom a problem in the daytime. Besides, I can see them long before they reach us."

That hardly reassured him. Why not spend a day with her, though? It wasn't an unpleasant prospect. But his distance from her had grown now that it was obvious she needed someone, needed to lean on him. "I can't help anybody now," he said. She looked down at the ground.

Finally the guilt—and a basic desire which made him feel worse—drove him to agree. "What about the market?" he asked as they left.

"It is taken care of now. Come."

The sun had reappeared, driving away most of the clouds. The afternoon was pleasantly warm. The river flowed broad and slow and was also warm—which would have surprised Michael, had they been on Earth. The water was clear enough to see long silver fish gliding in the depths, just above ghostly reeds. Eleuth lay naked on the bank and Michael lay on his side, facing away from her, his head supported in one hand. "How is the novice Sidhe doing?" Eleuth asked.

He couldn't read her tone, so he turned away from the river to look at her. "Fine, I guess. I don't know what it takes to be a priest here—a priest of Adonna."

"It takes compromises, my father said once. He once tried to worship Adonna like a Sidhe, but it wasn't productive. All the Sidhe have compromised. They worship Adonna, Adonna lets them live here."

"How can worship be coerced?"

"Some Sidhe are very dedicated to Adonna. They feel a kinship."

"What kind of kinship?"

"Adonna is like the Sidhe, Lirg said once. 'We deserve each other, we and our God; we are both incomplete and lost.' What is the God on Earth like?"

"I'm an atheist," Michael said. "I don't believe there's a God on Earth."

"Do you believe Adonna exists?"

That took him aback. He hadn't really questioned the idea.

This was a fantasy world, however grim, so of course gods could exist here. Earth was real, practical; no gods there. "I've never met him." Michael said.

"It," Eleuth corrected. "Adonna boasts of no gender. And be glad that you haven't met it. Lirg says—said—" She suddenly fell quiet. "Does it bother you when I talk too much about Lirg?" she asked after some seconds had passed.

"No. Why should it?"

"Humans might wish the talk to center on themselves. Not on others. That's what I've heard."

"I'm not an egotist," Michael said firmly. He looked at her long limbs, so lovely and pale and silky, and reached out to touch her thigh. She moved toward him, but the movement was too automatic, too acquiescing. He flashed on an image of Spart; what Eleuth would someday become.

"I'm confused," he said, removing his hand and rolling on his back. Eleuth gently lay her chin on his chest, staring up at him with large eyes gone golden in the low-angled sunlight.

"Why confused?"

"Don't know what I should do."

"Then you are free, perhaps."

"I don't think so. Not free. Just stupid. I don't know what's right."

"I am right when I love," Eleuth said. "I must be. There is no other way."

"But why love me?"

"Did I say I love you?" she asked. Again he was taken aback. He paused another minute before saying, "Whether you do or not," which was certainly witless enough.

"Yes," Eleuth said. "I love you." She sat up, the muscles on her back sleek like a seal's, her spine a chain of rounded bumps. The sun almost touched the horizon, orange in the haze of the Blasted Plain. Her skin looked like molten silver mixed with gold, warm and yellow-white. "On Earth, do humans choose those they love?"

"Sometimes," Michael said, but he thought not. He never had. His crushes had always been involuntary and fierce.

"A pure Sidhe male does not love," Eleuth said. "He attaches, but it is not the same as love. Male Sidhe are not passionate; neither are most Breeds. Liaisons between Breed males and females are usually short. Lirg was different. He was passionate, devoted to my mother." She sounded regretful. "Sidhe women are passionate, desiring, far more often. They are seldom fulfilled." She turned to face him. "That is why there are Breeds in the first place. Sidhe females and human males—almost never the reverse. Why are you confused?"

"I told you," he said.

"Not really. You don't love me? That confuses you?"

He said nothing, but finally nodded. "I like you. I'm grateful . . ."

Eleuth smiled. "Does it matter, your not loving me?"

"It doesn't feel right, making love and not reciprocating everything. Feeling everything."

"Yet for all time, Sidhe males have not loved their *geen*. And we have survived. It is the way."

Her resignation didn't help at all. It twisted the perverse knot a little tighter, however, and the only way he could see to forestall the discussion was to kiss her. Soon they were making love and his confusion intensified everything, made everything worse . . . and better.

As dusk settled, they walked back to Halftown, Michael trailing his shirt in one hand. Eleuth held on to his arm, smiling as if at some inner joke.

Chapter Twenty

The market courtyard was empty when they returned. Eleuth entered the house and began to stack her belongings in one corner. When she came to a brown rug, rolled and tied with twine, she paused and smiled, then undid the twine. "Do you have to go back right away?" she asked.

"No," Michael said.

"Then perhaps I can show you some of what I've learned." She lay the brown rug on the floor, smoothing out all the wrinkles, going from corner to corner on her hands and knees. "They'll leave me here for tonight, but tomorrow I must be gone. Lirg would be pleased with how far I've come; if I practice one more night here, it's almost like having him present." She kneeled on the rug and motioned for him to sit at one corner. "Lirg says the reason Breeds have a harder time with magic is because they're more like humans. They have more than one person inside them . . . but no soul."

Michael opened his mouth to express doubts about that, but decided he wasn't the one to judge.

"I'm not sure what he means . . . meant by that. But I feel the truth in it. Whenever I do magic, and I'm one person, it works. Sometimes my thoughts just split up, and many people talk in my head, and the magic fades. For a Sidhe, there is only one voice in the head, one discipline. So it's easier for a Sidhe to concentrate."

"Maybe that's what he meant—just concentration."

"No, it's deeper than that. Lirg said . . ." She sighed and sat up on her knees. "A Sidhe would be very upset to talk about his parents all the time. Breeds like to think they're Sidhe . . . but

I'm mostly human. Anyway, when you bring it all down to one person willing one thing, magic just flows. The next hardest thing is controlling it. Now little magic is easy to control. For a split second you tie up the Realm with your head and there it is, what you want done is done. The Realm flows for you. It's almost automatic, like walking. But big magic . . . that's very complicated. Shall I explain more?"

Michael nodded. His mouth was a little dry. Eleuth lay on the rug, staring at him steadily with her large dark eyes, her straight hair falling down around her shoulders and curling over one breast.

"The Sidhe part of a Breed knows instinctively that any world is just a song of addings and takings away. To do grand magic, you must be completely in tune with the world—adding when the world adds, taking away when the world takes away. Then it becomes possible to turn the song around, and make the world be in tune with *you,* for a few moments, at least. A world is just one long, difficult song. The difference between the Realm and your home, that's just the difference between one song and another." She closed her eyes and chanted. *"Toh kelih ondulya, med nat ondulya trasn spaan nat kod."*

"What does that mean?"

"It means something like, 'All is waves, with nothing waving across no distance at all.'"

Michael gave a low whistle and shook his head. "And you feel all that?"

"When it works," she said. "Now sit farther back, on the edge of the blanket. I won't be able to talk to you for a while, because I can't listen to you in-speak. Understand?"

"Yes." Maybe.

She stood in the middle of the blanket and held out her arms, then swung them to point at opposite corners, as if doing slow exercises. Michael looked at the corner on his left and saw a curl of darkness, as tiny as a thumbnail, seem to screw the rug to the floor. The rug tensed under his knees as if alive.

She held her arms down at her side and closed her eyes, lifting her chin. Her fingers straightened.

For the merest instant, four glowing pillars rose from each corner and passed through the roof as if it weren't there, into a greater darkness high above. She held out her hand, fingers clenched into a fist, and spun once. Her eyes flashed just as he blinked and in the moment his lids were closed, the room seemed bright enough to be seen clearly through the skin.

She knelt in front of him, held out her fist and uncurled it. A beetle lay in the middle of her palm, like a scarab but deep metallic green, with velvety green wing cases. It moved slowly, turning as if confused.

"That's very nice," Michael said, not sure whether to be impressed or not.

"It was a cold night, with clouds and the sky filled with light," she said. "It was a kind of road, hard and black, with white lines and golden dots and grass imprisoned in rock on each side, and trees in the grass." She pointed to the beetle. "This was . . . there. So I brought it back."

Michael blinked. "I—"

"I brought it for you from your home," Eleuth said. "You live in a very strange place."

The beetle crawled a half inch across her palm, then stopped and rolled over. Its legs kicked feebly and it was still. Eleuth looked down on it with concern and touched it gently with one finger. Drops of water glistened on the finger, as if . . .

As if it had searched through wet grass.

"Is it dead?" Michael asked.

Tears brimmed in Eleuth's eyes. "I think so. I have so much to learn."

It was dark and very cold when he returned to the mound. The windows of the Crane Women's hut glowed brightly. Spart waited for him between the huts, standing on one leg. She crooked a finger at him, lowered her leg, and strode to his hut. He followed. She gestured for him to pull back the cover and he complied. She snapped her fingers and the letters of the poem in the dirt glowed. "Where did that come from?"

"I'm a poet," he said, resenting her intrusion. "I write poetry. There's no paper here, so I write it in the dirt."

"Yes, but where does it come from?"

"How should I know? It's poetry."

"Do you know how old this poem is?" she asked, pointing to the last few lines. "In its Cascar version?"

Michael shook his head. "I just wrote it."

"It is dangerous to write such things. Your play with the Breed girl is making you a very interesting student." She walked away, her long limbs carrying her like a two-legged spider.

"It's *my* poem," he called after her. He heard a scratching noise behind him and saw Nare peering around the door into the hut's inner darkness. She mouthed a few words, her eyes focused on the glowing scrawls. "Tonn's *Kaeli*," she said, grinning at Michael. She straightened and followed Spart.

The air smelled of dust and electricity, though the night sky was cloudless. He lay on the grass reeds, shivering, and thought briefly of Eleuth and what she had done, then more lingeringly of Helena. He wondered what Helena was doing, and when he would get to see her again . . . and he wondered if she could ever be as affectionate as Eleuth.

(What Eleuth had done . . .)

It seemed almost too much to hope for.

Chapter Twenty-One

The few times Michael saw the Crane Women training Biri, they spoke Cascar and he couldn't understand precisely what was happening. They continued to work with Michael, and as the days passed and the weather grew colder, Nare finally devoted a day to teaching him how to harness *hyloka*, or drawing-of-heat-from-the-center. He was just beginning to get the hang of the discipline when she abandoned him, and, for a week, they concentrated on Biri from dawn to dusk.

On a bitterly cold morning, Michael came out of his hut and saw Biri in the middle of the mound with the Crane Women. They surrounded him with linked hands, their eyes closed and faces upturned to the cool blue sky. Snow fell around them in lazy, sauntering flakes. Michael sat cross-legged on the dirt before his hut door.

For hours, the group simply stood, doing nothing. Michael wrote poems in the hardening dirt and scratched them out, peering up now and then to see if anything had changed. He tried to recapture the sensation of an inner, separate voice, but failed.

Finally, Biri collapsed between them and the crane Women broke away, backing up, crouched over like birds of prey, their eyes wide and lips pressed tightly together. They went to their hut and left Biri where he lay. Michael went to him and bent over, feeling his forehead.

"Are you all right?"

"Go away," Biri said, eyes scrunched shut.

"Just asking," Michael said. Spart came running from the house, arms swinging.

"Go!" she screeched. "Leave him alone! Get out of here!"

"Forever, you mean?" he asked resentfully, running ahead of her shooing hands.

"Come back at dusk." She looked down on Biri, who hadn't moved.

"Is he all right?"

"No. Go now."

Michael walked across the stream, glancing over his shoulder at the frozen tableau of Spart and the prostrate Sidhe. He frowned and kicked at small rocks on the road to Euterpe.

The snow fell more heavily, forming speckled caps on the bushes and grass clumps by the roadside. He practiced *hyloka* as he walked, and felt a gradual spreading of warmth from the pit of his stomach.

How many days had he been in the Realm? His concentration was broken by the question and he became cold rapidly. He had lost count of the days; perhaps two months, perhaps two and a half or three. Everything had merged into training, running, casting shadows, with highlights of terror, of Eleuth's affection, and thoughts of Helena.

He frowned and bore down on *hyloka* again, feeling new heat rise in his chest and spread down his arms. He smiled and swung his arms experimentally. The chill was dispelled. When Euterpe was in sight, he quickened his pace. His face was flushed and his fingers tingled.

He thought of Biri lying on the ground in apparent agony and was very glad he wasn't a Sidhe. He felt almost giddy with relief that he was Michael Perrin. He was even glad to be in the Realm, because otherwise he wouldn't be so warm, standing in the snow; so warm and comfortable. He kicked his legs and didn't notice the thin trickle of smoke.

Michael was dancing by the time he reached the outskirts of Euterpe. He jigged past the outer houses, grinning and humming. He wondered vaguely why he was so happy, and turned up the street to Helena's alley.

A thin coat of ice crusted the cobbles in the central gutter. As he danced, his feet didn't so much crack the ice as melt it. They left steaming tracks. He leaped and ran around the corner of the alley, hollering as he passed between the blank stone walls. In his ecstasy, he seemed to find the inner voice again, and was about to chant a snatch of poetry when he came to the bottom of the stairs. He stopped, somewhat daunted. He didn't want to be less than dignified around Helena.

Michael's feet hissed on the steps. He stood by Helena's doorway, knocking on the frame. Something was burning. He looked around, puzzled, hoping it was only a cooking fire and not the building. The smell grew stronger. He lifted his arm to scratch his nose.

The sleeve of his shirt smoked. He stared at it for a moment, dumbfounded. Heat radiated from his skin. Flames curled from the edge of the fabric, small and dull at first; then the entire sleeve ignited. He clawed and tugged his way out of the shirt, casting it to the floor, where it sent up volumes of gray smoke. He dropped to his knees and pulled the book from its pocket, dropping it as his fingers scorched the binding.

The pants caught next and he kicked out of them, brushing bits of char and smoking fragments from his legs.

His breathing was deep and rapid. The walls of the hallway reflected an orange glow, but the clothing had extinguished itself. His whole body tingled and euphoria mixed with his astonishment and fear. He wanted to dance again, but instead decided it was time to do some hard thinking.

About what? About something left untended . . . let out of control. And that was . . . yes?

Hyloka. He hadn't stopped the drawing of heat from the center. He shook his head in comic exasperation and concentrated on the center of warmth, gradually damping it down. His hand was still ruddy, so he damped the impulse further. Normal skin color returned.

With the heat went the euphoria. Michael suddenly realized he was standing naked in the middle of the hallway, surrounded by the blackened remains of his clothes . . .

In front of Helena's door.

It was worse than any nightmare of embarrassment he had ever had. He had burned his clothes off his back. He bent to pick up the book, and without thinking he pushed on the wicker door. It opened—there were no locks in Euterpe—and he darted inside.

Several seconds passed before he was calm enough to realize she wasn't home. Chilled again, he looked around for something to wear. The closet—a wicker armoire—yielded a long skirt which he tied around his waist. He found a kind of short jacket which barely fit his shoulders and was about to sneak out when the wicker door swung open again.

Helena came in with several scraps of cloth draped over her arm and a sewing kit in one hand.

"Hello," Michael said by way of warning. She turned slowly and regarded him with wide eyes.

"What in hell is wrong with you?" she asked a moment later. He was shivering, mortified, but he managed a miserable smile. "I burned my clothes," he said.

"Jesus H. Christ." Helena propped the door open with her foot, as if contemplating escape. She glanced down at the blackened rags in the hallway. "Why?"

"I was trying to keep warm," Michael said. "It got away from me. I was, you know, drawing heat from the center.... Spart calls it *hyloka*—"

"You're only making it worse," Helena said, relaxing. She folded the fabric over the back of a chair and laid the sewing kit on the seat. "Start at the beginning."

Michael explained as best he could, and when he was done, Helena nodded dubiously. "So you dress up in my clothes. That's my only skirt, you know."

"I wouldn't fit in your pants," Michael said.

"Indeed you wouldn't. What are you going to do? Wear my only dress around? How many clothes do you have?"

"Just those," Michael said, pointing toward the hall. "I was—"

"Why did you come *here* to burn your clothes?"

His mortification turned into agony. He stammered and felt the start of tears. Then he saw she was enjoying the whole situation, egging him on. "I was coming to visit. It was snowing."

Helena suddenly started laughing. She bent over and fell back on the chair, knocking the kit to the floor. "I'm so-o-rry," she cackled. "I'm really so-o-o-rry!"

Michael saw the humor, but couldn't bring himself to join her. "I'll go now," he said.

"Not in my dress, you won't. What are we going to do? I don't have any men's clothes here."

"Borrow some, maybe," he suggested hopefully.

She restrained her mirth and picked up the sewing kit. "Actually," she said, walking around him, "you don't look half bad. Maybe I'll let you wear it."

"Helena, please."

"All right. I shouldn't laugh."

"I'm sure it's very funny," Michael said. "I'd be laughing, too, but it's me standing here like an ass, and in your apartment, too. And it's me wearing your clothes—"

"Why did you come back? I've seen so little of you."

"To talk. Up until a few days ago, they've been keeping me busy." He hoped she hadn't heard about Eleuth; he didn't know what kind of gossip network there was in Euterpe. No doubt he would soon find out. "You won't tell anybody, will you?"

"No. Michael, you are the most unusual person I've ever met, and you get weirder every time I see you."

"It's just this place, everything about it."

"Oh. You're normal, then."

"Yeah. . . . No, I mean, not like everybody else—"

"Enough, enough," Helena said. "I'll go find Savarin and tell him you need some clothes. He might know where to get them—fabric is scarce around here, you know. You can't just cook it off every chance you get." She giggled. "I'm even bringing home stuff mangled in the tubs at the laundry," she said, pointing to the fabric. "It's part of my job to patch it up."

"Don't tell Savarin. Don't bring him here, *please*."

"But we'll need an excuse. Some reason why you need new clothes."

"Tell him I wore mine out training."

"Sure. And walked naked through town to my apartment."

"Then make something up! Please."

"I'll be circumspect. I'll tell him it's a secret. You know what he'll think then?" She put on a prim expression. "Well, let him think whatever he wants." She went to the door. "I'll be back shortly. Don't go anywhere."

"You don't need to tell me that," he said.

She gave him one final glance, shook her head, and closed the door. Michael looked down at the blouse that barely fit across his chest, and the dress, and gave a helpless groan. He sat on the chair and rubbed his face with his hands, then lifted his head and looked around the small apartment.

Sitting on the wicker table near the chair was a rounded piece of what appeared to be driftwood. He wondered where it had come from; it was displayed prominently, like a kind of treasure. Wood was highly regarded by the humans. The Breeds were forbidden to trade wood, and he doubted Sidhe traders would supply any to humans. He wondered if he could procure some for Helena, perhaps a board from his hut; anything to make up for what he had just done.

Near the window looking down into the alley was a tall, columnar ceramic vase with three leafy sticks giving out one small yellow bud. He walked over and sniffed it, but there was no odor.

The rest of the room was quite spare. Still, after his hut, Helena's apartment seemed like the height of civilization.

An hour passed before she returned with a cloth bag and held it out to him. "Go into the back room and put these on," she said. "Savarin asked Risky for some leftovers. She had them from a tenant who disappeared years ago. They should fit."

Michael did as he was told and used the opportunity to examine her sleeping quarters. The bed was made of—what else?—wicker, with a mattress stuffed with vegetable fiber, not precisely straw. Over it were two plain, thin blankets. The area was barely large enough for a single bed. On the walls, more flowers had been hand-painted, clumsy but somehow charming.

Helena examined him critically when he returned through the curtain. "Well," she said, finger to cheek, "it's not the tailored look, but it will have to do."

"There's no pocket for my book," he said. He held up the volume, which was starting to look the worse for wear.

"I'll make you a pocket with some scraps," Helena said. "Give me the shirt." He removed the shirt and handed it to her.

"So you won't be needing any warm clothes, hm?" Helena asked as she cut out a patch pocket and began to apply it.

"I don't want to use *hyloka* again until I know how to control it," he said. He sighed. "There are so many really strange things to watch out for."

She looked at his naked chest as she sewed on the pocket. He shifted on his chair and pretended interest in the window. He wasn't scrawny but his skin was pale and he was self-conscious. He would never pass for a pin-up.

"You're getting heftier," she said. "Must be the training. Too bad baggy clothes hide it."

Snow was falling again. "Does it get real cold here?"

"Looks like winter's getting started, but you can't always count on it. When winter sets in for sure, it gets very cold. The laundry shuts down, everything stops. Winter is a good time to hide things. The Wickmaster hardly ever comes through then. He doesn't want to see how miserable everybody is. He has to keep us reasonably well-cared for, and what he doesn't see, he doesn't have to correct."

She finished the sewing and put the needle away. "There. A pocket." She passed the shirt to him and turned her chair around to watch as he put it on. "A regular ragamuffin. Have you thought much about what I said?"

He buttoned the front and slipped the book into place. "Said?"

"About our group."

"Oh. I've thought about it. I'm wondering what you'll do with a piano."

She stood and peered out the window into the alley, then drew closer to him. "It's not just the piano," she said. "It's bigger than that. The piano's nice, though." A distant look came into her eyes. "I'm all out of practice. My fingers are ruined." She wriggled them and made as if to pound a keyboard. "Stiff. Calluses. But like I was saying, we have other plans. Savarin thinks we can trust you. The Wickmaster seems to hate your guts. Of course, maybe that's just a ruse. . . . There have been humans who have gone over to the Sidhe." She looked at him sharply. "You're more mixed-up with the Breeds than with the Sidhe, and the Sidhe and Breeds aren't exactly close. But we have one reservation."

"Yes?" He felt vaguely guilty and grit his teeth.

"Why are the Crane Women so interested in you?"

"I think because of Lamia," he said. "But listen, if you don't trust me, forget it. Don't tell me anything."

"You don't know why you're being trained?"

"Savarin and I have been through all this before. I'm probably the most ignorant person in the Realm."

Helena laughed. "Don't be upset . . . well, we have to be careful. You know how serious things are. What do you know about the Pact?"

"That the Isomage, or David Clarkham, or whoever he is, fought a battle and won some concessions."

"He lost."

"Yeah, but he made the Sidhe agree to set up the Pact Lands. I suppose having Alyons watch over us was part of it."

"Savarin says Alyons was sent here as punishment for breaking a Sidhe law. But what I'm getting at is, if we put up some kind of resistance, or try to change things, the Pact is off. Alyons can do what he wants with us."

"You're not thinking of resisting?" He remembered Biri running around the rock, powdering it, and Biri was just a young, inexperienced Sidhe. What could a Wickmaster do, if all restrictions were off?

"Yes," Helena affirmed, her eyes wide with excitement. "Isn't it about time?"

"Is Savarin the leader?"

"Heavens no. Someone you have yet to meet."

"But I shouldn't know his name."

She hesitated, then shook her head. "Not until we're positive you can be trusted."

"Do you trust me?"

"I think so," Helena said after a moment. "Yes, I trust you." She smiled broadly and rocked back and forth in her chair. "Nobody could be an undercover agent and burn his clothes off on my doorstep."

"So what are you going to do?"

"We're still planning. Nothing's finalized. But if this really is winter, maybe we can get on with it. They've been planning ever since I came here, and long before. The central committee is very careful."

"Thanks for the clothes," he said, remembering how Eleuth had clothed him before.

"Nothing to it. Try not to destroy them."

"No guarantees," he said ruefully. "Sometimes the best intentions go way wrong."

"Don't I know it," she said. She fastened her gaze on him and bit her lower lip.

"What's wrong?"

"You're very handsome," she said.

"Bull."

"I mean it. You're attractive."

"I think you're beautiful." The words came out before he could assess them. Helena's expression didn't change for a moment, but then a slow, warm smile emerged and she touched his knee with her hands. "I mean it, too," he said.

"You're sweet. What time do you have to be back?" Her tone became businesslike and she went to the window again.

"Dusk," he said.

"That'll probably come early today. You want to learn why we're so positive we can resist, and succeed?"

"I suppose," he said.

"You'll have to be sure, now," she said sternly. "I'd have to take you someplace pretty unpleasant."

"How can I—? Oh, okay. I'm sure."

"Strong stomach?"

"I guess."

She frowned at him, then held out her hand. He took it and stood up.

"There are several lessons for you to learn," she said. He felt his heart quicken hopefully, but she put on a shawl and held the apartment door open for him. "I have friends in the Yard. They'll get us inside. There's somebody I want you to meet. A Child."

Chapter Twenty-Two

The Yard was at Euterpe's center, a broad, flat brick building surrounded by streets uncharacteristically wide for the human town. Helena marched ahead of him, an intent look on her face. "Nobody likes to go here," she said. "I don't go often. Savarin comes here more often than the rest."

The entrance to the yard was narrow, barely two feet wide, and blocked with a heavy woven wicker door a foot thick. Helena pulled a knob and glass chimes tinkled faintly within. A peephole slid open in the brick wall beside the door and a yellow, bleary eye peered at them.

"Sherebith, it's me," Helena said. The wicker door opened with a hollow scraping sound.

"Yes, Miss Helena. What can I do for you?" A yellow-faced, plump woman in a long gray gown stood in the half-open entranceway, arms folded, staring at Michael with neither trust nor liking.

"This is a friend," Helena said. "I'd like him to see the Yard and meet Ishmael. Michael, this is Sherebith."

Michael held out his hand. "Glad to meet you," he said. The woman looked at the hand, grimaced in disbelief and opened the door wider. "Come in," she said in a resigned tone. "He's been quiet today. The others are following his example. Thank whomever for small favors."

Sherebith led them down a dark corridor, the walls, floor and ceiling of which were made of close-spaced bricks the color of dried dung. Some light entered through narrow slits at intervals of six or seven strides; the only other illumination was from wax candles ensconced between the slits. Despite the musty smell, the floors and walls seemed clean and well-tended. Sherebith went first, followed by Helena and then Michael, who had the nagging urge to look over his shoulder.

The interior was silent. At the end of the corridor was another heavy wicker door, this one studded on the outside with more glass chimes. "Alarms," Helena said, tinkling one before Sherebith opened the door and set them all ringing.

Beyond was an open court about ten feet square, again made of brick and devoid of ornament. In each of the four walls was another door. Sherebith stepped to the door directly opposite and unlatched it. As the door creaked open, a damp thick odor wafted out, combining the worst traits of musty cellars and the sewer sludge Michael's father used on the family garden.

The candles burned dimmer in the thick air beyond. There were no slits for lighting, but covered ventilator holes in the ceiling admitted faint barred spots of day.

The room's opposite walls were lost in darkness. Square brick columns supported the low ceiling, each side holding a guttering candle. Michael saw pits dug into the floor, each about ten feet on a side and faced with brick and tile. Michael counted seven. "Compound three," Sherebith said. "I call it Leader of the Howl Compound, because of Ishmael. He's the big one. The instigator." She pointed to benches near each pit. "When the compounds were built, people thought perhaps the parents would like to come visit their children now and then. Nobody has, not since the first few months. Only me and the caretaker. I'm the warden." She smiled, revealing snaggled, yellow teeth. "I'm the only one who cares about them, who's kind to them, except the caretaker."

"What about Savarin?" Helena suggested gently.

"Him? He has reasons to come here. He gets them upset sometimes. No love for Savarin. Does he listen to them when night's down and they hear the calls from the Plain, things you and I can't hear? No." She pointed to her small, curled ears, hidden beneath straight strands of graying hair. "Calls from their real kin. The bodies mean nothing. It's what's in the bottles that counts, not the shape nor the labels."

She led them to the middle pit. Michael glanced into the other pits as they passed; the walkways were only a yard wide, and it was difficult to stay calm with the unknown on each side. Each pit held a single pale, reclining figure, some child-sized, some larger. He couldn't make out details.

Sherebith leaned over the middle pit. "Ishmael," she called

softly. "Ishmael, are you home?" A thin gray figure stirred in the shadows.

"Yes, Mother." The voice was thick, deep and cultured, imbued with an abyssal sadness. Michael felt a tug on some emotion that he could not immediately identify.

"I'm not his real mother," Sherebith confided with a slack-lipped smile. "But I'm the only one he knows."

"Ishmael," Helena said, kneeling on the walkway. The pit was as deep as it was wide, and the walls were made of slick, hard tile. The figure was naked and the pit was bare except for three bowls, receptacles for food, water and waste, all arranged neatly against one wall.

"Yes."

Michael's eyes had adjusted well enough that he could make out the details of Ishmael's face. It was small, round, dispro-portionate to such a tall body. The hands were large and hung from arms which began thin at the shoulders and widened to grotesque forearms and wrists.

"We have some questions to ask," Helena said.

"I'm not otherwise occupied."

"Has he been here since he was born?" Michael whispered.

"Almost," Helena said. "He was one of the first that we know of. He's been here since the War."

"Time passes," Ishmael said. "Questions." He sat down, leaning against the tiles and stretching his pale legs out on the floor.

"Who are you?"

"A sideshow for the guilty. A product of lust. Something so evil it must be evilly confined through all its endless life. An abortion walking. Victim."

"Don't listen to that crap," Helena told Michael. She glanced at him to gauge the effect Ishmael was having, then returned her attention to the pit. "Who are you?"

"An abortion!" Ishmael's voice rose. "Born of man and woman."

"You killed your parents."

"I don't remember." Coy, smiling.

"You tried to kill others."

"You are so informed."

"Who are you?" Helena persisted. "Your name."

"Call me—"

"Stop that," Sherebith said quietly. "His name is Paynim. He's one of Adonna's own."

"Paynim," said the figure, "Ishmael. No matter."

"He took the child's body when it was born. There are no souls here." Sherebith walked around the pit. "I am the only one who cares."

"Adonna cares!" Ishmael wailed. "Adonna bred me—"

"Buried you," Sherebith said, pacing behind Helena and Michael, making Michael edge uncomfortably close to the pit.

"Adonna freed me."

"You rose from the Blasted Plain. You still call to your friends there."

"No friends." Sad, deep.

"Then what are you?" Helena asked.

"Out of time, mired in the Realm, given form by Adonna. Ishmael."

"What are you capable of?"

The Child shook his head. Michael could barely make out his grin. The air was stifling. Michael wanted very badly to be outside.

"I stare at the Realm. I foresee."

"What do you foresee?"

"Rebellion."

"When?"

"Soon, soon."

"Who will win?"

Michael looked at Helena, then at Sherebith.

"The Pact will be broken. Alyons will lose everything."

Helena's expression was triumphant. "That's the second time he's used those words. He told Savarin the same thing. We'll win!"

Michael frowned. The Child's face was composed, hands folded in his lap. Sherebith kneeled beside the pit and looked up at them. "Nobody cares for them but me," she said. "I am the only one."

"And the caretaker," Helena reminded her.

"And him."

Behind them, a short lean man dressed in brown pants and a knee-length baggy shirt pushed a wicker cart across the narrow walkways. From the sides of the cart hung the paper and wicker bowls used by the inhabitants of the pits. Three covered containers poked from a recess in the top of the cart. Helena and Michael stepped out of his way and he passed along the narrow walkway, the bowls tapping against the side of the cart. Michael looked at the man's face. He seemed to concentrate on some inner melody, gliding under the bands of light from a ventilator; his eyes were sunken, useless, and as blue as a newborn kitten's. "The caretaker," Helena whispered into Michael's ear.

"The only one," Sherebith affirmed, gaze fixed on Ishmael in his pit.

Michael was cold when they emerged from the Yard. Sherebith closed the door behind them and latched it without a word. For the first time, Michael knew what it felt like to want to die—to get the misery over with.

That was the emotioon he had contracted from Ishmael.

Helena took a deep breath and brushed her hair back from her face. "Now you see why we don't go there often."

"They're kept in the pits . . . because they hurt people?"

"They're monsters," Helena said, walking across the road. "Didn't you hear him?"

"Yes, but he's been there . . . how long? Decades? That would turn anyone into a monster."

"I've only heard stories," Helena said, keeping one pace ahead of him. "They killed their parents, or they murdered other people. Or they escaped to the Blasted Plain and lived there and made raids on Euterpe until they were caught, or killed. And when they were killed, a foulness came out of them." She shuddered, her shoulders jerking spasmodically. "This isn't Earth, Michael."

"I know that," Michael said, his voice rising. "But Jesus— the way they're treated. If they're so bad, why not just kill them?"

"We can't kill them," she said. "Alyons can. Not us. He hasn't killed any of them for a long time. None have escaped for a long time. They're human . . . sort of. I don't wish to talk about it anymore."

"All right. Then about his prophecy. How do you know he's telling the truth?"

"Sherebith will tell you. Once you get past all the crap, Ishmael never lies."

"But maybe he misleads. I read about the sibyls—"

Helena turned on him, neck thrust out and fists clenched. "Look! We have little enough to go on, nothing to encourage us. We take our reassurances where we can."

"From Ishmael?" Michael said, his face flushing. "From someone you lock up as a monster?"

"A special monster," she said, relaxing slightly. "Don't try to set us straight about the Realm, or about what we're doing, Michael. We've been here much longer than you have."

That seemed to settle it. They were silent the rest of the way back to Helena's apartment. She walked up the stairs ahead of him. "You want to come in?" she asked.

He considered. "Yes. I want to know what I can do to help. I don't like Alyons any more than you do. Maybe less."

"Then come in," Helena said.

Chapter Twenty-Three

Helena busied herself cleaning up in the back room behind half-drawn curtains. Michael listened to water splashing, toilet articles clinking, Helena humming to herself.

He was disturbed. Something was wrong, but what exactly eluded him. The perverse mood brought on by Ishmael's words was passing; what was wrong, or seemed wrong, was much more mundane.

Helena. When she was away from him, he had doubts she could ever be more than she was at this moment—friendly, but distant. When she was in his sight, the doubts shrunk to mere points, blocked by his infatuation. She was quick, pretty, human. She would never look like the Crane Women. She came from Earth. From home.

Yet he didn't feel at ease around her. He was more comfortable around Eleuth than Helena.

Helena parted the curtains and smiled at him. "Thank you for waiting. I always have to wash myself off after visiting the Yard." She offered him a damp rag. He didn't feel any dirtier than usual, but to please her, he rubbed off his face and wiped his hands.

"There," she said, throwing the rag into a corner and sitting in the second chair before him. She adjusted her seat until it was square with his. "You know how much I feel for you," she said.

He didn't reply for a moment. Her eyes locked his; he had to make an effort to look away and swallow. "I know *that* you feel for me," he said, concentrating on the curtained window. "I don't know how."

"Now you're being obscure," she said. "I care for you a great deal. You are a very sweet boy. True, you're caught up in things you don't really understand, but so am I. So are we all. You do the best you can."

He shrugged, his thick red eyebrows drawn together. She smiled. "You're smart, attractive, and anywhere else I would probably be in love with you, right this minute. I'd want you to write your poetry for me. I'd play the piano for you." Her smile broadened. "You may hear me play a piano soon, anyway. If we were in Brooklyn, I'd take you—" She stopped and her face stiffened. "But we aren't. We have to see that. I can't love you, not like I should. Today you've seen why."

"I have?"

"The Yard. To love you properly, I'd want to give myself to you completely . . . and I can't." She searched his face and reached out to touch his cheek. "Don't you see? They've taken love away from us here. We might make a mistake, a slip. I couldn't stand the thought of having a Child."

He was dumbfounded.

"Poor Michael," she repeated.

"I don't see—" he began. But he did see. She was being perfectly reasonable. And yet . . . there was that wrong thing, that still-nagging point of disturbance.

"Friendship is very important here," she said. "We live by it. We all have to work together, or they'll overwhelm us. We all have to resist every way we can. I need you. We need you. As a friend."

He still didn't have any reply. He wanted to show her he knew what she was about to say, but he couldn't.

"We can't be lovers, Michael. Do you understand? I hope you do. I want to have you understand, now, before it gets all . . ." She waved her hand and cocked her head to one side. "All crazy."

"I understand," he said. It was too late. He felt it even more strongly now. Not being able to have her made him love her all the more. He knew it was perverse, but it wasn't a new emotion; it was just that the denial unveiled it completely. He had to be near her any way he could. "Friendship is important to me, too," he said with a weak grin. "I need friends here."

"Good." She laid her hand on his knee and regarded him earnestly. "We need your help."

"How?"

"If you truly want to be one of us, to resist Alyons and the coursers and to free us all from the Sidhe . . . you have to listen for us. Let us know what you hear."

He laughed. "The Crane Women don't tell me anything," he said. "I feel like a God damned mushroom with them." He was surprised by the bitterness in his voice.

"Yes. I know the joke," she said. "We all feel that way. But Savarin says you're right in the thick of things. There's a Sidhe living not ten yards from your hut, and the Crane Women are training you. I've told Savarin I bet you're already learning things no other human knows. Like how to burn off your clothes." She smiled. "We still don't know why you're being trained. Probably only Lamia could tell us that. But there *must* be things you can learn, knowledge you can pass on to us. You could learn about the land beyond the Blasted Plain—"

"I've been there," Michael said.

"See!" Her excitement doubled. "Wonderful! You could tell Savarin what it's like, what we'll find when we break out!"

"I'm not sure it's wise to even think about crossing the Blasted Plain," Michael said. "Even the Sidhe have to dust themselves with *sani* and use their horses for protection. It's dangerous."

"We know a little about the powder. Can you get some for us?"

"I don't think so," he said. "I don't know where it is, or even if the Crane Women have any. . . ."

"But if you could get into their hut, look for it. . . . They must have *some*."

"I wouldn't even want to try," he said.

"Why not? They're half human."

He chuckled. "The forgotten half. You should see their windows at night. Like they have a blast furnace inside. Orange light, flickering. You'd think it was on fire."

"Can't you even look?" The goad in her voice was not particularly sharp, but surrounded by the silkiness, the hint of doubt, it hurt.

"I'll let you know," he said after a pause.

"We'll need it soon."

"How soon?"

"Within a fortnight. Two weeks. Sorry—I start to talk like the old folks here." She gave him a questioning look, lifting her eyebrows. She was practically begging.

"I'll try," he said.

"Marvelous!"

"I better be going back now." He wanted to be alone, to think things over and subdue the buzz of confusion and disappointment.

"Don't cause any trouble," she said. "Don't try to run away again. Just work with us . . . help us. You heard what Ishmael said."

"I heard." They stood and she kissed him on the cheek, gripping his arms tightly.

For the next week, he hardly had time to think. The Crane Women suddenly integrated him into Biri's training, without explanation—and without reprieve.

The day after he'd spoken with Helena, they took Michael and Biri to a barren mound about two miles south. Coom supervised Biri and Spart kept watch on Michael as they tried higher and higher levels of *hyloka*.

The Crane Women were positively grim. Spart barked out her instructions, her voice growing hoarse as the hours passed. Before the day was out, Nare was instructing Michael on how to block his aura of memory—which, among other things, would prevent a Sidhe or Breed adversary from in-speaking. "Occult the knowledge," she told him. "Occult the knowledge, not just your immediate knowings, but the knowings of your mother and father, your forefathers . . . memories of your kind. No eyes will see, no minds will use what you do not wish them to have."

Snow fell more frequently during that week. The season was indeed going over to winter, in fits and starts, as if the air itself were undecided. But more days were cold than were not. Michael's *hyloka* kept him warm under the coldest conditions.

Spart schooled Michael on how to throw a shadow while asleep, and how to sleep like the dead, his heart barely beating, while at the same time his mind was alert. He controlled his breath until he seemed not to breathe at all. He explored his inner thoughts, paring them down to the ones most essential to his exercises.

For a time, he forgot about Helena and Eleuth. What little spare time he had, Michael spent exercising these new abilities, reveling in the potential that was being unlocked without resort to Sidhe magic.

He could not locate the inner voice that had briefly conversed with him in poetry. He did find, however, a good many other unexpected things in his mind. Some edified him, some astonished him, and others made him wilt with shame. When he complained he couldn't stand any more introspection and asked if this was just incidental to the other disciplines, whether it could be foregone, Spart told him that a warrior must know all there was to hate in himself, or his enemy would use it against him.

"Blackmail?" Michael asked.

"Worse. Your own shadows can be thrown against *you.*"

Biri's training seemed similar, but at a higher level. There was no repeat of the torturing circle-formation the Crane Women had exercised against him. Nevertheless, Biri became thinner. He was less talkative and seemed more resentful of Michael's presence. Michael stayed away from him.

In and around all the other exercises, there was running with and without sticks, physical training from a taciturn and frowning Coom, verbal harangues from Spart when he didn't pay attention.

He hated it, yet the training was exhilarating. He missed Earth even more but he began to feel as if he could survive in the Realm.

There was no training on the eighth day. Biri and the Crane Women left the mound before sunrise. Michael was asleep and had no idea where they went.

He walked around the mound in the early dawn, calling out their names, looking at the fresh footprints heading south, wondering if now was the time to look for the *sani* in the Crane Women's hut. He lingered near the hut, frowning, feeling he was about to betray them. Still, they were not exactly friends— taskmasters, tyrants, not friends.

Then why did he feel beholden to them?

He began to sweat and ran away from the mound, going to Eleuth's new quarters in Halftown. She was cleaning clothes and preparing for more of her own exercises; he half-listened as she described the Sidhe magic she now knew.

"If I brought a beetle back now, it would be alive," she said proudly, smiling at him.

"No need," he said gloomily.

"You are bothered."

He walked around the small single-room apartment, one of four units in a single-story wood building. The room was barely fifteen feet on a side, divided in half by a curtain; clean, neatly arranged, but somehow oppressive. Eleuth didn't seem to find it so.

"What are you going to do?" he asked.

"I'll be assigned another task soon," she said, looking down at the floor, eyebrows raised.

"Like what?" he pursued.

"The decision hasn't been made yet."

He was about to say something that might make her feel miserable but he caught himself. He was upset. He couldn't stand her calmness but that was no excuse to pass on his gloom. "The Crane Women are gone today," he said. "I don't want to stay on the mound. Would it bother you if I stayed here?"

She smiled; of course not.

She fixed a simple dinner for them. In perverse exchange, he briefly put up his wall against in-speaking, leaving her fumbling for words, without ready access to his memory of English. She was chastened, but remained outwardly cheerful.

After dinner was cleared, he asked her whether she could transfer someone between the Realm and Earth. He thought the question innocent enough; he just wanted to know how capable she was.

"Why are you angry?" she asked.

"I'm not angry." He shrugged and admitted perhaps he was. "It's not your fault."

"I feel that it is."

"Damned females, always so sensitive!'"

She backed away and he flung up his arms. "I'm sorry," he said.

"You wish to return to Earth?"

"Of course. I always have."

"You would consider it love if I returned you to Earth?"

The question took him aback. "Can you?"

"Would you consider it love?"

"What do you mean, love? It would be wonderful, yes."

"I'm not sure I can," she said. "I wouldn't want to fail you."

He paced around the room, scowling and mumbling. "Jesus, Eleuth, I'm just confused. Very, very confused. And angry. Yes."

"With whom are you angry?"

"Not at you. You've never done me anything but good."

She smiled radiantly and took his hand. "I would want everything I do to be good for you, to be love for you."

He felt even more miserable. What if he never did go home, would it matter much? Could he make a life here in the Realm,

even in the Pact Lands? Others had lived in worse conditions
and been happy, or at least not miserable. Eleuth sensed some
of his mental peregrinations and gripped his hand all the tighter.

"It could be a *good* life here," she said. Her hopeful tone
was like a dart in his temple.

"How?" he asked, shaking her hand loose. "I don't belong
here! I'm human, and you're—" He pounded his hand against
the wall. "And *she's* human, and that's the problem, isn't it?"

"The woman in Euterpe?" Eleuth asked, staring at the back
of his head.

"Helena," he said. He imagined it to be the most vicious
thing he could say: the name of the woman toward whom he
felt as Eleuth deserved to have him feel toward her. As Eleuth
wanted him to feel.

"Humans have many more troubles than Breeds, actually,"
Eleuth said. She didn't sound upset or jealous. He turned toward
her. Her face was composed, half-caught in the afternoon light
from a high window, eyes large and deep and calm.

"Please," Michael said.

"You could love her, and be with me," Eleuth said.

Tears began to flow down his cheeks. He was furious, every
thought part of a turbulent, rising whirl. "Don't say any more.
Please, no more."

"No," Eleuth said, standing and reaching for his shoulder.
"I'm sorry. I don't understand. I cannot be . . . jealous. Sidhe
women are not jealous. Who can be jealous of males who
cannot love, cannot attach?"

Michael sat on a bench and rubbed his eyes with his palms.
None of the calmness exercises would work now. He couldn't
bring down his level of misery, or control its effects on his
body, the tension in his neck and arms.

"I could love you while you loved her," Eleuth said. Michael
didn't seem to hear. She sat beside him and put her head on
his shoulder. "I could do many things for love, and what I
cannot do, I will learn." She stroked his back with one hand.
"It is all a Sidhe women ever expects."

He stayed with her that night and the next morning returned
to the Crane Women's mound. The huts were still empty. He
entered his own hut and stashed the book in the rafters, then
sat on the mats and tried to think of a poem. Not even an
opening line would come. His head was empty of words. Full
of turmoil; empty of expression.

By late morning, he made his resolution. He would search for the *sani*. He didn't know right from wrong himself; perhaps Helena and Savarin did.

In Biri's empty hut, the plaited mats were neatly folded in one corner. He looked everywhere in the hut and found no sign of the powder.

He crossed to the Crane Women's hut and stood by the door. Peering through the windows, he saw only darkness within. He tried to pry the door open with his fingers, but it seemed latched. He pushed, hoping it would open. It didn't. Then he pushed harder and something wooden clicked within. The door swung outward slowly.

The Crane Women obviously didn't feel the need of locks. So what—if anything, or anyone—did they have guarding the hut? The thought didn't give him much pause; he was beyond practical concerns.

The sunward window cast a shaft across the room, illuminating shelves stacked with bottles. The contents of one of the bottles wriggled pinkly in the beam. His eyes adjusted slowly to the gloomy corners. In the center of the room was a cylindrical brick oven, reaching almost to the roof, with four mouths opening around its circumference. A ceramic platform surrounded the oven, shiny white and indented with a regular series of pestles. A few mortars lay on the table, and small piles of powder of differing colors and roughness. The fire was out, but the oven still retained heat; he could feel it on his face and outstretched palm.

Across the room from each other were two sets of shelves, both packed tight with bottles full of teeth and small fragments of bones. Other bottles contained roots and vegetable matter. A bottle with a forked root had been the first to catch his eye; even now, the root squirmed.

Yet another shelf was devoted to bottles of dusts. None of the containers were labeled. If they had discernible uses, only the Crane Women knew what they were.

Beyond the closest set of shelves was a partition made of wooden boards, on which thin sheets of tough, pearly tissue had been stretched between pegs to dry. Below the sheets hung the skeletal forearm of a small clawed animal. The claws appeared to be made of gold.

On the other side of the room, partly hidden behind a drape of gray cloth, a glass box sat on a table. In the box were pieces of frosty crystal finely carved into abstract shapes. Each crystal had a single clear facet like a peephole. Michael pulled the drape aside with forefinger and thumb and opened the lid of the box.

The temptation was too great; he removed a crystal and held it up to his eye. Like a slide viewer, the crystal contained an image. Green rolling hills and a wonderfully vivid sky appeared to Michael. He was about to put it down and pick up another when a woman walked over the hills. With a shock, he realized she was a much younger Coom. Her name, the crystal informed him in no obvious way, was Ecooma. She smiled and swung her arms, her long, shapely legs outlined beneath a wind-blown red dress. Her face resembled Eleuth's, but was even more comely. She passed out of range of the crystal eye, prompting him to turn with it to follow her, but to no result. The crystal maintained one steady point of view.

A second crystal showed a high mountain pass. Swift clouds threw shadows on a snow-covered slope beyond. The naked female standing on a rock, undaunted by the obvious cold, was called Elanare. She stretched her arms out to the wind, long red hair trailing behind her. In her youth, Nare had been even more lovely than Ecooma,

He picked up a third crystal. Spart—Esparta—stood among a group of young human women, seated on marble benches in a small stone amphitheater. The women wore short white dresses tied around the waist; Spart wore a long black gown and her hair was tied up in a bun with sparkling gold thread. She was speaking to the women, and they laughed now and then as if surprised and delighted. Though her beauty was more subtle than that of Ecooma or Elanare, to Michael she seemed the most beautiful of all.

Gone were their distortions of face and frame, rolled back by time. He gently laid the third crystal in the box and reached for a fourth. The one he picked revealed a man and a Sidhe female from the waist up, arms around each other. The man was ruddy-skinned, with a thick brown-black beard, wry intelligent eyes and a sharp short nose. The Sidhe's facial features were so evocative and familiar that Michael was sure he must have seen her before, however impossible that was.

They were Aske and Elme, the crystal informed him, and there was good reason for their portrait to reside in the glass box. They were the mother and father of the Crane Women, and of seven other Breed children whose pictures resided in other crystals.

He put the crystal down quickly, his arm hairs tingling with
premonition. He quickly searched the rest of the hut for *sani*
and spotted a pouch resting on a small wooden table near the
door. He hastily sprinkled some of the contents into his palm
and saw the unmistakable golden flakes he needed. He poured
the flakes back into the pouch and re-tied the knot.

Now that he had found what he needed, Michael felt a
sudden tingle of panic. He looked around to see if he had
disturbed anything, knowing there was no way to conceal his
invasion from the Crane Women. Hopeless. They would catch
him, and what would they do?

He fumbled at the door latch and pulled it open sharply to
leave—

And jumped back with a yell. There stood Biri, covered
with mud and blood, his eyes wild and mouth gaping wide as
if in agony. Black blood oozed from the corner of his mouth
and dripped from his hands, spotting his *sepla*. He made small
whining noises deep in his chest like a hunted animal.

Michael retreated into the hut, horrified, his throat con-
stricting. Biri rolled his eyes back and twisted his head horribly.

"Michael, oh, Michael," he groaned. "What have I done?"

His body contorted and he raised his hands in supplication.
Then he straightened and ran. Michael went to the door and
looked after him as he leaped the stream and ran past the limits
of Halftown.

Nare, Spart and Coom walked onto the mound from the
opposite direction, skirting the piles of rock and bone and
staring at Michael in the doorway of their hut. He slipped the
pouch into his pocket surreptitiously.

Spart motioned for him to leave. She put her arm around
his shoulder and walked him to his own hut, then stopped and
turned him to face her.

"Was he hurt?" Michael asked, swallowing. "What happened to him?"

"You have witnessed Biri's shame," she said. "You must
tell no one. He has survived his test."

"What test? For the priesthood?"

"Yes," Spart said, her expression unusually grim. "Tarax
sent Biri's favorite horse across the border. Biri hunted it down
and slaughtered it. When he recovers, he will be ready to serve
Adonna." She focused her eyes on his and frowned, releasing
his shoulders. "What you have, what you know . . . you will
use it wisely?"

"I will," he finally said after swallowing hard twice.

The Crane Women entered their hut and shut the door behind them. Michael stared across the grasslands, tears on his cheeks, wondering if he would ever again feel like a whole person.

Chapter Twenty-Four

The snow fell quickly, leaving behind a blank white page on which was lightly sketched the horizon, Halftown, the huts and a few gray gaps in the clouds. The stream was dark and shiny gray, with a thin layer of ice projecting from each bank. Little ice-blades sliced the smoothly rushing water.

Michael stood on the bank and watched the stream. The falling snow seemed to calm him. His discipline isolated him from the cold. His mind felt just as isolated from reality, aloof. If he had done wrong, he thought, it was through no fault of his own. He was involved in a situation for which he was totally unprepared, in the face of which he was of necessity immature.

The pouch of *sani* rested in his pocket.

Biri sat outside his own hut, head bowed. The Sidhe hadn't spoken once, hadn't eaten. Coom had washed his hands and face and wrapped a reed blanket around him.

There had been some peremptory training for Michael that morning—a run with the stick across the fields, while Spart paced him and checked his skin temperature with long, black-nailed fingers. He had thrown a shadow for Coom, skilfully enough to delay her catching him by a few seconds. He had blanked his aura of memory well enough to prevent Spart from in-seeing. All this, as the snowflakes careened slowly down like drunken, frozen dandies, oblivious to the dark emotions around them.

"I'm going to Euterpe," he told Coom, who squatted outside the Crane Women's hut, keeping an eye on Biri as she pounded a rock to powder with a harder rock. She nodded.

He left the book in the rafters of his hut. He wasn't expecting trouble, but if any came, the book wouldn't help and he didn't want to lose it or see it damaged.

The road seemed longer, extended by the whiteness. When he came to Euterpe the town was as private and closed-down as a sleeping face. He walked through deserted streets, glancing at brick walls and tile roofs, worn-out wicker baskets piled in a heap, carts carrying buckets of frozen human waste. He saw everything as if for the last time. The sensation of fatedness was strong, emphasized by his numbness.

He took the familiar alley, approached the familiar entrance and stairs and climbed slowly and quietly. He reached for the bag. When he came to the wicker door, now draped with a cloth cover, he held his hand up to knock, then hesitated. He heard voices inside. Helena had a visitor.

He felt, if such a thing was possible, even more more deeply isolated and sick at heart. He pushed the door. It became party to his stealth and opened with only a faint scrape. The voices continued. He pulled aside the curtain to the bedroom, knowing it was wrong to invade someone's privacy, but feeling his own grievance was stronger.

Savarin and Helena lay on the narrow cot, covered mercifully by a dun-colored blanket. Helena saw him first. Her eyes widened. He lowered the curtain and backed into the front room, pulling the *sani* from his pocket and laying it on the front table. There was scuffling and creaking behind the curtain, and sounds of clothing hastily being put on. "Stay here," Helena said. "Don't come out. I'll talk to him."

She emerged from behind the curtain, combing out her hair with her fingers, looking at him sidewise. Her face was white. "Michael," she said.

"I brought it," he said, pointing to the wicker table. "What you need. What you wanted."

"I'm sure you don't understand," Helena said, coming closer. "It's—"

"Please," he said. "Enough. I'll go."

"Let me explain!" The note of desperation held him. "It's not what any of us wants. Savarin can't have children. Before he left Earth—"

"Please, enough," Michael repeated.

"He's safe, don't you see? You're not. You're not safe. That's the difference." She repeated these words a few times, coming slowly closer, holding her hands up. Finally she stopped, hands circling to form small shields. She struggled for something more to say. "We need your help still."

"You've had my help," he said. "You have the powder. I'll go now." As Helena called his name, louder and more frantically, he ran down the stairs and back to the street and out ot Euterpe.

He was hardly aware of his running. His long stride carried him without apparent effort. He seemed suspended within his body, isolated from the exertion, his breath smooth, the machine running even better without his interference. He passed a woman clutching a cloak about her head and shoulders.

As if on an endless cycle, he was going to Halftown. The awareness that it was all drawing to a close, that his adventure in the Realm was about to end, was very strong.

Chapter Twenty-Five

Halftown was also quiet in the mid-afternoon snowfall, its half-circle streets covered with shallow drifts. Michael wasn't thinking clearly and it took several extra minutes for him to find Eleuth's quarters. He stood outside the door, his mind almost as blank as the fields of snow between Euterpe and Halftown.

As he knocked, it occurred to him that not for an instant did he suspect betrayal behind the door. (Had Helena betrayed him? Or had she just done something which, in his youth, he couldn't begin to fathom?)

The door opened. Eleuth examined his downcast face and took him by the arm, leading him inside without a word spoken. She sat him on the bunk and took the small stool for her own seat. Several deep, jerking breaths were necessary before Michael could say, "I have to go back now. There's nothing more I can do here."

She nodded, then shook her head, and nodded once more. "Do you need my help?" she asked.

"Of course I need your help. I can't do it myself, or I'd have done it already."

"Then I'll help," she said. "We have to wait until dark, and we can't do it here. Somebody might see us, or feel what's happening. Until night, you'll stay here, have something to eat?"

"I'm not hungry," he said.

"You'll need all your strength," she said, pouring him a bowl of stew. After he finished eating, she took the bowl and pulled back the covers on the bunk. He sat down. She adjusted the pillow for him and he lay back with his eyes open. Deliberately, with another breath, he closed them. His face was rigid.

Even when she was sure he was asleep, his face remained stiff. She sat watching him for some time as the snow fell faster outside and the wind rose. Then she went around the room, removing objects from the dresser drawers, from shelves, and from the low table. She assembled the articles in a cloth laid over her lap: white face cream, though it really didn't matter, she thought; a few twigs from a flowering tree beyond the Blasted Plain; some stones from the Plain itself, dusty to the touch; and the dead green beetle she had summoned from Michael's neighborhood. When she had pulled in the corners of the cloth and made a bundle by tying them, she sighed deeply, pulled back a few loose strands of hair with both hands, and stared out the window at a white world she doubted she would experience much longer.

With darkness, the snow stopped and the wind died, leaving the Pact Lands in muffled silence. Michael awoke and ate more of the stew while Eleuth painted her face with the white cream. "It reflects the light," she explained.

The inevitable unreality of everything was coming down on him now in an avalanche. Why should he be dismayed by betrayal? None of these people existed. They were all phantoms; to find his way home, all he had to do was enact some formula which would bring him out of his trance, his waking nightmare.

He forgot all the proofs he had accepted in the past about the Realm's existence. They were dim, feeble things compared with his present pain. Eleuth tied a blanket-cloak around his neck, in case his discipline slipped in his distraction. Then she took his hand, lifting the bundle in the crook of her arm, and led him into the night. He followed her through the snow without speaking. Her grayish outline advanced into the darkness beyond Halftown and away from the road, the stream, the mound, taking him in a direction he had never gone before.

The grass was frosted with snow that powdered with the brush of their legs and fell on their feet, melting into their cloth shoes until they were soaked. Only *hyloka* kept their feet from freezing.

When they were far enough away from everything to suit her, she cleared the snow away for him to sit, laid out the cloth and arranged the articles and squatted opposite him. He could barely see her. Only a few stars peeped through rifts in the clouds. The cream on her face glowed slightly and he followed her movements that way.

"You wish to go home," she said, her tone more stern than he had heard it before.

"Yes," he said.

"You wish to get there by Sidhe magic."

"I do."

"There is some risk. Do you accept that?"

"Yes." He didn't much care.

"Do you accept this gift from me, given out of love?"

"I do." He felt a pressure in his chest. "I appreciate this very much, Eleuth."

"How much?" she asked, almost bitter.

He shrugged in the darkness. "I'm not worth much. I don't know why you feel so strongly toward me."

"You acknowledge that love?"

"Yes."

"Do you return it?"

He leaned toward her dim features. "I love you, too," Michael said. "As a friend. As the only friend I have here. Wherever we are."

"As a friend, then," Eleuth said, her tone less astringent. She laid the twigs out on the cloth in a circle, pointing toward the center. Near one of the twigs she laid the beetle. Next to another she placed one of the pebbles. The rest of the pebbles she piled on one corner of the cloth.

"Is that all you need?" Michael asked.

"That, and my training," Eleuth said. "I'm still not very good." She stood, took his hand, and made him stand in the middle of the circle of twigs. "For you, I wish I were a full-blooded Sidhe," Eleuth said, holding out her arms. She assumed the same pose he had seen in the crystal portrait of Nare. "But Lirg's blood is good and I rely on him, too. Wherever he is now." She danced lightly around him, spinning from one toe to the next. He turned his head to follow her. "Face straight ahead," she said.

After a few minutes she stopped, breathing more heavily than when she had begun. "Did the Sidhe pass his test?" she asked.

"Yes."

"Did he take his flesh, drink his blood?"

"I think so."

"He left the Crane Women this evening," she said. "He goes to his new home. Perhaps he will see Lirg."

"I don't know."

"Do you know what your friends in Euterpe are doing tonight?" she asked.

"No."

"All the Breeds stay in tonight. We don't know either, but we have our suspicions." She resumed the dance, reaching now and then to brush his shoulders with her fingers. "Michael," she said, her breath harsh, spinning around him. "Look straight ahead. It is time for you to go home . . . very soon."

Light sprang up around his feet. He glanced down and saw the twigs burning brightly from the outside in, like multiple fuses.

"Out of love," Eleuth said. She formed her arms into a circle. Two circles of light leaped from the arcs of her fingers, rose and fell around him, stopping at waist level. The twigs burned to their ends. He stood in the middle of a radiance of fire that rose around his feet but did not burn.

Eleuth stood rigid in front of him, arms held high, breasts pulled taut against her rib cage, stomach flat, heaving. Her hair was disarrayed and her eyes were closed. She twisted her head to one side. "I will guard," she said. "For as long.

As.

I.

Can."

Her eyes opened. They were black, rimmed with blazing red. He felt himself falling toward them. His feet lifted from the cloth. The circles tightened around his waist like belts, cinching close. The fire spread to Eleuth, crackling and hissing, searing away the darkness until the land around them was bright as day. When the flames touched her naval, she flinched and screamed.

The fire surrounded her. Arced outward to the snow-covered grass. Melted the snow into steam. Dried the grass and set it ablaze. She twisted in her own fire, mouth open to reveal darkness much deeper than the night. Michael rose toward her and felt the cold electric destruction of the power she had unleashed.

"Please," she said, barely audible over the crackle and roar. "I will guard. Careful! Out of love—"

She became smaller and darker, twisting in the fire until she receded to a black point.

Michael was no longer on the grassland but high above, looking out across the infinite expanse of the Realm, its forests, plains and mountains laid out beneath him like a topographical relief map. The river snaked far to the northeast through forests, scrub lands, blank desert and swamps. There was a mountain surrounded by a city with walls like a tangle of silvery roots—

And a black, spiky something beyond.

To the north he saw a broad lake glowing cobalt in the night—Nebchat Len, possibly. Beyond the lake stretched more forest, and beyond that massive jagged mountains. Looking down, he saw the Pact Lands mounted in the middle of the Blasted Plain, a yellow-green circle surrounded by warm, forbidding orange-tinted darkness. This darkness seemed to writhe, rise up to grab him. Then everything writhed—and vanished.

He could have been suspended in nothingness for all eternity. The sensation of time left him. In the void was a flicker of light, somewhere above where his head had been. He was aware of a canopy of leaves, then of something beneath his feet, hard and gray. His circle of vision expanded. His head filled with rushing blood, and the sensation of weight returned.

Michael closed his eyes and rubbed them. The rush of exultation was dizzying. He wanted to jump, to shout. He glanced at his wrist to see what time it was—what time the trance had come to an end. But his watch was missing. He still wore the clothes Helena had scrounged for him; his feet were still shod in cloth.

A flicker of fire played around his ankles. He stared down at the fire, watching it brighten, fade and brighten again. Suddenly it flared up around his calves until it obscured the sidewalk. Tendrils rushed to wrap his wrists like shackles and crawl up his chest like serpents.

"No!" he protested. "NO!"

He doubled up as if kicked in the stomach. Curled, he flew backwards into darkness, winding along a jagged reverse course and surrounded by a comet's tail of fire.

Chapter Twenty-Six

Michael lay on his stomach, gravel and dirt pressed to his face. His legs sprawled across dry grass. He opened his eyes to the twilight and saw dark bushes with greasy green-black leaves. Rolling on his back, he encountered a featureless gray-blue sky, low and oppressive. A few muddy stars glistened wetly in the expanse.

Something rustled nearby. The path on which he lay crossed a yard of sickly grass and ended at a red brick porch. Dull orange paper lanterns hung on the trellis arbor rising over the porch.

He got to his knees. The rustling became louder. He stood, turned and flinched from the touch of dry, cold fingers against his face.

The figure in the flounced dress was less than a yard away, arm bent at two crazy angles and pointing toward him. The shadow of the wide-brim hat still obscured the features, but Michael was more certain than ever that it was a woman, caught between the Realm and the Earth, probably as crazy as Lamia. He wondered what he had to fear from her.

She advanced, lurching as if one leg were shorter than the other, or improperly jointed. The sleeved arm stretched out again and Michael smelled dust, mildew, something metallic. He backed away several steps. He had been home—

You are home.

The voice, soft as the still twilight air, reached around his ears and touched the back of his head. *You are home.* He focused on the fingers of the hand. They were thin, colorless; they could have been twigs wrapped in strips of coarse cardboard. They flexed against each other with the sound of rustling leaves.

Beyond the guardian was the gate leading to the alley. He looked over his shoulder for the merest instant, trying to see if he could go back through the house—reverse his course— but there she was, barring the way. When he wasn't watching she could move with incredible speed. He faced her and slowly backed toward the gate.

Stay. Images of incredible luxury, voluptuousness. Gardens filled with flowers and thick vegetables, luscious ripe berries studding intense green bushes. Tomatoes red as arterial blood.

If he stared at her—she was gaining on him, lurching— she might catch him. Already her hands were reaching out, her fingers rustling in anticipation. If he turned to run for the gate she might leap quick as darkness and have him anyway.

She played him like a fish on a line. He was trapped, no way out this time. There was only one way for the trance to end—in her garden, caught between the projected paradise and the dry, somber twilight reality.

Reality. As real a doom as any.

Still, he had learned a lot since he had last encountered her. There might be one way to elude her.

He searched for the hidden impulse, found it feeble but present. Between the Realm and Earth it would work only intermittently, weakly. Still, he had no choice but to try. He threw a shadow.

The gate seemed an incredible distance away—only a few yards. Behind he heard drapes of fabric shustle frantically, sensed the arms closing around something, passing through empty air. The guardian screed like a bat or a falcon.

He ran down the alley. Sixth gate on the left. But he no longer had the key! He couldn't open the lock, couldn't pass through. He felt rather than heard his pursuer leaping after like a wave of foul dead air.

At the locked sixth gate, he did not hesitate. He ran to the seventh, some yards farther, and found it without a lock. He jerked it open, making the rusty hinges and spring scream.

The guardian's hand grasped his shoulder and flung him back as if he were made of paper. He toppled and slid across the pavement, rebounding from the brick wall opposite. The gate slowly closed, its spring softly singing. He knew he would never have time to open it again if it latched.

He would never reach it, anyway.

But the guardian held back, rocking on hidden limbs like a nightmare toy, a puppet pulled by idiots.

He pushed against the wall with arms and shoulders, leaping, using all his new prowess to make it through the gate. The gate clanged shut behind him.

Michael stood in a long, narrow lot, bordered on all sides by low red brick walls. Some distance away over the end wall he could see the outline of the rear of Lamia's house, the Isomage's ruined mansion.

Perhaps the sixth gate wasn't the only way.

Bordering the path that led to a gate in the distant second wall were two continuous trellises, thickly wrapped in dead brown ivy. He hurried between them.

"Not that way!"

He stopped. The voice had come from his left, as much a dry croak of pain as a warning.

"She will have you before you reach the end."

"Hide!"

"Watch for her!"

The voices came from the ivy-covered trellises. Against all his instincts he slowed to a walk, his legs cramping with fear and indecision.

Then he discerned them. They were caught in the vines, limbs entwined: corpses. Emaciated, skin slumping like dry leather, jaws gaping, arms and legs skeletal, eyes hollow. But their heads turned to follow him and they strained against their bonds, lips pulled back over yellow teeth.

"Don't let her have you! Die first!"

"Watch for her!"

"Not that way. She'll get you!"

In fact, the gate seemed farther away now than when he had begun. The closer he came, the more it receded and the longer the trellises were. And the more writhing mummified bodies he saw in the grasping dead ivy.

"If she has you, you never die..."

"If she loves you, you sleep..."

"And awaken here."

"Live forever..."

"But decay!"

Maniacal laughter all around. The corpses struggled horribly, pieces of skin flaking off to the ground. Some reached out to him, imploring; others strained their hollow chests against the vines, heaving and thrashing and shaking the trellises until they seemed in danger of falling over.

The guardian was on the same path now. He hadn't seen her pass through the gate; perhaps she didn't need to. As she walked, the wide hat swung slowly from left to right. She surveyed her past victims, lurching down the path to certain conquest over another.

She collected them. Had them, used them, placed them here. She savored her collection, her work well done. This was her paradise of vegetables and succulent fruits, the garden of her labors.

Stay.

He half-ran, half-stumbled crab-wise, trying to find the center of impulse again. But he had no clear way to throw another shadow. The guardian, dress flapping and pressing back against her distorted frame, had risen a foot or so above the path and was accelerating toward him like a piece of fabric on a spinning clothesline. She pitched head-forward in her flight until the hat pointed directly at him and the dress fanned out, a deadly trailing blossom.

He turned and fled from his doom, screaming.

Ahead of him, Eleuth stood on the path, so close he couldn't avoid colliding with her.

And passing through. He stumbled and fell on the ground. Glancing back, face contorted, he saw the translucent Breed woman spread her arms before the hurtling guardian.

They merged. There was a drawn-out cry as the fabric and distorted body tangled in mid-air and fell to the ground like a downed bird. Michael ran. The gate at the end of the lot was much closer. He reached it in a few strides, opened it, looked back at the guardian still crumpled on the pathway and saw Eleuth's final shadow gently spinning with the force of their collision. It floated off the path, fading, fading, until it was gone completely.

Michael stood on the field behind the Isomage's house. With a hollow clang, the gate latched itself and the wall vanished.

Once again he looked out across the Pact Lands, down the slope to the broad river. His breath was ragged, his elbows and knees were scraped and bleeding, his head hurt abominably.

The trance was far from over.

Chapter Twenty-Seven

It was late afternoon in the Realm. From miles away, Michael could smell smoke. A thick column of black rose over Euterpe. Hardly able to walk, he crossed the field and went to the front door of the Isomage's house. In the distance he heard thunder and indistinct shouts and screams. Then the wind shifted and all was quiet.

The parlor, ballroom and dining room of the house were empty and silent except for a noise like sand or dust falling. He wasn't sure what to do next so he climbed the stairs. He wondered if he should confer with Lamia, ask what had gone wrong with his journey and what was happening in Euterpe.

He didn't particularly wish to know.

The room of candles was deserted and dark. He crossed the wooden floor, footsteps echoing sharply even though he still wore his cloth shoes. The room's echoes were like returning knives—breath, heartbeat, rustle of his fingers against his chin.

He noted, with a start, that he was beginning to grow a rough beard.

He walked farther down the hall, away from the open landing. Shadows ruled the house; all the candles sat unlit in their sconces or lay shattered on the floor, as if someone had despised their light. "Lamia?" he called, quietly at first, then louder. His throat still hurt from his screaming in the Between. He brushed one hand against the wall, venturing into the darkest recesses of the hall. The wall vibrated like a bell at his touch; the entire house seemed alive, yet fearful, shrinking back.

He touched a doorjamb and turned into the doorway. From a half-drawn curtain, twilight snuck into a small sitting room. Lamia sat in a chair facing the window.

"Please," Michael said. "I need help."

She didn't answer, didn't move. He approached the chair cautiously, fearful of her bulk, her quiet, her fierce concentrated expression as she faced the waning light.

For a moment, the dim lighting and the folds of her skin had concealed the fact that she was unclothed. She sat naked and still in the large chair. Michael was convinced she waited for him to come close enough to reach out and grab. But nothing moved. She didn't even appear to breath. Was she dead?

He reached out to touch her shoulder. His finger curled back involuntarily into his palm and he forced it to straighten.

The skin gave way beneath his finger, first an inch, then two. Repelled, unable to stop, he continued pressing. She hissed faintly and her head folded in like a collapsing souffle. Her arm and chest began to collapse and she fell into a pile of white translucent folds, sliding from the chair to the floor.

Not Lamia, but her skin—shed completely. He bent down and rubbed it between his fingers. Such a familiar texture. He had felt something like it before—in the closet downstairs, when she had hidden him from Alyons.

She kept a closet full of her own shed skins.

But then, where was she? Hiding someplace, vulnerable, like a soft-shell crab or snake still damp and tender?

"Boy."

He swiveled on his heels and saw her in the room's opposite corner. She was dressed in dark gray and blended into the shadows. She was even more huge now, perhaps half again as tall and fat as she had been. Her voice was deeper, more appropriate to the mountain she was becoming. Everything about her was vibration as she stepped forward, from her cheeks to the flesh of her hands.

"You tried to go back, didn't you?"

His mouth was dry. He nodded. She came within two yards of him and stopped, momentum swinging all her flesh toward him like a cresting wave . . . and resilience drawing it all back until the motions damped themselves out. He couldn't see her eyes in the fleshy folds of her face. The nose—tiny and surrounded by flesh—was her last identifiable feature but for her hair, which was glossier and more luxurious than before.

"The Breed girl. I heard about her. Lirg's daughter."

"How did you hear?"

"Hear many things," Lamia said. "Even when I'm . . . not quite up to my usual. Why didn't you cross?"

"She didn't get me all the way. I mean, she did, but only for a moment. Then I was drawn back."

"The Guardian? Meet her?"

He nodded.

"And you escaped."

Nodded again, only once, to signify just barely.

"Your little Breed girl sacrificed herself for you."

"What?" Though he knew.

"She wasn't even half Sidhe, boy. She couldn't do all that and survive the consequences. Even so, her life wasn't enough. You're still with us." This seemed to amuse her, and a little tremor passed through her, accompanied by a deep muffled chuckle. "Do you know what happened while you were gone?"

"How long was I gone?"

"Days, I suspect. Do you know?"

He shook his head. Her smell was dust and roses and acrid, sweating flesh.

"Your little rebel friends decided to defy Alyons. The Wickmaster has never been even-tempered." Again the deep-buried humor. "There's nothing I can do. Not now. They could have picked a better time. Now Alyons has what he's always wanted—a chance at the humans. To level them, make them pay for intruding."

"What's he doing?" Michael asked, his throat almost closing off the question.

Lamia peered down at her shed skin. "The guardian. She's my sister, boy. We were Clarkham's wives. Lovers, actually. He brought us here. There were fine times then. Dances, all the people rallying around the new mage. The Isomage, he called himself then—equal to the Serpent Mage. Come to bring everybody out of the shadow of the Realm, into the light of his rule. Oh, he didn't hate the Sidhe. He didn't hurt them, not really. He could work magic with music, with what the Sidhe taught us long ago. He was very proud. Soon, he claimed he was the mage reincarnate—born again to avenge what the Sidhe had done to the original human race. His arrogance became too great for the Sidhe to bear. The Black Order sent their armies against us. That was the war... the war that made the Blasted Plain." For a long moment she was silent, the folds of her face working. "He was not the mage. He could do magic, but he couldn't win with it. He could only lose a little and call it a draw. He fled. He gave us up, my sister and me. The Sidhe made their Pact with him but he gave us up. He claimed he had buried powerful magic here, fatal to any Sidhe who transgressed the Pact. He'd fought well enough that the Sidhe had to believe him. So he bargained. He set aside the Pact Lands and put all his people—he thought of them as his own—right here. The Sidhe shrunk the boundaries by half, to let the Blasted Plain act as a barrier. Keep their females from human temptation. Keep themselves pure."

"Are they fighting in Euterpe?" Michael asked.

"What would you do if you knew? Go and save them all? They're fools. They only get what they deserve. Though I'd fight the Sidhe myself if I could. In a week, I'd be able to. If your rebels had waited a week for their foolishness. . . . But now I'm in my curse. I eat nothing and grow huge. I shed my skin like a snake and my flesh is fragile as unbaked clay. You, you could grab my arm and tear it off, if you wanted. Here's your chance." She held out her arm. Michael backed away. "But I'll toughen, as I always have before, and the power he left me, that'll come back. Then Alyons will pay, if he hasn't already."

"Please. What are they doing?"

"They made my sister into the guardian, to keep humans from using the Isomage's pathway. She still has a touch of humanity, maybe? She doesn't catch all who would cross. Not you . . . maybe she held back a bit, seeing what you are."

"Tell me!" he demanded, neck muscles cording, lower lip contorted.

"Scourging," she said. *"Scarbita.* Alyons is the *Scarbita Antros,* and there's nothing you can do."

Michael ran from the room, down the hall and stairs. The sky was on the thread's edge of night as he ran down the road, trying not to focus on the smudge of orange light against the night.

He was hardly breathing hard when he came within sight of Euterpe. Invoking *hyloka* had restored energy to his tissues and given his senses hallucinatory precision. The brick houses lay in heaps around a central bonfire. He saw mounted Sidhe driving people in lines and clusters ahead of them. Wicks flashed in the firelight. Overhead, the stars seemed to have turned away in fear. The ground glittered with excited pinprick lights.

He left the road and crossed a hill. Most of Euterpe was in ruins, some glowing as if electrified. For a long minute he stared at what seemed the ghost of the hotel, limned in glowing outline against the fountains of fire, everything else translucent.

As he watched, the outline evaporated and the hotel was gone.

Piano music drifted from across town. The courser's mounts reared back and they broke away from their captives to ride back through the flames. Not all of the resistance was broken.

Michael ran around the outskirts, stopping to listen for the music. It came from the last remaining stand of buildings—from the school. Sidhe on horseback darted up and over the flames as if maddened by the music.

The Wickmaster stood on a mound about a hundred yards outside the town, lost in thought. His golden horse waited patiently behind him. Michael tried to keep well back from the firelight, but the Sidhe turned and saw him. For a long moment their eyes held; then Alyons smiled, baring ghost-white teeth, and glided onto his horse.

Michael reversed his run and fled from Euterpe. He wasn't afraid; if fear was a chemical, it had long since been used up in his body. He acted purely as he had been trained. Now it was obvious that his education had been accompanied by a good many subliminal instructions. The Crane Women had tinkered with his aura of memory. He could visualize tactics, methods of escape he never would have thought of on his own.

There was one instruction which he couldn't quite bring to the fore; nevertheless, he acted on it. The Wickmaster's golden horse glided up behind at a leisurely pace, its master exulting. Here was his chance at the troublesome *antros,* with no one to hold him back.

Ahead, Michael saw the outline of giant teeth—a ring of stones, slightly darker than the night. He ran in that direction—into the jaws and to one side, backing up against a smooth round stone carved with spiral grooves. Alyons slowed just outside the ring. *"Hoy ac!"* he cried.

"Hello yourself, you cruel son of a bitch," Michael whispered.

"Antros! You need the Wickmaster's mercy. Come out and join your own kind. They aren't mistreated, only punished."

"Come in," Michael invited loudly enough for Alyons to hear if he strained; no louder. Alyons lifted his wick to the sky. The tip glowed dull red. His horse paced between the stones, weaving in and out. The Wickmaster chanted softly in Cascar.

He's worried, Michael thought.

"He enters the circle, he must come closer," said a voice behind Michael. He recognized Spart but he couldn't see her.

"Wickmaster!" he cried out. "What was your disgrace? Did you make your masters angry? Were you the lowest thing in the *Maln*, a traitor, or just something they could do without?"

"The *Maln*," Alyons replied coldly, just loudly enough for him to hear, "Still accepts me. I do my duty in the Pact Lands. I keep the human filth bottled up."

"They won't take you back," Michael taunted. "How did you insult Tarax?"

"Shy of the mark," Alyons said. Michael could feel his aura of memory being feather-touched. He blocked the probe.

"Antros!" Alyons' horse passed into the inner circle, but the Wickmaster was not astride. Michael backed up hard against the cold stone.

The point of the wick thrust up before his face and glowed bright. Alyons flowed into visibility in front of him and lowered the point to Michael's chest. The Sidhe's armor flashed and rippled like living skin. The maple-leaf insignia on his chest seemed to stand apart from the armor, floating with a vitality of its own and changing from moment to moment to oak, then laurel, then back to maple. Alyons pulled the wick back, preparatory to thrusting, singing in that weird way Michael had heard the Crane Women sing, as if searching for a tune and not finding it, only the tune was present all along. . . .

The dried grass behind the Sidhe flew straight up, swirling into the night. Around the inner circle of the stones, a spiral of dirt fountained upward, the wind of its passage lifting Alyon's hair. For an instant, the Sidhe poised with his wick and Michael again felt the nearness of death.

Then the Wickmaster vanished. Out of the ground, with the roar of a dozen freight-trains, rose a monstrous steel snake. It had been coiled beneath the grass, and like a spring it lashed out and gripped the Wickmaster in gleaming steel teeth. Clods of dirt struck Michael all over.

The snake lifted the Sidhe high into the air. Then, with the sound of strained metal snapping, it broke into sections. The sinuosities straightened and plunged into the dirt like stakes, forming a tripod. The snake's head shuddered at the top of the tripod, in the exact center of the circle of stones.

Alyons, held like a mouse, reached down to Michael with a trembling arm. Michael walked slowly around the tripod until he could see the Wickmaster clearly, then let up his memory block.

"The wood, the wood!" Alyons whispered. "Quickly! Call

the arborals . . ." His body twisted violently, jamming the teeth even deeper through his flesh. His bones ground against the metal loudly enough for Michael to hear and the tripod swayed.

Alyons died.

Michael had never seen anything like it. Muscles twitching, he looked up at the corpse, fascinated and sick at the pit of his stomach. Alyons had been trapped and executed and he had been part of it. He turned away from the tripod and the limp, bloody Wickmaster.

Spart faced him. Her hair blew back in the night breeze. "The coursers haven't finished," she said. "We must go."

"Who made this?" Michael asked, pointing at the trap.

"Clarkham, who calls himself Isomage."

"Why?"

"I do not know," Spart said. Her voice was harsh and scratchy and the wind made her shiver. "Perhaps it was his revenge for the imposition of the Pact."

"Did Alyons know it was here?"

"Obviously not," Spart said. She closed her eyes halfway. "No more questions." He followed her as she plodded through the grass. Euterpe's flames were dying. Snow fell again, and he noticed with curiousity that when it alighted on Spart, it did not melt, as if she no longer maintained her *hyloka*.

"I saw Lamia."

"So?" She continued walking without looking back.

"She can't do anything. She shed her skin."

Spart shivered. "Quiet," she said. Overhead was a rushing, wind-whining sound—one Michael had heard before. He looked up but saw nothing in the smoke-palled sky. Snow fell through the smoke as if conjured out of nothing.

Michael had no trouble keeping up with Spart this time; her pace was deliberate, less than brisk. "Use your training now," she told him. "The coursers are still out."

"Don't they know about Alyons?"

Spart didn't answer. He frowned at her back and shook his head. Even now, she had the ability to exasperate him.

They dodged between the smoldering ruins and piles of brick and within minutes approached the Yard. It, too, had been demolished. Michael peered over the remains of a thick wall. The pits were open to the night air.

In the least damaged section of town, they passed humans running, or standing in a daze; townsfolk with shackles around their ankles, staked to the ground; men and women huddled in corners, the smoke and diminishing flames adding to the glazed light of panic in their eyes. He didn't see anybody dead, or even seriously injured. Perhaps the Isomage's threat had restrained the Sidhe enough to spare the town from general massacre.

Spart clambered down stairs leading to a basement beneath a relatively intact two-story warehouse. She walked ahead of Michael in the dark, and he followed her by the sound of her footfalls, using his hands to guide him along one wall.

At the end of the corridor was a room lit by glass-chimneyed oil lamps. The floor was scattered with smashed wicker boxes and furniture. The brick walls seemed to have been sprayed with silvery glitter that sparkled in a way painful to the eyes.

In the middle of the room, shoulders slumped, Savarin sat amidst the litter. He barely glanced up as he heard them. His clothes and face were covered with the sparkling dust. He looked down at the floor, then, as if reminded of something, looked up again and fastened his dull gaze on Michael. "Traitor," he said. "You told them." His voice was flat and lifeless.

"I didn't tell anybody," Michael said but Savarin was obviously beyond argument. The teacher smiled in a sickly way, shook his head and resumed his examination of the floor. Spart pointed to the far corner of the basement room at a figure seated away from the glow of the oil lamps. It was Helena, her skin and clothes aglimmer. She sat with knees drawn up on a make-shift wicker piano bench. Before her, smashed into the corner, was the piano.

It had been gutted. Its painstakingly assembled inner works lay warped and twisted a few yards away.

He walked to her and reached out to touch her shoulder, but she pulled away on the bench, making it shake. "I know you didn't tell," she said hoarsely, turning her face away. She tightened her arms around her knees and pressed her chin against her wrists, rocking gently. "We didn't use the dust. They were here a little while ago. I was playing. It was my only chance to play. We used the piano, we played it. But we didn't use the . . . what you brought. Here it is." She handed him the bag. It was empty but for a few grains, the tie loose.

Spart grabbed the bag and pinched it angrily. She took Helena's hair in one hand and shook loose malevolent glitter. "They turned it, they wasted it." She chuffed in disgust and pulled him away from Helena. "They are not worth your time," she said.

Michael looked back at Helena, uncertain what he felt—sadness, perverse satisfaction at his betrayers laid low, horror and anger that people he cared for could be treated thus.

"Isn't there any more dust?" he asked.

"Not for us, not for them. If they try to cross now, the *sani* is turned. It will attract every monster on the plain." She shook her hand and wiped it vigorously, then pulled him up the stairs out of the basement. When he protested that he had to stay and help, her look asked plain as words, *What can you do?*

Nothing. He followed her.

On the streets, they ran for a short distance, then hid behind the intact corner of a collapsed building as coursers thundered by. "Where are we going?" Michael whispered.

"You are leaving," Spart said. "With or without the powder. It is your time. You go back with me to the mound, then you go on alone."

Only now did he remember the book left in the rafters of the hut. He had forgotten it in his haste to leave the Realm.

"Come!" Spart ran ahead. Instinctively, as the pounding of horses grew louder, he threw shadows. Spart became a crowd of people. The horses halted and reared behind them, screaming with excitement. Michael barely heard the curses of the riders.

They ran along the deserted and snow-covered road to Halftown. Mottled starlight fell between broken clouds. The smell of smoke subsided. Spart ran as fast as ever and he had difficulty keeping up.

Halftown lay empty and quiet before them. Spart slowed and walked him through the town, glancing at the empty buildings, then at Michael, as if to emphasize the solitude.

"Where are they?" Michael asked.

"They will serve Adonna, those who haven't escaped." That was the whining-wind sound he had heard—Meteorals sweeping in. The Crane Women's pact with the Meteorals had been abrogated. Now was certainly not the time to leave, not if he wished to retain any of his self-respect.

"I can't leave," he said. "I have to find Eleuth. I have to help."

"If you stay," Spart said, "the coursers will take you and imprison you with the others. You will be unable to do anything for them. If you escape, perhaps you can help . . . from outside." She was not telling the whole truth—though a few weeks before, he wouldn't have been able to detect her evasion. And it was Spart who had trained him to be sensitive.

"Besides, you cannot find Eleuth. She is dead."

The double confirmation—this time from an unimpeachable source—hit him very hard.

"She did her best," Spart said. "She did well, considering."

There were tears in his eyes as they approached the mound. The Crane Women's hut was intact, but his own had been knocked over. Biri's had been removed entirely. Michael searched in the rubble for the book and found it pinned between a shingle and a beam, undamaged. He pocketed it.

Nare and Coom stood behind him. He looked between them, nothing to say, virtually nothing to think.

"Soon, you are empty," Nare said.

"Ananna," Coom reiterated. "Ready. Now, never."

Spart grinned sympathetically. "One more thing, and then you go across the plain, find the Isomage. You must leave your hated parts behind."

"What?" he asked softly.

"If there is a part of yourself you don't like, you can be rid of it. You still have too many people inside of you. But that can be an advantage for a while. Sacrifice them. When you are in great danger, make one of the selves you don't like into a shadow. Send it forth. It will be real, solid. It will die for you."

"That is something you can do, we cannot," Nare said. Coom nodded agreement.

"Where do I go after I cross the plain?"

"So positive," Nare said, lifting her eyes.

"Follow the river to the sea. No matter how far you stray, always the river," Spart said.

"And what will happen to you three?"

Nare and Coom were gone already. He seemed to remember their leaving, but not clearly. Spart held her hand in front of his eyes. "In-speaking," she said. "Out-seeing. When you are ready, they are yours. The only outright gifts, man-child. Be grateful. We are never generous."

Then she was gone, too. He turned to see if they were running from the mound, but there was no sign of them in any direction. The mound was now empty.

Only dust and old sticks, a few stones, a broken mortar and some pieces of glass showed that their hut had ever existed.

Michael was on his own.

Chapter Twenty-Eight

The border between the Pact Lands and the Blasted Plain was less well-defined now. Michael suspected the circle of corruption was closing, and that soon the Pact Lands would not exist.

He stood on a ridge not far from the river, looking down at the indistinct smudge of red and gray and brown creeping across the frosted grass. Where the border crossed the half-frozen river, whirlpools of mud and bloody-looking water left pinkish foam on the ice and shore.

With no *sani*, with no weapon but his stick, he was indeed empty—empty-souled and empty-handed. For a moment, after leaving the Crane Women's mound, he had hated himself, but even that was gone now. He was a pair of eyes suspended over a vast mental desolation, swept clear of youthful obstructions—but swept clear of youthful ideals as well; of all things beautiful and inhibiting.

He slid down the ridge and across the ambiguous border.

What impressed him most, the deeper into the Blasted Plain he walked, was the silence. There was only the gentle thump of his feet in the dust, raising little puffs. The dust fell back into place, undrifted by the slightest breeze.

Winter had not touched here. The morning light was patchy and orange and vibrated occasionally as if all the air were a plucked string.

Michael walked quickly at first, then broke into a run. He passed brown pools and smoking crevices, skirted a lava pillar and picked up his pace. The pillar crawled with tiny elongated shadows.

After an hour, his way was blocked by a chasm. It was about ninety yards across, the rim separated like book-pages into razor-thin slices of translucent rock. Sand lay flat across the bottom. At regular intervals, conical depressions blemished the sand like the marks of giant bootspikes.

He walked along the edge for a while, hoping to find a way across. It was a drop of about twenty-five feet to the bottom and he didn't fancy a trek across the sand, but finally impatience and the chasm's seemingly endless length changed his mind. He experimentally kicked at the rock slices. With moderate impact, they crumpled into shards, and he was able to dig and kick an angled descent to the bottom.

The sand was gritty and hard-packed. He walked quickly and carefully, avoiding the depressions.

Thus far, he had seen none of the Blasted Plain's inhabitants—unless the worm-shadows of the lava pillar qualified. He was hoping his passage might be easy when a hole directly in front of him enlarged suddenly. He had to scramble to keep from slipping over the edge.

A bulbous protrusion was visible in the center of the pit. Michael backed away, but not far enough to avoid being sprayed with sand as the protrusion burst like a bubble. He wiped his eyes and heard a deep pleasant voice say, "You don't know what a *relief* it is to be free of Euterpe."

Ishmael, the Child who had prophesied in the Yard, climbed out of the pit. He stood before Michael, lank and naked. His long, pale dour face was free of wrinkles but still seemed ancient. He lifted one hand on its thickened wrist. "I've been away from my friends much too long." His thick-jointed finger flicked, and from depressions all around leaped more figures, not all of them as pleasantly shaped as Ishmael. "How may we help you, human?"

"Let me pass," Michael said. The emptiness inside helped keep his voice steady.

"All pass who will. Would you like guides? These areas can be hazardous, you know."

"No, thank you."

Ishmael sucked in his breath and coughed up a laugh, his eyes jerking wide. "We're the only kin you have here. Don't take all that propaganda they fed you seriously. We're not nearly as bad as our parents make us out to be."

"Perhaps not," Michael said. "But I'll manage on my own." He glanced at the others. There were seven or eight, all with some resemblance to humans, but for at least three the resemblance was passing at best. Their hairless arms hung to the ground or grew into their thighs; their faces were bad parodies. Ishmael approached Michael slowly, arms held out as if to show his good intentions.

"After all that time, we're in the mood to help," he said. His tone became more like a radio announcer's—slick, cultured, less and less believable.

So which part don't you like? Make ready.

"For so long, our talents have gone unappreciated," Ishmael said, full of self-pity. "Our emotions have been neglected."

"Stay back," Michael said.

"Back, back it is," Ishmael said, stopping. He knelt down and peered up at Michael from large yellow-green eyes. "Brother. Born of man and woman. Just like us."

"Quiet," Michael said.

Ishmael took a deep breath. "Where is your powder, traveler? Only a fool would cross the Blasted Plain without powder or a horse."

I believe, Michael thought, *that I would willingly cast off most of what I once was. Like my foolishness and blindness. Can I cast off those things?*

No answer. It was his own decision, his own risk.

Or my reckless defiance. If I had looked at things more closely, and opened my mind to how they might turn out, perhaps Eleuth would still be alive, and Helena—

No, there had been little or no fault in his behavior toward Helena. He couldn't make a shadow from unpleasant memories.

I wish to cast a shadow of the self that took advantage of Eleuth.

For a moment, two Michael Perrins stood in the same spot on the Blasted Plain. Ishmael opened and closed his long fingers. His mouth opened wider and wider until it seemed he had no jaw; his lips peeled back across flexible but very sharp teeth. His face became all mouth, all teeth, the eyes receding and the tongue darting out thin and silvery like a knife blade.

The skin of the Child's shoulders split and blood poured down his chest and arms. Rank brown nettles and thorny vines crawled from the split skin and twined around the mouth, then slid down the rest of the body, the thorns piercing and grabbing hold.

"Time to become real," Ishmael said, his tongue clacking.

The other Children went through their own transformations. Both Michaels remained calm.

What I did was not all that bad, said the Michael about to be sacrificed.

But you cannot be all of me, ever again, said the Michael about to escape. *You are past.*

He stepped aside. The Children moved with astonishing speed toward the shadow Michael, wrapping thorns, teeth, arms, claws and unnamed organs of destruction around him. The shadow screamed and Michael felt a sudden weakness as he ran across the chasm.

Ishmael lifted his mouth from the consuming and wailed, lumbering to his feet to follow, but Michael was already kicking aside the sheets of rock and climbing the opposite cliff. He sliced his hands and lay one shin open from knee to ankle, but made it over the top and stumbled on. The pain didn't slow him much, once he was back on the powdery flatness. The dust flew up into his wounds and his blood fell back into the dust, beading like tiny rubies.

He clutched the book in his pocket. The book was sanity, words from home, arranged by those who had never been where he was now, who had lived in relative normality and worked in quiet to craft their poems. His fingers rubbed the leather spine through the cloth, and he thought of who and what he had just left behind to perish.

Atonement. Survival.

Yet strangely, the emptiness was less profound now. He had lost; he had gained.

He could see the far border of the Blasted Plain, and beyond, the mist and the tall, snow-dusted tips of trees. The lava pillars had become sparser and smaller, more like vertical stacks of slag doughnuts than pillars.

At the border the mist swirled opaquely, like a spill of milk in water. From where he stood it looked tangible, more spider's web than fog. He was less than a hundred yards from the border, yet he slowed, then stopped.

Something long and sinuous stretched above the mist and peered down at him. It was the skull-snail, heads and blood-red eyes searching, body dragging the macabre shell behind. Michael tried to judge how slowly it moved and how much chance it had of catching him if he ran across the final stretch.

It emerged from the mist with an audible sucking sound, its body rippling peristaltic. The skull-shell lurched behind, dragging a smooth furrow in the dust.

What did it want? It wasn't moving so fast he couldn't outrun it; it didn't seem to be threatening, as ugly as it was. Its multitude of stalked eyes focused on him, outer edges arterial, inner circle venous. The body glistened like oil on a dirty puddle. Michael half-crouched and held his ground, back prickling at the thought that the Children might have followed him out of the chasm, or were burrowing beneath to pop up in front of him again.

The skull-snail halted, its momentum pushing it a yard or so farther in the dust. The shell changed colors, jagged bands of brown, black and red crossing its surface. The arm which issued from the "nose" cavity rose seven or eight feet higher and formed a very human mouth.

"Take me with you," the mouth said. The voice was female, unfamiliar to him. "Take me with you," it repeated more quietly. "I am not what I seem. I do not belong here."

"What are you?" Michael asked, glancing around quickly to see if he was being decoyed.

"I am what Adonna wills."

His memory was being tapped, but he didn't opaque the aura. The skull-snail's voice sounded like a Sidhe's and he was curious to know why.

"Who are you?"

"Tonn's wife," the skull-snail said. Tonn had been the Sidhe mage mentioned at the *Kaeli*. "Abandoned. Betrayed. Take me with you!"

Michael walked a wide circle around the creature. It made no further move toward him. "You are a mage. Take me where I might live again. And I will tell you where Kristine is."

"I'm sorry," Michael said. "I'm no mage. And I don't know who Kristine is."

He passed through the bitter-tasting mist and over the border. The skull-snail raised its eyes higher but fell silent as it watched him go where it could not. He walked two dozen yards into the wintered forest before he began to shudder uncontrollably. The creature's plea echoed in his head, the voice so lovely—the shape so grotesque, as if a curse had been laid on by a particularly creative and perverse sorceror.

He lay down on the icy grass in the snow-shadow of a majestic oak and cleansed his hands with rime, then rubbed his face and eyes.

It felt like years had passed since he last slept. He damped his body's pains, tried to ignore the signs of suppuration in his wounds and relaxed in the now-dripping grass until his eyes closed.

It was night when Michael awoke. A light breeze whispered through the tree leaves overhead, brushing their silhouettes over the clear gem-like stars. Flakes of snow wobbled down from the leaves, melting as they struck his clothing and skin. The fresh cold smell of frozen grass sap and crushed leaves met him as he rolled over on his side.

He had strayed north of the river when he had crossed the chasm. Now, to wash his wounds and clean off what remained of the dust from his passage, he stood on wobbly, prickly legs and tried to find the water again. The cut on his shin hurt the worst and his leg felt swollen. His hands were tender, but he wasn't using them nearly as much. For a moment, Michael felt light-headed, and then his feet splashed in the cold reedy shallows and he wriggled his way through the ice.

He sluiced his wounds thoroughly, then bound them with the reeds, spreading some of the astringent sap on them as the Crane Women had taught him, it seemed centuries ago. In a few minutes his light-headedness passed and he stood in the shallows and removed his clothes to wash more thoroughly.

As he sat on the bank, allowing the night breezes and his heightened body heat to dry him, he listened to the noises of the woods. He had no idea whether he was past the worst of it or not. He felt at peace, however. After so many months in the barren Pact Lands, and the difficulties of his training, he had time to be truly alone, to search for himself in the middle of all his experiences. What he found—now—didn't displease him, but he knew rough edges remained, even entire personalities still to be sacrificed.

And however peaceful it seemed here, he had not left the Realm.

He wished for some light so he could read the book, but the starlight, while bright, was inadequate, so he massaged his legs with his wrists and forearms and tried to connect with Death's Radio.

Failing that, he whistled for a few moments before he caught himself—looking around guiltily—and then began to make up a poem, speaking under his breath.

How often death is simply love.
Make way, make way for the new!

He couldn't go anywhere with that fragment, nor could he
force more lines. Being at peace, it seemed, was ill-conducive
to poetry—at least for the time being.

And what in hell did he mean, anyway? Eleuth had killed
herself for love—he had killed a part of himself, a kind of
counter-sacrifice. . . .

The leaves rubbed against each other, tree-boughs swayed,
snow fell, the grass hissed faintly and the river rumbled in its
bed, making the frozen reeds snap.

"Antros . . ."

Michael was instantly on his feet. His *hyloka* vanished and
the cold sucked up his warmth. A few yards away, standing
in the darkness with wick in hand, was the tall, unmistakable
shape of Alyons.

Chapter Twenty-Nine

Michael tried not to show his terror. He tried to restore his warmth and control the beating of his heart, which threatened to explode in his chest.

He had seen Alyons crucified by the steel snake. He had watched the life and blood drain from the Sidhe, and had heard him call for the Arborals....

And now Alyons stood before him, grinning as if nothing had happened. Michael knew the Sidhe were even less likely to return from the dead than humans, yet here was evidence to the contrary—solid-looking, terrifying.

Alyons advanced slowly and stared at a point over Michael's shoulder. "Why so frightened, human?"

There wasn't a thing Michael could say that wouldn't seem ridiculous.

"You thought you could be rid of me so easily? That you could save your people from their own stupidity?"

Michael kept still. His *hyloka* flickered back, but he shivered from fear anyway and the returning heat didn't seem to help. "I didn't—"

"Yes, man-child? Stupid, weak man-child."

"I didn't kill you," Michael said.

"No matter."

"I didn't ... enjoy seeing you die."

The Sidhe shrugged. They faced each other in silence for a long minute. The Wickmaster's coat flapped in the gentle night breeze; his red hair looked black in the starlight. His eyes were distantly reflective, like mirrors seen from miles away. Finally, Michael backed off. Alyons didn't move.

"You *are* dead, aren't you?" Michael asked. He could feel nothing inside Alyons; there was no aura. Or . . . he hadn't yet learned how to use the boon.

"I am dead," Alyons confirmed. "Beyond hope even of the trees. And if you didn't kill me, then you led me to the circle, tempted me in. It's all the same."

"I didn't know."

"If you had known, I wouldn't have been trapped," Alyons said. "I would have read your knowing. Or do you think I was a complete fool?"

"Sidhe don't leave ghosts," Michael said. Evidence to the contrary . . .

"True."

"Then what are you?"

"I am grief, *Antros*. Your grief, my grief. I am emptiness, not even one left. My horse wanders and does not take a rider now. You have wronged me twice, man-child."

"I don't understand."

"You drew me to my death, yet you did not claim your prize. You disdained."

Michael was now several yards from Alyons, one foot behind the other, prepared to turn and flee.

Alyons gestured to the woods. A horse emerged from between the trees. It was wounded on its withers and rump, and its eyes were wild with recent danger.

"Kill a Sidhe, claim his horse. Disdain the horse, double the insult. You are very stupid, man-child."

"What do I do?"

Alyons pointed to the horse. "Take my *epon*. Do not waste all that I was. Surely, a Sidhe horse will be valuable to you . . ."

Indeed, it would, but Michael no more wanted Alyon's horse than he desired the Wickmaster's company. "I can't," he said. "I don't even know—"

"Tell it, 'I am your master, you are my soul.' It will know you then."

"Why do you want me to have it?"

"I have no wishes, no wants. It is the way things have been done. Only a human would not know instinctively . . . it is the way."

"You're a shadow," Michael said, revelation dawning.

"With no wishes, no wants . . . and no time limit, if the horse is wasted." He folded his arms as if prepared to patiently wait forever.

"You'll go away if I take the horse?"

Alyons nodded once. "I am not here now. It is only your ignorance that shapes me from darkness. I am nothing but grief and violation."

"Then I take the horse," Michael said. The shadow pointed his wick at Michael and the horse paced over to him, turning behind Michael to face the image of its former master.

"The grief remains," the shadow said, growing darker. "But the violation is ended. . . ." Then, with a harsh braying laugh, the image became as black as the distant trees and blurred into nothingness.

Michael convulsed violently, throwing aside his fear in a single paroxysm. The horse regarded him with large, puzzled gray eyes. He reached out tentatively to touch its muzzle.

"Gift horse," he said. "You must have crossed the Blasted Plain alone . . . or perhaps he, it, led you." Michael peered into the night where Alyons had stood, as if the shadow might still be there, awaiting its chance. A hundred thoughts plagued him. What if a Sidhe could impress his essence in an animal after death—what if the horse still obeyed the Wickmaster? It could throw him, kill him. . . .

Yet as Michael probed, there wasn't the slightest taint of the Wickmaster in the animal. And he could certainly use a horse in his journey.

He lay back in the snowless lee of the oak and regarded his undesired mount for an hour before going to sleep again.

The day was well along before he awakened. The horse kicked frost from the grass and ate breakfast. Michael was ravenous; *hyloka* had to get its energy from somewhere, and he suspected he wouldn't stay warm for long without substantial food.

"Where do we find something to eat, hm?" he asked the horse. It shook its mane and kept an eye on him as it ate. Michael stroked its flank softly, then approached its head and whispered slowly, carefully into its ear. "I don't know if you understand English, but I am your master. And I hope I have room . . . now . . . for you be be my soul." The horse nuzzled his palm and jerked its head back.

"Ready to go, eh?" Michael said. No sense trying to mount as the Sidhe did. He climbed on as best he could, gripped the mane and nudged the animal.

The horse tensed its muscles under him uncertainly and tossed its head. Then it broke into a trot. Michael laid himself low against its neck to keep trees branches from swiping at his face.

There was very little food in the wintered Realm. He survived off a scant supply of red berries gleaned from bushes and was glad for them, and for the crazy character of the Realm's seasons, that bushes should bear fruit in winter. With so little food, his *hyloka* became undependable, and he quickly learned how to concentrate what warmth was left and light fires with his index finger. It wasn't as neat a trick as the ones Biri had performed, but it made him suspect that his abilities strayed at least a short distance into the domain of magic. He warmed himself by the fires and melted snow for drinking. The horse survived well enough on frozen grass, but gladly drank some of the snowmelt, and stayed close at night when the fire burned and smoked.

After some days of that kind of fire-lighting, Michael noticed that the finger was losing its nail. He was soon able to peel back the skin and remove the nail completely. He thoughtfully tossed it in the middle of his most recent blaze and watched it blacken and shrivel. The consequences of certain kinds of discipline began to worry him from that moment.

Within a week, he traveled about two hundred miles—there was no way he could be sure of the distance, if distances were ever reliable in the Realm—staying near the icy river. He was hungry all the time and growing thinner. He longed for the porridge the Crane Women had fed him, so bland and so wonderfully filling. . . .

On the eighth night, huddled close to his fire with woods all around (and this was a *small* forest!), the horse standing nearby with its head lowered and eyes hooded, Michael thought about killing the animal and eating it. Part of him remembered Biri immediately after his ritual horse-eating; another part fondly remembered the taste of solid food. He tried the grass, but it was bitter and clearly not fit for humans. He tried bark, or rather chewed on it while searching for grubs, but the bark tasted like quinine mixed with lemon rind and grubs didn't exist in the Realm. He did manage to make a fair tea from the bark, using a queer scooped-out rock as a pot in the middle of the fire, and rolling a cup from the unstewed bark. He thought some of the trees might be laurel, because the leaves were shaped and smelled like the bay leaves his mother had used in cooking; others were obviously oaks, but lacking acorns (and he wasn't sure he could have prepared acorns for eating, anyway—did one do more than just steep them in hot water after crushing?). By far the majority of the trees were now huge conifers with needles thick as iceplant leaves.

He saw no other animals.

On the ninth day, the pines gave way to more oaks and laurels; the air grew warmer; the snow became patchy.

Within ten miles—about an hour on horseback—the seasons began to change. The trees had never lost their leaves and the grass had never browned off; when the Realm's erratic and premature spring appeared Michael found his first food and wept for joy.

There were fruit trees everywhere, standing unarrayed in wild orchards, bursting with fruit untouched by any but himself. Apples, pears, peach-like fruit with brown-striped skin, large cherry-like clusters that clearly tasted alcoholic. There was even a pulpy, salty fruit that grew on the laurel-like trees and satisfied his craving for meat.

He was relieved of his troublesome thoughts about Alyon's golden horse.

Michael stayed in the wild orchard for two days, even taking the risk of getting mildly drunk on the wine-tasting pulp of the cherry-fruit. The horse cropped grass contentedly nearby. As Michael lay with his back against a tree trunk, he thought of the *Kaeli* and wondered what the animals had been like that had carried the Sidhe between the stars. He closed his eyes and tried to imagine such a journey, made without fireball launchings or spaceships; simply riding on the backs of the original *epon*, stretched out across space like quicksilver or molten gold. . . .

He read a few poems from the book, savoring them, his mind warmed by the fruit, his stomach full. He was content as never before, even with the past horror and his own shame—perhaps because of it. He thought of himself as a comet head at the source of a vast tail of experiences, flowing out behind him, growing longer and richer. Gradually his reverie muddied and he slipped into a doze. The book tumbled from his fingers and lay in the grass, the wind turning the pages deftly, sighing when it found what it wanted.

An Arboral female stood at Michael's feet, regarding him with unblinking green eyes. She walked over to the horse and patted it affectionately, though Arborals had no use for *epon*. Then she looked up at the Meteoral who had luffed the pages in the book, and a face between the tree branches winked at her. She knelt down and applied a blue-green paste to Michael's forehead. The paste sizzled, releasing vapors which poured down the sides of his nose and into his mouth.

Both of the Sidhe melted into the woods.

Michael saw a palace of silk and gold, as airy and light as a vast tent, rising above a mountain of ice and granite. A huge cataract of melt-water poured from the caverns in the mountain's side. He was led by a shadowy guide from enclosure to enclosure through the palace, and found within a great king— an oriental *Khan*—bemoaning the fate of his lost fleet, destroyed by a demon wind far to the east. The Khan had dreams also; dreams of great plains of grass and high snow-capped mountains and trackless desert and wild horses stalked by sturdy bow-legged men with hard, flat determined faces and lank black hair . . . all of that in the Khan's past. Now he ruled the greatest empire of all time, stretching from the Eastern sea across the mountains and plains, south to the mountains of the snow devils, north to the tent-pole of the world.

The Khan's face changed, becoming that of a pale, gray-haired Caucasian, looking younger than his years, sitting on the Khan's throne. He was not of the royal line. The plains of grass faded, the empire vanished into far history, and the pale usurper regarded his palace with an expression of repressed rage and boredom, of impatient waiting. . . .

Waiting for Michael.

The paste had evaporated. The visions swirled and Michael opened his eyes slowly. He had never dreamed in the Realm, and he didn't believe what he had seen was actually a dream. It had a certain quality, a stamp, which indicated he had once again had a message from Death's Radio . . . this time, without the use of words.

After tying up a supply of fruit in his shirt, Michael reluctantly left the orchard and followed the tree-lined river, which now turned east, sometimes doubling back in a lazy loop or wrapping around mist-shrouded islands. As the horse walked patiently on, Michael stared across the river at the largest of the islands and fancied he saw battlements in rocky crags. He always stayed on the left bank; it was equally easy to fancy Riverines lurking in the water, ready to deliver him up to Adonna's forces if he was so indiscreet as to try to ford.

He ate sparingly of the fruit, which stayed at the peak of ripeness. Like all Sidhe food, little was sufficient.

In the dusk of his fourth day away from the orchard, the horse took an opportune gap in a wall of shrubs and followed a very old, almost overgrown trail up a gently sloping mountain. They spent the night near the crest, Michael sleeping in an open spot near a weathered cairn, the horse nearby, blinking sleeplessly in the dying firelight.

Michael awoke and saw a silvery band crossing the pre-dawn sky. He rubbed his eyes and looked up again. A mother-of-pearl ribbon of light stretched from horizon to horizon at an angle of about thirty degrees. It had moon-like mottlings, and in fact could have been a severely elongated moon, though it seemed about four times broader. As dawn came, the ribbon dissociated into blurred disks, which broke down further into an indistinct contrail and vanished.

After breakfast—a chunk of meaty fruit—he walked the horse up to the crest to get his bearings. They looked down the opposite side of the mountain into a long, broad valley. The horse snorted with eager recognition; the atmosphere above the valley was as golden as its skin, and the trees—thick as lumpy moss, from this vantage—seemed suspended in another season entirely, not spring but autumn. They made up a patch-work of browns, oranges and golds. Despite the warmth of the colors, the morning air filling the valley like liquid in a bowl was quite chill.

Michael looked for some time before finding the structure hidden far to one side of the valley. It was dark, angular and ornate, but he couldn't make out much beyond its general shape. It resembled a tall Oriental pagoda.

"Can you think of any reason we should go down there?" he asked the horse. The horse couldn't. "Nevertheless, we're going."

Caution had kept him from crossing the river, but he discarded caution now. The compulsion was strong—and had nothing to do with Death's Radio.

Chapter Thirty

The slope down to the valley was about ten degrees, never greater than twenty. On the mountainside, the green trees of the regional spring gradually gave way to autumnal colors until few traces of green remained. The flowers beneath the horse's hooves were transforming from blues, pinks and reds to a uniform golden yellow.

The deeper into the valley they traveled, the darker the sky overhead became, until they were bathed in rich shadowy gold, like the twilight in a smoky old oil painting.

Michael's eye caught a last gleam of blue in a patch of flowers a few yards off the trail. He stopped the horse and dismounted to inspect them.

Four tiny blue flowers, luminous and enchanting, defied the auric suffusion. He could hardly take his eyes off them. He bent down on one knee and cupped them in his hands, then leaned over to smell them. They had little scent, but their color alone was sufficient. He picked one and removed the book from his pocket. Opening at random, he pressed the blue flower between two pages, arranging its petals carefully.

With a sigh—half drowsy and half nostalgic for the colors left behind—he remounted and continued toward the pagoda near the opposite slopes.

A wider winding trail became visible between the trees. Michael guided the horse onto this path and they followed it to a clearing. In the middle of the clearing stood the building, black and shiny as obsidian, sitting on a foundation of glazed dark bricks which absorbed the gentle rolls of the clearing. Surrounding the foundation were bushes glistening with waxy yellow-green leaves and large yellow flowers. Around the bushes stretched a lawn of smooth straw-grass, somewhere in color between ripened wheat and bleached bone.

Michael lifted his eyes to the tower. The first impression of a pagoda-like structure was misleading, he saw now. The tower had seven levels and was taller than it was wide. It seemed to have been carved out of foamy black lava, with the exposed pockets in the rock serrating every edge evenly. The effect was that of lace doilies and wickedly sharp obsidian daggers.

Wisdom clearly demanded a rapid retreat. Yet the house or palace was the most striking piece of architecture Michael had seen in the Realm. He wondered whether the Sidhe had built it. They seemed so little interested in the material arts.

He dismounted and took the horse by the muzzle as he had seen Spart do, leading it toward the dark polished granite gate set in a high courtyard wall. The horse's hooves clopped over ochre-swirled tiles of yellow stone. The top of the courtyard wall was protected by sharp upright crystals of golden quartz. Michael looked around, listening, hoping for a faint breeze to relieve the moribund silence and stillness.

The gate had no knocker, but mounted in the wall to one side was a polished wooden dowel tied to a gold chain. The chain passed through two circular eyes mounted in the stone and vanished into a hole.

The horse whickered and nudged Michael's back. He patted its forehead. "Nervous?" he asked. Strangely, he wasn't, and that made him wonder if the place was enchanted. "You be nervous for me," he said. He was becoming more drowsy; the valley swam in the color of so many half-remembered dreams. Part of him felt right at home, protected by the half-light, captured in a pleasant reverie. . . .

He gripped the dowel and gave it a firm tug. "Hello? Anybody live here?"

A mirror mounted on a wooden frame swung out from the gatepost, swayed briefly and ratcheted downward until it jerked to a stop about three feet above Michael's head. It angled slightly toward him. He looked into it and was startled to see a tiny face peering right back. All he could clearly make out was an unruly tuft of black hair, two glistening eyes with tawny pupils and a physiognomy not precisely human, yet certainly not Sidhe.

The mirror was apparently connected with a series of other

mirrors that conveyed images into the building—and vice versa. The face appeared to speak, and in a tinny distant voice said something he couldn't make out.

"Pardon?"

"Hoy ac!" the face shouted, barely audible.

"Hoy," Michael said. "I need a place to stay the night." Oh, did he now? part of him asked.

"Antros?" the face asked, showing astonishment.

"Yes," Michael said. "I'm human. May I come in?"

The gate creaked, swayed and swung wide, scraping over an accumulation of pebbles and dust in the courtyard. It apparently hadn't been opened in years. Michael walked inside and drew the reluctant horse after him.

The courtyard was deserted. Black stone walls surrounded a well carved from onyx. A black marble crow perched on the rim, water pouring from a slit in its throat. The crow's beak lifted to the dark swirling brown sky and its stone eye regarded Michael with calm curiosity. At the opposite end of the courtyard was another gate, already open.

A small man stood in the gate. He wore a silky golden robe, its hem pooling around his feet. Michael automatically sought the man's aura of memory. It was unfamiliar and difficult to read, neither human nor Sidhe.

"Hello," Michael said.

The small man nodded. A wispy black beard hung to his chest, and his features were slightly oriental. His sallow skin was glossy like fine leather. He hid his arms in the sleeves of the golden robe.

"Sorry to bother you."

"No bother," the man said in perfect English, and without probing Michael's aura. "Not many visitors pass by, certainly no humans. Introduce yourself."

"I'm Michael. Michael Perrin."

"And I am Lin Piao Tai. What may I do for you?"

"Your valley . . ." Michael gestured beyond the gate, which swung slowly shut, groaning and vibrating. He guided the horse around the fountain, closer to the man. "It's very unusual. It seems to be in a season of its own."

"A perpetual season," said Lin Piao Tai. "You're traveling, and you need a place to rest. Although I daresay you haven't been bothered by any of the Sidhe, since for a circuit of hundreds of *li* they scorn these forests. All but the Arborals and Meteorals, and I daresay they haven't shown themselves."

"No," Michael admitted. "I haven't seen anybody until now."

"Just as well. Come in. Leave the horse here. My servants will see to it." Michael patted the horse and followed Lin Piao Tai through the second gate, into the house.

The gate swung behind Michael without any visible help. Just inside the gate, a second fountain was set into a nook. The walls of the nook and the smooth, slightly feminine cup of the fountain were made of pure jet, while the interior of the cup and the floor of the surrounding pool were formed of smooth gray porcelain. The pool itself was illuminated by pale golden candles set in glass cylinders around the rim. Goldfish gleamed in the rippling water, their scales reflecting radiantly in the walls when they swam close. Lin Piao Tai walked down a black corridor, motioning for him to follow.

"Come."

Michael came to the end of the corridor.

"Welcome to my home, Michael—if I may call you that."

Michael looked around the large room. The ceiling was at least twenty feet high, made of a warm yellow wood intricately carved with designs of birds and fish. The walls were covered with panels of black and rich brown framing gracefully rendered screens of mountains, forests, and flowing rivers, floor to ceiling, the panels serving as fronts of drawers, closets and recesses.

"You must be hungry." Lin Piao Tai pulled the train of his robe aside and with a bare brown foot, drew back a straw mat from the floor, revealing a pit with several pillows spread around the outside and a low table in the center. "My servants will bring food—human food for you, I assume, though no meats—and tea. Be seated, please." Michael descended into the pit and found welcome warmth under the table. A ceramic pot filled with coals kept the entire pit warm.

Lin Piao Tai joined him, arranging his robes to make a kind of sack in which he perched, legs crossed, like a pupa. "Have you traveled far?"

Michael saw no reason to hold anything back. "From the Blasted Plain," he said.

"I am not familiar with . . . ah! Yes! I remember. Your people are kept there now. They used to wander at will, you know."

Michael's attention was distracted by the figures entering the room. They wore black robes and stood no more than four feet high, slender, with stylized metallic gold faces suggesting neither male nor female. Their hands were jointed and supple.

Whether they were robots or something else, Michael couldn't
decide, and he felt it would be impolite to ask, or to probe Lin
Piao's aura.

The servants brought in trays with food and pots of hot tea
and set them without sound on the table, bowing and retreating.
Michael reached for a jellied cake and savored the rich sweet-
ness. "Delicious," he said. Lin Piao poured him tea. "They've
closed the Pact Lands down, I'm afraid," Michael said, isolated
from the memory. He felt so calm—had felt very much at ease
since entering the valley—and what, after all, was wrong with
that? Everything was so elegant and peaceful.

"I suspected that would happen eventually. You humans—
if you pardon my opinion—are rather troublesome. I've had
many dealings with humans in the past. But, on the other hand,
I've had dealings with the Sidhe, as well, and I must say I
prefer humans." He smiled at Michael. "You don't seem to
know what I am. You are aware I am not Sidhe . . . yet not
human, either. My kind is most rare now, all credit to the
Sidhe. Rare in my form, at least. Doubtless you've seen my
kin on Earth. How is Earth, by the way?"

Michael tried to think of one word that summed it all up,
and couldn't, so he boiled it down to three. "Desperate. Cruel.
Beautiful."

Lin Piao beamed as if with nostalgic pleasure. "Some things
never change," he said. "I am a Spryggla. My kind is as ancient
as the Sidhe or the first race of humans, but we allied with
neither during the wars. You know about the wars?"

"A little," Michael said.

"Eat hearty," Lin Piao said, passing covered bowls to him.
"How fortunate you could drop by. We have a thousand things
to talk about. I just know it. A thousand things."

Michael ate from bowls of steaming noodles in savory broth,
and spiced vegetables in eggshell-thin procelain cups. As he
ate he told Lin Piao what had happened to him in the Realm,
and whenever he excised something from the narrative, he
found himself slipping it back in a few minutes later. He was
wary enough, however, not to mention the book, which was
still in his pocket.

"Fascinating," the Spryggla said, shaking his head after
Michael had finished. "Now I assume you wish to know more
about me."

"Certainly," Michael said. That seemed polite, and he *was*
curious.

Lin Piao's voice changed timbre, increasing in pitch and becoming more sing-song in delivery. The overall effect was entrancing.

"Of the thirty races," he began, "the Spryggla were those naturally suited to mold the dirt, grind the stones, make the bricks and plaster and erect the buildings. We loved places in which to live, and we loved them at a time when Sidhe and humans were content to wander under the broad and roofless sky. We built the first walls, and made the lands within them our own. We erected the first houses and the first granaries, and then the first fortresses. At first, we were not appreciated. The others thought we were possessive and greedy, but that wasn't so. We were just preparing ourselves for the finest of our accomplishments, the cities.

"Soon others saw our worth, and the worth of our cities, and accepted both. They lived under our roofs and within our walls. The rain became a controlled blessing. It was our choice whether to go out in it, or not. The wind became less vexing. There were no animals on Earth at that time; they were created much later, some by the humans, who were excellent in the vital arts, others by the Urges . . . but I stray.

"We built magnificent cities, all dust now I'm afraid, buried beneath the oceans or crushed in the mouths of the hungry Earth. We were essential. Ah, those times were *para daizo*— paradise, that is, within walls . . . but troubled. Soon each kind of glowing light, each intelligence, grew intolerant of its fellows. Tempers became short, and in those times tempers could be formidable, because our powers were formidable. Factions developed in each race, fomenting dissent and urging separation. There was excitement and intrigue, and no one really suspected where it would all lead. We were powerful but innocent. Knowledgeable but naive."

Michael had eaten his fill and sat back against a cushion to listen. He felt a thrill of expectation. Here at last was the story, simply told, and who cared if it was biased or not, true or distorted?

"Gradually, individuals gathered others around them and became leaders. They called themselves mages. There were four principal mages, called Tonn, Daedal, Manus and Aum, and their power grew at the expense of all the others. They were too strong to really desire war with each other but the lesser mages brought on the conflict through their own ambitions. The war lasted for ages.

"It was not entirely a bad thing, that war. Nobody died... not forever. We were like young gods then and injuries of combat, while distressing, were remediable. But gradually we learned the desperate arts of tact, and lying, and deceit, of gamesmanship and honour. Then we learned distrust and our magic grew stronger. The war became earnest. Enemies found it necessary to either be polite or to attempt to destroy each other. There was no middle ground. All the perverse pleasures of combat became engrained—the pleasures of triumph over another, of defeat at the hands of a stronger, of tragedy and loss, contest and victory. These are strong discoveries, and run deep in our blood even now."

Michael nodded, his eyes half-closed. He was awake, but he didn't need to see Lin Piao to appreciate his story. "The other races—what did Tonn turn them into?"

"I am coming to that. Finally, it was discovered how to kill. To kill so that the dead would never return to the Earth. All had immortal souls then, but we were bound to the Earth with such desires that death was abhorrent. War became serious indeed. Hate was a thing to be breathed, lived, wallowed in.

"There were winners and there were losers. The losers were treated badly. When the humans under the mage Manus vanquished the Sidhe, they imposed the worst punishment yet—they stripped the Sidhe of their souls. And when the Sidhe regained the upper hand, strengthened by the desperation of complete extinction, the mage Tonn put an end to the war. The Sidhe did not have the means to steal our immortality, but they could put us in more humble packages. The Spryggla, followers of Daedal, had always been proud of the work they could do with their hands, so Tonn took their hands away from them and put them in a place where there was no need to build—the sea. They became whales and dolphins. Humans were turned into tiny shrews, to exhibit their true character. Others were turned into other beasts. Some had their souls divided among millions, even billions of smaller forms, like the Urges, who were all transformed into one of their own creations, the cockroach. Aum's people, the Cledar, were music-makers, and their art was stolen by the Sidhe, who called it their own. Then Aum and all his kind were turned into birds."

Michael's eyes had closed, but he listened carefully to every word.

"Of all the races, the Sidhe preserved only a few of the Spryggla, that we might build for them. They let us live in comfort, and in time we grew accustomed to our fate. We were given work. They took my ancestors off to the stars with them, and we built great things out there. They returned to the Earth eventually, and I was born."

"How old are you?" Michael asked.

"I don't know," Lin Piao said. "How much time has passed on Earth?"

Michael opened his eyes. "How should I know?"

"Perhaps I will describe something for you, and then you can decide. When I was last on Earth, the greatest human ruler of all time reigned." He spread his hands, his voice carrying a hint of sarcasm.

"Who was that?"

"He was a scion of Genghis Khan. His name was Kubla. From shore to shore of the great lands, he demonstrated the new power of the humans, rising again over the sad Sidhe."

"That was seven hundred years ago, I think," Michael said.

"Then I am three thousand and seven hundred years of age, by the time of Earth. And how old are you?"

"Sixteen," Michael said. He started to laugh and choke at once. Lin Piao Tai made a gesture of magnanimity.

"And yet here you are, traveling the Realm, free and independent. Marvelous. You seem tired, my friend, and evening is coming. Perhaps you should rest."

"So soon?"

"Time in the Realm still surprises you? My servants will make up a bedchamber."

"How did you come to the Realm? Why did you leave Earth?"

"Tomorrow," Lin Piao said. Michael followed as the Spryggla went to a wall and pulled back a panel, revealing another dark corridor. In a small, sparsely furnished room, a feather mattress rested on finely woven reed mats, while on a nearby table a tall candle flickered in a glass dish beside a plate of cold tea and crackers—"For the night, should it last longer than expected and you become hungry."

The accommodations were the most luxurious Michael had seen in the Realm. He lay on the mattress, pulled the blanket around his chin and was asleep in seconds.

> *Beware, beware, his—*
> *Shh! Hiss!*
> *On a dreamless plain, voyagers*

Voyage, their eyes shut tight; listen
To the dripping voices. Children
Grow, discard ashes, cinders.
Judas selves linger, ponder;
Judas others ponder, linger;
Rude as strange words in the not-dream
Ponder, linger, and always scheme...

Michael jerked awake, shivering. He felt in deep danger.
His body was wet with sweat; the mattress and blanket were
soaked. The candle had burned halfway and flickered with
his sudden breath, making the close gray walls dance like
gelatin.

He turned his head to the other side of the room and saw
one of the gold servants standing a few feet away, its head in
shadow. Michael reached out and lifted the candle. The servant's face rearranged itself in blocks like a clockwork puzzle
or toy. Suddenly all the pieces slid into place and the face
became a smoothly sculpted blank. It bowed to him, but remained where it stood, as if posted to guard.

Michael felt under the covers and found the book, still in
his pocket. He lay back and tried to remember what had jerked
him awake. Perhaps another brush with Death's Radio. The
contacts seemed to come more often now, but he seldom remembered them.

A bell chimed in the hallway outside the room. Lin Piao
Tai walked slowly past, carrying a gold and crystal lantern with
a leaf-shaped reflector. He winked and smiled at Michael, then
motioned for him to follow. "A fine morning," he said as
Michael left the bedchamber, buttoning up his shirt. "The finches
are singing in the gardens, the lilies are in bloom, breakfast
awaits."

They sat under a rose and golden dawn in the middle of an
immaculately groomed garden. Lin Piao had ordered a golden
lacquer table set on the slate flagstones to one side of the
meandering pathway, laid with dishes of fruit, cooked grains
and more spiced vegetables. Michael was ravenous and ate an
amount that surprised even himself. Lin Piao Tai picked at his
food, watching his guest with obvious delight.

"There is no finer satisfaction than catering to an appetite,
and no greater compliment than eliminating one," he said.
Michael agreed and wiped his mouth with a raw silk napkin.
"Today, I would enjoy having you tour my grounds. You should

see what a fine place I've made of my prison."

"Prison?"

Lin Piao's expression tilted slightly toward sadness, then brightened again, as if on cue. "Yes. I have been audacious in my time, and now I pay for it. The Sidhe do not forgive."

"What did you do to them?"

"I served. Shall we walk?" He led Michael through the gardens, pointing out the various tiers and banks of flowers, all, of course, of assorted golden and yellow hues. A fine mist gently blurred the gardens as they came to the end of the path, blocked by a tall black lava wall. "I was a faithful servant," Lin Piao continued. "In those days, the Sidhe had long since returned to the Earth. They had dissipated themselves between the stars, you know—you've heard most of this before? Good. It tires me to relate Sidhe history. They were not as vigorous as they had once been. They still used Spryggla, and we still did their bidding, though our numbers had diminished even from the few of times past."

He pulled his golden robes aside and sat on a smooth onyx bench. "There was a conflict. Two factions of the Sidhe— perhaps more—were disputing over how they should conduct themselves on Earth. The Realm had already been opened to Sidhe migration, you see, and many Sidhe had come here, rather than remain in the lands of the new human race. In their squabbles, the factions created various songs of power, hoping to outdo each other. One faction planned to give the humans a song of power. I am confused as to the motives behind this— or even which faction engaged in such foolishness—but I believe it was the Black Order, and that they wished the humans to be just strong enough to force all Sidhe into the Realm, where Tarax could control them in the name of Adonna. Praise O Creator Adonna!" He winked at Michael. "They've done their worst, but it doesn't hurt to follow the forms.

"I was highly regarded in those days, and so I was given the task of designing a palace for the Emperor Kubla, who would have it revealed in a dream. When Kubla Khan built the palace—and it was inevitable he would, given the strength of the dream and the beauty of my designs—in all its forms and measures it would embody an architectural song of power, making the Emperor the strongest human since the wars. I faithfully designed the palace, and others under my command prepared the dream . . . but a strange thing happened.

"The dream was transmitted improperly. Kubla was tantalized no end by his vision, but he could not remember it clearly enough to construct it properly. And when I was placed in his service on Earth, the workers were plagued with slips of hand and diseases of the eye. The Black Order was foiled. They blamed me. In their court—a most fearsome place, and may you never see it!—they tried me and found me guilty of bungling. For that, I am confined to this valley." He leaned forward, looking up into Michael's face. "Spryggla have magic too, you know. Magic over shapes of matter. We can be very powerful, though not as powerful as the Maln. They took away my magic, all of it except that pertaining to things yellow or golden. They imprisoned me, and I have done as best I could. Not done too badly, do you think?"

"Not badly at all," Michael said.

"I'm glad to hear it. You're the first company I've had in decades. Now and then, some of the Sidhe call on me, give me commissions. It was I who conferred with Christopher Wren, and earlier than that, with Leonardo and Michelangelo. . . . But perhaps I shouldn't be telling you these things."

"Why would the Sidhe want you to help them?"

"It all has to do with the factions, the songs of power. . . . No, there's certainly no need for you to suffer through all my past exploits, past failures. That's what they were, you know. Never quite as magnificent as first conceived, always interfered with in the final construction. I'm under a kind of curse." He became emphatic. "But not through any fault of my own! I am most unfortunate, caught between warring Sidhe, dragged this way and that. . . ."

"Who was your last guest?" Michael asked.

The Spryggla's face darkened. "Someone I'd rather blot from memory. Most unpleasant. Besides, I am honored by a far more welcome guest now, and I must make the most of his company before he leaves!"

They walked back to the black stone house. "My powers are strictly confined to the valley. While I am limited to yellow and gold. I can work moderately well with the neutrals, blacks and whites and combinations thereof. Reds and browns do not interfere with my abilities, but of course I prefer yellows. And I can never leave the valley. So, as you can see, I lavish my creativity here." He sighed. "I fear I change my surroundings frequently, otherwise I would end up in a tangle of baroque embellishment. I would go quite mad."

"May I look in on my horse?" Michael asked.

"Of course, of course! How fortunate that I designed quite wonderful stables just before you arrived. Your horse is there now, very comfortable, I trust."

One wing of the house opened to the stables, which were made of gleaming black wood with natural oak stalls. Michael followed Lin Piao along a row of empty stalls, trying to remember something he had forgotten, something important. . . .

With an effort, it came to him. Lin Piao swung wide the door to his horse's stall. Michael entered and patted the horse on the rump, checking it over to make sure it was being properly cared for. (Why would he suspect otherwise?)

"I have to leave soon," he said. Lin Piao nodded, his permanent smile somehow out of place. "I have a responsibility."

"Indeed."

"I have to find the Isomage. So I can help my people."

Lin Piao nodded. "An honorable journey."

"I appreciate your hospitality."

"Yours to command as long as you wish."

"Everything seems fine," Michael said, closing the stall door. "Thank you."

Lin Piao bowed. "If I am too zealous of your company, please inform me. I am used to being alone, and perhaps haven't retained all the social graces."

"I don't mind," Michael said. Indeed, he didn't. He was starting to wonder what it would be like to be on his own again, without these marvelous surroundings, and this wonderful source of information.

"At any rate, I have work to do," Lin Piao said. "If you will excuse me, make yourself at home. The servants will respond to your needs."

They separated and Michael returned to the garden to sit and appreciate the flowers, the peace. He was becoming used to the limited colors. He had always liked yellow—liked it more and more now—and felt quite at home.

With nightfall, they supped in the main chamber. Lin Piao told him of the vicissitudes of working with the human Kubla, of the Khan's quiet melancholies and towering rages. "He was so nostalgic for his people's beginnings, for the steppes. We had tailored the design of the palace to impress him all the more. It was like a Mongol tent, one that might be found in the highest of the seventeen heavens—much larger than the grubby yurts his forebears slept in. All its walls were made of silk. It was a beautiful thing . . . in conception. But when I saw it built on Earth . . . the finished *thing . . .*" He laid a bitter emphasis on *thing*. "I was dismayed. Heartsick. All my work, my conferences with the Sidhe . . . for naught. It was a travesty. It didn't float, it loomed. It was encrusted with Mongol ornament. It was gaudy. Yet I could not make it otherwise. I was only an advisor, an architect. I could not overrule the Khan. He was desperate to capture what he had seen in the dream. Politics, my dear Michael, is a plague found wherever groups of beings gather. I imagine even termites must deal with politics." He smiled. "But you grow sleepy."

Michael's eyes were so heavy he could hardly keep them open. Lin Piao led him to his chamber, and as he pulled the covers over himself, he heard the Spryggla say, "It's very simple, why there are no dreams here. It is to keep the ways clear. . . .

"You . . . or I. We are the ones."

Then, oblivion. And in the oblivion, almost immediately, Michael struggled. Death's Radio was on him strongly now. He was not dreaming; he was struggling to stay on the ground. There was a great city seen from high in the air; he was almost as high as he had been when Eleuth tried to return him to Earth, but all his seeing focused on the great city, and to one side of the city, black and spiked like the nasty seed-ball of some evil tree, the temple . . . The Irall. Michael recognized it immediately. The temple of Adonna, and he was being drawn toward it. . . .

He twisted under the blankets and came awake. He was groggy at first, and almost immediately forgot what had aroused him. There was a noise in the dark room. Michael's eyes seemed glued shut by the secretions of sleep. He took his fingers and pried them open, then rubbed them.

In dim golden candlelight, Lin Piao stood by the sleeping mat, clutching something. There was a look of exulting on his face, and exaltation.

"You have brought it to me," he said. "As it was ordained. To me. Across the worlds. The Song. My Song."

For a moment Michael didn't realize what the Spryggla was holding. It was the black book of poetry Waltiri had given him on Earth.

"That's mine," he said groggily.

"Yes, yes. You have kept it well. I thank you."

"My book," Michael reiterated, struggling to his feet. He reached out for it, but was restrained by two of the golden servants, who stepped from the shadows and held his arms in firm, warm-metal grips.

"You don't even know what it is," Lin Piao said contemptuously. The change in his tone was abrupt and it shattered whatever remained of Michael's lethargy. "Didn't I tell you, I worked to transmit the dream? And now I see they've tried again, but this time not in architecture . . . in poetry! And again, somebody interfered. I had heard rumors that your Isomage had part of the Song of Power. Now I know what he has been waiting for. For you, for this!"

He held up the open book so that Michael could see the page he was referring to. "A human poet is sent the Song in a dream. He remembers it, begins to write it down line for line . . . and is interrupted! Practical business, a person from Porlock, sent no doubt by the meddling opposing faction of the Sidhe. And when the poet returns to his paper, the dream is obliterated, only a part of it written down. But Clarkham must have the part never recorded on Earth! And now you have brought the segment not allowed in the Realm, the poem Coleridge recorded, forever a fragment." Lin Piao's eyes flashed as he swung the book up and began to read.

> "In Xanadu did Kubla Khan
> A stately pleasure dome decree
> Where Alph, the sacred river, ran
> Through caverns measureless to man
>   Down to a sunless sea."

He turned the page.

> "So twice five miles of fertile ground
> With walls and towers were girdled round—"

The Spryggla suddenly broke off with a choke and batted at the book with one hand as if a wasp alighted on it. He began to dance, holding the book out at arm's length and squealing like a wounded rabbit. "Traitor!" he cried. "Human!"

From between the pages fell the blue flower Michael had plucked at the edge of the golden valley. It landed on the floor, flat and lifeless but startlingly brilliant. Amid all the gold and yellow it stood out like a jewel.

Lin Piao danced away from it, still squealing. He dropped the book as if fearing it contained more. One of the servants released Michael's arm and darted for the flower but at its touch the blossom leaped and seemed to take a breath, expanding and contracting.

"No!" Lin Piao wailed. "Not this, not now!"

The servant tried again to pick up the flower, lifting it from the floor and sweeping it as high as it could reach, rushing for the door. But the flower left behind a trail of blue with every motion. The trail seemed to drip color like a swath of paint and then diffused and broadened, pulsing, alive. Lin Piao shrieked as if he were being murdered and followed the servant, staying well away from the trail of blue.

The second servant released Michael's arm and backed away. Its face rearranged itself in blocks. Michael quickly dressed and picked up the book. The trails of blue had faded. For a moment everything was quiet and seemed perfectly normal.

Then a smile confronted him in the doorway as he tried to leave. Merely a smile, nothing else; bright blue lips with electric blue teeth. It zipped away. Michael peered around the doorframe, looking from one end of the corridor to the other. Empty and quiet.

He was on his way to the stables, walking through the main chamber, when he saw brilliant veins of blue creeping under the walls, linking to form a cobalt carpet which spread over the floor. Liquid blueness dripped from all the closets and drawers and doorways, splashing across the floor, each drop trailing a thread. Michael could not avoid the invasion. It passed under his feet, tingling but painless, and crawled up the opposite wall. Faintly, from which direction he couldn't tell, he heard Lin Piao cursing.

Michael's numbness wore off rapidly. The Spryggla's magic was failing. He was frightened and pleasantly excited at the same time. The feeling of power, of overwhelming transformation, was like a tonic. He wanted to dance on the blue floor, slap his hands against the blue walls. "Free!" he shouted. "Free!"

He wasn't sure what he was free of. Had Lin Piao actually manipulated him, drugged him? He didn't know, but his thoughts were much clearer and his sense of purpose very strong.

He had to get out. He found the door leading to the outer hallway. The black stone seemed unaffected; even the fountain bowl and luminous pool were as they had been when he first entered. Now, however, he saw waves forming in the pool. The ground vibrated underfoot. As the vibration increased in frequency, the waves in the pool took on a pattern, a tesselation of geometric figures. The water rose up in bas-relief, like gelatin formed in a mold.

Michael watched the process, fascinated, until the tesselations suddenly broke down into blue smiles. The smiles lifted from the pool and flashed past him to do their work.

Michael exited to the courtyard and stood there, trying to remember his way to the stables, when Lin Piao came rushing through a side door. His golden robe was singed at the edges and his black hair had turned white. The Spryggla stopped and fixed Michael with a hate-filled stare.

"You did this! You invaded my home, my valley! Monster! Human! I can find a way to destroy you—"

"I mean you no harm," Michael said coldly. "If I can do anything to help—"

A servant came through the door Lin Piao had just used, swaying back and forth as if about to fall over. Its once-golden surface was now the color of tarnished gun-metal. Its robes were charred and tattered. They fell away in shreds. Lin Piao backed off in terror. "It's spreading! Stop it, stop it!"

"How?"

"I admit, you are the one, you are the intended. Now stop it, make it go away! I will stay here forever, I will be content—"

Blue cracks appeared in the black stone walls. The cracks joined and the stone crazed as if struck by a hammer. Indeed, the sounds coming from within the house suggested something pounding to get out.

"I don't know what to do," Michael said. "I'm not a magician."

"And I AM!" Lin Piao screamed. "How could this happen to me?" His eyes widened and the skin of his face paled almost to white as he saw a great chunk of stone fall from the wall. Above, the pagoda-like tower teetered, crumbling, all its serrated edges bathed in blue fire. Bolts of fire spread in fans to all corners of the house and walled grounds and crackled out to the valley.

Michael knew there was no place where he could flee fast enough. Not even throwing a shadow would help. The ground lifted under his feet and the paving stones separated, leaking a bright blue glow. He closed his eyes and opened them just as he was abruptly tossed high into the air. All around, fountains of electric blue rose to the sky, catching the warm dark ochre of night and transforming it into cold, star-specked black.

Michael's stomach lurched. He was without weight or substance, wrapped in eternal cold, eternal ice. Lightning played between his fingers and his hair stood on end. All the wool carpets he had ever scuffed across, all the cats he had ever rumpled, came back to haunt him.

He closed his eyes again and lay on the ground, shaken, breathless. The air smelled electric but the ground was still.

There was a long silence. He waited for more but the quiet held. Even before he opened his eyes he felt for the book. It was secure in its pocket.

He looked around. There was little amazement left in him, but all that remained was engaged by what he saw. The house had disappeared, and the gardens with it. In their place was a spreading field of blue flowers. Blue flowers blossomed all over the valley. The trees of the valley were losing their autumn foliage. The new leaves were rich emerald like the forests outside.

He felt for bruises. For once he had come through an experience in the Realm without cuts, scrapes or contusions.

Michael turned to see the other half of the valley. Right behind him, fist raised as if to strike, stood Lin Piao Tai. Michael drew back, then stopped. The Spryggla was motionless.

He was, in fact, solid blue.

He had been transformed into a statue of lapis lazuli, complete with his expression of horrified anger.

Twenty yards away, the Sidhe horse whinnied. They walked toward each other, and Michael greeted it with a pat on the nose and an incredulous smile. He had survived, and the horse had survived. They were none the worse for the experience.

But whatever forces had been unleashed to restore the unknown balances of the Realm had not ignored the horse's golden coat.

From tail to nose, Alyon's mount was now a dazzling shade of sky blue.

Chapter Thirty-One

Snow was falling on Lin Piao's prison-valley by the time Michael reached the crest of the hill and turned to follow the river. He stopped the horse and looked back through the snow veils. He couldn't make out the spot where the house had stood; the valley was covered with blue velvet, soon to be white. He was hardly surprised by the abrupt reversal of seasons; it was Adonna's whim and to question it, he thought with a grin, would not be following the forms.

He was still unwilling to give the Sidhe horse full rein, so he never rode it faster than a trot. Several more days were spent crossing through forest. Again, food became scarce. Michael hardly noticed. His hunger had lessened. What he really needed, as night followed sunset and yet again three times, was an indication he was heading in the right direction, doing the right thing, and not just moving from point to point on a map of foolish incidents.

At night he kindled a fire with his nailless finger and sat by the flames, reading from the book. His interactions with Death's Radio had stopped; his sleep was undisturbed. He read "Kubla Khan" several times, but he had acquired most of it by heart in junior high school. The words seemed at once silly and sublime, pellucid and obscure. Coleridge's preface to the poem was also in the book, reinforcing some of what Lin Piao had said, but Kubla's dream and the building of the palace were not mentioned.

If Lin Piao had been telling the truth, and Michael saw no reason to doubt the broad outlines, he was in possession of part of a Song of Power. If the Isomage had the second half—

the part Coleridge had been prevented from recording—then together, they might be able to break the dominance of the Sidhe and save the humans and Breeds.

Or did he misunderstand the process? How could a Song of Power be both architectural and poetic? Lin Piao had mentioned encoding; perhaps poem and pleasure dome, as originally broadcast by the Sidhe, could be abstracted into a principle, an aesthetic equivalent. . . .

At that point, his mind was lost in vagaries and he closed the book, lying back near the fire.

Proportion, after all, was important in both architecture and poetry.

"Go to sleep," he told himself wearily.

The next morning, at the edge of a broad savannah, with what looked like a mountain (and likely was not) in the hazy distance, Michael found a snare.

It had been tied to a sapling and fitted with a very sensitive rope-and-stake trigger. It hadn't captured anything yet. The horse sidestepped it with a nervous nicker. The snare had obviously been designed to catch a small animal; the sapling couldn't support anything large. The bait was forest roots placed near the trigger in a loop of rope. The roots were still quite fresh.

Michael looked around the bushes and thinning trees. No Sidhe would set a trap for a meat animal; what if it was a magician's snare, set to catch a specimen for some rite? He had seen bones around the Crane Women's mound and hut. But he suspected a human had set the snare. There was something about the snare, a humanness in the casual and elegant way it had been constructed.

He didn't know whether to be hopeful or wary.

He didn't have to wait long. The river broke through the last of the forest and made its half-frozen way across the savannah, straightening and flowing faster in a deeper bed. Michael tried to discern what the towering shape in the distance was, but couldn't. He was positive it wasn't just a mountain.

He was walking the horse on the sandy river bank, skirting patches of river ice and snow, when he felt an imposition. Nothing more than that; simply the awareness of a presence, aware of him.

He stopped and pretended to check the horse's hoof. The imposition grew stronger. He took a deep breath and felt for the aura of memory. He had never needed to probe a purely human aura; now, sensing one—a man—he found it quite easy to search.

He knew how far away the man was, but not the direction. Whoever had set the snare was following him at a distance of about a hundred feet. The frosty grass was barely two feet high. "Anything I can do for you?" he called out on impulse. The man was forty or forty-five Earth-years old. Not a native English-speaker, but he seemed to be able to speak English well enough. "I'm not a Sidhe, you know. I found your trap set in the woods."

Slowly, a heavy-set bearded man with short spiky gray hair rose from a low crouch in the grass, shaking his head and smiling through a broad moustache. "Good trick," he said. "You smell like a Sidhe. I didn't know what you were. *Bozhe moi*, a human, out here!"

The man was a Russian, Michael realized, and a hunter. He didn't come any closer. He stood in the grass, dressed in skins and furs with a cloth bag over his shoulder and a fur cap perched on one side of his head, ear-flaps untied.

"Well," the man said after a pause. "Not like a Sidhe, that is, you don't exactly smell like one. Not sure what you were. I followed you to the Spryggla's valley. You went in, came out. . . . Big changes. I followed you here."

"Then you can teach me a few things," Michael said. "I didn't even suspect you were around until I saw the snare."

"Not much of anybody here, you know." The hunter began walking toward him, eyes flashing with caution. "Sidhe don't come here much at all. This whole area, south to the mountains and east to the city, west to . . . the Isomage's hole. Euterpe. You from there?"

Michael nodded. "And you?"

"They never caught me," he said. "I was a dancer." He held out his arms and looked down at his solid frame. "I came here when I was fourteen. *Christos!*" He wiped his eyes with a gloved hand. "Memories. Just seeing you brings them back. Forty years or more. I don't know. Been here . . ." Now he wept openly, standing ten yards away and shaking, wiping his eyes and finally turning away in shame. "Just a boy," he sobbed. "You're not much older than I was, then."

Michael was embarrassed. "They didn't catch you?" he repeated, trying to calm the man.

"Too fast! Much too fast." He wiped his face with his sleeve and faced Michael again, coming a few steps closer. "I haven't talked with a human in . . . I've forgotten how long. I hunt, eat, sleep, go to the city and visit the Sidhe. . . . Your horse. That's what made me think you might be a Sidhe. Where did you get it?"

"From the Wickmaster of the Pact Lands."

"Alyons?" The hunter stepped back in awe. "How?"

"He's dead. He thought I was the one who killed him. I wasn't. But he—or rather, one of his shadows—gave me the horse."

"Alyons is dead?"

Michael nodded again. "Killed in a trap set by the Isomage."

"I was there during the Isomage's first battle, long ago," the hunter said, shaking his head. "I watched the pillar of magic, all the colors and monsters you'd ever hope to see. Some of it caught me, changed me, but I escaped. It aged me." He bit his bearded lower lip and looked up at the sky to blink back more tears. "I became the age I am now. I was just watching, but the magic caught me. I fled. Never stopped until I came to the city." He pointed to the hazy mountain-shape. "A Sidhe woman took me in, taught me. I was very slender back then. But this is all premature. We need names. I am . . . *Christos!* I've forgotten." He blinked. "I am . . . Nikolai! There."

"I'm Michael." Nikolai removed his glove and they shook hands.

"Your hands are very warm for not being warmly dressed," Nikolai marveled. "The Sidhe have taught you, I suspect?"

"Breeds," Michael said. "The Crane Women."

"Do I pry if I ask where you are going?"

Michael didn't feel ready to answer, so he smiled and shrugged.

"I understand. At any rate, you go to the city. The river passes the city, and you follow the river, correct? Do we continue together?" He stared imploringly at Michael, bushy eyebrows lifted. Michael agreed.

As they walked on, Nikolai revealed the contents of his bag. He had strips of dried meat, tied neatly in pale white bark. "From something like a rabbit, big eyes," he said. "Stupid for a Sidhe animal." There were pieces of roots used to bait the snare, and fruit much like the kinds Michael had eaten in the orchard. He also had nuts and a bag of acorn flour. He took out a wood-bole pipe. "To smoke, I have this leaf, dried. Quite tolerable. Never smoke around a Sidhe. They enrage with jealousy. They can't smoke, you know."

"You're tolerated in the city?"

"They welcome me, they do! The females, you'll see. Sidhe males don't live there much now. Very cold. Prigs, I say. The females will welcome you, too. But the horse . . . I don't know about the horse. You tell the truth, that Alyons passed it on?"

"Yes."

Nikolai shook his head dubiously. "We'll see. It's a wonderful place, the city. Built for the Faer by Spryggla, ages ago."

That night they camped on a snow-free stretch of sand on the inner bank of a bend in the river. Nikolai offered his pipe to Michael, who refused it politely. Nikolai took a deep puff and blew the smoke across the still night air, just as the stars settled overhead. "My story," he said, "then yours. Agreed?"

Michael nodded. Nikolai began his story and spun it on at great length, in much more detail than was necessary. Hours stretched on, but the hunter seemed tireless. Finally Michael lay back and rested his head on his arms. Nikolai offered him a small pillow filled with flexible leaves. "Go ahead," he said, "doze. Won't bother me." And indeed, it didn't.

The core of the story was that Nikolai Nikolaievich Kuprin had been brought to the United States from Leningrad to dance in the Denishawn school. He had been dancing since the age of seven—"Really dancing, not just tottering like when I was four"—but not necessarily by choice. Music had always held more attractions for him than dance. Along with the grueling dance practice schedule, he had tried to study piano, and finally had become proficient enough to play accompaniment for the other dancers. "It happened when I was playing Stravinksy," he said, voice softening. "I was at my family's *dacha* in California, in Pasadena, on leave of absence. Nervous exhaustion. They let me play the piano because it relaxed me. I was doing 'Rite of Spring' for the next season's presentations. . . ." He lifted his shoulders and sighed. "Fourteen, I was. I knew nothing of our world, let alone this! Alyons' coursers almost captured me, but I was naturally canny. They were distracted by the conflict. That was when I came near the battle and saw the finale."

He looked down at Michael, who was nearly asleep.

"A little black-haired boy, watching," he said, eyes welling with tears. "What they did, the monsters they unleashed. The hatred for my people. It's wondrous I can like any of the Sidhe now. Wondrous."

That was the last word Michael heard that night, or heard clearly; Nikolai continued long after he was asleep.

In the morning, Nikolai was still awake by the embers of the fire, staring out across the misty savannah with bright eyes and an alert expression. "One more thing I learned," he told Michael. "Humans do not have to sleep here. Perhaps you can stop sleeping now, too."

The season was changing yet again. Two days later, the enormous city of the Sidhe covered almost the entire northeastern horizon. The sun was warming, driving out the snow and freeing the river of ice, which crackled and snapped all night as it broke up, and sometimes boomed like cannon. Nikolai suggested they camp on a boulder in case the water rose and flooded the savannah.

Michael offered to let Nikolai ride the horse but he refused. His attitude—half reverence, half fear—worried Michael. There seemed to be something the Russian wasn't telling, perhaps out of politeness, perhaps assuming that Michael already knew.

In the afternoon, less than five miles from the city, they rested beneath a broad laurel-like tree that stood alone on the grassland. "The city is a hundred miles from side to side, roughly guessed," Nikolai said, tugging experimentally on a low-lying branch. The smell of grass and damp soil swirled around them, driven by puffing breezes. "It's surrounded by five walls, with four gates in each wall. Now those towers on the left . . ." He pointed a leaf and sighted along it with his left eye. "That's where the music masters work. Sidhe music. Never heard it, myself. My female acquaintances say it would blast a human brain to blissful ash. Interesting experience, perhaps. And over there, in the golden dome, are Sidhe factories. What they produce I've never been told. Nothing goes in, nothing comes out, but they make, nonetheless."

In the warming sun, the city glistened gold and white and silver, with blue-gray walls and pale gray bridges and roads surrounding a central mountain of Realm granite. Atop the granite a needle-slim spire rose several thousand feet above the savannah, studded with crystalline structures. "We can't see it from here, but on the other side, about ten miles beyond the city wall—"

"The Irall," Michael said. "Adonna's temple."

Nikolai stiffened. "You've been here before?"

"I've seen it . . . from above. In visions."

"What else have you seen?"

"A Sidhe who trained with me showed me the mountains where the Black Order raises initiates for the temple."

"Those mountains lie far to the north," Nikolai said. "Always in snow, wrapped in snow-clouds, black rock with age-old blue ice sheets."

"You sound like you've been there," Michael said.

"Near."

On the western slope of the city's mountain was a building shaped like a rhombus twisted into a two-turn spiral, about a mile high and three-quarters of a mile across at its base. Around the base were huge tree-trunk supports holding up floors without walls, open to the air. Higher, the trunks branched out and multiplied until they formed a solid thicket around the upper floors. With the trunks and branches providing vertical stability, the Spryggla builders had arranged for transparent panels of many different colors to cover the upper levels, a single color panel to every region separated by a branch. The effect was a miracle of variety and color. Several similar structures, of different size and height, grew up around the mountain.

Closer to them, on the southern slope, was a low flat building consisting of a mesa-like upper surface braced by thousands of the tree-trunk supports. Each trunk was hung with clusters of dwellings arranged in a pleasing haphazard fashion around the building's circumference. Atop the mesa—barely visible as a green fuzz from a distance—was a thick forest. Yet another building had floors arranged like a stack of cards given a shove and slanted. A third had floors tilted to intersect other floors at angles of thirty degrees or more, the whole resembling a crystal latticework.

Between the larger structures were profusions of street-level houses, following the contours of the foothills, covering the lower slopes of the mountain and spotting the heights between ambitious roadways.

Michael regretted he hadn't had more time to talk with Lin Piao. If the Spryggla could build cities like this, they were something very special; he had never seen anything like it and didn't expect he would again.

Nikolai clearly enjoyed Michael's fascination. "The city is always impressive," he said. "Look over there." He pointed with proprietary glee. "That building. They make it like a small mountain, the walls come out in ridges. Caves in the walls. Never been there. What kind of Sidhe lives there, do you think?"

Michael wouldn't hazard a guess. The horse walked along beside them, looking ahead with ears perked, as if it knew it would soon be in more familiar company and looked forward to it. As impressed as he was, Michael wasn't quite so enthusiastic. The few experiences he'd had with the Sidhe didn't lead him to relish the prospect of further contact. Nikolai tried to reassure him.

"Listen, in the country, it's like they're bumpkins. Rude, unsophisticated. This is the city. Females are very different. Not many males. They welcome me, welcome you. We'll get along fine."

"What about the horse?"

"He's your horse, is he not? Alyons willed him to you."

"I don't have any proof," Michael said. Nikolai had nothing to say to that.

The walls of the city had been assembled from huge blocks of stone, covered with a bluish ceramic glaze. Nikolai urged him up an incline onto a roadway paved with white stone slabs. The roadway pointed straight as an arrow to a broad, low mouth-like gate in the shadow of the outermost wall.

"We come in from the rear. This is the face the city turns to the grasslands. Not much traffic, a little-used gate."

The gate resembled the entrance to a huge dark cavern. The wall appeared to be hundreds of feet thick, yet it was only a hundred feet high, making it more of an elevated causeway around the city.

Nikolai stopped at the edge of the roadway and put down his bag. "Here is where I change clothes, stash my food, domesticate myself to the ways of the Sidhe. You are disgusted if your cat brings home a dead animal, no? The Sidhe would dislike my foodstuffs and choice of apparel." He pulled out a simple tunic and pair of pants, stuffed his other clothing into the bag, and hid it in the hollow trunk of a nearby tree.

There were no visible guards. Nikolai led Michael a little ways into the darkness, then stopped and sat down with his back against the glass-smooth inner surface. "We wait a few minutes."

In more like an hour, Nikolai peered off into the darkness and nodded to himself. "There," he said. "She comes."

Far off in the gloom, a single figure approached them.

Michael stood and made himself as presentable as possible while Nikolai looked on. "Who is this contact of yours?" Michael asked.

"An attendant to the Ban of Hours," Nikolai said enigmatically.

The Sidhe woman was taller than Michael by a foot, and Michael was somewhat taller than Nikolai. Her most striking feature was her face, which was marked with horizontal stripes of orange bordered by lines of charcoal gray. As she walked gracefully up to them, Nikolai gave her an exaggerated theatrical bow. She hardly looked at him, keeping her gaze on Michael. Her eyes were pale gray-blue, like the edges of clouds set one against another. Her lips were narrow, almost severe, in a typically long Sidhe face. She wore a purple-brown cloak edged with a satiny strip of flame red. Beneath the cloak, glimpsed briefly as she walked, was a cream-colored gown with appliqued floral patterns of pure white.

She wasn't what Michael would have called pretty, but she was extraordinarily exotic.

"Hello," she said. Michael felt his aura being delicately feathered, with nothing of Alyons' bluntness or the Crane Women's forthright probing. The sensation was pleasant.

"Sona rega Ban," Nikolai said. "I introduce my friend, Michael Perrin. He wanders as I—"

She ignored both of them now, looking at the horse. She smiled and turned back to Michael, then reached out and gripped his upper arm in warm, gentle fingers. "I am Ulath," she said. "Of the line of Wis. Your friend is most unusual, Nikolai. The Ban of Hours will enjoy him, don't you think?"

"I certainly hope so," Nikolai said.

"This is your horse?" Ulath asked Michael.

"Yes."

"I've never seen a blue horse, even in the Realm."

"There's a story behind that, *rega Ban,"* Nikolai said. "I'm sure he'll tell it again, when the time is proper."

"Come," Ulath said, "and be welcome to Inyas Trai."

"That." Nikolai said, "is the name of this city, and I advise you not to say it aloud, even when you are alone."

"A superstition, Nikolai," the Sidhe woman said, her voice deepening.

"My lady," Nikolai said, bowing again. "We are but poor—"

"None of your humility. It doesn't belong here."

"No, indeed," Nikolai said, straightening and smiling at Michael. "There is nothing humble about the city of the Sidhe."

The tunnel branched in two in the depths of the wall, one branch leading off into reddish darkness, the other toward a half-circle of daylight. To Michael's relief, they walked toward the daylight.

They emerged onto a narrow street which wound between walls of tan and white buildings. The street was profoundly quiet. Michael felt as if he were at the bottom of a deep river gorge. Crystalline circular mirrors set in the walls reflected daylight all around, throwing luminous patches onto the streets at intervals of a few yards. As the sun passed overhead, new networks of reflection shifted into being, and new patches appeared as the old faded.

Ulath walked a steady two paces ahead of Nikolai and Michael, her robes rustling richly and her thick dark red hair swaying back and forth, a seductive pendulum counterbalancing the roll of her hips.

Nikolai looked around with bright interest, smiling now and then at Michael and silently pointing out one or another feature of Inyas Trai. After a few minutes, having passed only three other Sidhe—all female, and all dressed in some variation of Ulath's garb—they arrived at a broad rugged stone laid into a high-walled, shadowy alcove. Two natural steps provided easy access to the stone's flat surface. Ulath climbed the steps and looked back at them. "Does he know of stepping stones?" she asked. Nikolai shrugged.

"Do you?"

"No," Michael said. Ulath then faced him fully and by the most marvelous kind of out-seeing Michael had experienced, filled his head with the most important particulars of Inyas Trai.

To get from place to place in the huge city, stepping stones simply and directly took one from here, to there. Each stone had seven correlates. A passenger had only to think of the desired correlate, and he was whisked away. Inyas Trai had no vehicle transportation. One either walked, rode a horse (of which there were few in the city) or used the stones.

They stepped. The alcove brightened and faded and they stood in the middle of another stone, at the edge of the roof of a very tall building. Wind whipped Michael's hair. They were nearly level with the peak of the mountain and the air was quite cool. A sweet, spicy odor met them, wafting from slender bamboo-like stalks on one side of the stone. Michael was the last to step down; he was still "seeing" and absorbing the information Ulath had provided.

The city was populated almost entirely by females. Males didn't appreciate urban life; centuries ago, they had retreated to the woods around the Irall, rarely if ever returning. Females ran the city; the Ban of Hours, Ulath's mistress, was the equivalent of a counselor in the city heirarchy.

Michael blinked. He had suddenly become aware that in out-seeing, Ulath had deftly avoided his aura's barriers and plucked out a substantial chunk of personal information. She smiled at him apologetically and walked on, robes and hair swinging.

"Where are we going?" he asked Nikolai in a whisper.

"To the house of the Ban of Hours," Nikolai said. "She keeps the Sidhe records of the city. I will introduce you to Emma, and then I will go on my pilgrimage."

"You didn't mention a pilgrimage."

"You're welcome to come," Nikolai said. "I go to the mountains to witness the Snow Faces. The season approaches."

Michael followed them through an orderly grove of small, thick-trunked trees. They kept to a brick pathway with low railings on each side. "Who is Emma?" he asked.

"You'll see," Nikolai said, his face expressing the tenderest sentiment. He touched his cheek with his fingers and shook his head. "You must promise . . ."

"Promise what?"

Nikolai shook his head violently. "Never mind," he said, whirling and pointing his finger. "Did you see?" Ulath walked on, ignoring them.

"See what?"

"One of the Ban's Arborals. They tend her library."

"The trees?"

Nikolai nodded gravely. "Come. We mustn't lag."

The house of the Ban of Hours was made of wood, magnificently carved and fitted. The roof was high and conical, eight-sided for the first half of its height, then broken into three progressively narrower sections with fewer sides, the highest having three. A tower at the apex was made of brass and carried a silver crescent moon. Two wings protruded from beneath the central structure's conical roof at a forty-five degree angle, flanking a triangular courtyard. Flowers grew in disorganized profusion in the courtyard; roses of all colors, including blue, scented the air and also seemed to warm it. Ulath glanced back at Michael.

"The Ban of Hours has lived here for ages," she said. "Since long before the city was built."

"They moved the house here," Nikolai said.

They took a path beside the flowers and entered the Ban's house through a tall, narrow black door at the apex of the triangle. The interior of the rotunda was surrounded by slabs of black marble veined with green. These blocked direct light from windows set in alcoves in the outer wall. Soft, whispering voices issued from behind the slabs. Michael felt dozens of feathery touches on his aura. He gently rebuffed them and the voices stilled. Nikolai stood by Ulath in the center of the room. Both seemed to be waiting.

"The Ban of Hours is very powerful," Nikolai said. "There is confusion in her presence, and time is not the same. Do not be afraid. She will not harm us."

After a few minutes, Ulath shuddered and bowed her head. A tall female dressed in white entered from an adjacent hallway and approached them across the smooth stone floor, seeming to glide more than walk. From high in the tower's interior came a buzzing. Michael turned away from the glare of the Ban's presence and looked up. The lines of the tower spun, filled with golden bees. His thoughts became smooth as he watched the insects. The Ban took his hand and led him behind a marble slab and up a spiral staircase to the second floor. At the end of a hall lined with brilliantly illuminated windows, they came to a wood-paneled room with a floor cut from the single bole of some huge tree. At the center of the floor's concentric graining was a wide, low basin of water. The basin was attended, but Michael could not see by whom or what. The Ban asked him to wash his hands, and when he did so, an incredible perfume filled the room.

"We are in the presence of a poet," she said, taking his wet hands and leading him into another adjacent room.

The walls of this room were draped with fine white linen and the floor was covered with woven reed matting. The Ban of Hours held her arms out to him, her hands glowing with warmth and magic. Michael went to her and she folded him to her breasts. "Yes, there has been pain," she said, "and error. It is the way of both our homes. But you know me, do you not?"

He did, and softly, he began to weep.

Chapter Thirty-Two

Hours later, fed and left alone in a comfortable sleeping chamber at the end of the southern wing, Michael removed his book from its pocket and hefted it in one hand, frowning.

He had met the Ban of Hours—but he did not remember what she looked like. Ulath he remembered clearly enough, and all the other details prior to the meeting. But he recalled neither the ban's appearance nor the sound of her voice. He had an impression of a tall Sidhe female dressed in white, but what sort of dress—long, flowing, pale or diaphonous?

No matter how hard he tried to recall, his memory was no more specific than that. Probing Nikolai's aura had proven fruitless; such probes were not very good at eliciting information from recent events, and Nikolai had evidently not been in on much of the meeting to begin with.

Michael's room held a brass bed with a quilted comforter, a bowl of water on a marble stand and several framed paintings of scenes from Earth. It took him some minutes to realize that the paintings were genuine Corots, with one Turner. So the Ban of Hours was a connoisseur of things Earthly—including, it seemed, himself.

He undressed and washed himself with water from the basin. Again, the rich, heady smell filled the room—

And like a catalyst, the smell opened his gates of memory sufficiently wide to release one segment.

The Ban raised her eyes and regarded Michael with a warm smile, dimples forming just beneath her prominent cheekbones. Her eyes were inclined slightly upward, almond-shaped and deep-set, sapphire blue flecked with silver. "You are determined to go to the Isomage, no matter what the cost?"

Michael nodded.

"No matter that it makes you the pawn of those you know nothing about?"

He nodded again, less certain. The Ban sighed and leaned forward across the inlaid vine patterns of a table top. Between them was a bowl of sliced prepared fruits.

The segment ended. He dried himself with a linen towel and crawled under the soft bedclothes. The sheets were cool at first, gradually warming against his bare skin.

Tomorrow, he thought. Nikolai would introduce him to Emma—whoever that was—and they would prepare for the trip.

The Ban had approved the trip. That much he also remembered. As for the horse—Ulath had said it was being well taken care of by Sidhe grooms. It was, she had hinted, in sore need of good currying and having its hooves trimmed.

"No Sidhe would ever have history in a book," Nikolai said at breakfast. "Written words bind. Long memory is best. The past stays alive then; it can change like any living thing."

"So the trees remember?"

Ulath, bringing a bowl of prepared fruits—

The Ban had told him about Emma Livry. . . . What about her, though?

—smiled at him and laid the bowl on the table. "The impressed ones remember," she said. "Sidhe such as myself, who have served the Ban. When we have outlived our usefulness in her service, we have ourselves impressed in the wood. It is pleasant, so I'm told, to be released from all the cares of the Realm, and to have only the past to guard, to cherish."

Sun lay bright in the crystal window of the refectory. All around, Sidhe females in a bewildering variety of clothing and skin colors ate decorously while lying on their stomachs, as Michael had heard the Romans once dined. Nikolai lay next to Michael, peeling a blue apple and nodding. "I have often wondered what the pure life of the mind would be like," he said. "Halls of memory, corridors of thought."

Ulath lay beside them and rolled on her side to look at Michael directly. Michael felt a flush of embarrassment. He dropped his piece of bread and reached to pick it up. Ulath stopped his hand with her own.

"The Ban is very impressed," she said. "She wonders about you. You come to us, trained like a Sidhe, riding a Sidhe horse.

No human has ever done these things in the Realm. The Ban is curious, as are we all." She pointed to the other females in the refectory.

"I'm most jealous," Nikolai said, eating a candied peach.

"You are recently from Earth," Ulath continued. "What is it like there?"

Michael glanced around the room and realized everyone was listening. "Lots of machines now," he said. That hardly seemed enough. "We've been to the moon."

"I was on the moon once," Ulath said. "Lovely gardens there."

"Pardon?" Michael wiped fruit juice from his hands on a white linen napkin. The walls of the Ban's room—

Emma Livry, yet another pawn—

"That doesn't sound like our moon," he said, recovering quickly. "It's dead, no air, no water."

"There are gardens for those who see," Ulath said.

"Ulath has been around," Nikolai confided to Michael. "She knew King Arthur personally."

Ulath regarded Nikolai with mild disapproval, then returned her attention to Michael. "None of us has been very successful at reading you," she said.

"Oh?" Michael thought he had been read very thoroughly by Ulath.

"Not where your motivations and plans are concerned. In Inyas Trai, it is polite to be open. Nikolai is very open."

"Nothing to hide," Nikolai said. "Unless some of the males are around."

"There are no males here now," Ulath said. "We are curious about Michael. . . ."

He didn't feel it was wise to open up completely. He told them he had come to the Realm by accident. He mentioned Arno Waltiri's music, skipping a great deal after that—touching only briefly on the Crane Women—and told them about Lin Piao Tai, without mentioning the book. Ulath listened intently, and when Michael was done, stroked his arm. Her touch was cool and electric, quite different from Eleuth's.

And from the touch of the Ban of Hours. "No matter that it makes you a pawn of those whose wishes you know nothing about?"

"Come on," Nikolai said somewhat gruffly, standing and rearranging his city clothes. "Let's go find Emma."

Away from the Ban's house, beyond the groves of trees

they came upon a small stone chateau. The chateau was sur- rounded by poplars and larches. On one side, a mirror-smooth lake diffused the morning sun with a glazed sheen. Swans crossed the lake like small carnival rides, their expanding wakes troubling the rafts of water lilies.

The heavy wooden door of the chateau was set into an archway carved with foot-high saints. Michael had never gone to church and didn't recognize them. Nikolai crossed himself before one, set at eye level, and murmured, "St. Peter." He took the heavy iron dragon's head knocker in hand and pounded the door twice. "She is quite charming," he said while they waited.

The door opened. A small thin face framed by lank black hair poked out and regarded them with sharp, narrow brown eyes. "Nikolai," the face croaked, and the door opened wide.

It was a woman—of sorts. She was barely four feet tall, thin as a stalk of grass, wearing a black shift with long sleeves. Her skeletal hands were gloved in white. The corners of her mouth seemed turned down by nature, and her high quizzical eyebrows carried a message: *I'm easily hurt, don't mess with me, I bite instinctively.*

"Is Emma available?" Nikolai asked.

"For you, always," the woman said. "But who's this?" She looked at Michael as though he were some garden slug brought in by the cat.

"An acquaintance," Nikolai said. "From Earth, Marie."

Marie's face softened ever so slightly. "Recently?"

Michael nodded.

"Come with me," she said. "She's upstairs, dancing."

They followed Marie up the stairs to the second floor. Down a short hallway with powder-blue walls, they found a half-open double door. Marie pushed through. "Emma," she sang out harshly, "we have visitors. Nikolai . . . and a friend."

The room was very like Lamia's dance studio on the upper level of the Isomage's house; smaller, however, and filled with sun from a broad skylight.

Standing to one side, dressed in a calf-length dancing outfit, was a girl not much older than Michael. Her black hair was drawn back and tied into a bun. Her long graceful neck and arms were as expressive as the swans in the lake outside. She descended from her point and rushed to hug Nikolai. *"Mon cher ami!"* she cried. "I am very, very glad to see you!"

She pulled back a step and twirled him around once, then turned to Michael.

"Pay no mind to him, he is a heartbreaker," Nikolai said. "I know."

"He is human!" Emma said, delighted. She held out her hand and Michael took it. It was flushed, warm, delicate as a flower. Slightly paler than the fingers, however, was the back of the hand, where the skin puckered faintly as if from a long-healed burn.

"From Earth," Marie husked. "Recently."

"Oh! *C'est merveilleux!*" She clapped her hands with child-like delight. "Nikolai, you found him and brought him here, so he could speak with us, tell us about home?"

"Partly," Nikolai said. He confided to Michael, "I would do anything to make Emma happy."

Marie brought in a small table and they pulled wooden chairs away from the wall and sat. "Marie," Emma said, "bring wine and some of those delightful cakes the Ban gave us."

She turned to Michael and smiled dazzlingly, then closed her eyes and positively wriggled with delight. "Where are you from?"

"California."

"Do I know . . . California? Yes, I do! In *les Etats Unis*. I have never been there. It is a desert, and very dry, no?"

Marie brought cakes, wine and glasses and poured and served all around. The cakes were sweet buckwheat. When Michael had satisfied Emma's curiosity about California, she asked him if he had ever been to France. "No," he said. Her face fell.

"Is it that you can tell me anything about France, how it is? What year is it!"

"1985, when I left," Michael said.

"Left? You left of your own will? Oh . . . I was taken. Not that I am not grateful." For a moment she looked as if she were about to cry, but she brightened immediately and touched his hand. Nikolai looked at the contact with undisguised jealousy. "So what was Paris like, France, when you left? So many questions!"

Michael looked to Nikolai for help. "When did . . . uh . . . Emma leave?"

"1863," the hunter replied darkly. "A bad year for her."

"Very bad," Emma said, but not as if she felt it. "So it has been . . . more than a hundred and twenty years. I have hardly known the time. They have been good to me, but sometimes I think I am their toy."

"They love you," Nikolai admonished, then raised his brows and pursed his lips. "As much as they can love, I suppose."

"I dance for them," Emma said. "Their attitude, it is so funny! They tell me Sidhe can dance with far more control, grace, even spontaneity, than can I, yet that is only to be expected. I dance, they say, with a special magic, because I have no magic! It is all physical, no sorcery, no illusion. Ah, but if I had stayed on Earth—"

"If you had stayed on Earth," Marie said, "you would be dead."

"But if *that* had not happened," Emma went on, undaunted, "Nikolai tells me I would have changed the shape of the dance! I mean, the way everyone thinks of dance, ballet."

"You are a legend," Nikolai said. "Michael knows nothing of dance, however. He is a poet. So the Ban tells us."

"Then I will show you dance," Emma said.

"Your practice is over today," Marie said. "You must not overdo."

"Marie is so silly sometimes," Emma said, giggling. "She forgets. Here, I cannot overdo! They protect me. Ulath, the Ban . . . I feel like a . . . how is it? A flower in a conservatory, kept under glass." She shook her head saucily. "I am so delicate, such a fine little toy. Nikolai doesn't think of me that way, though. He knows dancers are tough."

"You are the sister I never had," Nikolai said.

"I am older than he, aren't I?" Emma asked, searching the faces around the table. "He is from Earth after I, so I am older. Yet we look so different in time! This place, don't you agree, Michael, it is very strange.

"But no matter. If you wish, you will have me dance for you, perhaps when the Ban requests . . . or anytime."

Nikolai told her they had to leave soon, and she followed them to the door, looking quite distressed until she blew them a kiss, smiled, and ran back up the stairs. Marie stared at them forlornly and closed the door.

"How did she get here?" Michael asked. "Like you, like the others?"

"No. The Sidhe brought her here, perhaps the Ban or Ulath or another, even. She is Emma Livry; haven't you guessed?"

"I've heard the name. . . . The Ban . . ."

"Emma Livry, one of the finest dancers of her time—but

she never had a chance to be as accomplished as her promise. She was just twenty years of age, a beautiful girl. Her dress caught the flame of a gas jet. She was burned," he screwed up his face, "horribly. I am not sure exactly how it was done, but the Sidhe of Inyas Trai came to her, took her. They healed her and kept her here. She delighted them, so young, so beautiful." He inhaled deeply. "Sometimes even the Sidhe do something worthwhile."

Emma Livry. The rest of the meeting with the Ban was suddenly clear as could be, and her words:

"I venture to guess Nikolai is almost as ignorant of what really happened as you. This dispute over Songs of Power . . . over the human question . . . it was raged in all quarters for centuries."

"I know about the pleasure dome," Michael said.

"Good. Then you are not completely unlearned. That was a minor episode, man-child. There have been episodes far more cruel and senseless. Nikolai will no doubt inform you that Emma was a very promising young dancer who met with an unfortunate accident. It was not an accident.

"Early in her career, she was approached by David Clarkham. Oh, he had another name at that time—"

"He's that old?"

"Even older. Do you know who or what Clarkham is?"

"Only that he calls himself the Isomage."

She smiled again, conveying an entirely different meaning. "He approached her with plans for a major ballet in which she would have the starring role. She would dance a quite revolutionary solo. And in that solo, Clarkham would incorporate yet another form of the Song of Power. Not as architecture, not as poetry, but as dance. He knew that the Maln had gone to great lengths to discourage the transmission of a Song of Power to the humans, when they realized what humans would be able to do with it—not just drive the remaining Sidhe from Earth, but re-unite the Realm and Earth. First the Maln sabotaged their own early schemes by sending a person from Porlock to Coleridge. When Clarkham came along with his plan to bring power to himself by realizing a Song, he knew he had to have a great human artist enact the design. Emma Livry was his first choice. The Maln discovered him, however, and before she could dance in his ballet, they . . . arranged her accident."

"Why didn't they just kill Clarkham?"

"He was much too strong."

"But humans aren't supposed to be capable of working strong magic!"

"Only now do you question Clarkham's character and abilities?"

Michael ignored the gently barbed inquiry. "What did they do to her?"

"She was wearing untreated tarlatan. She wished her costume to be pure white, without the dinge of flame retardants. She was waiting backstage. All the Maln had to do was increase the length of a gas jet when she fluffed her dress. She became a pillar of fire, like a butterfly caught in a candle. She ran across the stage, and the flames ate the wind. Poor butterfly. . . ." The Ban lowered her eyes. "For eight months she lingered in agony. She was so dedicated to the idea of art, such a pure individual, that she invited pantomimists to come look at her writhing, the better to understand the reality of pain."

Michael made a face and shook his head.

"You are disgusted?"

"That's very bizarre."

"Perhaps to someone with incomplete understanding. But a Sidhe understands. There is nothing but the Song, and all things are the Song. Finally, even the Maln relented, and we were allowed to take her away from the pain. We left a changeling in her place, to die for her, and we healed her, on the condition that she never leave Inyas Trai. She never has. We cherish her. Even Tarax has been known to visit, to watch her dance, and Tarax hates your kind with a bitter passion."

The Ban lifted her hands from the table and stood.

"Does that mean I'm in danger?"

She said nothing, merely gazed at him, through him, to more important problems beyond. "You are a pawn," she said. "In the midst of great forces involved in age-long struggle. You are better equipped than most, but you are still ignorant, and it is not my place to inform you." She looked at him tenderly. "Though you come to my bosom, and remember me in dreams, and know me for what I have been to your kind in ages past, I have my limitations, too. I cannot protect you beyond the dictates of the geas of Adonna."

Nikolai touched Michael on the shoulder. "No lollypoddling," he said. "You look disturbed. Something wrong?"

Michael shook his head. "No. Not yet."

Chapter Thirty-Three

The stepping stone where their pilgrimage would begin lay on the north side of the history grove. No one accompanied Michael and Nikolai as they walked through the grove. Nikolai wore heavy clothes to protect him against the upcoming cold; Michael's clothes were considerably lighter.

Arborals tending the trees stood in the shadows of their charges, male and female both green and naked. They watched but said nothing as the pair passed. "I rather like them," Nikolai said. "They do their work, bother no one, never complain and stay faithful to the Ban. I could live here among them and be quite happy."

"Why don't you just stay in the city?" Michael asked.

"Ah, that's another matter. The city is full of tension. Most of the time the males hide in their woods, or hunt in the hills around the Irall. Then there is peace here. But the males return for their *Kaeli,* and then the Ban must be vigilant to keep her humans and Breeds from being hunted out and taken away."

"But Tarax watched Emma Livry dance!"

"Tarax, friend, does not know about you and me. Emma he may tolerate, so long as his power is matched by the Ban's— but the Ban can do nothing to protect us if we are found."

"So Emma and Marie receive special treatment. . . . How did Marie come here?"

"She has always been here, tending Emma. I have never asked." Nikolai looked at Michael sternly. "Perhaps you shouldn't, either."

"Are you upset with me?" Michael asked. The stepping stone was visible through a thin stretch of saplings too young for the history groves.

Nikolai took a deep breath. "No. Envious, perhaps. Worried. You are . . . high profile. They seem to dote on you, as they have never doted on me."

"Yet the Ban won't protect me, any more than she'll protect you."

"I have never spoken with the Ban," Nikolai said. "Not that I recall. And you have. Those who attract the attention of the Sidhe face two possible fates. The first is imprisonment, perhaps degradation. Emma is imprisoned, but not degraded, at least not in any way we understand or that she will ever know. She dances; as she says, she is like a flower in a conservatory. I think she enjoys being the flower, being able to concentrate on dance. I would not enjoy that. The Sidhe tolerate me, enjoy me, but they are not attracted to me."

"What's the second possible fate?"

"I don't know," Nikolai said. "Perhaps what happened to Clarkham."

"Is he human?"

Nikolai lifted an eyebrow. "You seem to know more about him than I do."

"I don't know everything. He's been alive for a very long time, and he seems to know a lot about magic."

Nikolai sighed. "Well, for this journey at least, let us travel with light hearts. The Ban has approved, and there is little that will happen on a journey the Ban watches over."

"Nikolai, do you remember what the Ban looks like?"

"No." The stepping stone was deserted, merely a dark flat boulder resting on a white gravel circle. Clouds whisked overhead, shading the sun. Wind carried some of the flower-scent from the gardens around the Ban's house. "Nobody knows what she really looks like, except perhaps Ulath. It is her weapon against Tarax and the Maln."

Nikolai stood on the edge of the stone and reached for Michael's hand. He pulled gently and Michael accompanied him across the stone's surface. Suddenly, they were surrounded by intense cold.

Michael was almost instantly blinded by a dazzle of white. He covered his eyes with his hands and felt for the opposite edge of the stepping stone. Nikolai took him by the arm and guided him down and into a rock-walled wind-shelter. "Caught me by surprise," Michael said, rubbing his eyes and blinking.

"Much colder than when I was here last season," Nikolai said. The stepping stone perched on the edge of a broad shelf of rock, looking over high jagged peaks. Snow filled the valleys between the peaks, brilliant and white and as smooth as the surface of a pail of milk. Snowflakes swirled violently in the wind that howled around the stepping stone and made the walls of their shelter rattle and vibrate.

"How far do we go from here?" Michael asked, hoping to brace his *hyloka* for the ordeal.

"A mile or so. We wait for the others. Never travel alone, especially with weather like this. Adonna must have a bad toothache today." He grinned and brushed a seat clear for them on a bench-shaped boulder. The interior of the shelter was dark and powdered with drifted snow. "Will you be warm enough? Ulath seemed to think you wouldn't have any trouble. The Sidhe can come here naked if they wish. Perhaps you could, too?"

His *hyloka* was finally taking hold. "I'll be fine," he said. He cut back his temperature when he felt his pants become warm. This was hardly the place to repeat the incident at Helena's apartment.

Nikolai clasped his gloved hands and stared down at the rugged black stone floor. He sniffed and glanced across at Michael. "What are you most afraid of?" he asked.

Michael shrugged. "All sorts of things. Why?"

Nikolai looked out into the snow. "For talk."

"What about you? What are you afraid of?"

"I will admit I am afraid of dying here. If I die here, I become nothing. I never go back to Earth. So I am afraid of not being good enough to stay alive. I know I'm afraid, and I live with it. But you . . . do you know what you're afraid of?"

Michael thought of the Ban's comforting, warm arms. "There are lots of things that frighten me, like I said."

"What in particular?"

"I'm thinking. Don't rush me. Okay." He looked up at the rock ceiling. "I know. I'm afraid of being normal."

Nikolai grinned broadly. "Thank God. I was worried perhaps you didn't know. Then you would be dangerous. What are you going to do with your fear?"

"Avoid being normal."

"And if you succeed?"

Michael laughed and felt the cold in his stomach dissipate. "Then I'm going to be sorry I have such a hard time getting along with people. With the Sidhe, with women, my friends . . . whomever."

Nikolai stood and peered around the edge of the shelter. "They're coming. Be prepared. Almost anybody can show up here."

"What are the snow faces?"

"A mystery," Nikolai said, sitting again. "In a place where everything is a mystery to us, we can see something that is mysterious even to the Sidhe. I like that. That's why I come here."

The first pilgrim to join them in the shelter was wraith-like, tall and deathly thin. Michael noticed bright red hair beneath a white hood, and the pale gray eyes of a pure Sidhe. But the look the pilgrim gave Michael and Nikolai had no menace in it, only deep exhaustion—of both body and mind. Michael probed his aura and saw nothing but darkness, as if even memory had guttered out. The Sidhe nodded cordially to Nikolai and sank to his knees on the rock floor.

Five others trooped in one by one: three more Sidhe, one human—heavily wrapped in white—and a Breed. The Breed was a young, strong-looking male, tall and with stiff pale blond hair, dressed much like Michael. At first, Michael couldn't tell if the human was man or woman, old or young. It wore two wooden cups over it eyes, with slits to see through—a precaution against snow-blindness. When Michael probed the human's aura, he pulled back as if burnt.

He had never touched such naked spiritual pain and ugliness. He was left with the impression of foul cancers and leprosy, creeping vermin and monstrous, all-consuming greed.

The five new pilgrims gathered in the lee of the barricade. The trio of Sidhe removed their outer garments and stood naked in the dark nook, hardly glancing at the others. The exhausted-looking one regarded Michael with deep-sunk eyes, then probed his aura gently. To be polite, Michael allowed him access to certain information—language, vague origins.

Nikolai had met them before, apparently, and introduced them to Michael. "This is Harka, Tik and Dour." Harka, the tired-looking one, nodded. Tik and Dour might have just entered maturity; they were younger and more robust and they lacked the calm jaded equanimity of the older Sidhe. "The one bundled up, that's Shahpur—last name I've forgotten—"

"Agajeenian," came a muffled voice through the wrappings. The voice was pleasant, a surprising contrast to what Michael had briefly touched within.

"And I don't believe we've met before," Nikolai said to the Breed.

"Bek," the Breed said, lifting his palm. "My first time. When are we off?"

"When the wind lets up," Shahpur said. His voice seemed more beautiful each time he spoke, very like a Sidhe's. Michael wondered if he had been mistaken in the first probe and tried again. The foulness was indescribable and for a moment he had to struggle to keep from throwing up. The Sidhe stayed away from Shahpur, who said nothing more.

Nikolai tried to keep up conversation. His efforts died. Soon they all stood or sat behind the barricade with only the whistling roar of the wind and the crack and rumble of distant avalanches.

Light was fading, making the shelter even darker. Suddenly the wind stopped its bitter assault, leaving only a hollow and fading echo, like the moan of a dying horse. The silence was profound, almost having its own sound as Michael's ears adjusted. Shahpur looked around the edge of the barricade and moved out onto the trail. Bek followed, then Harka, Tik and Dour. Nikolai and Michael left last.

"Sometimes I think this is a shameful thing for them," Nikolai said, nodding at the figures ahead. "I wonder why they even come. Harka grows worse every year. If he was human, I'd say he was dying, but Sidhe don't get physically sick."

"He's blank inside," Michael said. "Maybe they have another way of getting sick. What's wrong with Shahpur?"

"Ah." Nikolai shook his head. "He is cursed. Like me, he wanders the Realm, but the Sidhe caught him once. He escaped, but not before they had their fun with him." The heavily bundled figure turned stiffly around and regarded them for a moment. Nikolai pursed his lips and shut up.

The path followed the contours of a nearly vertical face of granite. Far below, pinnacles of rock spiked through roiling layers of cloud. Their feet crunched the snow gathered in wind-blown patches along the path and their breath cast almost tangible mists that hung in the air like markers of their passage.

Tik, Dour and Harka were the first to reach a narrowing of the ledge. They turned with their backs to the abyss and sidled along the face, at one point stepping over a yard-wide gap where the ledge had spalled away. Shahpur, Michael and Nikolai had a more difficult time spanning the gap, and Nikolai's foot slipped on the opposite side. Michael grabbed hold of his hand and drew him along to a wider portion, where they lay against the face and took several deep breaths.

"That was not there before," Nikolai said. "The path gets more dangerous every season."

The ledge widened to a broad, rounded lip, giving them at least the illusion of security. Around a blade of rock that had fallen long ago from some higher spalling, they saw the object of their journey. Shahpur followed the leading Sidhe and the Breed, and Nikolai pressed ahead of Michael, panting and cursing.

They all gathered on a broad rock stage before a deep cave-like hollow. "The mountain," Nikolai said. Many miles away, yet as clear as if it stood just yards before them, was Heba Mish. "No one knows how tall it is, not even the Sidhe."

Far below the rock stage and cave, clouds poured into a deep chasm, leaving behind wisps which slowly unwound and vanished. At the bottom of the chasm, a deep blue-green slope of ice accepted the falling cloud and scattered it into broad rivers of mist, which slid down worn, rounded grooves. Michael felt dizzy, peering over the rim of the stage. He lifted his gaze and followed a sheer flank of delicately poised snow on the mountain. The white mass reached three-quarters of the way to the peak before being sullied by outcrops of black rock.

"Now we wait," Nikolai said. As if at a signal, the three Sidhe and the Breed moved back into the cave, leaving the humans to listen to the silence.

"What are we waiting for?" Michael asked.

"The Snow Faces," Nikolai replied.

Night came and Michael lay comfortably enough on the chill cave floor. Nikolai slept restlessly beside him. Shahpur sat on his haunches, appearing to be awake. The Sidhe sat with legs crossed, lined up against the opposite wall of the cave.

Michael couldn't sleep. He kept trying to probe Harka. The wraith-like Sidhe's aura was virtually empty of any memory, as if he had been created just moments before, with no ancestry and no past. Michael wondered if certain Sidhe chose to wipe their lives away. There was a way it could be done with the discipline, boiling memory off with a kind of focused *hyloka*. . . .

Nikolai grumbled and opened his eyes. "Waiting is miserable," he said. "Especially here."

"How do you know the right time to come?"

"I have my contacts. Word gets passed along. Arborals whisper, or I listen to Amorphals in their deep cavern homes. Or another wanderer, like Bek or myself or Shahpur, hears about it and the pilgrims begin their journeys. Then we gather. I've always used the stepping stone from Inyas Trai. Others hike and climb. Some never say how they arrive; they just do. Not always, not every season . . . sometimes not for years.

"I've heard the sign first appears in a pool in the Irall. The pool is very deep, with ice at the bottom, and the Sidhe watchers know, when it turns black as night, that the season is coming. They pass the word in secret. . . . Adonna might not approve of Sidhe regarding a genuine mystery." He rearranged his legs and closed his eyes again. "In the morning, perhaps, when the wind rises again."

Michael lay in a state between sleep and waking, much like the state he had been in on his second night in the Realm, while perched on the rock waiting for the warmth of dawn.

Orange light slowly filled the cave, accompanied by a low, deep hissing. Michael stood, stretching his cramped legs. Nikolai did likewise, complaining bitterly.

The sun was rising beyond Heba Mish, reflecting from the westerward mountains and casting a dull purple backlight on the snow slope. Clouds in the east became bathed in flame, green and orange and lavender. Several shafts of light broke through the clouds and dashed themselves against the unseen side of Heba Mish, creating an aurora-like edge of yellow around the peak.

High above, the pearly ribbon broke down into its separate arcs and faded. Snow had fallen in the darkness and lay glittering outside the cave.

Nikolai and Michael walked onto the rock stage. The clouds pouring into the chasm had been depleted. Now there was just a hollow invisible rush of air. Cracks had formed in the ice and occasional deep bass rumbles and explosions rose to their ears as the cracks broadened and the ice calved.

"Here it comes," said Shahpur behind them. Far off, the hiss increased in volume until it was discernible as a combined wailing and roaring. Icy breezes slapped at them and rushed through the cave with a ghastly jug-blowing hoot. The Sidhe and the Breed came out onto the stage, their hair pinned back by the rising wind. The hooting became continuous.

With sudden violence, the wind drove them back and threatened to blow them from the stage. Michael felt himself flung

down, then lifted until his feet were inches above the rock. He
hung suspended for a seeming eternity as Nikolai and the others
clawed for purchase, lying spread-eagled on the stage. Then
the balance of pressures shifted and he fell back. The roar was
now a painful scream; wind rushed down the gap between the
mountains, pouring into the chasm and leaping over to begin
its climb up the white, snow-covered flank of Heba Mish.

The flank's delicate balance was upset. With barely heard
reports, it began to disintegrate. Mile-wide sheets sloughed off
and descended like ragged paper on a cushion of air. The sheets
broke up and the wind snatched at their fragments, powdering
them, grabbing and lofting great billows of snow.

Amoeboid, the billows obscured the side of the mountain,
then the rock outcrops, and finally shot above the peak.

It seemed like hours before the snow reached its zenith.
Again the wind stopped. For breathless minutes the billows
hung in a curtain above Heba Mish; then they descended.

"Now," Nikolai said.

Michael squinted, trying not to lose any detail. The curtain
broke up in residual pockets of unstable air. The pockets sculpted
the falling snow, slicing away this extremity and that, forcing
the cloud to push outward here and slide inward there. A shape
slowly emerged from the turmoil.

"Number one," Nikolai said. The features abruptly clarified.
It was a man's face, young-looking, lightly bearded. Michael
didn't recognize it. The face spread over Heba Mish, miles
wide, and then decayed. The clouds continued their descent
until more features formed. Very indistinct at first, then crystal
sharp, came the second face—a Spryggla, Michael was certain,
because of its resemblance to Lin Piao Tai. The next face was
so familiar he sucked in cold air and almost disrupted his
hyloka. Familiar—but who was it? Narrow nosed, strong and
youthful, sharply chiseled. . . .

"Two and three," Nikolai said. "Now it will fall, make one
more, and all will be finished."

Michael stared at the face, trying to recall where he had
seen it before. "I *know* him," he muttered. "I know who that
is!"

But his memory balked. The fourth face formed, that of a
stern and impressive Sidhe, eyes haunted. Michael didn't care.
He was so close, and the memory seemed so important he
wanted to strike himself, pull his hair—anything to force the
answer.

And it came.

The third face was not quite identifiable because of its youth—the man had been old when last they met.

It was Arno Waltiri, now falling into random drifts down the ravaged flank of Heba Mish and into the ice chasm miles below.

Chapter Thirty-Four

The Sidhe were the first to leave, walking back along the same path but climbing a few yards up to another ledge to avoid the stepping stone. They were not returning to Inyas Trai; they had other destinations which could be reached only by hiking out of the mountains. Shahpur remained on the stone stage, his covered face unreadable, his mind as horribly repellent as before. Only the Breed, Bek, elected to return with Nikolai and Michael to Inyas Trai. "I've never been there before," he said. "And I've run from Sidhe coursers long enough. The city sounds like a haven, for the time being at least."

Nikolai didn't encourage him, but the Breed had made up his mind. Where humans were welcome, surely Breeds would not be despised.

The ledge was even more treacherous after the passage of the winds. Snow had fallen from the sides of their mountain and compacted to slippery ice under their feet. Michael was very tired and glad to see the stepping stone.

He felt as if he had lived a dozen lifetimes, and left something unresolved in each one. He was a many-formed ghost caught between at least two realities, neither of them quite solid and convincing. Who had Arno Waltiri been, that his face should be carved in clouds of snow in the Realm of the Sidhe?

Perhaps Clarkham was not the goal of his travels after all, not the one to return him to Earth or help the humans in the Realm. But Waltiri was dead . . . or rather, Michael had been informed of his death. In the "real" existence of Earth, such a message—such information—was certain. Nobody in Michael's experience had ever been so cruel as to lie about the death of a friend, and he had no reason to suspect Golda.

Perhaps she hadn't known, either. Or perhaps he had deceived them all.

Perhaps he hadn't even been human.

Michael's thoughts were deeply mired as he stepped up on the stone. Nikolai and Bek followed, Bek with hands trembling, as afraid of the Sidhe as Michael would have been, once.

And should have been, now. In the instant between stones, he heard voices engaged in conversation. Whether the hearing had been arranged as warning, he was never to know. The voices discussed his status in Inyas Trai, his position with the Ban of Hours, the status of humans in the Realm—and mention was made of the Council of Eleu and of the Maln.

He emerged in warm sunlight. Neither Nikolai nor Bek stood beside him on the stone. Ulath and four male Sidhe in pearly gray waited on the gravel surrounding the stone. Ulath's expression was tense, grim. He could feel her aura pulsing angrily, sense her restrained power.

The male Sidhe were coursers from the Irall. He gathered that much before they became aware of his abilities and sealed their memories.

"I remind you," Ulath said, "that he is protected by the Ban of Hours."

The shortest courser stepped forward and held his hand out to help Michael down from the stone. Michael hesitated, then took the hand, realizing he would exhibit his fear otherwise. He didn't know what he would do next. He doubted he could successfully cast a shadow with so little preparation, and so many Sidhe on alert.

"I am Gwinat," said the Sidhe who had offered his hand, "I am your intercept. You are in possession of a horse of the Irall."

"It was given to me," Michael said.

"That is irrelevant. No one, especially a human, can be in possession of a horse from the stables of Adonna's temple."

"It was the horse of Alyons," Ulath said, glancing between Gwinat and Michael. "You are well aware of that."

"And for stealing that horse, Alyons was sent to the Blasted Plain. That was his punishment. We could not reclaim the horse—he put his imprint on it and it would have been of no use to the temple. Sidhe law does not recognize the return of stolen property, anyway—certainly not horses."

Ulath touched Michael on the cheek. "Alyons' shadow took

revenge on you," she said. "After Alyons' death, the horse had
to be returned to the Irall, or left to die."

"He gave it to me," Michael said hollowly. Then, suddenly
crafty, "And I've come to return it."

Gwinat smiled in appreciation, then shook his head. "You
were his enemy, and you killed him; no?"

"I didn't want to be his enemy. I didn't kill him."

"Come." The coursers drew up around him, cutting off any
hope of escape. Ulath withdrew her hand and backed away.
He probed her fleetingly and found regret but no deep sorrow.
"The Irall does not approve of the Ban's policy toward humans," Gwinat informed her.

"The Irall has no power over the Ban. She was appointed
by Adonna. What does Adonna say?"

Gwinat smiled snakishly and bowed his head. "We will
remove this one. That is the law."

Michael

What? Who is it?

Go with them

He looked at Ulath but she hadn't sent any messages, and
it hadn't felt like the Ban—or Death's Radio. Who, then?

He walked between the coursers, onto the stepping stone
which led to the streets below, then through the streets to
where their horses—and Alyons'—waited. A small number
of Sidhe females watched as the coursers allowed Michael to
mount the sky-blue horse, mounted their own, and rode with
him through the northern gates of Inyas Trai. Gwinat turned
to look back through the gates, still smiling.

"I don't see what even a human would find of value in
there," he said softly. "The Spryggla took their revenge on us
when they built it, just as Alyons took his revenge on you,
eh?"

Michael looked straight ahead, down a wide stone road that
passed straight as a shadow through an avenue of black stone
pillars, and beyond, to the gates of the temple of Adonna.

They were taking him to the Irall.

Chapter Thirty-Five

The Irall loomed, its black central tower smooth and round and featureless, tapering to an anonymous needle point. Around its base were irregular clusters of smaller towers, all inclined toward the center. The towers rose from a smooth dome of silky gray rock.

Gwinat and the coursers led Michael down the dark stone road, between pillars as shiny as polished metal yet as black as night, with gleams buried in their depths like eyes, enjoying his discomfort, his fear.

Nothing the Crane Women had taught him could possibly have prepared him for this.

The entrance was surprisingly small, just wide enough for three horses abreast, and perhaps two heads taller than the coursers riding on either side of Michael. The walls of the tunnel were cupped like the walls of a glacial cave, and the floor was littered with what looked like dried flowers. The air smelled sweet and dusty, not unpleasant, yet not quite pleasant. Suggestive, haunting, like the smell of

> old roses cupped in hands
> hidden far beneath the sun
> petals falling one by one
> scented, black in always-dark.

The message came through stronger than he had ever felt it before, just as the light from the tunnel's entrance was cut off by a bend in the path. The coursers pushed on, having no need for the light. Michael, trying to listen for the voice again, heard Gwinat dimly: "We're to take you to the Testament."

As Michael's eyes adjusted, he saw the tunnel had broadened and was filled with a faint greenish glow. Ahead, on walkways to either side, two long lines of figures shuffled in single file, eyes staring forward. They were Breeds, and each carried a green ceramic basin filled with black liquid. Michael tried to examine each face as they passed, looking for Lirg, but there were far too many and he wasn't sure he could remember what Lirg looked like anyway.

The tunnel opened onto an immense smoky chamber, its ceiling lost in darkness. The walls on either side were pocked with holes thirty to forty feet in diameter, their lower edges stained by a continuous rusty dripping. The horses splashed in an inches-deep layer of silty liquid rippling across the floor. Alyons' horse—or rather, Adonna's—twitched its ears and withers uneasily.

The next chamber was like the inside of a cartoon beehive, circular horizontal ribs stacked layer upon layer to form a dome. In the middle of the chamber was a depressed amphitheater with yard-high steps leading down to a rusty pool of water. All Michael could smell now was stale water.

The coursers escorted him around the amphitheater and led him down a side hallway. They passed a line of marching Sidhe, dressed only in gray kilts.

All of Adonna's attendants were male, apparently; the Irall was a male sanctuary.

"What is the Testament?" Michael asked.

Gwinat turned to him. "The trial chamber of Adonna's judges. The meeting place of the Maln." He did not need to probe Michael's aura to speak English.

"I thought that was in the mountains," Michael said. Gwinat smiled at the absurdity of trying to correct human misperceptions.

"I mean, that's where you train priests." Michael remained quiet for a few minutes, then said, "It's obvious I'm guilty, under your law. Why should you try me? Isn't the Maln all-powerful? Or is my ignorance some excuse?"

"Your guilt is an excuse," Gwinat said.

Michael had to think harder than he had ever thought before. There had to be some way out of the situation, some supreme effort or cleverness the Crane Women had instilled that he had temporarily forgotten.

Ahead, an electric blue glow suffused through the tunnel

like a fog. The horses took them through wreaths of bluish mist. The mist curled with sentient gestures, curious, cold.

The air cleared and Michael saw they were advancing across some tremendous open space, the interior of the dome itself; all the other chambers had been contained in the walls of the Irall. Long minutes passed before he sighted a stone table on the otherwise bare floor, and in tall stone seats surrounding the table, four Sidhe in black robes, facing inward.

The coursers led Michael in a circle around the table. The four Sidhe in black watched him closely. The floor crawled with dim patches of blue mist, shot through with transitory lines of green and black.

"Tra gahn," said one of the four, rising and pushing back the stone chair with a grating rumble. He looked into Michael's eyes and made a gesture to Gwinat. Gwinat took Michael's arm and pulled him from the horse, setting him on the ground with a wrenching pain in his shoulder.

As he turned, he saw that a stone amphitheater now surrounded the table. On the risers stood a crowd of plumed, dazzle-robed Sidhe males. They all stared at Michael and picked at him with a silent chorus of sharp-edged probes, seeking a way through his defenses.

"Do you recognize me?" asked the Sidhe standing at the table. Michael turned, and nodded. "Who am I?"

"You are Tarax."

"And you know your crime?"

Michael nodded again, knowing it was useless to argue.

Tarax removed his black robe, revealing a blood-red cloak. He then pulled back the cloak, unveiling not another layer of clothing, nor his body, but a forest of leaves, as if his head were supported not by flesh and blood but by a tree. Birds flew from the leaves high into the darkness, their wings beating steadily. The wingbeats faded.

Gwinat leaned over him. "Tarax says you are quite guilty," he said, "And that you are the one they want. Even had you been innocent, we would have the authority to take you from the Ban now. Adonna wants you."

Chapter Thirty-Six

They led him away from the table. The risers vanished as quickly as they had appeared, and the beautifully dressed Sidhe with them.

"We are going below," Gwinat said. Michael detected a hint of pity in the Sidhe's voice.

The center of the dome of the Irall was occupied by a pit perhaps fifty yards across at its rim. Concentric steps descended to a narrower opening of ten or twelve yards. Gwinat urged his horse down the steps, pushing Michael ahead. The coursers followed. A cold breeze blew up from the center. "Mount," Gwinat said, extending his hand. Michael took hold and was lifted onto Gwinat's horse, sitting before the Sidhe.

Michael's eyes widened as Gwinat booted the animal's flanks. It tossed its head, reared and kicked off into nothingness. The coursers leaped after.

He closed his eyes momentarily. His stomach twisted and his eyelids fluttered involuntarily, then opened. He blinked against the wind. They plunged down the hole into darkness. Gwinat kept a tight grip with one arm on Michael's waist. To each side, the coursers' beasts stretched out in silvery, elongated poses of leaping, tails twisting and waving behind, manes unfurled and gleaming like fire, lips drawn back from gnashing teeth. They seemed to pull at the air ahead with their teeth, legs straining for solid ground and finding none.

The darkness was broken only by hanging swatches of luminous green moss on the smooth-bored stone walls. Michael turned to look at Gwinat. The Sidhe's teeth were bared; he seemed to be grinning, grimacing and preparing to scream all at once.

Michael shielded his eyes with his hands. The dry wind stung. The stone walls gave way after several minutes to ice as clear and deep as flawless blue glass.

Far ahead—below—a tiny dot of dim rainbow-colored light appeared, then rushed toward them. Michael prepared for destruction. He felt the horse's muscles relax beneath him. He leaned close to its neck and clasped its mane with what must have been a painful grip, but the animal didn't protest. The walls of the hole vanished; they had fallen for at least a quarter of an hour and now glided over a maelstrom of cloudy, turbid light.

They were now beneath the bottom of the Realm, beyond all solidity, into darkness and terrifying creation. The horses navigated through an upside-down forest of ice stalactites with bases hundreds of yards thick. Below, small brilliant globes of indefinite size flitted over the maelstrom.

Michael silently prayed; not that he would have been heard above the rush of wind which filled the void, pasting his hair to his head and threatening to tear him from Gwinat's grip. "Lord," he mouthed, "I thank you for all I have lived, all I have seen. I am sorry I never acknowledged You, and I hope this is not all for nothing. . . . If I die now, I know I have done nothing worthwhile, and have brought pain and death—" He thought of Eleuth's spinning, fading shadow in the Between, and then of the Ban of Hours' accepting, forgiving arms. "I know I am nothing in the face of this, and that this is nothing before You. . . ." He was repudiating all his weak attempts at disbelief, and all of his young materialist philosophies. And he was doing it clumsily, with inelegant words and far too many repetitions of the word "nothing." He was half-crazy with fear, and yet he realized he was editing his own prayers, his own supplications. . . . He was worried about style in the face of extinction.

Gwinat tightened his hold as Michael began to tremble, then shake. With some surprise, the Sidhe realized that the boy was laughing. Tears blew back from the human's face and struck Gwinat's, streaming across his cheeks. For a moment, the Sidhe felt it might be best to simply drop the human into the maelstrom and be done with him. There was something weird and dangerous in this laughter and weeping, something he could not fathom. But he held on and the boy became calm after a time.

The horses pitched downward, away from the ice pillars. Michael was through praying. He was filled with a wordless, profound silence. Only one thought crossed his mind as they dropped away from the Realm's underside: This must have been the way the Sidhe crossed between the stars. Taking their own wind with them in the emptiness of space, traveling in hordes of millions, so many they would have seemed like a comet's tail from far away, glittering like pearly motes against the stacked razor's-edge blackness.

Ahead, drifting over the Maelstrom, was an oval object like an elongated bean. The bean-shape clarified into a cylinder about twice as long as it was wide. Spinning slowly on its long axis; it appeared to have been lathed from a solid piece of brass. The cylinder pointed down toward the maelstrom, irregular blotches of verdigris rolling along with its outer surface.

They approached the top. The flat expanse loomed like a wall, pierced by an irregular gaping entrance at its center. Michael wasn't able to get an impression of its size until the very last, just as they entered the hole.

The cylinder was perhaps a mile in diameter.

For a moment there was confusion. One of the coursers got ahead of Michael and Gwinat. His animal's hoof twitched a few feet from Michael's face, then swung back and caught Michael on the side of the head. He was knocked from Gwinat's arm and fell away, seeing nothing but warm, mellow red, dimming rapidly to deep brown. . . .

Michael's awareness returned in stages. First he smelled dust, acrid and irritating. He sneezed. Then came the pain. His forehead felt on fire. His eyes were open, but he couldn't see until the darkness irised and revealed another, even more profound black. He was in chains.

His wrists and ankles were shackled to a brass bar with a ring on each end. Chains extended from the rings to another bar a few yards away. Shackled to that bar was a skeleton, clothes and dried skin floating in tatters on its translucent yellow bones.

He was weightless. All around was the ineffable presence of something huge, moving. Within a feeble gray illumination Michael could see nothing but chains, bars and more bodies.

He was floating in a graveyard. He shut his eyes and probed outward to the limit of his range. Only uncertain murmurs came back to him. The impressions were strong enough to convince him that he was at the center of the brass cylinder, and that the cylinder was an outpost of the Maln—an extension of the Irall.

Michael probed again, and suddenly withdrew cringing as a voice blasted him. He threw up his shields, but they were not strong enough to mask the power, and the hatred.

"For your crimes, *antros*, for all the creatures that have died that you might eat their flesh; for all that have loved you and been betrayed, for all the so very human things you have done. Together we face a mystery, *antros*."

It was the voice of Tarax. The Sidhe emerged from the darkness, standing on a brass platform.

"Who are you?" Tarax asked, white hair floating in a nimbus around his head.

"I am a poet," Michael said, feeling none of the hesitance or awkwardness he would have once experienced on naming his occupation, his obsession.

"That means nothing to me. Who are you, that you should be protected, that I am prevented from killing you." Now even Adonna requests you. Frankly, I am puzzled. Who are you?"

"What does Adonna want?" Michael's throat was dry from inhaling the acrid dust.

"I do not know. I have served Adonna for a long, long age, and kept his secrets, and admired his creation—"

"His?"

"You are his now. I do not need to be discreet with you. In fact, I have only one function to perform, and since time means nothing to Adonna, I do not need to be hasty. I know these things about you: that you are an evil; that your worst crime is not the theft of a horse. It is being human... and helping the one who calls himself Isomage. You would bring a Song of Power to him, would you not?"

Michael felt the pressure of the book against his hip. Tarax's platform drew closer and the high priest of the Maln reached out with long fingers to touch the chains bonding him to the other bodies. "This is my only task, to release you and send you down the axis to the Mist. For all these," he gestured at the hundreds, thousands of corpses, "I have done the honors, and come back a short time later to find them here, returned by Adonna, who took from them what he needed. Most have been Sidhe. Few humans have earned such a demise."

Tarax's robe suddenly came to life. Gray stripes rose from the black fabric, writhing and forming knotwork designs. He touched Michael's chained feet and shoved him slowly, steadily away from the floating graveyard. "Michael Perrin," Tarax announced loudly. *"Antros."*

An exit opened in the opposite end of the cylinder. Michael looked ahead and saw the rainbow light of the maelstrom. Behind, the graveyard receded into a lattice of brown points, and then was enveloped in obscurity.

He closed his eyes and swallowed hard.

When he opened them again, he drifted through the hole and saw the flat cylinder wall rushing around him, rotating endlessly, brass and verdigris illuminated by the flickering light of what Tarax called the Mist.

There was activity below. Something rose toward him from the Mist. Darkness sparkled. A pseudopod of night, full of potential, extended and enveloped him. Forms flashed all around, passing in a parade of metamorphosis; faces, bodies, less pleasant shapes. Michael moaned and tried to stop seeing, but couldn't

There is no magic but what is allowed in our heads.

"No!" He recognized the tone, the intention.

Universes may co-exist in the same wave-train, operating as the harmonics of a complex of frequencies. Analogous to the groove in a phonograph record, which is easily distinguished into horns and strings by the practised ear—horns one universe, strings another. We may exist in all universes, but 'hear' only one because of our limitations, the valve of our desires, our practical, physical needs. All is vibration, with nothing vibrating across no distance whatsoever. All is music. A universe, a world, is just one long difficult song. The difference between worlds is the difference between songs. All Sidhe know this when they do magic.

Michael had been struggling, but now he was limp, horrified, waiting. He had not anticipated this. He knew the voice very well—had been searching for it recently, hoping for answers, help.

The book was withdrawn from him, and with it, memory of the poem Lin Piao Tai had sought, the first half of the Song of Power the Spryggla had thought the Isomage needed. His only secret, his last defense, was now gone.

"You're Death's Radio," Michael said.

I am the Realm. My body is the Realm, and my mind is the Realm.

"Why have you helped me, if you hate me?"

I do not hate. The Creation is flawed. Holding it together

*has become very tiresome. And there is not as much time as
once seemed possible . . . not an eternity.*

The voice became less hollow. At the same time, Michael's
focus sharpened and he saw the darkness and the clouds of
chaos eddy inward, flashing green and yellow and blue, becoming rosy, giving off halos of brilliant red.

Before him, standing on the cut-stone field high in the mountains first revealed to him by Biri, was an extraordinary figure.
He was a Sidhe, certainly, but like no other Sidhe Michael had
seen. Despite the lack of wrinkles, the full redness of the hair,
the apparent strength of bare arms and legs, the figure looked
old and weary. His eyes were black as the void and without
whites, and his teeth were stone gray.

He wore a short kilt and a loose tabard tied with a length
of golden rope. The kilt was decorated around the hem with
branches and leaves in gold thread. Michael glanced down but
could not see his own body; he was simply a pair of eyes, at
least for now.

"So you recognize me?"

Yes.

The Sidhe came forward. "I went to some trouble to disguise
myself. Still, you've been very perceptive. It wasn't my voice
you recognized, was it?"

No.

"My delivery. Even a god can't disguise his inmost self, I
suppose.

How long have you been . . . a god?

"Not long, actually. Twenty, thirty thousand Earth years.
But quite long enough. Do you know what I am?"

A Sidhe.

"Yes, and a very old Sidhe, too. Not of this younger generation. All the Sidhe alive today—with very few exceptions—
have forgotten me. All they know is Adonna. They forget Tonn,
who led them back to Earth, who opposed his own daughter
and the Council of Eleu. I was the leader of the Council of
Delf. Do you know who Tonn was, boy?"

The Sidhe mage.

"Good memory. There were four mages, boy, remember
them?"

Tonn, Daedal . . .

"Manus and Aum. Others, less powerful, the mages of the
lesser kinds. All are animals on your Earth now, not strong
enough to re-evolve, or content with their lot. Only humans

struggled back, hated us so much.... Now so few of your fellows remember why they struggled back. Perhaps only one . . . the Serpent Mage. I imagine *he* remembers, oh, yes!"

Michael didn't respond.

"You won't remember this exchange, either. Not for a while. Wouldn't do the great majority of the Sidhe any good to know that Adonna was once one of them. A mage is impressive, but a god must be infinitely more impressive. Aloof. I know my people, how to chastise them and keep them in line. But life in my Realm is just not enough. I've labored long and hard to keep the Realm going, to reconcile all its inconsistencies . . . all the poor judgments of my own creation. And I've sacrificed, too. Whatever personal life I may once have had . . . the respect of my offspring . . . and my own wife."

Michael remembered the skull-snail on the Blasted Plain.

"Yes, yes," Tonn said, coming even closer, until he seemed right next to Michael. "The time has come for a change. Perhaps the Council of Eleu was right. Perhaps Elme was right. It is time for the Sidhe to return to the Earth. Ah, if only poor Tarax could hear me now! He'd lose the very foundation of his life. He'd melt with shame. You, a pitiful human child, must carry the burden—not a powerful and faithful Sidhe. But then, Tarax is remarkably ignorant. All my people are ignorant, except perhaps the Ban of Hours."

Michael conjured back an image of tall figures around his bed on Earth, discussing him. You? he asked.

"No, indeed," Tonn said, pulling up a block from the stone field with the palm of his hand and sitting on it. "Not even the Maln, or the Council of Delf. The Council of Eleu chose you, and they would be very distressed to know I concur. But before any of our plans can be carried out, some obstacles must be cleared away. Some old greeds. We do not precisely agree, but each of us has a use for you."

Then I have no will of my own?

"You have all the will you'll ever need. And you won't need this." He held up the black book. It faded from his hand. "Nor will you need Death's Radio. Time now for forgetting. . . ."

The stone field's blackness intensified and smeared up to take in the sky and clouds, to sweep around Tonn and obscure him.

Once, poets were magicians. Poets were strong, stronger

than warriors or kings—stronger than old hapless gods. And they will be strong once again.

The cloud of creation was back in its place. The receding blackness sparkled and churned.

Chapter Thirty-Seven

Michael walked and whistled tunelessly, caught himself whistling and stopped abruptly. He looked around warily, his armhairs tingling. Then he frowned and sat down, wondering why he was still alive. He had been in the Irall.

He felt for the book. It was gone. He looked around frantically, pushing aside the grass to see if he had dropped it. Everything in his memory was jumbled.

The broad river flowed nearby, noisy as it rushed slick and turbulent over boulders. A few hundred yards beyond the river was one wall of a canyon, and much closer—overshadowing—the opposite wall. Both were gray stone streaked with rusty red, jagged and scarred as if the river's gouging had been neither gentle nor discreet. Each wall rose at least five hundred feet and stretched for as far as Michael could see. Trees clustered in fives and tens along the banks, leaves swaying in a cool, persistent breeze—a canyoned river of air to complement the river of water.

"What happened?" he asked, taking a step one way, then back, then another. He remembered meeting Death's Radio, a tall fellow in a kilt and tabard...but who had that been? He remembered being told certain things, but he couldn't recall what the things were.

Tarax he remembered quite clearly, and he shivered.

"Michael! Michael!"

Two figures clambered down a rugged trail in the canyon face nearby.

"Nikolai!" he shouted. His difficulties were temporarily driven out by joy. "You didn't make it back to the city!"

"And you did?" Nikolai and Bek ran across the river sand, skirting patches of grass. Michael and Nikolai embraced and Michael was surprised and embarrassed at how good Nikolai's warm, strong body felt in his arms. Bek stood to one side, smiling faintly at the reunion.

"I was captured," Michael said.

"We were filtered out, then...by the Ban," Nikolai said. They laughed and embraced again. "We were sent here. And so were you. By the Ban? Did she rescue you?"

Michael explained as much as he remembered, which wasn't very helpful. He described the interior of the Irall, the ride below the Realm, and the cylinder above the Mist. "After that...I think I was dreaming."

"Here? Most unlikely," Nikolai said. "Whatever it was, it must have been real."

"My book was taken away. I've forgotten some things." His face fell. Thinking of the book automatically sent his mind back to "Kubla Khan." He couldn't remember past the first few lines.

"But you survived! No one has ever come out of the Irall alive—no human, anyway."

"And no Breed," Bek said, running his hand through his silky blond hair. "Nikolai told me you were special. Now I believe him! A special *antros.*"

Michael was ready to be offended by the word used so often as a curse, but he probed Bek deftly and found no animosity. Bek returned the probe and met Michael's instant shield. The Breed smiled broadly and shook his head in appreciation and wonder.

By evening, they had gathered dried sticks and grass for a fire. They ate from Nikolai's foraging of the day before— some fruit and roots—and rested, saying very little. Nikolai cast proprietary glances at Michael now and then.

The fire became smoke and ashes and a few crackling embers. Bek and Nikolai slept. Michael felt as if he had slept an age and might never sleep again. He sat with his arms wrapped around his knees and looked at the drifting smoke, wondering how he could feel so good when he had lost the final thing of importance to him, when he had no future and no foreseeable prospects. When he was still in the Realm.

He was alive. That was enough. So often he had resigned himself to death—or worse. He thought of the weightless graveyard and the acrid dust.

Even if Clarkham turned out to be useless to him—and vice versa—even if he was a pawn—

He heard a rustling in the grass. What he saw, beyond the sandy oval where Nikolai and Bek slept, made his back go rigid.

Biri stood in the grass, dressed in a black robe with red shoulders and arms. He stared fixedly at Michael and held out his hand, beckoning.

Michael stood and brushed sand from his travel-stained pants. He followed Biri away from the camp until they were out of earshot, their conversation covered by the river's tumult.

"Is this some sort of crossroad?" Michael asked, his voice almost failing him. He cleared his throat.

"No crossroad. I've brought something that may still be of use to you. It is yours, by law. You have survived your punishment, and it has been imprinted." He gestured to a copse of trees. There, visible in the light of the pearly band, was the blue horse. It nickered and walked forward. Michael reached out to it hesitantly. It nuzzled his palm.

"I've gone through a lot because of this horse," Michael said. "This isn't another trick?"

Biri shook his head. "Tarax was furious not to find you back in the cylinder, dead. He released the horse, but not in the same place he was commanded to release you."

"What are you doing here?"

"Fulfilling Adonna's ruling."

"And . . . ?"

Biri looked down at the ground. "Because of Adonna, I have no horse. Because of Tarax, I have no faith in Adonna or the Irall. All my training has been for nothing. My people are dying. We are withering inside. I blame Adonna." The look he gave Michael was almost pleading. "I went to the Ban of Hours. She and her attendants are the only ones who seem to know something has gone wrong in the Realm."

"The Council of Eleu," Michael said.

"Yes. What do you know of them?"

"Not a great deal."

"Would you like to know more, as much as I know?"

Michael nodded. If Clarkham was an unreliable savior, then the Council of Eleu might be able to help.

"Ride with me, then . . . or rather, since I have no horse, allow me to ride with you. While your companions sleep."

"Where to?"

"Not so very long ago, I would have thought it an accursed place and shunned it. Now I am much less certain. It is not far, if we ride."

Michael looked back at the camp and the sleeping shapes of Nikolai and Bek. He knew Nikolai was asleep, but Bek...

"Why shouldn't they go with us?"

"The human has never undergone discipline. He would not survive. The Breed..." Biri shrugged. "It would not matter to him. He is without a people, a loner. He does not care that he is a Breed, otherwise it might have some importance to him."

Michael considered briefly. "Lead on."

The blue horse allowed both of them to mount, this time, unlike with Gwinat, Michael riding behind and Biri in front. "I was in the Irall," Michael said.

"Yes."

"Did you see me?"

"Yes."

"Why didn't you help?"

"No one interferes with Tarax. Besides, you were going to Adonna. Even initiates know the futility of trying to cross Adonna."

Michael urged the horse forward. Then, fully aware of the consequences, he gave the Sidhe animal a chance to run... and to fly. "Tell us where to go," he told Biri as the horse's body blurred and silvered under them.

"South," he said.

Chapter Thirty-Eight

For a time the horse followed the river and canyon. Michael couldn't tell if they were flying or running, or even precisely where they were. Everything was disarrayed. With a twist of his head the world became a different place, filled with streamers of light and rushing clouds.

"Abana," Biri shouted. "Tell the horse *abana."*

Michael repeated the word, and what was left of the Realm dissolved. The night became twilight, the streamers and clouds oriented to form a gray-blue heaven. Below, city lights moved across the grassland like water flowing on a wrinkled cloth. "It looks like Earth!" Michael shouted. The wind tasted electric on his tongue.

"It is one of many Earths," Biri said. "The Earths between your world and the Realm. Where the horses go when they *aband."*

The city lights coalesced into streets and buildings, tilting and swaying far below. Everything was greenish, a very memorable tint indeed—the tint of the Between where Lamia's sister stood guard. "How many Earths are there?"

"Far more than can be counted," Biri said.

"And the horse crosses over?"

"We are only visiting. We are not actually there unless we fall off. The horse grazes the surface, skips along the Earths surrounding the Realm."

The city lights vanished and everything became mixed and indistinct again. To Michael's hand, reaching around Biri and grasping, the horse's mane felt like cold fire. The horse turned to look back at them. Its eye was cold and deadly blue, like a ball of ice lit from within. Its lips drew back and its teeth were as sharp and long as a tiger's. Between the Realm and the Earth—or Earths—it was a very different beast indeed, a true nightmare.

"We're getting near," Biri said.

The horse shivered and the swirl became less intense. He could feel the horse's muscles tighten beneath his legs, preparing to run instead of *aband*.

The Realm returned. The horse galloped over a rocky field studded with tiny trees. The night air returned, cold and dry. The sky was filled with sharp white stars.

Michael brought the horse to a stop. "How far did we travel?"

"Too far to walk," Biri said, sliding off the horse to the left. "We cannot ride the horse into the protected circle."

Michael dismounted and they walked across the field, stones driving hard into Michael's soft-shod feet. Ahead, vaguely outlined in starglow, was a dirt and stone mound, very much like the barrows Michael had seen in history books.

"We have those on Earth," he said.

On one side of the mound was a arch stone blocked by a circular slab half-buried in the ground. Biri reached to the left of the slab and withdrew a round boulder about six inches across. As if the boulder were clay, he scooped a hollow in it and shifted it from hand to hand. With one finger he planted a fierce white glow in the hollow. "A lantern," he said.

On the right-hand edge of the slab was a series of notches. He placed the fingers of one hand into certain grooves, then touched others in different sequences. The slab sunk into the ground with a grumble.

"Now we enter," he said.

The stone lantern showed a dank, root-lined tunnel stretching about ten yards into the mound. The floor was cut stone. The air smelled musty and chill. Biri led the way.

In the center of the mound was a chamber about thirty feet in diameter. The chamber's stone walls shone with damp. Silvery-white beard-like fungus hung from the wet surfaces.

Surmounting a stone bier in the middle were two transparent quartz coffins placed within a few inches of each other. In each was a skeleton. Biri stood on one side of the bier and Michael walked slowly around to the other, peering through the crystal sides.

"Do you know who they are?" Biri asked, his voice soft in the echoing chamber.

"I don't think so," Michael said. The bones in the left-hand coffin resembled translucent ivory and were draped in a diaphanous white gown; in the right-hand coffin, the skeleton was opaque and brown with age and wore nothing but dust and rags. In one hand it clutched a polished wood staff with a bronze head.

Michael completed his circuit and stood beside Biri. "Most of my people reviled her," Biri said, touching the quartz with the tips of his fingers. "When we returned from the stars, we were too weak to destroy your kind. Some Sidhe, including the Mage, revealed themselves to humans as gods and tried to hinder their development, but your kind was not always reverent. They grew and matured and found their own skills anyway. Your kind even used the lies and dreams the false gods revealed, like a flower uses manure.

"She thought we should live in peace with you, but at first, her ministers refused to carry out her plans. She was queen; she had guided us home, and she was a powerful sorceress; they couldn't fight her openly. But she began to wander the Earth, trying to find a solution. In time her ministers were able to convince most of the Sidhe that the queen was mad, that she had succumbed to the stresses of the journey, that—as often happened then—her powers had broken her mind.

"So she gathered together her own followers, and formed the Council of Eleu. While other Sidhe tried to control humans, the Council spread knowledge among them. While the mage, Tonn, spent centuries portraying your gods Yahweh and Baal, and others, the queen opposed him, and tried to encourage humans to develop their own finest qualities. Tonn was stronger.

"And, finally, the queen declared she had fallen in love with a human. She rejected the cold and heartless union with her own males." Biri's face betrayed no irony, or even awareness of self-criticism. "Sometimes, even now, her followers believe she truly was mad at that time, but she did indeed love the man, and when he died, as mortals will, she placed his body here. Then, for a thousand years, the Council of Eleu worked with the queen to raise humanity to a level where other Sidhe might be able to accept them as equals. But her enthusiasm had died with her husband; in time, the queen herself died, and was placed beside the one she loved, instead of in a tomb of honor or in a tree where she might pass on her wisdom.

"Tonn founded the Black Order to oppose her wishes, and put Tarax in command. The Black order, the Maln, fought every action of the council of Eleu. To this day they oppose each other, and the Council of Eleu must work in secret."

"This is Elme and Aske," Michael said. Biri nodded.

"Adonna is a corrupt god," he continued, "growing more and more senile with time. I cannot serve him. I must serve those who oppose him, and oppose the Maln."

"You want to help humans?"

"It seems I must, doesn't it?" Biri smiled grimly.

"The Crane Women are Elme's daughters?"

"Elme and Aske had forty children, the first Breeds. Twenty of their offspring married humans, and had children by them. . . ."

"How long ago?"

"As far back as nine thousand years on Earth, and as recently as eighty years. Those with less than an eighth Sidhe heritage revert to mortals again, but can still work some magic. Their children spread around the Earth, and many of them lived for thousands of years, surviving many generations of descendants.

"Long, long ago, Elme held court in a beautiful garden, surrounded by high stone walls. She sought the advice of the Serpent Mage, the last of the original humans."

Michael's eyes narrowed.

"Do you know of it?" Biri asked, regarding him curiously.

Michael stared at the skeleton in the radiant gown and didn't know how to react. Finally, his eyes welled up, as if all his life he had heard just parts of a wonderful and sad story, and now it had been completed for him.

Chapter Thirty-Nine

They returned the way they had come. Michael hardly noticed the pyrotechnics; he held on to Biri and the horse and turned his thoughts inward.

He had learned things no history class on Earth could ever have taught him. He suspected there were far more things of which he had heard only partial truths, or no truth at all.

The horse stopped on the ledgetop overlooking the camp and pawed the ground with its hoof. Its fangs were no longer apparent and its eye was gentle. Michael swung down from the horse and looked up at Biri.

"I don't trust you," Michael said. Biri returned his gaze with expression unchanged. "Oh, I think you've told me the truth about Aske and Elme, and what you know of Sidhe history. You'd have no reason to lie to me about that. Perhaps you know I've heard a lot of the story from others. But I don't necessarily believe you've abandoned Adonna."

Biri smiled ironically. "You'll entertain the thought, however?"

"I'll consider it as a possibility," Michael offered. "But everything is going too smoothly. Everybody wants me to go to the Isomage. Only the Ban of Hours told me I was a pawn, caught between two forces—the Council of Eleu, and the Maln. I trust her, I think."

"She is a worthy female," Biri said, nodding his respect.

"I think it's time I acted on my own," Michael said. "I want to return to the Pact Lands."

"They no longer exist," Biri said. "Your people and the Breeds have been moved, put in new communities."

"Camps, you mean," Michael said. "Take me to one of the camps."

"They are closely guarded. Tarax wants no more like you to come to the notice of the Council of Eleu."

"You and I together, we can—"

"I have forsaken Adonna," Biri said, shaking his head firmly, "but I will not fight my own kind."

"Yet you want to serve the Council. You can do that by helping humans."

Biri said nothing.

"I'm not sure that going to the Isomage isn't what the Maln would have me do. They released me from the Irall, and that makes me suspicious."

"What would the Council have you do?"

"I don't know."

"Who has opposed you most?"

"Human-hating Sidhe."

"The Maln."

"I just don't know . . ." Michael said, confused again.

"It seems obvious," Biri said.

"Then why didn't Tarax kill me when he had the chance? I'm not very strong. Any Sidhe could have killed me. You could, right now, just by raising a finger."

"Perhaps you are not as weak as you think."

"Oh, no?" Michael laughed. "You just hollowed out a boulder and lit a fire in it. It's all I can do to keep myself warm."

Biri dismounted and squatted on the ledge to peer into the canyon. His red-shouldered robe made him look disembodied in the starlight, as if his bust floated on a gray platform over the canyon. "You call yourself a poet," Biri said. "The Sidhe have long regarded poets with respect."

"I am sixteen, maybe seventeen years old by now," Michael said. "In my lifetime, I've written maybe five halfway decent poems, probably less. In the Realm I've hardly had time to write any. And when I've tried, I've heard somebody else's voice in my head giving me suggestions, or just creating things for me. I'm more a pawn than a poet, believe me."

"So what do you intend to do?"

"Maybe sit right here, travel with Nikolai and Bek. See what I'm really capable of before I make any decisions." He paused, then said under his breath, "From what I've learned, I can't see Clarkham being any help. I'm not even sure he's human, or really cares about humans."

Biri nodded. "If you are a pawn, do you think the forces using you will allow you to remain aloof?"

That stumped Michael. He sat beside the Sidhe and dangled his legs over the canyon. "At least they won't have me behaving like a silly puppet."

"If you are being used, either by Tarax or the Council, you face very powerful adversaries if you defy them."

"So what do you suggest I do?"

"Not much, perhaps. Advance in your discipline. Finish your training."

"The Crane Women are gone," Michael said. "I don't expect them to pop up around here anytime soon."

"I can train you," Biri said. He held his hand out in the direction of the camp. "Tonight, while they sleep. Then you can decide." His smile in the dark was radiant, feral. Michael's back prickled.

"And if I decide against the Council?"

"My allegiances haven't solidified," Biri said. "Perhaps you can guide me."

Michael thought for a moment. "Won't Tarax come after you, try to take you back?"

"Why? I am useless to him, useless to Adonna. I am just another disaffected Sidhe. They won't waste their time on vengeance. Only miserable Sidhe like Alyons engage in such silliness."

Michael stepped over to the horse. "So teach me."

"Beginning now," Biri said, getting to his feet.

Chapter Forty

It might have been the longest night in the history of the Realm. To Michael, it stretched on forever...and it was not pleasant. Biri walked with him away from the canyon until they stood in the middle of a broad belt of sand and small boulders.

"First, you must realize you are alone," he began. "For a Sidhe initiate, his aloneness is confirmed by the murder of his horse; there can be no closer relationship and no greater shock than being required to kill his most treasured companion."

"Do I have to kill the horse?" Michael asked, suddenly queasy.

"No. Your feeling toward the animal is shallow, uncertain. You were not raised with it. The *Mafoc Mar* did not pick it out for you from the fields when you were young; you did not grow to youthful maturity with the horse by your side. You must find something else."

"Maybe another shadow-self?"

Biri shook his head with irritation. "That doesn't concern me."

They stood in starlight bright enough to cast shadows.

"No swords, no baubles. Those are all human misunderstandings of magic, human preoccupation with technology. Magic lies purely in the mind. The Sidhe are among the most dishonorable, unreliable creatures on all the faces of Creation, but they have one thing—concentration. What they want, they focus on completely."

Biri sat down in the grass and gestured for Michael to do likewise. "You are alone," Biri said. "You are the only thing in existence. You will never truly know there are others. Because humans have souls is no reason to believe they differ from the Sidhe in this, that they are eternally alone."

Michael shook his head. "What about friendship, love?"

"Love does not occur to the Sidhe male," Biri said. "But I can demolish love even so. Did you love the real person, or your image of the person? Did you love an external, or what the person was to you?"

"But there has to be someone, something, to love or to be disappointed with."

"Only yourself. Alone. Life is alone, love is alone."

"But then you don't exist. Nobody else exists."

"Together, we are alone. That is the peculiarity of our being. We never know true community. Not even Sidhe, who can reach inside each other's aura of memory, out-see and in-see; not even Sidhe can avoid being alone. You can never rely on another, not to the core of your being. You can never ultimately trust in another . . . for how is that possible, when you are alone?"

Biri seemed to vanish, leaving Michael on the grass. Alone.

He pulled up a sprig and contemplated it, feeling dead inside. If he was unique, solitary, without any support in all of reality—including his own internal reality—if even his mind was alone, with just one voice, and all else illusory—

The deadness was replaced once again by enormous calm. How often could he have devastating realizations, and then have them smoothed away like a waveless ocean?

How many more revelations would there be, ending in the same assurance of mastery, all illusory?

The blade of grass was alone. Together, they were alone. They were alone together.

The ground of the Realm was alone. The blade of grass was alone with the ground.

Words flowed within him, arguments, changing shape and meaning, having no meaning. He gave them up only after a tremendous, jerking pain swept him.

"I am in love with words," Michael said. "They are my horse. I ride them, use them. But I can never kill them. Even if I cannot use words to get where I am going." The realization of his dependence was enough.

His aloneness suddenly became apparent, without words, truth, meaning or thought.

The only way one can truly be alone is to be at one with everything, everybody. . . .

The entire universe, having only one voice.

All the faces of creation, alone.

Michael became aware of what he had been doing when he performed the small tricks the Crane Women had taught him. "To be alone is to be difficult to spot."

He could improve on that. "Aloneness means isolation from needs." He could last indefinitely without food or water.

"I only fight shadows. If I am alone, there is no enemy to fight." And ultimately, no need to fight. "It is crazy to fight when you are alone."

He put down the blade of grass and looked up at the multitude of stars. Biri had helped him build this structure piece by piece, carefully. Now it began to collapse. The whole thing was ridiculous. How could he ever believe such nonsense? Yet as it collapsed, it did not take the calm or sense of mastery with it; they remained.

They had built a boat, crossed a river, and the boat had crumbled just as he stood on the opposite shore.

Biri came up behind him.

"It's all wrong," Michael said. "It doesn't make sense."

"That is the sign over the gate of your acceptance," Biri told him in Cascar. "For a Sidhe, being alone is exaltation, being alone is ridiculous. You must never trust us . . . or our philosophies."

"Then I shouldn't trust you at all?"

"Never trust a teacher."

He didn't seem to be joking. Michael was far from convinced he knew what this final discipline was all about, undeniable though its effects were. And if it was such a discipline that made the Sidhe behave as they did—that segregated males and females, and led to such odd behavior in the males—then he would just as soon be rid of it, effects or no.

But there was nothing he could do now. He felt stronger, better able to cope. They returned to the canyon, Biri following Michael down the path.

The eastern horizon was brightening. The long night was finally over. Nikolai and Bek still slept as they approached the camp. The fire had died down to smoking ashes. Biri stayed away from the sleeping figures, staring off down the river.

"What do you plan to do now?" Michael asked him.

Nikolai woke up, rolled over and stared in groggy surprise at the Sidhe. "Who's that?" he asked, scrambling to his feet. Bek sat up on the ground. Biri ignored them.

"I think I will go to the Isomage," Biri said.

"That's where we're heading," Nikolai said, glancing at Michael.

"Not necessarily," Michael said. "Why go there?"

Biri smiled his feral smile. Nikolai shivered and backed away from the camp. "He wears the cloak of the Maln's initiates!"

"Perhaps because he has some answers," Biri said. "And if you do not go there, somebody has to. Besides, he isn't far from here." He gestured downriver. "The river flows into the sea. The Isomage's lands are on the delta." He turned to walk away.

"Where have you been all night?" Nikolai asked, staring at Michael curiously.

"I'm not sure," Michael said. The Sidhe merged with shadows near the canyon wall. When the day brightened, he was nowhere to be seen.

"I've always been interested in the Isomage," Nikolai said. "A tragic, perhaps fearful person." They gathered fruit from the low scrub trees near the river. "Would it be dangerous to go there just to satisfy curiosity?"

"Probably," Bek said. Nikolai frowned and bit into a tiny pear.

"Then we just stay here, or we go back to the Pact Lands—except you say they aren't there any more, and we can't go back. I'm confused."

"At least the Sidhe knows where his answers are to be found," Bek said.

"They may not be the answers I'm looking for," Michael said. "If I'm looking for answers. And I don't know why he's going to Clarkham."

"Perhaps Clarkham can tell him about the Council. Or tell us."

"I take it both of you want to go on, find Clarkham?"

Bek considered a moment, then nodded. Nikolai shrugged. "I'm contented wherever I happen to be, so long as none of the Maln are aware of me."

"Then you should go to Clarkham. I'll make up my own mind, in my own time." Michael stalked back toward the camp, pockets filled with the tiny fruit. Nikolai jogged after him.

"Michael, Michael, what is wrong? What did the Sidhe say to you? You have changed. . . ."

Indeed, he no longer felt a need for anyone's presence or advice. He felt an ugliness growing inside, replacing the initial calm Biri's discipline had given him.

He stopped, staring beyond a fire much larger than the one they had left. "Brothers," came a muffled voice from behind the fire. Wrapped in white from head to toe, Shahpur walked around the flames, arms folded at chest-level. "We've been told you need an escort." Harka, Tik and Dour emerged from behind a nearby boulder. Michael looked over his shoulder and saw Bek approaching, his pace measured and confident.

"They're all together," Nikolai told Michael, eyes wide with concern.

"The Isomage welcomes you to the vicinity of Xanadu," Shahpur said. Nikolai groaned.

"Grand, grand!" he cried, swinging his hands out. "Now you do not have any choice. Nor do I."

Chapter Forty-One

Harka greeted Michael wearily and sat on the sandy river-bank with Tik and Dour standing beside him. The two younger Sidhe seemed nervous; only Bek and Harka remained at ease, Harka perhaps being incapable of anything more. Shahpur could not be read.

"We have been watching over you, of course," Harka said. He did not fend off Michael's probe; he was, if anything, even emptier than when Michael had last peered into him. His emptiness was as disturbing as Shahpur's horrible fullness.

"I don't need protecting," Michael said.

"The Isomage thinks otherwise. There wasn't much he could do while you traveled between the Pact Lands and here, in Sidhe territories. But he had us meet you in the mountains, and even dared to send Bek into Inyas Trai with you. Now that you approach his domain, we are much freer. We can help when necessary."

"By help," Shahpur said, "Harka means we must insure you come to Xanadu. It is the Isomage's wish."

The Sidhe, however low their status, still retained certain skills. Michael could tell that just by lightly skimming their auras. He could not escape. He still felt strong, but it was not any sort of strength he could immediately apply; Biri's discipline had somehow confused even his rudimentary skills. If Biri had been with them, the match would have been at least equal; there was nothing he could do to resist now, however.

"It's what I've been planning all along," Michael said. "No coercion necessary."

"Excellent," Harka said. "The Isomage will be very pleased.

He doesn't have many visitors, as you can imagine."

"What about me?" Nikolai asked.

"All who have helped the man-child are welcome in Xanadu. Shall we begin now, or must you rest after your . . . strenuous night?"

"I'm rested," Michael said. Nikolai squared his shoulders and nodded agreement.

"Fine. It's a pleasant journey. We can be there by late evening. Of course, if we could all ride . . ." He looked enviously at the horse. "But we can't. Bek will tend the *epon.*"

For the next ten miles, the walls of the canyon grew higher until they walked through a deep chasm in perpetual shadow. Mosses and ferns crowded the river bank, some towering high overhead to form a dense canopy, casting everything in verdant gloom. The river became a deep, swift-running torrent no more than thirty feet across.

In its translucent volume, Michael saw Riverines flashing by like trout, dodging rocks and reed banners in their plunge toward the sea.

They approached the canyon's end by late afternoon. The walls declined abruptly and the river broadened, pouring out onto a wide, forested plain. The plain was brushed by swift patches of fog; overhead, the sky melted into a color between butter and polished bronze. The trees on the plain took up the bronzen color and became a pale, umbrous green. Golden-edged clouds cast long shadows over all.

The plain sloped gradually to an immense flat sea, placid as a mirror in the last light of day, reflecting the sky and adding only a darker hint of its own character.

In the red glow of sunset, they hiked through the nearest spinney of trees, still following the river. The water sighed and hissed over a broad course covered with small stones. Where the Riverines went when the water was only inches deep, Michael couldn't decide.

Harka urged them on through the evening shadows. The forest trail was overgrown and difficult to track even in good light, but the cadaverous Sidhe seemed to feel an added urgency. Bek, Tik and Dour followed some distance behind. Shahpur stayed near Michael, his white form making barely a noise as he passed through brush and over dry leaves.

Harka puzzled Michael. There was a familiarity about his emptiness . . . but Michael had never encountered a Sidhe with Harka's affliction. If these beings worked for Clarkham, it was possible he had performed some sort of magic on them—subjected them to a *geas*, perhaps. But how could Sidhe be controlled by someone not a Sidhe?

Again and again, Michael concocted plans of escape, and discarded them. His deep-seated anger and confusion fermented. Why had Biri subjected him to such a weird, ridiculous philosophy? Perhaps, Michael thought, to create the stymie he was in now.

Nikolai became more and more apprehensive as they neared the shore of the sea. Finally, the pearly ribbon of light appeared and illuminated their path out of the last stretch of the forest. They walked across sand to the still water's edge.

"It is dangerous to approach Xanadu in the dark, even for the desired visitor," Harka said. "We stay here for the night."

Nikolai followed Michael a few yards up the beach. The others made no move to stop them. Michael bent down and dipped his hands in the sea's glassy surface. The ripple caught the ribbon light and carried it yards away from the beach. The water was neither warm nor cold. Michael brought a wet finger to his lips. It was only faintly salty—more of a mineral tang, actually.

"There's nothing you can do?" Nikolai whispered.

Michael shook his head. "Why try? This is where you wanted to go—and I, too, at first."

"You decided against it."

"If I change my mind, how can I be sure I'm the one changing it? If my mind is changed for me, does an escort make any difference? Perhaps they're merely making us do what we should be doing, anyway."

"I have always felt apprehensive about that Harka," Nikolai said. "But to know he works for the Isomage!" The Russian clucked his tongue, then looked at the Breed, Sidhe and cloaked human from the corner of his eye. "Surprises, surprises. What will we do when we see Clarkham?"

"I'm sure he'll let us know what's expected."

The night passed quickly. Michael did not sleep. He sensed a growth of the poison within, a combination of hatred, suspicion and strength that was dismaying. Biri's discipline was blossoming and the flower was ugly.

Dawn disrupted the eastern sky and shattered the arcing ribbon light into fading fragments. The air hummed once again like the beginning chords of a symphony. When the sun was fully above the horizon, the hum subsided. The bronzen sky brightened to pure butter.

Harka walked past Michael and Nikolai, who lay in the sand, and gestured for them to follow. "We have an appointment and we're already late."

Their path took them at a tangent away from the still sea. Within a mile the sand acquiesced to grass—a perfectly kept rolling lawn spaced here and there with peaceful gingko trees, rustled by leisurely warm breezes. Once the sun reached a certain angle, it blended with the rest of the sky, leaving only an illuminated featureless bowl.

Harka pointed to a green hill which rose with dignified gradualness to a rounded peak about five hundred feet higher than the sea. Surrounding the hill were walled forests and gardens, and atop squatted a pale ivory dome, its size uncertain from their distance. In one side of the hill was a deep gash bordered by trees; even from miles away, the sound of water plummeting from the gash was audible. The water came in a torrent down the hillside facing away from the sea and began a sinuous river.

"The Isomage's palace," Harka said solemnly.

They approached a stone wall about fifteen feet high, made of blocks of dark marble. There was an open bronze gate, the doors chased with dragons. The gate's only guard was a twelve-foot-tall granite warrior, his fierce oriental eyes fixed on the lifeless sea, one hand holding a gatepost like a spear. As they passed through the gate, Nikolai regarded the warrior with unabashed wonder.

Within the circumference of the first wall, animals of all description played, browsed and hunted, though the hunts seemed never to succeed. Michael spotted a huge tiger, head hanging as it stalked a herd of translucent deer. The deer, legs like rods of glass, pricked up their ears and bounded away, flushing pheasants from a jade-colored bush. The pheasants flapped wings like sections of stained-glass windows as they ascended; then, tiring, they dropped into a nearby gingko.

The second wall was constructed of glazed brick and was only eight feet high. Steps mounted up one side and down the other. There was no guard, real or stony.

They now climbed the slope of the hill. At one point they halted and stared out over the river and ocean. Michael estimated they had covered three miles from the outermost wall,

which meant the whole circuit was about five miles in radius.
The walls were circular, broken only by gates placed at the
four compass points and by the meandering river, which emp-
tied into the sunless sea without stirring a ripple.

The third wall was a hedge barely five feet tall but ten thick
and studded with long thorns. The gate in this wall was a
pedestrian tunnel beneath the hedge. The plaster walls of the
tunnel were covered with frescoes of pastoral Chinese life,
depicting a long-moustachioed, round-faced emperor enjoying
the peace and fertility of wise rule.

They now passed around the hill, out of sight of the sea. A
stone causeway guided them up one side of the fountaining
chasm, through a wide strip of cedars. Bridges crossed over
verdant rills filled with flowering trees and thick, fragrant bushes.
The ground beneath them seemed to breathe, each breath punc-
tuated by a sudden roar of water and a deep grinding rumble.

Through the gap of one particularly long rill, Michael saw
the torrent flushing thick chunks of ice, jagged and pale green
in the dark waters. The ice bounded from side to side and was
finally shattered to milky slush at the base of the hill.

The steps ended in a graceful carved wood pavilion equipped
with silk-padded benches. They rested for a few minutes to
allow Harka to regain his breath, then crossed the flawless lawn
spreading over the hilltop.

Two hundred yards from the dome, a circle of black minarets
lanced up from the lawn. They were spaced at intervals of fifty
feet and had external staircases spiraling to bronze crow's nests
at the top. The cages were vacant, but Michael had the strong
impression he was being watched, if not from the towers, then
from the pavilions of glass, stone and wood that decorated the
grounds.

The dome itself was constructed of silks held aloft by curving poles. The poles were set in walls of alabaster. Now he
could judge the dome's true size; it was at least three hundred
feet high and twice as broad.

They entered the pleasure dome through a spidery arch carved
of green soapstone. Harka bade them stop with his uplifted
hand and turned to Michael.

"The Isomage meets you as an equal," he said. "That is a
great privilege. He is at peace, yet eternally occupied with his
work. He invites you as a guest, and as a fellow of Earth. Do
you harbor him any ill will?"

"No," Michael said. Clarkham had never done anything to him, had never, in fact, *been* anything to him but a distant goal.

"No," Harka said wearily, "You do not. Nor does your companion." Nikolai regarded the Sidhe with patent mystification. "Enter, then, the fulfillment of the dream and the song."

Chapter Forty-Two

The interior of the silken dome was effulgent with milky light; the air enveloped Michael with warmth and incense. They walked across a black marble floor veined with ice, a layer of chill air flowing over their feet. Nikolai stuck close to Michael, swiveling his head to see everything at once.

The poles supporting the silken tent converged high above, where a gap in the fabric showed the sky. At the center of the enclosure, up a flight of wooden steps carved with dragons and horses, beyond a teakwood fence topped with gold rails, stood a full-sized house: white plaster walls and curtained windows, a sloping red tile roof, all surrounded by perfectly trimmed oleander bushes.

"That's Clarkham's house," Michael said. "That's where I began..."

The front door was open but they didn't enter. Instead, Harka led them up the steps and around the yard to the back. The rear of the house was quite ordinary, with a brick patio and a well-tended garden of tree roses, outdoor redwood furniture with gaily covered pads, an umbrella-shaded round table on curved metal legs. It was extraordinary only in that it was *here*, a comic discrepancy in an exotic *chinoiserie*.

A dark Sidhe female trimmed the tree roses with bronze pruning shears. At each snip, the roses on the tree she pruned glowed and the air filled with a sweet, sharp fragrance. She glanced up and saw the group gathering beyond the lawn's brick border. She smiled, put her shears down on a folding wooden stand and smoothed her gold-trimmed gray gown.

"Finally!" she exclaimed. "We've been waiting a very long

time for your arrival." She walked across the lawn and held out her hand to Michael. He grasped it by the fingers and she beckoned him onto the lawn. The chill of the ice-veined marble was immediately replaced by the warm summer softness of grass. She kissed him decorously on the cheek and led him across the lawn. "Please come," she called back to Nikolai. The others bowed and backed away. Nikolai hesitated, confused, then stepped up onto the grass and followed.

"David has been very patient," she said. Her voice was as sweet as any Sidhe voice Michael had heard yet, like an inviting smile. Her hair was lustrous, silky black. Her brows were slightly asymmetric, one angling higher than the other, and her lips were more full than the lips of other Sidhe.

They entered the glass doors and passed into the rear room of the house, where Michael had once watched moonlight spill over the bare wood floor. Here, the room was furnished as a study, with an oak roll-top desk in the corner opposite the doors, full bookcases along two walls and an upright piano placed before the gauze curtains of the bay window.

"My name is Mora," the Sidhe said. "We don't have long before he comes down to meet you. Before then . . ." She reached beneath the peplum of her gown and produced a rose from an inner pocket, handing it to Michael. "To decorate your room. You'll be with us for some time, David says."

Michael accepted the rose. "My name is—"

"Oh, we know, we know!" Mora said, laughing. "And this is Nikolai, a friend of Emma Livry."

Nikolai nodded formally and regarded the books and piano with obvious longing.

"Now, I must return to the garden," Mora said. "This is a special season, rare and brief." She laid a finger on the rose in his hands. "This will keep for some time."

She left by way of the French doors, shutting them behind. Michael and Nikolai listened to the tick of a pendulum wall clock mounted over the desk.

Footsteps sounded on the stairs, paused and resumed. The study door opened and a gray-haired man of middle height, appearing perhaps fifty or fifty-five years old, entered. He wore an open-collared shirt and brown slacks and was shod in fawn-colored moccasins. His face was broad and pleasant and there was a faint growth of ruddy beard on his cheeks.

"Michael?" he asked, extending his hand. "Michael Perrin."

Michael took hold of the hand and shook it firmly, feeling,

as always, awkward over such ritual.

"Very pleased to meet you. I'm Clarkham. David Clarkham. Welcome to Xanadu—or has Mora welcomed you already? Of course. She's a marvel. I'd have a hell of a time running this place without her. I trust you had an interesting journey?"

Michael was at a loss for words. He nodded.

Clarkham offered his hand to Nikolai. "Mr. Kuprin. I've admired your daring for years now. We met briefly once, though you may not remember. When I visited Emma in Inyas Trai. I was quite heavily disguised."

Nikolai frowned.

"Yes," Clarkham said, smiling. "Successfully disguised. It's getting toward supper, and I've laid out quite a feed to celebrate your arrival. I'm sure you're hungry. Food in the Realm is such a chancy thing. Come with me and I'll show you your rooms, let you wash up. I have another guest here, someone you know, I believe—a Sidhe. He'll be joining us for supper. There's so much to discuss, yes indeed!"

Supper was more of a feast. It was served as the muted sunlight filtering through the silken dome began to wane. A table was arranged on the patio, near Mora's glowing roses, and she brought out bowl after covered bowl of baked vegetables, spiced grains, fresh fruit salads and compotes and green salads. Bread came wrapped in linen in wicker baskets, hot and fresh-baked, and was served with spiced vegetable butter, the milk of Sidhe horses not being suitable for regular butter.

Michael and Nikolai sat on one side of the table, Clarkham at the head next to Michael. When Mora was through serving, she sat opposite Nikolai. It was then that Biri strolled onto the patio from the house. He smiled cryptically at Michael and sat beside Mora.

"Fine!" Clarkham said, passing the first bowl of food, "We're all here. Mora has done her usual magic"—he winked at Michael—"in the kitchen. What a fine evening this will be."

Michael was less enthusiastic. He ate—he was very hungry—and listened, but he said little. Most of the talk was from Clarkham; domestic pleasantries, the state of the garden, the quality of the weather around Xanadu, what the coming spring might portend for the grounds.

Michael tried not to stare at Biri. Above all else, he wanted to ask two simple questions—why the Sidhe was on such familiar terms with Clarkham, and what Biri's purpose had been in meeting Michael in the canyon.

Biri volunteered nothing, in fact seldom spoke directly to the newly arrived guests. When the meal was done, Clarkham suggested they go inside. Night had fallen and the interior of the pleasure dome had grown somber. Biri stood and passed his hand behind each of a string of paper lanterns hung across the patio just above head level. They began to glow with a guttering yellow light.

The scent of roses was noticeable even inside the house. Michael glanced curiously at the electric lights—the first he had seen in the Realm. The illumination seemed harsher and more grating on his eyes. With that final touch, the house might as well have been on Earth, for all the sensation of normality and comfort—Earth in the 1940's, perhaps, considering the furnishings. Michael was not comforted, however. He had been lulled by appearances too often before.

Clarkham brought out brandy in a crystal decanter and poured snifters for himself, Nikolai and Michael. "The Sidhe love human liquor entirely too much," he explained. "Mora never touches it—says it spoils her heritage. Biri, I suspect, has never touched a drop in his life. The Maln wouldn't approve, would they?"

Biri shook his head half-sadly. "Alas, no."

"I, however, can drink, and I hope my guests are willing, too." He caught Michael's eye and passed out the glasses. "Master Michael wishes to know what sort of being I am."

"A sensible question," Mora said. They sat in the living room on comfortably overstuffed chairs and a couch, all upholstered in fabric prints of jungle leaves and exotic birds. A fire had been laid and crackled warmly in the fireplace.

"'What is he?'" Clarkham mimicked. "A question asked often, young man, for the past few hundred years, at least. Much less time has passed here, of course."

"You're not a Sidhe," Michael said, deciding to participate in whatever game was being played. "You're not a Spryggla."

"Heaven's no!" Clarkham exclaimed, laughing.

"Arno Waltiri thought you were human," Michael went on.

"No, you have that wrong, young man. *I* thought *Waltiri* was human. I doubt very much if Arno was at all deluded by my masque."

Michael was taken aback. Clarkham noticed his surprise. "My dear fellow, the game is very complex, and everybody has a stake in it. One can't rectify sixty million years of misery and injustice overnight, or without some turns in the maze."

"Waltiri's dead," Michael ventured, no conviction in his voice.

"Let's say I have my doubts," Clarkham said. "He is a very capable and crafty individual."

Michael couldn't bring himself to ask what Clarkham thought Waltiri was, but Clarkham's tone irritated him. Everything seemed to irritate him now—the light, the company, even Nikolai—as if he were filled with hornets.

"I was born on Earth," Clarkham continued. "In fourteen hundred and ninety-nine. My mother had come over from England some centuries earlier, where she had served as *cubicularia* to Queen Maeve herself, before the Queen took to an oak in the Old Forest and her retinue scattered to the islands to escape the charcoal burners. They eventually downed the queen's oak, by the way. Perhaps some of Maeve's venerable smoke resides in the glass windows of a fine English cathedral. But she is no more, and my mother is long dead, too, though she was not mortal. My father *was* mortal, Michael. I am a Breed, if you have not guessed—fifty-fifty. From my mother I learned Sidhe magic, and from my father—well, my father gave me a form which does not unduly reveal my fay ancestry. That is what I am." He waved his hand at Michael. The hornets hummed softly within.

"And you, sir. Question answered one for one."

Michael spoke without hesitation. "I believe I am supposed to be a poet."

"Oh. And are you?"

"Yes."

"Just what I've been waiting for," Clarkham said, exhibiting his satisfaction around the room with a contemplative rub of his chin. "We never have enough poetry."

"To my regret, I have none of my poems with me," Michael said. "And my book was stolen."

"Which book?"

"The book Arno gave me."

"Indeed, indeed," Clarkham mused. "Arno was always quite generous, when he needed something done. Did he give any advice with the book?" Clarkham asked.

"He suggested I shouldn't be afraid to take risks."

"To come here, that is."

"I suppose."

Mora broke in. "I'd love to hear some of your poetry."

"I'll have to write some new," Michael said.

"Splendid," Clarkham said. "Biri's been telling us a little about your journey. Quite remarkable. I'm saddened to hear what happened in the Pact Lands. I understand Alyons paid dearly for his excesses."

"Your trap killed him," Michael said. Mora gave a tiny, barely noticeable shudder.

"And he thought you were responsible," Clarkham said. "Poor fool. Never did know which way the wind blew. Not all Sidhe are brilliant, Michael; take that as a lesson."

"I'd thought you might be disappointed to hear I haven't brought the book."

Nikolai glanced between them, bewildered and uneasy.

"Heavens no!" Clarkham said. "What use would I have for it?"

"I don't have the first part of the Song of Power."

"Which one? I've dealt with so many in my time."

"The poem. Coleridge's 'Kubla Khan.' I don't even remember it."

"Then perhaps you'd care to read it again? I have it, right here." He stood and went to a bookshelf, pulling out a book from between two heavy leatherbound volumes. He handed it to Michael with his finger deftly insinuated between the appropriate pages.

Michael glanced at the poem. It was the same text—including the introduction—as in the book Waltiri had given him.

"You thought perhaps the Maln was trying to prevent you from bringing this to me?" Clarkham chuckled. "I've had it for decades. I once told a crazy old Spryggla that I needed it, but only after the fool tried to ensorcel me. For all I know, he spread the word, though his range seemed quite limited."

"He's dead," Michael said. "Or at least, turned to stone."

"And who was responsible for that?"

"Indirectly, I was."

Clarkham took a deep breath. "You are very influential, Michael. You eliminate age-old traditions left and right, break tabus, pioneer new ground. No, it isn't the old material I'm interested in. You have arrived here with potential. The potential is in your poetry. You are in the same position as poor Mr. Coleridge."

Michael turned to Biri. "You've gone over to him, haven't you? You really did want me to come here."

Biri nodded. "Adonna has no influence here. I am free of him"

"Ah, fine old Adonna," Clarkham reflected. "Biri tells me you survived even the Irall. I've never been there, myself. I likely would not have survived. I have been a thorn in Tarax's side for many years. Adonna, I suppose, made you forget the meeting. Typical. He's a very old, very weary mage, and he assumes too much responsibility. Valiant in his way, however."

Michael suddenly recovered a memory of Adonna—Tonn— in his kilt and tabard, holding a staff.

"Seeing more clearly now?" Clarkham inquired.

"Seeing what?" Nikolai asked, *sotto voce*.

"I'm remembering some things," Michael explained. Nikolai was obviously not competent to be anything but a spectator in this game. Who else was playing?

"May I ask who, or what, Adonna really is?" Nikolai looked around the circle. Mora took pity on him.

"At one time, he was the Mage of the Sidhe. He made the Realm—a masterpiece, nobody denies that—but he was overly ambitious. He has always opposed the Isomage."

"I never could muster up enough *hubris* to call myself a true mage," Clarkham said. "Others may have, but not I. The mages have earned their positions, their esteem. I simply hope to accomplish what they set out to do, long ago."

"Quite humble," Nikolai whispered.

Michael leaned forward in his chair. "You brought me here for a reason. Your wife—one of them—cleared the way for me. The other allowed me to escape, when perhaps she could have added me to her collection."

Clarkham kept a perfect poker-face, revealing nothing.

"Please tell me why I am here."

"This evening? I was willing to let you rest..."

"Now is as good a time as any."

Clarkham held up his hand and looked at Mora and Biri. "Very well. You are here to finish the final Song of Power. That much must be obvious to you."

It was far from obvious, but Michael nodded.

"I, in turn, will use the Song of Power to gain control of the Realm, and restore liberty to humans and Breeds."

"You'll use it for nothing else?"

Clarkham tilted his head to the right and tapped his forefinger on the endtable, then his middle finger. "You've met Tarax. You know what the Maln is capable of."

"And you've helped me remember Adonna. He doesn't seem such a fiend."

Clarkham's face reddened. "Tonn appears to you as he wishes. Sidhe of his age and accomplishment are very little less than gods, Michael, and enormously devious. I have worked for centuries to simply be able to resist him, and I have succeeded—but I cannot overcome him. It isn't because he is a nice fellow that I wish to conquer him." The muscles of Clarkham's cheek worked visibly and his eyes narrowed. Then, with obvious effort, he brought himself again under control. The ingratiating smile returned. "It isn't an issue I can always be calm about. Tonn is not quite the monster Tarax would have him be, no. But Tonn knows his Sidhe. He designed the Realm for them, and he rules them with a severity which he relaxes only for the Ban of Hours. Can you guess why?"

Michael shook his head.

"Because she was the daughter who stuck by him when Elme defied him. Even though he turned their mother into an abomination, in a fit of . . . I'm not sure what you would call it. Horrid anger. When Elme married a human, it was Tonn who orchestrated her banishment, and devised all her fell tortures. When he couldn't break her to his will, and when the Council of Eleu supported her, then and only then did he put all his power into creating the Realm. He hated humans desperately, Michael."

"Perhaps he's changed his mind."

Clarkham looked surprised, then laughed shortly and sharply. "Obviously he's exercised some influence over you, and without revealing his true nature. For that reason, I suppose I should be a little wary of you."

In the ensuing silence, Nikolai regarded the occupants of the room with growing discomfort. "Michael is for the humans and the Breeds," he spoke up finally. "Michael is a good fellow."

Mora smiled and Biri grinned. Clarkham laughed heartily and without malice. "Of course. He has struggled long and hard to get here, to help his people and mine. We will work together, and all our goals will be achieved. For now, after such a long journey and an excellent dinner, it's best we retire to our rooms and enjoy a comfortable night's sleep. Mora will show you where everything is." He stood and stretched casually. "Good evening, gentlemen."

She led Nikolai and Michael upstairs and showed them the bathroom, their bedrooms and places where linen could be

procured. She left a scent of roses in her wake. Michael was
distracted from his jumbled thoughts by her black, shining hair
and teak-colored skin.

There was a fine king-sized bed in his room, the sheets
folded back neatly and the white cover pulled down to reveal
warm woolen blankets. On the valet near the oak dresser hung
a complete change of clothing—slacks, shirt and sweater with
new-looking brown shoes made of very supple leather. When
he put them on in the morning, he would be better dressed
than he had usually been on Earth.

The bedroom walls were decorated with soothing abstract
pastel patterns of brown and gray and blue. In one corner sat
a tiny rosebush in a brass pot, and beside that, a writing desk
with an inlaid leather pad. A goose-neck reading lamp cast a
soft glow over the bedstead. A bookshelf near the door was
filled with interesting volumes—Gerald Manley Hopkins, Yeats,
Keats and Shelley, as well as novels old and new.

He shut the door and sat on the bed. With all the comforts
of Earth arrayed before him, he should have felt touched, even
despite his caution. But there was no room in him for sentiment.
He removed his clothes and put on a terrycloth robe. Then he
went into the hall, chose a towel from the linen closet, and
entered the bathroom.

Hot water, soap, white enamel basin and tub and marble
countertop, fern-leafed wallpaper, tiled shower stall. He show-
ered for a long time, until his exhaustion was unavoidable, and
dried himself with his eyes closed.

When Michael returned to his room, he found Clarkham
standing beside his bed. Clarkham held a box of paper in one
hand, his thumb clamping down a fine black fountain-pen with
gold banding and a clip. "For your convenience," he said,
placing the items on the desk. His expression was almost be-
seeching as he took a step toward Michael. Clearly, he was
interested in being friendly, but something came between them,
a so-far muted antagonism that might break from its cover at
any moment.

"Sorry," Clarkham said after the moment passed. He walked
around Michael and stood in the doorway. "I'm still having
difficulty deciding what you are."

Michael shook his head. "I'm not a sorcerer, if that's what
you mean."

Clarkham smiled grimly. "Unaware sorcerers are the most
formidable, sometimes. But take no heed of my prattling." He

made an offhand gesture at the desk. "Exercise your talents whenever you feel the urge. We will all be a receptive audience."

Clarkham left, closing the door behind.

Michael doffed his robe, put on flannel pajamas laid near the bed and crawled under the covers. He reached up to turn off the light. Every gesture was so alien, so familiar.

He slept. And this evening, he dreamed.

Chapter Forty-Three

The rose had turned to glass. It lay on the dresser, perfect in every detail, and rang softly when Michael touched it. He picked it up by the stem and inserted it into the lapel of his shirt. It poked from the sweater, still sweetly scented.

As he came down the stairs, three sheets of paper in one hand and the gold-banded fountain pen in the other, he realized that all that had gone before had been trivial.

In bed, he had written five short poems on one sheet. They were more exercises than finished works; tests of his skill. They showed that his ability had not withered. If anything, even while not in constant use, it had grown.

He passed through the french doors onto the patio.

> It was an Abyssinian maid,
> And on her dulcimer she played,
> Singing of Mount Abora.

Mora, however, was not singing of Abora, but of a paradisaical place called Amhara. Michael probed her lightly and she allowed him into her weave of Cascar words with a smile and a willingness that was quite erotic. Clarkham, seated across the umbrella table from her, did not seem to notice or care. She played her lute-like instrument, occasionally pausing to experimentally tune a string.

Nikolai had already eaten breakfast and sat on a white-painted wrought-iron bench near the low brick wall separating the patio from the garden of tree roses. Biri was not present.

"I dreamed of you last night," Michael told Mora.

"Yes?" She stopped playing.

"You were singing, just like now, with your lute."

"It is a *pliktera*," she said. "Where was I playing?"

Michael didn't answer. He turned to Clarkham and handed him a sheet of penciled poems. "Is this what you're after?"

Clarkham read the poems quickly and laid them on the table. "You know they're not."

"How can I be sure what you need?"

Clarkham stared at Michael steadily. Nikolai shifted uneasily in his seat. Beyond the rose garden, across the black marble-and-ice floor and near the perimeter of the dome, stood Shahpur, Harka, Bek, Tik and Dour. Far too many for Michael to take on if they combined their power. . . .

"I tried to help you last night," Clarkham said.

"You sent me a dream. Not much help." For a brief moment, Michael felt sorry for the Isomage.

Clarkham laughed sharply. "I've dealt with far more songs of power than you, young man."

"I don't need suggestions in my sleep. I've had quite enough from others."

"From Tonn?"

Michael nodded.

"And who else?"

"Whomever. I'm free of them now. I'm on my own." The image came to him clearly; falling free, living up to his purpose. He was full of strength.

The strength of a bomb.

Arno Waltiri had begun the process. The Crane Women and Lamia—Lamia unwittingly, he assumed—had carried it further; Michael had been forged under their hammers. His journey had annealed him and filled him with the necessary images—images which he would transform beyond all recognition. Clarkham himself had set the timer with the dream sent during the night—awkward as it was, so sublimely ignorant of what was necessary.

"How pompous," Clarkham said. "You're only a boy. You've lived what, sixteen, seventeen Earth years? I'm older than the city in which you were born."

"Wherever you went, you left disaster and disappointment. Even in the beginning . . . when you worked for the Maln." It was just a guess, but apparently an accurate one.

Clarkham's eyes narrowed and his hands clenched into fists on the table top.

"You were the person from Porlock, weren't you?" Michael continued. "The Maln sent you to interrupt Coleridge. You did your job, but afterward you began to wonder if a Breed could serve Sidhe interests and his own at the same time. And you wondered what Coleridge would have written if you hadn't interrupted . . ."

Clarkham rose to his feet.

"Years later, when you had developed your own magic, you tried to get Emma Livry to dance a song for you. You must have come very close then, because you drove Tarax and the Maln to burn her."

"I loved her," Clarkham said, his voice a menacing purr. Mora looked up quickly and turned away from his glance.

"Who else did you touch?" Michael asked. "And how much better off would they have been if you had simply left them alone? Besides Arno, of course."

"Do you know who Waltiri was—is?" Clarkham asked.

"No," Michael said. He didn't really want to know.

"His people are *birds*, Michael. The Cledar. He was the one who seduced *me*, not the other way around. I had found a way into the Realm centuries before, but it was his music that opened a gateway through my house that I could not close. He was the one who attracted attention to me in the Realm, and brought the Sidhe down on me to destroy my house and enslave my wives. It was his kind that taught the Sidhe how to use music . . . and he let me believe *I* was the one controlling things. He was a mage, boy, the last of his people. I'll let you decide how long he has been waiting for this moment, and where he is, now. And how I have turned the tables on him, and on Tonn."

He stretched his arms, yawning to release his tension. "I suggest we stop this ridiculous talk. Time enough to discuss motivations and peccadillos when the song is completed. And I know you well enough, boy, to have complete faith in the necessity of your finishing the song. It's inside you already, isn't it? Whether my dream last night helped or not."

"It was a comic opera dream," Michael said. "Do you think that was what Coleridge was trying to say?"

Biri came through the patio doors with a tray of glasses and a clay pitcher dripping with condensation. Clarkham frowned and waved the pitcher away. "I have it on authority," Clarkham said. "I have always known the shape of this song, but not its fine details."

"Perhaps the song's secret lies in how its vessels transform it."

"Now you're becoming obscure," Clarkham said, taking his seat again.

"What was your dream?" Nikolai asked.

"I was in the original pleasure dome. I dreamed of Mora playing, singing. I was a poet—a wild, untamed poet, living in the forests around the palace. Mora was in the emperor's service. She was loved by the court astrologer, a magician—and I loved her, too. We would meet in the cedars. The astrologer became jealous. He advised Kubla to send his fleet to invade Japan, the Eight Islands. And he arranged for press gangs to kidnap the wild poet and send him with the fleet as a galley slave."

Nikolai listened, enthralled. Mora folded her hands on the table top. Biri had set the tray down and was pouring a glass. "And then?" Nikolai asked.

"Then the astrologer planned his marriage to the Abyssinian maid, knowing the fleet would be sent to the bottom of the sea, and his rival with it. A great wind rose and destroyed the emperor's ships, just as the astrologer had forseen, and all aboard drowned. But the young poet's will was so strong he could not be kept away, even in death. He returned to haunt the palace."

"That's what Coleridge was going to write?" Nikolai asked.

"Nobody knows what he was going to write," Michael said. "Why do you need us at all?" he asked Clarkham. "Why not just complete the song yourself?"

"The Isomage is well aware that form is crucial in a song of power," Biri said. "It takes a poet to give it form."

"Indeed," Clarkham said.

"And you think I can equal Coleridge?"

Clarkham considered, then shook his head, no. "You haven't his lyric ability, boy. But you can still give it *form*. You can still finish the song."

"Then I choose not to," Michael said with great difficulty. "You don't deserve the power. You abandoned your wives, and you abandoned Emma Livry. How many others did you hurt? Arno simply gave you what you deserved—some of your own medicine."

"The poor, sad German," Mora said, eyes downcast.

"I was not responsible for Mahler," Clarkham said without looking at her. "Or for his child. That was not my work at all."

he smiled at Michael, abruptly calm and friendly. "I've been through a great deal, my boy. I must not be stopped now."

"Then go on without me. You fed me the dream. Give it form. If I can't equal Coleridge, perhaps you can."

"I'm not a poet."

"No!" Michael shouted. "You're a parasite. You want power you don't deserve."

"At the very least, I'm a symbiote," Clarkham said. "I interact, inspire. You've been too influenced by Tonn, I suspect, to fully understand my relationship with artists."

"Tonn said poets would rule again someday. I will not allow you to rule."

Clarkham inhaled deeply and let his breath out through his teeth with a faint whistle. "Commendable courage. And stupidity." He pointed to Nikolai. "Look at him."

The corpse in Nikolai's chair was a mass of finely shredded skin and muscle. Blood pooled under the chair. Clarkham raised his finger and Nikolai was restored. "I wouldn't have to be so immature," Clarkham said, "if I were dealing with a worthy opponent. But I'm not. So we'll get our preliminaries out of the way. Produce the final portion of the song, or Nikolai will become what you just saw. But not now. Our emotions have been engaged. There must be time to reflect, prepare."

"I don't need time," Michael said. He had given Clarkham his last chance, and the Isomage had passed it by with a threat. "I can write it down now."

"I insist," Clarkham said.

Mora contemplated the tree roses in the garden, her face impassive. Nikolai simply looked as he had the night before, out of his depth and bewildered. He hadn't felt a thing.

"Let Mora give you and your friend a tour. There's much to see here. The pleasure dome was quite a remarkable pattern, and I've gone to a lot of trouble to recreate it. It would be a pity if the object of my efforts were to plunge ahead without full benefit of such labor." His smile was almost sweet. "We'll conclude our little dance later. It's a lovely day. Off with you." He lightly fanned a hand in Mora's direction and left the table.

"You must not underestimate him," Mora said as she led Michael and Nikolai across the marble and ice floor. "The Isomage is a very powerful sorcerer."

"I'm sure he is," Michael said.

She turned and regarded him with a pained expression.

"Then why do you anger him?"

"Because for months now, I thought he was the one who would show me the way home and help the humans in the Realm. Now it's obvious he just wants power. He wants to be another Adonna."

Mora shook her head slowly, almost pityingly, her large eyes steady on Michael's face. "No one comprehends the whole. That is what the Isomage has said, and he must be correct. There is always mystery and surprise."

"Besides, he won't harm me until I've given him what he wants. And"—Michael felt the hornets hum within—"I don't care anymore. I'm ready to give it to him. So let's tour and get it over with."

Mora cocked her head to one side. "You are saying that a poet from Earth, given a chance to tour Xanadu from end to end, is not even interested?"

This bothered Michael. The opportunity was unparalleled, certainly; but he was not sure he could be enthused by anything now. "I suppose," he said.

"Then come. We'll start at the top. . . ."

To one side of the dome, in the middle of a neat circle of cedars, was a black marble staircase leading down into the hill. Mora removed a lantern from a brass plate on the wall and preceded them down the steps. Nikolai followed her closely, and Michael trailed a few steps behind.

"How do you serve Clarkham?" Michael asked her.

"As he wishes me to," she answered, barely audible over the whistle of the wind in the shaft.

"And how is that?" Michael pursued, aware he was touching sensitive areas.

"When the Isomage came here, there was nothing but sea. The Maln had ceded it to him in the Pact. He was bitter and exhausted. He had nothing. He had lost everyone he loved; there was only Harka and Shahpur, and they were of little use to him then. He had his power, but no . . ."

She held her hand up in the air and Michael felt her probe him for the right word.

"Inspiration?" he suggested.

"Yes. I also was lost, cast out because I had loved a human. I wandered by the sea, and the Isomage took me in. He was no longer alone, and his strength to imagine returned. That was when he started on the pleasure dome."

"How did the Isomage create all this?" Nikolai asked as

they descended into darkness and cold.

"He did not," Mora answered, her voice echoing. "The song already has a variety of forms. He simply took the song as it existed and let it shape the Realm within his territories."

Michael felt the walls with one spread hand; they were ice veined with rock now, and very small veins of rock at that. Ahead was a roaring grumble. The steps vibrated in rhythm with the rise and fall of the grumble.

"The Realm is built on ice," Mora said, "but that ice does not begin for miles yet. This is ice required by the song, cold in the midst of dark. It melts to form the river. And the river—"

They turned a corner and cold blue-green light fell on them. Moisture dripped from smooth slick walls of ice. Rivulets gathered in gutters to each side of the stairway. "The river empties into the sea," Mora said. "It waters the grounds first, so that ice leads to life—cold to warmth. That, too, is part of the song. Some things are not mentioned in any manifestation of the song." She stopped and pointed. Deep in the ice were twisted, elongated fish with the heads of cats and deer. Michael looked closer and saw they were not real, but illusions created by fine cracks; looking again, he saw not fish but frozen reeds capped with eyes. "The song must always be more than its singer can convey."

The steps ended as the floor leveled and they walked directly on ice. Nikolai stumbled in a narrow crack and Michael grabbed his arm. "Not safe for tourists!" the Russian commented wryly.

The ice around them brightened to a pale blue-green, more alive than the dead green of thick glass. Mora led them on to an expansion in the tunnel. "Come," she said, beckoning toward a broad ice bridge.

Above, vaults of ice and marble formed curious traceries, vegetal fans of mineral mixed with the translucent water. Below, the accumulated melt careened from the right and cascaded to the left. The cavern bearing the melt was easily five hundred yards across. The chunks of ice seen from afar now took on more meaningful proportion; they were the size of houses, even mansions. And not all the chunks were ice. As Coleridge had described, pieces of rock were mixed in the tumult. The ice bridge—twisted and doubled-back, obviously natural yet too convenient—took the blows of the rushing bergs and boulders without a shudder.

They walked along the span, Nikolai reluctantly, afraid of

slipping off the rounded surface. The air smelled of cold and mist and was filled with noise: high-pitched grinds and squeals, pounding spray, a deep and momentous impression of motion.

They crossed the bridge and passed into a narrow, low-roofed tunnel, once more as much rock as ice.

Near the exit, rock predominated. They emerged into the dim overgrown light of a deep wedge in the hill—Coleridge's "romantic chasm." Deeper still, a hundred yards below, where they stood on an unfenced ledge, the melt fountained, carrying its ice and rocks in a frothing torrent. Trees formed a canopy over the ledge, glistening with drops of spray. Nikolai shivered.

The ledge took them to the rim of the chasm, overlooking the gardens. The sinuous river flowed like sluggish bronze beneath the warm sky. On the opposite side of the chasm were the steps they had climbed to reach the dome on their arrival. Michael stared down at the base of the falls and the bobbing ice in the deep blue pool there.

"Now we descend to the gardens," Mora said. Michael resisted her hand on his arm.

"We're just wasting time," he said.

"*Please*," she said.

"Either I do what I was brought here to do, or I leave—now," Michael said sternly. Mora backed away and folded her arms across her breasts. Nikolai stood awkwardly to one side, thumbs hooked in his belt.

"Why do you wish to hurry things?" Mora asked. "There is always time."

Michael looked down the slanting path and saw Harka and Shahpur seated on flanking boulders. There was obviously no chance of escape. "Lead on, then," he said.

The empty Sidhe and the white-wrapped human accompanied them without comment on the rest of the tour. Michael paid little attention to the gorgeous landscaping, the mazes of perfect and ever-blooming flower gardens, the delicate, jewel-like Sidhe animals. In the early afternoon, Nikolai professed to being tired and hungry, and they made their way up the opposite side of the chasm and returned to the soapstone gate. Harka, Michael and Shahpur hung back a bit before entering the silken tent. At Harka's signal, Michael stopped. Shahpur approached and nodded his shrouded head at the Sidhe.

"We think it wise to warn you," Shahpur said to Michael. "The Isomage will not accept much more defiance."

Harka sighed. "He has been here a long time, with little to do, and not all of his thinking is clear. He still has great bitterness."

"He is powerful," Shahpur said. "He will do you great harm. . . ."

"You know that we are different," Harka said. "I have not always served the Isomage in ways that pleased him. He punished me."

"And you still serve him?"

"We have no choice. Now, we warn you only because *he* thinks you could learn from us. We tell you only because *he* wills it. I fled from the Maln with Clarkham; I was his partner. We quarreled, and he gained the upper hand. He poured my self from me like wine from a jug. I have only the hollowness. Shahpur . . ."

"Once, the Isomage was filled with hatred and it bred a disease in his brain like worms in rotten meat," Shahpur said. "It made him weaker, so he cast a shadow. But the shadow was too strong to simply fade away. He had to cast the shadow *onto* someone. The Isomage chose me. I carry his past foulness."

"He has treated us this way," Harka said, "and yet we have never done him great wrong. If you defy him, refuse him what he most desires, he will consider that a very great wrong indeed. Even empty, I shudder to think what he will do to you, to your companion."

"Then I won't defy him," Michael said. "I'll give him just what he wants."

"What did the humans and the Sidhe lose when they separated?" Clarkham asked after they had finished the early dinner. Bek and Tik cleared away the plates as Mora brought out a tray of brandy snifters. "One lost magic, and the other lost a sense of direction. Bring them together again—that's inevitable—and both will benefit. Ah, but how to bring them together smoothly? Who understands both Sidhe *and* humans?" Clarkham lifted his snifter and urged Michael to do the same. "Not Tonn. Not an old, decrepit mage losing control of a universe he himself made. Not Waltiri. Not Tarax, a hard and resolute Sidhe with no sympathy for the old enemies. Only a Breed."

The brandy was obviously one of Clarkham's evening rituals. Michael sipped the smooth but potent fluid. "How?" he asked.

"How would I unite them?"

Michael nodded.

"Very carefully. Which do I add first, the water or the acid? An old alchemical problem—"

"Always add acid to water," Michael said, recalling Mrs. Perry's chemistry classes.

"Yes. Now I would say the Sidhe are acid, and the humans are water. . . . Adding humans here hasn't done any good. The Sidhe have simply spit them out, isolated them. But take a few Sidhe and return them to the Earth . . . perhaps the results will be better."

"We're doing well enough on our own," Michael said, disputing his own words before they were out. "We don't need Sidhe."

"The Earth is a mess, Michael. No one can see into the minds of others, and that makes for a nasty and selfish people. What wonders you make are hard and dangerous wonders, without intrinsic poetry. You fight battles a Sidhe would not even have to acknowledge—against disease, natural disaster, your own confusion."

"And you want to be in control of the mixing?"

Clarkham nodded. "Yes. Can you think of another Breed so qualified, with so many . . . experiences under his belt?"

Michael shook his head. "You would be the wise one, the benevolent master."

Mora stood behind Clarkham, her hands on his shoulders. Clarkham covered one hand with his own. "As selfish as any."

Michael's eyes went to Harka, lingering at the edge of the patio.

"It wouldn't be an easy job. Frustrating. Infuriating," Michael suggested.

The early evening light and the glow from the paper lanterns reflected gaily in the snifters and cast a mellow subdued air across the patio.

Clarkham leaned forward and spread his hands on the cleared table. Between his hands appeared an image—the Earth, as immediate and real as ever Michael had seen it, minutely detailed. "All that would be required is to lay a song over it . . . with the cooperation of humans and Sidhe, guided by the appropriate leader—myself—and the misery would vanish. The world would return to the paradise it had once been. . . ."

"Amhara," Mora whispered, her face warming to cherry-wood brown.

The globe between his hands rushed at Michael. Michael did not flinch. The image expanded to fill his vision, and he seemed to pass through clouds, over wine-colored seas, over broad white beaches and jungles and sharp, jagged mountains. He could smell the air, clean and somehow exuberant, filled with pleasure and challenge. The image vanished like a bubble but the impression lingered.

"Youth," Clarkham said. "A young world again, rid of the guilt, wiped of the sin and the hatred."

"With you in command," Michael reiterated. At that moment, he launched his heretofore withheld probe. Clarkham expertly blocked all but the foremost barb. That portion returned to Michael a brief and horrifying impression of the inner Clarkham—and a realization.

Use.

Foulness, hatred, almost as repugnant and intense as that within Shahpur. How often had Clarkham shed his darkest shadow? How often had his inner foulness regenerated? He carried a malignancy that could not be eradicated, only reduced, to grow anew.

Shahpur was human; an unprotected soul is flypaper for a cast-off shadow, especially in the Realm.

When Michael had given Clarkham what he wanted, Clarkham would give *him* what he could no longer comfortably contain. A spiritual excretion. How could he counter that?

And why should I judge him so harshly? Isn't there a darkness and foulness within me?

Clarkham did not react to the probe. "I will lead. Yes," he said. Only a few seconds had passed. "Who else would you suggest?"

"No one," Michael said.

"Then let us put aside our quarrels. You have the key to help bring paradise to Earth, to help me re-unite peoples separated for much too long. Let's cooperate. Our ends are the same." Clarkham gestured for Mora to bring out the pen and paper. She returned to the house and came back with a writing tray, setting it before Michael.

"And something special to drink," Clarkham ordered.

Michael reached for the two remaining sheets of paper and began to write. The fountain pen lay its ink in smooth thick lines across the fine linen-grain surface.

> The triple circles round him tighten
> While from Avernus rise to frighten
> The ghosts of voyagers dead while wandering
> From edge to edge his shadow Realm . . .

That was just a warmup. He stared at the white paper, turning his mind away from the surroundings. It was like casting a shadow, he thought; the words inside could be drawn out, given shape, sent forth. And they would be deadly.

Again Biri brought out the clay pitcher and thick heavy glasses. He poured a translucent creamy-colored fluid and passed the portions around.

Clarkham sipped from the glass Biri gave him and toasted Michael. "The veritable milk of paradise," the Isomage said.

> Weave a circle around him thrice . . .

The drink was milky-sweet and biting, with an alcoholic tang. All in all, it was delicious. "Kumis," Biri said. "The drink of Emperor Kubla."

The kumis began to act in Michael almost immediately. He wrote down the last two lines of Coleridge's fragment:

> For he on honey-dew hath fed
> And drunk the milk of paradise.

And then it was upon him. It flashed and sparkled and came so fast he hardly had time to record it all. He knew he would not have another chance. He tried to catch as much as he could, and he exulted. There was no outside source for this; it came from inside, purely from himself, or rather, that self which connected him with Coleridge, with Yeats, with all the fine poets. That moment when there was nothing but the Word, and it came in perfect waves.

> And so the ice, cross ages dripping,
> Undermines the silken palace,
> Falls beneath the cedars, ripping
> As if the years themselves with malice
> Seek to still great dreams by gripping
> The gardens, walls and golden towers,
> Rending from the Khan his powers . . .

Perhaps twenty lines passed so quickly he could not write them down. They were not essential.

> As wave to wave, in storm sea floundering,
> His galliots beach, unguided at the helm.
> Thou Khan, who eats the fruit of Faerie,
> Who hastes to leave when bid to tarry,
> Listen to the sweet soft critic,
> That dusk-wrapped maid on sweet strings playing,
> "Palace, towers and gardens," saying,
> "Cannot save your soul from pity
> Nor build from song a timeless city."
> The Caverns roar with rising waters . . .

The ground trembled. Clarkham steadied himself against the table.

> Drowning to the highest mountains,
> Flooding all the Khan's great slaughters
> Beneath the whirling, vaulted fountains.

There was more, much more, and it did not simply spin through his head and vanish. The song was created and completed, and Michael knew immediately it was not the Song of Power Clarkham sought. It never had been. From the very beginning, when they had commissioned Lin Piao Tai to build the palace, the element of destruction had been plain.

Coleridge's poem, and Michael's share in it, were simply decoys, traps meant to snare and destroy those, like Clarkham, who stood in the way of the ultimate combatants. Waltiri, mage of the birds, the Cledar, had sent Michael; the Crane Women and the Ban of Hours had cooperated; Tonn and the Maln had let him pass.

Clarkham grabbed the sheets as soon as Michael stopped writing. He read them, eyes widening. "Traitor," he said "This is not—"

"It's finished. It isn't all there, but I've finished it," Michael said, suddenly exhausted. Clarkham crumpled the pages and threw them down on the table. Mora reached for the *pliktera* beside her chair. Clarkham turned to her, but she would not look at him. The ground shook again as Nikolai backed away from the table. From the chasm, the pulse of ice catapulting to the river bed quickened. Clarkham swiveled to face Biri, who stared at him implacably.

"You!" Clarkham said. "You're the traitor. You're still loyal to Tarax!"

"There was no disputing the boy's mission," Biri said. "Tarax and Adonna willed it, as well as the council of Eleu. All are united against you. Even you willed it. The boy would have turned away, but you brought him here. He would have refused the song, but you forced him to write it. On your own head, Isomage."

Clarkham's face darkened with rage. His hands trembled, waiting to spill their power.

"Better leave," Michael whispered to Nikolai. The Russian didn't need any more encouragement. He leaped over the wall, dodged through the rose garden and vaulted the fence to the icy marble floor. Fine cracks shot across the marble surface behind him, throwing chips of stone into the air as the ground shuddered. Michael reached down to retrieve the pages. He flattened them out and held them behind his back.

"What shall I do with you all?" Clarkham asked. More than ever now, Michael pitied him—and feared him.

Biri took Mora's hand. They walked away from the Isomage, down the brick steps to the lawn. The light passing through the silken dome was reddening and the fabric rippled under the rough touch of a new wind.

Clarkham faced Michael alone on the patio. "Get out!" he cried. The black marble screamed and separated along the ice veins. The lawn rippled and showed gashes of soil. The roses shook. Most of the staked trees had turned to glass; the blossoms shattered and cast their fragments on the dirt.

"GET OUT!"

Michael turned his back on the Isomage, neckhair prickling. He fully expected to have his flesh riven from his bones, but Clarkham was concentrating all his power on keeping the palace together.

One of the curved supporting poles snapped with the report of a gunshot. The pole fell and tore out a length of silk. The plaster and brick walls of Clarkham's home split. Chunks slipped away and crumbled on impact. The house's timbers groaned in agony.

As Michael crossed the lawn, barely able to keep his balance, he heard Clarkham shout his name. He looked back and saw the Isomage standing spread-legged on two separated pieces of the patio. The Breed's hair flew out from his head. His hands and arms crackled with energy.

He held up a wickedly glowing finger.

"You may not go!" he shouted over the uproar.

Coils of viscous light oozed from his fingers and expanded above the rose garden and lawn. They sank around Michael, forming a serpentine net of bright green strands.

Michael felt his eyes grow warm, then hot. The shadow he cast was a dark, enveloping thing, alone and indescribably nasty. He spung away from the shadow, passed through the web and leaped to the broken marble, his own hair charged with power.

> And all should cry, beware, beware!
> His flashing eyes, his floating hair!

The shadow contained all of Biri's Sidhe discipline, all of the poisonous, virulently inhumane nonsense about aloneness and self-mastery through isolation. It was the philosophy of a discouraged, dying race and it had served its purpose—it had filled Michael with the basic will to destroy. Now he had no use for it—except as a defense.

Clarkham leaped to a more stable position and drew in the green web. The shadow struggled, made a sound like crushing rock and exploded. Darkness scattered the web and dissipated under the fiery dome light.

Clarkham shouted in a language Michael had never heard before, then extruded another web, this one intensely blue.

Michael turned his face away and held up the poem. The lines of ink hissed and crackled. The words shot out in lances of fire over Clarkham's head, setting the house aflame. In seconds, the rear wall and tile roof became a furnace of quicklime, wood and clay. The glass in the french doors exploded and the frames shrunk like blackened matchsticks. Glowing embers wafted up in the rising heat and ignited the silken tent.

"My work, my work!"

Michael looked down and saw Clarkham running toward the house. The flames beat him back, but he unrolled a sheet of ice from nothingness and plunged inside. From the corners of the pavilion, Shahpur and Harka ran to help their master. Shahpur's wrappings issued trails of smoke.

Strains of music rose from the vibrations of the hill and palace. Michael ran to escape the falling shreds of burning tent. Only when he was through the soapstone gate did he realize he must be hearing the original Infinity Concerto, as it had sounded decades before.

Mora and Biri waited for him on the lawn beyond the dome's foundation. Nikolai struggled to stand upright a few yards behind them. Biri led the way down the side of the chasm, away from the hill and the fire spreading from the dome to the orchards and cedar forests. In their flight, they passed Bek, Tik and Dour, who seemed to melt into the smoking trees.

They didn't stop until they stood by the granite guard near the gate of the outermost wall. Biri still held Mora's hand. Her face was a mask of grief and remorse.

Nikolai danced from foot to foot, watching the conflagration. "Jesus, Jesus! Look what you've done! I have never seen anything like that! What in hell *are* you, Michael?"

Michael looked at the papers still clutched in his hands. All the writing had been neatly burned out, line by line, leaving brown-edged shreds held together by margins.

The hill sagged. The conflagration was now a pillar of smoke and fire reaching up to smudge the sky.

"That dream is ended," Biri said, lifting the ruined pages from Michael's hand and scattering them over the grass. "You are free to go now."

"Go where?"

"Home."

"What happens to everybody else? To the humans?"

"That is Adonna's concern. You have served your purpose. You are spent." Biri regarded him with contempt. "You threw off Sidhe discipline. In our eyes, you are nothing now."

Do not reveal yourself. He is merely a wheel, not an engine.

Michael recognized the voice now; it was Waltiri. He felt the power still residing in his mind, and smiled at Biri. He did not need to dispute the Sidhe.

The hill was now level with the plain. Water flooded from its perimeter in high-vaulting fountains, spreading to form a lake. Ice bobbed lazily in the water. At the center of the lake, a whirlpool formed, its horrible sucking sound audible even at the outer wall. Michael felt a tug in the center of his stomach.

"Clarkham made one mistake," Biri said as they watched the lake vanish. "He trusted a Sidhe." The words struck Mora deeply. She backed away from him and threw down his hand.

"Nikolai," Michael said. "Will you be all right?"

"I am fine," Nikolai said. "Why?"

"Something's happening."

"Your gateway is falling through the Realm," Biri said. "Down to the void. Go home, man-child."

"Michael! Wait!"

Nikolai lunged for him, but a thread pulled tight—the long thread of his existence in the Realm. The grass, scraps of paper, walls, Biri and Mora, Nikolai, all took off around him in a violent spin. He arced high above the Realm and was drawn with incomprehensible speed over the river, grasslands and forests—

Cometing through the Irall, Inyas Trai, across the barren mound of the Crane Women and through the flat, burned village of Euterpe—

Through Lamia's house, where the huge woman lingered in shadow, discarded by all now that her work was done—

Across the ruined field to the softly flickering gateway—

Down the alley, past the slumped figure of the guardian sitting under the trellis—

And into a warm, dark early fall breeze.

Filled with the sound of leaves scattering over pavement, the smells of fresh-mowed grass and eucalyptus, the sensation of complex and ever-changing solidity.

Crickets.

And in the distance, a motorcycle.

Chapter Forty-Four

He stood beneath the moon-colored streetlight, half in the shadow of a tall, brown-leafed maple. Four houses down and on the opposite side of the street was the white plaster home of David Clarkham. It had been deserted for forty years and its lawns were overgrown; its hedges thrust uncontrolled branches in all directions; its walls were cracked and spotted with mud. There were no curtains in the front windows. The FOR SALE sign on the front lawn leaned away from the house, shunning it.

The house was empty.

Michael pulled the hair back from his eyes and felt the growth of silky beard on his cheeks. He looked down at the sweater and shirt and slacks that Clarkham had given him to wear.

In the lapel of the shirt was the glass rose.

He removed it and smelled it. The scent was gone.

Chapter Forty-Five

Michael sat across from his parents in the living room, his discomfort growing with the silence. His mother had stopped weeping momentarily, and his father looked down at the carpet with a face full of pain and relief, the end of grief and the beginning of helpless anger. "Five years is a long time, son," he said. "The least you could have done—"

"There was no way. It was impossible." How could he tell them what had happened? Not even the glass rose would convince them. And five years! It seemed less than five months.

"You've changed," his father said. "You've grown a lot. You can't expect us to just...accept. We grieved for you, Michael. We were sure you were dead."

"Father—"

His father held up a hand. "It will take time. Wherever you were, whatever you were doing. It will take time. We..." Tears were in his eyes now. "We've kept your room. The furniture, the books."

"I knew if you were alive, you'd come back," his mother said, brushing strands of red hair from her eyes.

"Did you ever talk to Golda Waltiri?"

"She died a few months after you...went away," his mother said. "She sent a letter for you, and there's a letter from some lawyers." She looked down at the carpet. "Such a long time, Michael."

"I know," he said, his own eyes filling now at the thought of their pain. He got up from the chair and sat between them on the couch, putting his arms around them both, and together

338

they hugged and cried and tried to push away the strange time, the long time apart.

After dinner, after hours of catching up on news and telling his folks repeatedly that there was no way he could describe what had happened—not yet, not without more proof—he took the stairs to his room and stood amid the books and prints and the writing table he had now completely grown out of.

He opened the letter from Golda and the papers from the lawyers of Waltiri's estate and lay back on the pillow. Golda's handwriting was elegant, old-world, clear, spread with conservative margins across green-lined airmail paper.

Dear Michael,

I have not told your parents, because I know so little myself. Arno—mysterious husband! I hardly know how to describe my life with him, wonderful as it has been—Arno requested that our estate be placed in your care, upon my joining him (dare I hope that? Or is something more powerful at work here?), which I believe will be soon, for I have been under great strain. Do not feel bad, Michael, but much of this strain has come from withholding certain facts from your dear parents, who have been so kind to me. But what can we tell them—that you have followed my husband's suggestions—and, despite his last words, perhaps even his wishes? I do not know where you have gone, and I am not even certain you will return, though Arno, apparently, was. I am not so old that I may be excused the confusion I feel, but excuse me, dear Michael, for I do feel it. That, and the sadness, the sensation of being in circumstances for which I am totally inadequate either in knowledge or mental capacity. Perhaps, on your return, you will know why Arno has made this request, and what you should do with our resources, which are not small. You will also control the rights to Arno's work. There are no other specific requests, and all of these will be detailed in letters from our lawyers. Dear boy. Turn a glass down for us—one glass only, since Arno never drank wine, and told me to drink for him when celebrations were on—when you have safely returned and your loved ones rejoice. As all our people have said for centuries, dear Michael; May there come a time when all shall share their stories, and all will be unveiled, and we may revel in the cleverness and the beauty of the tales thus told. So clumsy, this note, for a young poet to read!

He folded the letter and put it into its envelope, then removed the legal instructions and skimmed them. He would be financially secure; his duties would be to organize the Waltiri papers and provide for their publication, and oversee the publications currently in progress; he could live in the Waltiri home if he so wished.

The letters slid down his chest as he sat up and folded his strong brown arms around his blanketed knees. Of all things now, he wished he could speak with Golda, have her help him with his parents, perhaps put all their minds to rest.

If it would have done Golda any good to know—as much as Michael knew—what Arno Waltiri was, and that he was not dead. Not in any human sense.

And what about the humans in the Realm? Helena, and the others? Adonna—Tonn—had said all would be well, once Clarkham was removed. Michael simply could not believe that, but there was nothing he could do. Not here, not now.

He went to the bathroom to wash his face. Steam rose from the basin of hot water, curling around his face. He breathed deeply, drawing the steam into his lungs to clear away the sorrow and stress. He looked up through the steam into the mirror.

The position—the angle—wasn't quite right. Familiar, but . . .

Michael presented a three-quarters view. The realization was like a cold razor sliding along the glass. He stared at the first face of Hebal Mish, the first visage sculpted from clouds of snow. He had changed so much he hadn't even recognized himself.

At first he was frightened. He stood in the hall outside the bathroom, then went to his room and flung open the window to breathe fresh air.

It wasn't over. It would never be over; and he was more involved in it than ever.

In the depths of the night, a bird began to sing.

Notes and Acknowledgments

My special thanks to those who helped with this novel: to Terri Windling who revived it; to Poul and Karen Anderson, exacting readers; to Jim Turner, Ray Feist and David Brin for critiques and encouragements; and of course to Astrid, who read it endlessly in its various printouts. My debts of inspiration are many—portions of this book go back thirteen years—but Jorge Luis Borges is at the top of the list, and once again, Poul.

The book, of course, is not finished. This is the first half. The second half, *The Serpent Mage*, will conclude the tale.

The language spoken by the Sidhe is not completely artificial. Many readers may recognize Indo-European roots and borrowings from various extant languages; most will likely not recognize that other words are derived from some very obscure Irish cants. If you're curious to find out more, please refer to a marvelous book by Robert A. Stewart Macalister, *The Secret Languages of Ireland*, first published in 1937 by the Cambridge University Press. It's still in print from Armorica Book Company/Philo Press. A good university or public library should also have it. Lovers of languages—or dabblers, such as myself—will find it fascinating.

Appendix

The Film Scores of Arno Waltiri (Highlights)

1935	Ashenden
1939	Queen of the Yellow River
1940	Dead Sun
1941	Sea Scorpion
1942	Warbirds of Mindanao
1942	Ace Squadron
1943	Yellowtail
1946	Northanger Abbey
1948	Descartes, a.k.a. The King's Genius
1950	Let Us Now Praise Famous Men
1951	Some Kind of Love
1958	The Man Who Would Be King
1963	Call It Sleep